Bello:

hidden talent rediscovered

Bello is a digital-only imprint of Pan Macmillan,
established to breathe new life into previously published,
classic books.

At Bello we believe in the timeless power of the imagination,
of a good story, narrative and entertainment, and we want to
use digital technology to ensure that many more readers
can enjoy these books into the future.

We publish in ebook and print-on-demand formats
to bring these wonderful books to new audiences.

www.panmacmillan.co.uk/bello

Richmal Crompton

Richmal Crompton (1890–1969) is best known for her thirty-eight books featuring William Brown, which were published between 1922 and 1970. Born in Lancashire, Crompton won a scholarship to Royal Holloway in London, where she trained as a schoolteacher, graduating in 1914, before turning to writing full-time. Alongside the *William* novels, Crompton wrote forty-one novels for adults, as well as nine collections of short stories.

Richmal Crompton

THERE ARE
FOUR SEASONS

BELL

First published 1937 by Macmillan

This edition published 2015 by Bello
an imprint of Pan Macmillan
Pan Macmillan, 20 New Wharf Road, London N1 9RR
Basingstoke and Oxford
Associated companies throughout the world

www.panmacmillan.co.uk/bello

ISBN 978-1-5098-1036-9 EPUB
ISBN 978-1-5098-1034-5 HB
ISBN 978-1-5098-1035-2 PB

A CIP catalogue record for this book is available from the British Library.

Typeset by Ellipsis Digital Limited, Glasgow

Visit **www.panmacmillan.com** to read more about all our books
and to buy them. You will also find features, author interviews and
news of any author events, and you can sign up for e-newsletters
so that you're always first to hear about our new releases.

Four seasons fill the measure of the year;
There are four seasons in the mind of man.

KEATS

Chapter One

"BY whom was a body of royalists raised in Scotland," said Miss Thompson, reading the question from the book she held in her hand, "and what was the success of their leader?"

"By a young and gallant hero, the Earl of Montrose," repeated Vicky glibly, "who performed many brave actions but was defeated after a short and brilliant career and obliged to retire amongst his native mountains."

Vicky was standing in front of Miss Thompson, her hands behind her, her heels together, her feet, in black strap-over shoes, turned out at the correct angle. She wore a dress of red linsey, piped with white, a white cambric pinafore with tiny frilled pockets, and long black woollen stockings. Her hair was cut in a fringe in front and hung down behind in a cascade of well-brushed curls.

"Very good, Vicky," said Miss Thompson approvingly as she closed the book. "You are making excellent progress. Now get your slate and pencil and I will set you your sums."

Miss Thompson was short, but her upright carriage and the black bombazine dress and bustle lent her figure a certain dignity. The bodice was buttoned tightly to her neck, its high collar fastened by a large cameo brooch, finished off by a tiny white frill. Her faded hair was taken straight from her brow and gathered into a chignon net. She wore a small black silk apron, edged with black lace, and black silk mittens. This constituted, as it were, Miss Thompson's official costume, and she would never have dreamed of confronting her pupils in any other. The only modifications she allowed herself were a black woollen shoulder shawl and black woollen mittens over the silk ones in winter. Her pursed-up mouth gave an impression of severity that was belied by the rather timid, short-sighted eyes behind the thick steel-rimmed spectacles. Despite her spectacles, her nose was almost touching the slate as she set Vicky's sums—division on one side and multiplication on the other—forming her figures with meticulous exactitude. Miss Thompson always paid more attention to the formation of her pupils' figures than to the actual results of their sums. The latter seemed to her, in fact, quite unimportant.

Vicky took the slate to the table and resumed her seat, bending her small shining head diligently over her work. Her toes swung clear of the ground, and her curls fell over her shoulders, making, as it seemed to her, a little tent for her face. The fancy pleased her, and she shook them over still farther to make the tent more complete. Miss Thompson sat at the head of the table, her feet on a footstool, her work-basket in front of her. She was engaged in scalloping a piece of white flannel that was to be a petticoat for Vicky. She had, at first, been a little affronted to learn that she was expected to be nurse to her charge as well as governess, but it was such a light post and she was so fond of Vicky that that had long ceased to rankle. It was, indeed, the highest post that Miss Thompson had ever had.

Vicky was not only intelligent but docile and easily managed—easily managed, that is, if one went about it the right way, and Miss Thompson always made a point of going about it the right way. The absence of parents, too, was a great advantage. Miss Thompson generally found parents even more troublesome than pupils. They were either over-indulgent or exacted impossible standards of behaviour, and, in either case, of course, put the blame of their children's faults on the governess. Vicky's papa seldom came to the house at all, and as to her mama—well, the less said about her the better. Miss Thompson discouraged gossip and always began to talk about the weather when the servants mentioned Mrs. Carothers, but she knew that Mr. Carothers had divorced her four years ago when Vicky was three years old.

Distressing as the situation was, every cloud has its silver lining (Miss Thompson was fond of setting that proverb as a copy for her pupils), and it was certainly pleasant to be in the position of mistress of this house, in sole charge of a dear little girl like Vicky, with no one to criticise her or spy on her or snub her. Cook and Emma, the housemaid, were very respectful, and life was pleasanter for Miss Thompson than it had been for a long time.

Vicky had stopped making a tent of her hair and was now doing her sums. She liked sums. Each had a definite beginning and end. Each was perfect and complete in itself. She formed her figures slowly and carefully, taking an almost sensuous pleasure in their waves and lines.

"Finished, dear?" said Miss Thompson, fastening her needle in the piece of flannel and putting it into her work-basket.

Vicky threw back her curls and handed up her slate.

"Excellent, my dear," said Miss Thompson. "Your ones are much straighter, and your eights are better. I don't think you've got the answers quite right, however. Let me show you."

"No, I'll do it again," said Vicky quickly.

Vicky always hated to be shown, and Miss Thompson could never make up her mind whether this was a fault or a virtue. She contented herself with saying, "You should say 'please,' dear," and Vicky, with a perfunctory "please," took her slate back to her place, rubbed out the sum with the little damp sponge that hung by a string from one corner, and set to work on it again, while Miss Thompson prepared copy-book, ink, and pen. To-day's copy was "Evil Communications Corrupt Good Manners." Miss Thompson always wrote the first line herself, partly to show that it really would all go into one line, and partly because she was proud of her flowing copperplate hand, which, indeed, could hardly be distinguished from the copy.

"Now remember, Vicky," she said, when the sum had been done again correctly and the slate put away. "Upstrokes thin and downstrokes thick, and keep well within the lines."

After the copy came sewing. Vicky was hemming a handkerchief for Papa. It had been Miss Thompson's idea, and Vicky had at first been very much excited about it, but now that she was on the second side she was secretly rather tired of it. As she sewed, her glance went to the photograph of Papa that stood on the mantelpiece. He had dark eyes, thick black hair, and sweeping black side whiskers. Vicky thought him the most handsome man in the world. Mama had been beautiful, too, of course, but Mama was dead. She had left home suddenly for a holiday and died while she was away. Cook had told her about it (it was before Miss Thompson came) and Vicky had thought that someone ought to buy her a black dress, but no one did. Cook snorted and said "Black dress indeed!" when Vicky suggested it. Vicky didn't mind very much about Mama's being dead. It made Papa belong to her the more, and it was Papa whom she had always loved best. She had read a good many stories about motherless little girls who were their papa's only joy and comfort (there was one in particular called "Little Betsy and her Papa"), and she was gratifyingly like the illustration of those stories, with her blue eyes, pink and white cheeks, and golden curls.

She loved to think of herself as Papa's only joy and comfort—sitting on his knee or being swung up in his strong arms like the little girls in the illustrations of her story-books. One part of her was aware that nothing of the sort ever happened when he came home, but it was now so long since she had seen him that she had almost replaced the dim memories of his last visit by the illustrations of "Little Betsy and her Papa" and other similar stories.

Though she was tired of the handkerchief, she worked at it industriously, not only because it was being made for the indulgent devoted papa of her dreams, but also because she was a very precise little girl, who always did whatever she was doing very thoroughly, consciously enjoying the feeling of self-satisfaction that this gave her. A task that she could not master would throw her into a passion of angry frustration. Once Miss Thompson, feeling unusually enterprising, had tried to teach her what she called the "theory of music," but the resultant scene had discouraged her so much that she had not continued the experiment.

"I don't understand," Vicky had stormed, "and I hate it ... I hate it," and had ended by throwing the book across the room in a miniature transport of rage. Certainly Miss Thompson's explanations had not been particularly illuminating, and by mutual consent the subject was dropped.

Vicky's thoughts wandered from Papa to her walk this afternoon. She was going with Miss Thompson to engage a new gardener's boy. George, the old one, had left to "better himself" and they were to call at a cottage in the village to interview a boy whose name had been given to Miss Thompson by the schoolmaster.

"Put your things away now, dear," said Miss Thompson, "and get ready for lunch."

Vicky folded up the handkerchief and put the books into their places on the shelf. There was never any trouble in making Vicky clear her things away. She hated untidiness as much as Miss Thompson herself.

Miss Thompson cleaned the slate and put it into the table drawer. She'd enjoyed the morning, as she generally enjoyed mornings with Vicky. How nice it would be, she thought dreamily, if children could stay always at the stage Vicky was at now!

The gong sounded and she went to supervise Vicky's toilet for lunch, but even that was no trouble. Vicky never seemed to get dirty like other children. Miss Thompson had never before known a child of that age who cleaned her nails without being told. . . .

The Hall, which had been built by Mr. Carothers' grandfather, was not a large house, despite its pretentious name, nor was it built in any very distinguished style of architecture; but it was pleasant and spacious enough, standing against its background of trees, and the red brick had mellowed with the years to a restful weather-beaten tint. A gravelled terrace ran along one side of the house, enclosed by a stone balustrade, from which a double flight of stone steps led down to the lawn. Beyond the lawn, separated from it by a railing, was a wooded stretch of pasture always referred to as the park.

Vicky and Miss Thompson came out of the front door, down the terrace steps, across the lawn, and through the park to the road that led into the village of Six Elms. Vicky walked happily and sedately beside Miss Thompson. She was still feeling excited at the thought of interviewing the gardener's boy.

Miss Thompson, of course, would do the actual interviewing, but she would be there, part and parcel of it all. It made her feel grown-up and important.

She wore her red cashmere pelisse, trimmed with fur, and a small hat pulled forward over her brow, with ribbons hanging down behind. The pinafore had been taken off, revealing rows of small flounces on the red linsey dress, and the strap-over shoes changed for a pair of black buttoned boots. Her small gloved hands were hidden in a tiny muff. Her curls hung down her back in ordered array. She looked very neat and trim and demure as she walked along the country road beside Miss Thompson.

Miss Thompson, for her part, looked eminently ladylike in her black waisted jacket and the black bonnet whose broad ribbons were tied in a bow beneath her chin.

She was smiling proudly down at Vicky. She loved to walk with her through the village like this, showing off her looks and pretty clothes. It delighted her to hear people say, as they often did, that the child could not have been better cared for by her own mother. And Mr. Carothers was so generous. She could buy what she liked for her and no question was ever raised. The smile faded from her lips and she heaved a gentle sigh. If only it would last. . . . But in Miss Thompson's experience of life it was only the unpleasant things that could be counted on to last.

It was March, and the atmosphere held that dazzling clarity of early spring in which every detail of the landscape stands out sharply. Dark tussocks in the elm trees showed where the rooks were building, and their sleepy notes floated down through the pale clear sunshine. The red glow of the silver birch saplings told of rising sap. In the fields new-born lambs lay so still that they looked like white gloves dropped by a passing careless giant or, galvanised into fantastic jerky life, leapt and reared like miniature steeds trying to dismount invisible elfin riders. Vicky forgot her sedateness and laughed delightedly, climbing onto a gate to watch them, the buttoned boots perched on the second rung, the neat gloved hands holding the top one, the small muff hanging free.

She climbed down reluctantly to follow Miss Thompson, but soon the wild flowers on the hedgerows—coltsfoot and celandine and ghost-like anemones—attracted her, and she darted from one to another, naming them in a tone that claimed and received Miss Thompson's approving "Quite right, Vicky."

Vicky kept a collection of pressed wild flowers, and her neatness and precision made it a small masterpiece. Miss Thompson was as proud of it as Vicky herself, and it was always shown to any visitors who came to the house.

As they approached the village, Vicky pushed back the curls that had fallen over her shoulders, put her hands into her muff, and began to walk again sedately beside her governess.

They stopped at a small thatched cottage, whose ramshackle porch seemed about to collapse beneath its weight of jasmine, and Miss Thompson knocked at the door.

A thin harassed-looking woman in an apron, her sleeves rolled up to her elbows, her arms covered with flour, opened the door.

"Come in, miss," she said respectfully, standing aside to let them enter.

The low-raftered kitchen seemed very dark after the bright sunshine outside. The tiny window, hemmed in by curtains and a row of geraniums, admitted little light. The room, however, was spotlessly clean. A fire burnt in the grate, and the air was full of the pleasant scent of baking bread. The table was covered with flour and pieces of dough.

"Sorry I'm not quite straight, miss," said the woman, looking flustered and anxious in the presence of the "gentry." "I've just been doing the baking. Sit down, will you, miss?" She hastily dusted a wooden chair. "I'll call Andrew."

She went to the back door and called "Andrew!" in a thin tremulous voice.

Miss Thompson sat down on the wooden chair, and Vicky stood by her. A fat baby, who had been sitting under the table playing with a piece of dough, crawled out and squatted there, gazing up at them. A solemn little boy appeared at the cottage door, his thumb in his mouth, his eyes fixed on the visitors.

Miss Thompson said "Good afternoon" in her most gracious tone, but the little boy did not reply.

"You should say 'Good afternoon, miss,' " went on Miss Thompson severely.

The little boy removed his thumb from his mouth and inserted his fingers in its place, but said nothing.

Miss Thompson pursed her lips and drew herself up. She was always somewhat sensitive of her dignity as representative of the Hall.

A quick whispered colloquy could be heard in the background. Evidently Andrew had arrived and was being given his instructions. Then he came slowly into the kitchen—a lanky boy of about thirteen with a pale freckled face, wearing a suit that he had obviously outgrown, his face shining from a hasty wash, his hair damply plastered down. He looked tense and nervous as he took up his position in front of Miss Thompson and touched his forehead respectfully.

"Good afternoon, miss," he said.

The woman shooed the little boy away from the door, picked up the fat baby, and stood in the background, her eyes fixed anxiously on her son. The baby, who still held a piece of dough in her hands, began to pat her mother's face with it, but the woman did not move.

Miss Thompson was pleased by the boy's respectful manner and began her questioning and admonition on a condescending note. "How old are you, boy?" "I hope you're prepared to work hard." "Are you quite strong?"

The boy answered in a voice hoarse with earnestness. Though he tried to focus all his attention on what the lady was saying, he was really conscious of nothing but Vicky. He had seen her before, of course, but not at close quarters like this. Her beauty and daintiness took his breath away. He felt that somehow his nearness to her was an outrage. He wanted to go miles away from her . . . and yet he wanted to fall at her feet and worship her.

Vicky was fully conscious of the effect she produced in the dark little kitchen. She saw herself, indeed, exactly as Andrew saw her—a glamorous being from another world. She took his interest and admiration for granted. He belonged to the Poor—a class that in the very nature of things must look up to and admire her. He was ugly and shabby, while she was beautiful and well dressed. This, too, was part of the natural order of things. The little girls in her story-books went to visit the Poor and shone like angels in their squalid rooms. Vicky, conscientiously and yet with a feeling of deep gratification, shone like an angel in the little kitchen. Her wide blue eyes wandered from Andrew to the woman, from the woman to the baby who was plastering dough on her face, but she didn't see any of them. She only saw herself in her fur-trimmed pelisse and flounced dress, her hands in her muff, her curls falling down her back. This pale freckled boy who stole looks of furtive admiration at her was merely a sort of mirror reflecting her. He had no independent existence.

"You may come for a week on trial, then," Miss Thompson was saying, "starting to-morrow. Belson, of course, will tell you your duties when you arrive."

"Thank you, miss," said Andrew.

He was to live within sight and sound of this vision of loveliness and grace. It seemed almost too much. A lump came into his throat at the thought.

"I hope that you will be industrious and obedient and respectful," went on Miss Thompson.

"Indeed he will, miss, thank you kindly," put in his mother, firmly taking away the piece of dough that the baby was now trying to push into her eye. "I warrant he will, I do indeed."

She went on to say that she herself had been in service and was anxious to get her children into "gentlemen's houses."

The father, Miss Thompson knew, was a farm labourer—steady and respectable, or Miss Thompson would not have considered engaging the boy.

"Mr. Carothers," she went on, "is very little at home, but when he does come he likes to see everything in good order."

She took her leave of them, noticing with approval that the boy again touched his forehead, and went out, followed by Vicky. The solemn little boy was standing at the gate with two fingers and a thumb in his mouth. He stared at them stolidly as they passed.

Every evening, mingled with Miss Thompson's pleasure at being left in sole charge of her pupil, was a slight regret that she could not send her down, beautifully dressed, to an admiring drawing-room for the conventional "children's hour." She felt jealous for the child's beauty and good manners, because there were so few people to appreciate them. It was the irony of fate, she thought, that, when her pupils had been rough and unruly, there had always been parents to find fault with her, and now, when for once she had a pupil who was perfectly behaved and perfectly mannered, there was no one to accord her her due meed of praise.

But after tea, when the regulation time for the "children's hour" arrived, Miss Thompson would give herself up entirely to the entertainment of her little charge, and the two of them would play draughts or dominoes or arrange scraps in the scrap-book and pressed flowers in the wild-flower book, or Miss Thompson would read aloud from *Sandford and Merton, Ministering Children, or The Wide Wide World*. There was something essentially childlike about Miss Thompson, and she entered into all these games and interests as whole-heartedly as Vicky herself. The woman and child lived in a warm, happy, intimate world, in which nothing existed but themselves and their concerns. Precise and tidy, giving meticulous care to details, living a life of unchanging routine, they were more like a couple of elderly spinsters than a pupil and governess. Vicky, as a rule, hated to deviate from their routine by even a fraction. Tea at five, games from half-past five to six, reading aloud from six to half-past, scraps or painting from half-past six to seven. At seven came bed with prayers and a Bible story. Vicky was a devout child and prayed for the poor and sick and wicked every night and morning. She enjoyed doing this, not only because it made her feel that she was helping to make them better, but also because it made her feel rich and well and good.

To-night Vicky won at draughts, and Miss Thompson at dominoes. Vicky was a good loser though she loved to win. Then they put some scraps into Vicky's scrap-book, Miss Thompson as deeply interested in their arrangement as Vicky herself. (Miss Thompson would sometimes lie awake at night, planning new arrangements for the pages of the scrap-book and wild-flower collection.)

"Seven o'clock, Vicky," said Miss Thompson at last. "Time to go to bed."

Vicky looked up from her scrap-book.

"I haven't finished the page," she said. "I can't leave it in the middle of a page."

"There's no such word as 'can't', dear," said Miss Thompson. She had made this fallacious statement on an average a dozen times a day since she began her teaching career. "Put the book away now."

Vicky's dislike of leaving anything half-done fought and conquered her dislike of deviating from routine. It was bedtime but she wanted to finish the page. She went on slowly and carefully arranging the little coloured pictures.

"Vicky!" said Miss Thompson, and then weakly, "How much more have you to do?"

"Only this page."

"But you've only just begun, dear. You won't finish for a long time. No, you mustn't stay up any longer. Put it away at once."

She came towards Vicky as if to take the book. The small face was suddenly distorted with anger, the cheeks flushed, the blue eyes flashing.

"Don't take it. . . . I won't go to bed. I *will* finish it. . . . Leave me alone. . . . Go away."

She had spread her arm over the book as though to protect it from attack, and her voice was choked with tears. Miss Thompson knew the symptoms. If she persisted, the child would fly into a rage, hitting, biting, kicking, and, when finally put to bed, would cry for half the night. These crises did not often occur, and Miss Thompson, who valued discretion above valour, had learnt skill in warding them off. A child should, after all, be led, not driven. Vicky was really no trouble at all if managed in the right way, so Miss Thompson proceeded to manage her in the right way.

"Very well, dear," she said graciously. "I'll allow you to stay up a little later to-night just for a treat."

Chapter Two

VICKY came down to breakfast the next morning in high spirits. Miss Thompson was rather silent, not because of last night's little scene—for she considered that she had dealt with that very wisely—but because she had received a letter from Mr. Carothers saying that he was coming home that day and would arrive some time during the evening. It was short and laconic, and it depressed Miss Thompson unaccountably.

"I have various arrangements to make," ran the letter, "and I think it best to speak to you about them in person."

What "arrangements" had he to make? The feeling of insecurity that was to Miss Thompson part of the very air she breathed seemed to locate itself as a dull aching constriction on her chest. She had always thought that this post was too good to last, but surely it wasn't going to come to an end as suddenly as this. . . .

"I have had a letter from your papa, Vicky," she said. "He's coming home to-day."

Vicky raised shining blue eyes from her plate.

"Oh, how *lovely*!" she said.

Probably the most real emotion in Vicky's life was her love for her father, and even that was mixed up with a jumble of sentimental day-dreams in which she figured as heroine. She saw her father's sudden decision to return home as a proof of his devotion to her. He could not bear to stay away from his darling a moment longer. Perhaps he was bringing a box full of presents for her. He would take her abroad with him. Betsy's papa had done that, because Betsy was such an agreeable little companion and reminded him so constantly of her dead mama. Vicky saw herself being an agreeable little companion to Papa and reminding him constantly of her dead mama as they travelled about through the deserts and jungles that were Vicky's mental picture of "abroad."

Miss Thompson rose from her seat and went over to the window.

"The boy's come," she said.

She had felt responsible for Andrew since engaging him, but now that he was actually working in the garden under Belson's direction her responsibilities ceased.

Vicky finished her breakfast and ran to the window, too. There he was, the pale lanky boy who impersonated for her the whole class of the humble and admiring Poor, digging one of the beds on the lawn.

"May I go down to the garden before lessons, Miss Thompson, please?" she asked.

"Certainly, dear," said Miss Thompson. "I'll call you in when I'm ready for you."

Miss Thompson was so much disconcerted by the letter she had just received from her employer that she was only too glad to be left alone. The fear that it heralded the end of her pleasant placid existence in this house still oppressed her. She felt like a fox in its hole who hears the feet of the huntsmen coming to dig it out. She thought of the un-ruliness of some of her former pupils, the unreasonableness and rudeness of their parents, and the constriction in her chest became a physical pain.

Vicky went downstairs and ran across the garden to where Andrew was working. This thin ugly boy in the shabby clothes had an irresistible fascination for her. In his presence everything about herself that she admired seemed to become still more admirable. His ugliness emphasised her beauty, his clumsiness her grace, his undeniable commonness her own refinement.

"Good morning, Andrew," she said sweetly.

"Good morning, miss," he said.

He didn't look up from his work, and she began to feel somewhat disconcerted. She stood by him for some moments, not knowing what to say next. Finally she said:

"Are you digging?"

"Yes, miss," said Andrew, still without looking up.

She was silent again, wondering whether to say "Do you like digging?" and deciding against it on the grounds that he would probably just say "Yes, miss" again without looking at her. She felt vaguely aggrieved that he hadn't looked at her as she stood there in her red linsey dress and pinafore, with her curls over her shoulders.

She began to kick at the ground with her shoes, but still he took no notice. A sudden inspiration came to her, and she ran indoors to fetch her skipping-rope. Then she took up her position by Andrew and began to skip as fast as she could, passing the rope to the right and the left, passing it twice under her feet as she jumped, and finally running lightly round the lawn, skipping as she went.

She stopped at last, breathless. He was still digging as if she were not there. She felt strangely put out and was wondering what to do next to attract his attention when Miss Thompson opened the schoolroom window and called, "Come indoors now, dear. It's time for lessons."

Vicky went slowly across the lawn to the side door. At the door she turned sharply to see if the boy were watching her, but he was still busily engaged in digging. She shrugged and pouted, then ran upstairs to the schoolroom.

The morning passed slowly. Both Miss Thompson and Vicky were distrait. The feeling of apprehension weighed ever more heavily on Miss Thompson's spirits, while Vicky still felt disconcerted by the lack of response shown by the boy at work in the garden. She kept making excuses to go past the window so that she could see what he was doing. Once or twice she moved the curtains, hoping that he would look up at her, but he didn't.

By lunch time Miss Thompson had one of her headaches. Miss Thompson was vaguely proud of her headaches. She was herself, she knew, supremely negligible and uninteresting, but the headaches gave her a certain spurious distinction and importance. They only came on when she had been worrying and, she felt modestly, marked her out as a sensitive and highly strung organism. She was too conscientious, however, to presume on them and only gave in when she could really hold out no longer.

The lunch was, as usual, beautifully cooked and served (that was another point: she had never been in a place before where the maids took any trouble with the schoolroom), but Miss Thompson could eat nothing.

"I wonder if you would mind playing quietly in the garden by yourself this afternoon, dear," she said at last, when Vicky had finished her second helping of pudding, said her grace, and got down from her seat. "I have rather a headache, and I think I'll go and lie down."

"Yes, of course I will, Miss Thompson," said Vicky demurely. "I'm so sorry about your headache."

Secretly she felt delighted. It would give her another opportunity of approaching the strange unresponsive creature in the garden and forcing him to recognise her sovereignty.

She washed her face, tidied her hair, and went down to the garden. The boy was weeding the lawn now, kneeling by the side of a gardening basket, digging out daisy roots with a little fork.

Vicky went up to him and stood by him in silence. She remembered suddenly that she hadn't told him that her papa was coming home.

"My papa's coming home to-day," she said importantly.

He went on weeding without answering her.

"I expect he'll bring me lots of presents."

She waited for some comment but, receiving none, continued, "He's going to take me away with him. To London and Paris and probably abroad. I don't suppose you'll see me again after to-day."

Andrew deftly dug up a plantain root and put it in the basket without speaking.

"I haven't any mama," went on Vicky, trying to instil a note of pathos into her voice. Surely that would interest him. But apparently it didn't. He moved his basket a few yards away to do another patch. Vicky followed.

"I'm all my papa has now, so of course he's wrapt up in me," she went on.

He made no comment. There seemed nothing more to say on that subject.

"I'm seven," she said after another pause. "How old are you?"

He'd have to say something now, she thought with satisfaction.

"Thirteen, miss," he replied, and moved still farther away.

She had made him speak, but it seemed somehow to bring the conversation to a close.

She looked around. In the park over the railings she could see Judy, her pony. It was characteristic of Mr. Carothers that, having realised that his daughter was of a suitable age to learn to ride, he had purchased a pony, but had made no further arrangements. The old coachman had retired on a pension soon after the pony arrived, and no other had been engaged as the carriage was now never used. Belson, the gardener, looked after the pony and had once made a half-hearted attempt to teach Vicky to ride, but after two or three falls Vicky had decided to put it off till she was older. Miss Thompson, who considered riding far too dangerous for her darling, had heartily concurred, and so Judy spent a happy existence in the park, the monotony varied by an occasional harnessing to the garden roller, when she trotted up and down the lawn with sacking tied round her hoofs. Now, for the first time, Vicky wished that she could ride. She wanted to canter round the park on Judy before the eyes of the gardener's boy. Surely he'd admire her then. . . .

"That's my pony there in the park," she said.

Andrew lifted his eyes, glanced at the pony, and lowered them again to his weeding.

"I can ride it," went on Vicky.

Still he said nothing.

She suddenly became angry.

"I'm going to ride it now," she went on. "You can watch me if you like."

She ran to the railings.

"Judy!" she called.

Judy, expecting the piece of sugar that Vicky sometimes remembered to bring her, came trotting up, and Vicky climbed onto the railings and sprang on her back, clutching at the mane. Judy started off at a canter. Vicky held on triumphantly, but she couldn't resist turning her head to make sure that Andrew was watching, and in that moment she shot off the smooth round back to the ground.

For a second she was too stunned to do anything but lie there. Then she began to cry—loud childish sobs of pain and fear and anger. She felt herself raised gently in a pair of thin strong arms.

"That's all right, missie, don't cry . . . you're not hurt that bad. . . . There, there!"

Andrew had had a disturbing day. The radiant vision of perfection who had appeared suddenly in his home yesterday had turned into a very conceited little girl, intent upon showing off. And now again she had turned into a hurt and frightened baby whom he was comforting, just as he would have comforted the fat baby at home had she fallen on her head.

Vicky hid her face on his shoulder, ashamed of her tears but unable to check them, clinging to him blindly for consolation.

He carried her to the garden seat and put her down.

"You're all right, missie," he said reassuringly. "Now, don't you cry no more."

Still sobbing, she pushed her hair out of her eyes.

"I'm not all right," she said. "I'm nearly killed. I——"

Miss Thompson came running across the lawn, her face pale and tense. She had been roused from sleep by the sound of Vicky's cries and had hurried down in a fever of apprehension. She would never forgive herself if anything had happened to her darling to-day, just when her papa was expected.

Examination, however, showed nothing worse than a badly bruised knee and forehead.

"Thank you very much, Andrew," said Miss Thompson. "I should have been down in a moment, of course, but it was quite right of you to go to help Miss Vicky. . . . Come along, darling."

But Vicky continued to sob, though less violently now, and protested that she couldn't walk, so Andrew lifted her up and carried her indoors. She still clung to him, hiding her face on his shoulder, frightened and ashamed, but taking comfort from the firm clasp of his arms about her.

"You can go upstairs yourself, dear," said Miss Thompson when they had reached the foot of the stairs. It was really hardly fitting for the gardener's boy to be seen in the upper regions of the house.

Andrew gently set Vicky on her feet. She was so shaken that she had forgotten all her affectations. She raised her tear-stained face to him and he bent down and kissed it, then tiptoed clumsily to the side door and out into the garden. Miss Thompson was slightly shocked. It had surely been rather "familiar" of him to kiss the child. But there had been something so natural in the raising of her face and his response that one couldn't feel seriously annoyed.

She took Vicky to the bathroom and bathed the bruises. Fortunately her fringe hid the one on her forehead. It would have been dreadful for the child to have been disfigured by a bruise the first time her papa saw her after all these months. What a good thing the accident hadn't been worse! And Vicky was generally so careful—not one of those children who were always falling about and hurting themselves.

"Whatever made you do it, darling?" she said, as she combed the golden fringe gently over the rising lump.

"I wanted to ride Judy," said Vicky in a small unsteady voice.

"But why?"

"I don't know," said Vicky after a pause.

Now that the pain and fright were lessening she was beginning to feel humiliated by the incident. She had had a mental vision of herself flying gracefully round the park, seated firmly on Judy's back, and she could hardly bear to think of the scene that had taken its place.

Miss Thompson was holding up a dainty white muslin frock, trimmed with bows of blue ribbon. It was Vicky's best frock and had only been worn once before.

"I think you might put this on after tea, dear," she said, "ready for when your papa comes."

Vicky's feeling of humiliation vanished. What did Andrew matter, after all? He was only a gardener's boy. She didn't care whether he thought she could ride or not, or, indeed, what he thought of her.

Papa was coming home—Papa who adored her, who couldn't bear to stay away from her a moment longer, Papa laden with wonderful presents for her, Papa who was going to take her abroad with him. She saw herself walking round the garden with him, hanging on his arm. Andrew would look up from his weeding and touch his forehead respectfully, and she would smile at him very graciously. The picture restored her cherished sense of importance, blotting out the ignominious picture that the afternoon had left on her mind.

"I wonder when he'll come," she said excitedly.

"I don't know, dear," said Miss Thompson. "You can stay up till eight, but if he hasn't come then you must go to bed, of course."

"He's sure to come and see me in bed if he comes late," said Vicky with happy conviction.

After tea Miss Thompson dressed her charge in the white muslin frock, tying a pale blue silk sash round her waist.

Then they went to the schoolroom, where Vicky knelt on the window-seat, her eyes fixed eagerly on the corner of the drive that could be seen from it, and Miss Thompson sat at the table sewing with fingers that were not quite steady. Neither of them thought of suggesting the usual entertainments.

The evening wore on. Emma brought in the lamp, setting it down in the middle of the table and hovering in the doorway as if she would have liked to discuss the master's visit with Miss Thompson, but Miss Thompson shot a warning glance at Vicky and pursed her lips.

Suddenly Vicky gave a cry of joy.

"A cab! A cab! Oh, it *must* be Papa."

Miss Thompson folded her sewing and put it into her work-basket, her heart beating unevenly.

"I'll go down and receive him, Vicky," she said. "You'd better stay here till you're sent for."

Vicky made no demur. The beloved little daughter should, of course, be leaping downstairs into Papa's outstretched arms, but now that Papa was actually here Vicky somehow felt much less like the beloved little daughter.

Her heart, too, was beating unevenly, and she was rather glad of a respite before actually going into Papa's presence.

Miss Thompson smoothed her black silk apron, drew a deep breath, and went downstairs.

She reached the hall just as Mr. Carothers was entering it. He was a handsome man above medium height, with a rather stern expression and luxuriant black side whiskers. He wore a tall hat and heavily caped ulster. Waving aside Miss Thompson's nervous suggestion of tea, he handed his hat and coat to the maid and took out his watch.

"I can only stay a few moments, Miss Thompson. I have told the cabman to wait as I wish to catch the 6.40 back to London."

"Oh, but——" began Miss Thompson.

He silenced her with an imperious wave of his hand.

"I can say what I have to say in a very few words," he said. "Shall we go into the drawing-room?"

They went into the magnificent shrouded drawing-room. It had never been used since Miss Thompson had known it. The Venetian blinds were drawn, the chairs and the chandelier covered with holland. The bearskin hearthrug was rolled up, the Aubusson carpet hidden by drugget. In the dim light the piano, chiffonier, and inlaid cabinet looked unreal and ghost-like, the lustres threw out a faint subdued gleam. Even the wax flowers beneath their glass cases showed wan and colourless. An ormolu clock on the mantelpiece had stopped at twenty-two minutes past ten.

Mr. Carothers motioned Miss Thompson to a holland-covered chair, and she sat down, simply because her knees were too weak to support her any longer.

In the interview that followed her worst fears were justified. Mr. Carothers was marrying again; would be married, in fact, within the month. His new wife would be making the Hall her home, and they thought it best for all concerned that there should be what Mr. Carothers called a "clean break." In other words, he gave Miss Thompson a month's notice, thanking her for her services and assuring her that he would do all he could to assist her in finding another post. Then he took out his watch again.

"And now I'm afraid——" he began.

Miss Thompson mastered her emotion sufficiently to say:

"But you'll see Vicky, won't you?"

He frowned as though her suggestion were distasteful.

"Victoria? Surely that is not necessary? I think that you can probably explain the situation to her better than I can. It can mean little or nothing to a child of that age."

He strode into the hall, took his coat from the hook where the maid had put it, and shrugged his broad shoulders into it.

"Oh, but, please ..." protested Miss Thompson, thinking of Vicky upstairs, waiting so patiently, dressed up so beautifully. "She'd be so upset. ... If you'd just speak to her I'll call her. ..."

She ran half-way upstairs, called "Vicky" in an unsteady voice, and then, standing in the shadow of the wall, began to cry silently, making furtive little dabs at her cheek with her handkerchief.

Vicky came down slowly, her curls hanging over her shoulders, her eyes bright with excitement. At the bottom she stood, trying to still the beating of her heart, waiting to be swung up in his great arms and kissed.

Mr. Carothers looked at her and frowned again, as if the sight of her were as distasteful as the mention of her name had been.

"Well, my dear ..." he said awkwardly.

Then he bent down, brushed his moustache about an inch from her face, put on his hat, and went out to the waiting cab.

Chapter Three

THE new Mrs. Carothers sat at a desk in her boudoir, writing to an old school friend. She was a handsome woman, with fine dark eyes and glossy dark hair, massed—in the style of the day—into a thick loosely woven plait at the back of her head. She wore a dress of checked brown and grey barege, trimmed with cross-bars of brown faille and rows of flounces. The over-dress was looped up into a large bow behind, emphasising the fashionable bustle.

"The workmen have gone at last," she wrote, "and we have more or less settled down. The place had been neglected for so long that simply everything needed doing. While the child was here alone with her governess they managed with a cook and a housemaid, both of whom I have got rid of, as I consider that the fewer left-overs from the old *ménage*, the better. Actually there is now no one but a gardener's boy, and he was here only for a few weeks before we came. The gardener, fortunately, was old enough to be pensioned off, and I have engaged a new one who has already improved the place considerably. It was very old-fashioned. There was not even a croquet lawn. My old nurse has come to look after the child till we find a good school for her. We hope to find one soon, especially as I am expecting a certain happy event in the spring, and should like her out of the way by then. Edmund wants her out of the way as soon as possible in any case. She's ridiculously like Rosamund, and you can imagine that he does not exactly relish being reminded of Rosamund at every turn. I cannot tell you how shamefully that woman treated him right from the beginning. He says that he cannot even be sure that the child is his own, which is another reason why he would like her packed off to school as soon as we can arrange it. One would be sorry for her if she were not so insufferably affected and conceited. She has been hopelessly spoilt by her governess who was apparently an utter fool.

"There are some new people at the Vicarage. . . ."

Vicky still felt bewildered by the changes that had taken place around her during the last few months. An army of workmen had invaded the house, and the rooms had re-echoed all day to the sound of hammering. Every room had been redecorated. A large conservatory had been built on to the drawing-room, and a smoking-room added at the side of the conservatory. Vanloads of new furniture had arrived, pictures by modern artists—Leighton, Alma-Tadema, Landseer,—crates of "curios" from places on the Continent where the newly married couple were staying. One of the bedrooms had been turned into a boudoir for the bride—the chairs, couch, and footstool upholstered in yellow satin, an inlaid French writing-desk at the window, an embroidery frame and painting easel behind the door. The china door-knob and finger-plate were hand-painted, and the thick soft carpet showed an elegant design of pink and yellow flowers.

Cook and Emma departed, and new servants began to arrive, among them a butler and a page, resplendent in tightly fitting uniform and a row of buttons. A new coachman and a groom took up their quarters over the stables, and the old carriage was replaced by a shining new one from London. Gas had been laid on, too, and Vicky loved to see the little "batswing" of flame leap up at the touch of the long taper.

She wandered through it all, enchanted. It was like watching a spell actually taking effect before her eyes. The house was a Cinderella, shedding its dinginess at the touch of the Fairy Godmother's wand. Vicky was, as usual, in her own eyes, the central figure of the picture. The grand new furniture, the shining mirrors, the bright new carpets and wall-papers existed only as a background for her. She was the little princess and the grand new house her palace.

She had cried inconsolably on the night of her father's visit, but when morning came she had explained his behaviour quite

24

satisfactorily to herself. He had had to go back by the next train on account of Business (that mysterious agency that had gentlemen at its beck and call), and he had been almost as heartbroken by the short meeting as she was. She had wandered into the kitchen garden after breakfast and found Andrew hoeing a lettuce bed.

"My papa came last night," she said, "but he only had just time to see me and dash off again. He was terribly disappointed. He'd wanted to stay here and then take me abroad with him, but he had Business in London and couldn't."

"Yes, miss," said Andrew, feeling rather uncomfortable, for he had already heard Cook's version of the affair.

In the days that followed Vicky found that she could do pretty much as she liked. The schoolroom was being turned into another dressing-room, and there was no place in the house where Miss Thompson could conveniently give her lessons. Moreover, Miss Thompson had naturally lost interest in the lessons. She spent most of her time writing letters of application for posts in her flowing copperplate handwriting and weeping in her bedroom. She shrank with all her being from a return to the life of the normal schoolroom, to noisy unruly children and interfering parents. She felt hurt that Vicky seemed so little affected by the prospect of separation from her—Vicky, flitting excitedly from room to room, chattering to the workmen, and watching them at work.

When the actual day of her departure arrived, however, Vicky wept all morning, and Miss Thompson felt slightly consoled. But, though Vicky's tears were genuine enough, there was an undercurrent of excitement even in her distress. It was the end of the old happy order of things, but it was the beginning of a new and still happier order. She saw herself driving out in the new carriage with her new mama, saw herself in the spacious new drawing-room surrounded by a crowd of visitors. She would occupy, of course, one of the lovely new bedrooms that were being papered in hand-made Morris paper, with designs of flowers and fruit (the one next Papa and Mama perhaps. . . . She would go in and wake them in the mornings).

Her attitude to the new mama had undergone several changes

since she heard of her. At first she had felt indignant at being deprived of her cherished imaginary position as Papa's little joy and comfort. Then she had felt pathetic, for all stepmothers were of necessity cruel and she would probably be ill-treated now for the rest of her life. Then Miss Thompson had suddenly remembered that the stepmother of one of her old pupils had been a most devoted parent, and after that the new mama took her place among the shadowy admirers who thronged Vicky's dreams.

Mr. and Mrs. Carothers had not yet returned from their honeymoon when Miss Thompson went away. She felt distressed at leaving Vicky with no one to look after her but the maids. She wanted to hand her formally into her successor's charge, to explain that she was an affectionate child and had a beautiful nature but must be led, not driven.

"You'll write and tell me everything, won't you, darling?" she said tearfully as she kissed Vicky good-bye and gave her bag to Andrew to carry down to the waiting carriage.

Vicky didn't take much notice of Andrew nowadays. The large new staff and expensive new furniture seemed to have placed him immeasurably beneath her. She often went out of her way to meet him so that he would have to touch his forehead to her because she enjoyed that, but she did not speak to him except to say "Good morning" in her little princess voice.

The days after Miss Thompson's departure passed quickly and happily. She queened it to her heart's content over both servants and workmen, and looked forward with joyful eagerness to the moment of Papa's and Mama's return.

The actual moment of their return fulfilled her highest expectations, for she stood alone at the top of the steps to receive them, dressed in the white muslin frock and blue ribbons—but only the actual moment. It was all over almost before it had begun ... two perfunctory kisses, and she was whisked off to a room at the top of the house which had been hastily furnished as a nursery, in the charge of a uniformed individual, called Nurse Tanner, who had arrived in the wake of the bridal couple. The change was so sudden and so complete that at first Vicky felt stunned by it. From being the petted companion of Miss Thompson, the adored "Little Missie" of the workpeople and servants, she was suddenly subjected to a nursery discipline that she had never known in her short life before.

There was much coming and going downstairs. Carriages wheeled up and down the newly gravelled drive, horses were led by grooms to the front door for Mr. and Mrs. Carothers and their guests, there were dinner-parties, tea-parties, luncheon-parties, but for all the part that Vicky played in it she might not have been there. She never oven set foot in the gorgeous bedroom where she had imagined herself waking Papa and Mama in the morning; she was never sent for to the spacious drawing-room, though it was full of visitors almost every day. She was not even allowed to go up or down the sweeping staircase that she had used all her life till now. A staircase connected the nursery with a side door into the garden, and Vicky and Nurse Tanner used that.

Nurse Tanner was a middle-aged woman, good-tempered but a firm disciplinarian. She was conscientious in the training of children and the care of their health, but had little personal affection for them. Far away, indeed, were the days when Miss Thompson had taken as much interest in the arrangement of scraps and dried flowers as Vicky herself.

"Now then, Miss Vicky, take your mess off that table," Nurse Tanner would say briskly.

Far, too, were the days of Miss Thompson's long and patient explanations of any problem that Vicky propounded.

"Don't bother me with your questions," Nurse Tanner would say, "I've no time for them," while at any hint of the tantrums that had brought Miss Thompson so promptly to heel, she was shut up in the big nursery cupboard, where she could kick and scream as much as she liked, but was never let out till she had said she was sorry and promised to be good.

Banished from the glamorous life she had imagined for herself, Vicky shed many tears of disappointment and chagrin. She decided to say, if anyone asked why she was crying, "I'm crying for my real mama, who's dead," but she was denied even that satisfaction, for no one asked her why she was crying.

In spite of all this, however, she was just settling down to her new existence, getting used to the grimness of Nurse Tanner, and adjusting herself to the routine of the nursery, when she became aware of further impending changes. There were whispered consultations between Mama and Nurse Tanner over something called an inventory—"Two school dresses, one Sunday dress, two hats . . ."

Vicky, pretending to be absorbed in her games, because she had learnt that people forgot to whisper if they thought you were not listening, gathered that she was going to be sent away to school. At first she didn't know whether to be aggrieved or excited about it. Rather to her surprise she found that she would be sorry to leave the nursery and Nurse Tanner. They had by now acquired the charm of the known. They held no further shocks or surprises for her. They formed the rut into which she had unconsciously been digging herself all the time that she imagined herself martyred and ill-used. Moreover, though she had no part in the glamorous life of the house, the coming and going, the laughter and music and parties, still she existed there on the edge of it. She knew when there was to be a party, could sometimes manage to escape to the top landing and look down upon the flower-decked heads and sweeping trains in the hall below. It was a sad change from her dreams, but it was better than nothing. And now she was to be uprooted again and flung into the unknown.

But she felt excited as well, for her dreams seized avidly upon the blank canvas to paint on it the picture they loved so dearly. She would be clever and popular. She would win all the prizes. Papa would at last love her and be proud of her. For that was the goal of all her dreams—the winning of Papa's love. She built up endless little fictions to prove to herself that Papa loved her, but she knew now in her heart that he didn't.

When Mrs. Carothers told her that she would be going away to school next term, Vicky received the news docilely and demurely, without comment.

"You see, dear," said Mrs. Carothers, who felt a slight compunction at the banishment of the child, "Papa and I want to do the very best we can for you, and at this school we've chosen for you you will have excellent teaching and be looked after far better than we could look after you here. Do you understand?"

"Yes, Mama," said Vicky.

"She wasn't even interested," said Mrs. Carothers to her husband afterwards. "She seems a stupid little creature in some ways, though Nurse says she's sharp enough on the whole. She's certainly pretty. . . ."

Mr. Carothers' lips had taken on the grim lines that any mention of his only daughter seemed to bring to them.

"My dear Eleanor," he said, "need we discuss her?"

Preparations for the change now went on openly. Nurse Tanner laid aside certain tiny garments (which, she told Vicky, she was making for a sister's child) and set to work on Vicky's outfit—measuring, sewing, trying on. . . .

One morning Mama came into the nursery straight from riding, still wearing, her habit—tall silk hat, close-fitting bodice, and flowing skirts. She carried a riding-whip in one hand and held up her skirts with the other.

Nurse Tanner rose to her feet respectfully. Though her mistress had spent her childhood under Nurse Tanner's stern rule, Nurse Tanner was now scrupulous to accord her all the marks of respect that she considered due from employee to employer.

"Good morning, Nurse."

"Good morning, ma'am."

"Good morning, Vicky."

"Good morning, Mama."

"As you're going to school next week, Vicky, I thought that perhaps you'd like to have a picnic before you go. You may ask the Vicarage children and walk over to Darrock Woods with them. Andrew can take the dog-cart with the tea by road and meet you there. Would you like that?"

"Oh yes, please, Mama," said Vicky eagerly.

"A picnic!" she cried, when the door closed behind her stepmother. "How lovely!"

"Yes, and you'd better behave yourself between now and then," said Nurse Tanner grimly, "or there'll be no picnic for you nor nothing else."

Vicky was not depressed by this sinister pronouncement. She hardly heard it, indeed, for Nurse Tanner's daily conversation consisted chiefly of similar premonitions.

A picnic. The Vicarage children. Vicky had been to tea at the Vicarage the week before to meet the new Vicar's children. There were three of them—Roger, aged eight; Mark, six; and Mabs, four.

Roger was a grave, silent little boy, tall and fair and very thin, who kept a watchful eye upon the other two, ready always to quell Mark's over-exuberance or go to Mabs' help when she was hurt or frightened. Mark was square and sturdy, with rosy cheeks and dark curly hair. He very easily became over-excited, and then he would begin to show off, shouting "Look at me" or "See what I'm doing." Roger's "Shut up, Mark," would repress him, but only for a short time. Mabs was a roly-poly of a child, with rosy cheeks and brown curls like Mark. She was very shy and prone to tears, and was always running to Roger for comfort and protection.

Vicky was glad that Andrew would be at the picnic, too. She looked on Andrew as her special possession. She had gone with Miss Thompson to engage him. He had been there in the days when she had queened it over Miss Thompson and the servants. She felt it vitally important somehow that Andrew should see her as the radiant and beloved "Little Missie" of her dreams. And there was no doubt that, lately at any rate, he hadn't done. He had heard Nurse Tanner's scoldings and seen her in tears many times in the last few weeks as he worked in the garden.

The picnic would restore her prestige. She saw herself playing with Roger, Mark, and Mabs, while Andrew waited in the background with the tea-basket, watching her. She would order him about kindly but imperiously. She felt still more excited when she learnt that Nurse was not to be in charge of the party. Instead, the maid from the Vicarage was to be in charge—a large untidy girl called Violet, who was supposed to help in the house as well as look after the children, and who did as little of either as she possibly could.

Vicky sulked somewhat when she was told that she must wear her everyday blue gingham frock and pinafore for the picnic (Nurse Tanner had made short work of the elaborate little toilettes provided by Miss Thompson), but she did not dare to argue the point, for she knew that Nurse Tanner would have thought nothing of putting a stop to the whole outing even at the last minute.

The day dawned fine and sunny, and the morning passed off without anything worse than a "Now, Miss Vicky, do you want to go to that picnic or not?" when Vicky dallied over her porridge at breakfast.

Violet and the Vicarage children called for her soon after lunch, and the party set out. Roger and Mark wore sailor suits and Mabs (Vicky was relieved to see) a pink cotton frock.

Vicky walked in front with Roger and Mark, and Mabs walked behind, holding Violet's hand.

"Andrew's bringing the tea in the dog-cart," said Vicky importantly. "He's our gardener's boy."

"Oh, we know Andrew," said Roger. "He comes to help in our garden on his half day."

It was rather a shock to find that anyone else had any claim on Andrew.

"Oh, his half day," said Vicky, as if that did not count.

"Look at me," shouted Mark. "I'm walking on my toes."

"Shut up, Mark," said Roger, and continued, "Andrew can tell a bird from its note—every bird, not just the ordinary ones."

But Vicky didn't want to talk about Andrew. She couldn't have contemplated any life in which Andrew wasn't there in the background, but he was only a servant, not important enough to be talked about.

"I'm going to school next week," she said. "I'm having all the extras—French and dancing and meat for breakfast and milk."

"Are you?" said Roger. "The milk'll probably be sour. It's nearly always sour at our school, but they make you drink it."

"I'm going to school because Papa wants me to be well informed," went on Vicky. "He'll miss me terribly."

As usual, it became true when she said it, but she wished that Roger would say something in reply. His saying nothing made it seem just a little less true than it would have seemed if he'd agreed.

"Look at me," shouted Mark. "I've got a caterpillar walking on my finger."

"*Isn't* it a long way?" said Mabs pathetically.

"Would you like to hold my hand, Mabs?" said Roger, and Mabs came and walked between Roger and Vicky, holding Roger's hand.

She looked shyly up at Vicky from beneath her thick lashes and turned her head away, overcome with confusion whenever Vicky looked at her. She had short fat legs, and dragged her toes in the dust every now and then to make a little white cloud.

Mark was stamping and singing and pretending to be a soldier. He had taken a stick from the hedgerow and was slashing with it in all directions.

"Put that stick down for goodness' sake, Master Mark," said Violet. "You'll have my eyes out next."

Vicky noticed with envy that none of the Vicarage children ever dreamed of doing what Violet told them, and that she didn't even seem to expect them to. Probably no one would have been more surprised than Violet if Mark had put his stick down. Even Mabs only stopped dragging her toes in the dust for a few seconds after Violet had reproved her, then started again.

Vicky and Roger kept up a desultory conversation over Mabs' hat. Vicky was very anxious for Roger to like her and kept trying hard to impress him.

"I've got a pony," she said.

"I know," said Roger. "I've seen it."

"I can ride it awfully fast."

"I've never seen you riding it."

"No, I don't ride it in the road. I only ride it in the park."

There was another long silence. Evidently Roger wasn't interested in the pony.

"I know the names of all the wild flowers that grow round here," she went on. "I'll tell you some."

She named the flowers that grew in the hedgerows as they passed.

"Did you know all those?" she said.

"No," said Roger.

He didn't seem interested in wild flowers either, but there was an ingenuous admiration in his eyes as they rested on her that Vicky found very gratifying.

They had reached the wood now, and Roger unfastened the big wooden gate and pushed it open for them.

"I'll be glad of a sit down, I can tell you," said Violet as she entered. "I'm just about wore out with all that walk in the heat."

They went down a narrow path that wound in and out of the trees till they came to a small clearing. At one side was a beech tree whose leaves seemed to hold the sunshine like tiny luminous cups till it splashed over upon the ground beneath.

Violet sank down and leant against its trunk with every sign of extreme exhaustion.

"Walking about in the heat!" she repeated. "Even the animals know better."

Violet was a strong healthy girl, but objected to exercise in any form, and was fond of pointing out that the animals never took any unless they were compelled. Her greatest grievance was her daily walk with the children.

"If you've got to go somewhere you've got to go somewhere," she would say, "but walkin' for the sake of walkin'—it's not natural."

Still panting, she took from her bag a paper-backed novelette and became deaf and blind to all that went on around her.

"What shall we do till tea-time?" said Vicky.

"Hide-and-seek," suggested Roger.

"You'll never find me," shouted Mark.

"Can I hide with you, Roger?" said Mabs anxiously.

"May she?" said Roger to Vicky. "She can never think of places to hide in by herself and then she cries."

They played Hide-and-seek and Catch among the trees, and

Vicky became, almost for the first time in her life, an ordinary shouting romping child among other shouting romping children.

At last they stopped breathless and sat down on the grass.

"What time is it, Violet?" said Roger.

The third time the question was asked Violet tore herself reluctantly from the attic room where the kidnapped heroine was defying the villain and looked at her watch.

"Five to four," she said and returned to the kidnapped heroine.

Mark and Mabs wandered about, picking flowers. Roger and Vicky remained seated on the grass. Roger's eyes were fixed on her gravely. She was flushed and bright-eyed with the game. She turned and met his gaze.

"What are you thinking of?" she said curiously.

"I'm thinking how pretty you are," he said simply.

All her self-consciousness returned. She blushed and tossed back her curls.

"Oh no, I'm not," she said, with an affected little laugh.

Suddenly there was a cry of "Andrew," and the three children ran down the path to the gate, where Andrew had appeared with the dog-cart. Vicky sat alone on the grass, feeling aggrieved and resentful. They needn't all have run off to Andrew like that—even Roger, who'd just said that she was pretty.

In a few moments they returned, hanging round Andrew, all chattering to him at once. A wave of jealousy surged over Vicky. Andrew was *hers*. They'd no business to behave as if he were theirs.

She said, "Good afternoon, Andrew," in her little princess tone, but they were all making so much noise that no one heard.

Andrew touched his cap to her, set down the tea-basket, and went back to the dog-cart.

"He won't have tea with us," said Roger regretfully.

"Of *course* he couldn't have tea with us," said Vicky rather sharply.

During tea her excitement returned. Cook had provided a splendid tea, and the Vicarage children were loud in their praises. There were milk and lemonade, several kinds of sandwiches, a sponge cake, an iced cake, and apples and oranges.

"I wish *we* had picnics like this," said Mark, with his mouth full.

Violet was trying to look after the children, eat her own tea, and go on reading her novelette at the same time. She snapped at the Vicarage children and refused to answer their questions, but her manner to Vicky was respectful and polite. She was overawed by the child's prettiness and grand manner, by the social position of her parents, and the fact that she had tried several times to establish friendly relations with Nurse Tanner, only to be snubbed on each occasion.

"Pity you can't behave like Miss Vicky here," she said to Mabs, who had jam all over her face.

Roger was waiting on Vicky assiduously, and Mark was telling her about a game they played at his school, and about a fight he'd had with another boy, in which, of course, he had come off victor.

Vicky listened, making appropriate comments, aware in every nerve of her guests' admiration. Her happiness was a golden cloud, buoying her up. She seemed to soar blissfully into the air. . . .

They finished tea, and Andrew came for the basket. The others crowded round, helping him pack the things, and going back with him to the dog-cart. Vicky sat alone again, frowning, all her happiness gone. How silly they were! Andrew could perfectly well have carried the things himself. Roger came running back.

"Come on, Vicky. We're going through the woods with Andrew."

"With *Andrew*?" said Vicky, opening her blue eyes wide.

"Yes," said Roger impatiently. "We've been with him before. He's wonderful. He knows where every bird's nest is. He's going to show us a fox's hole. He knows where you can catch fishes in the stream, too. He comes to the woods on Sundays and watches the birds and things. I'm coming with him next Sunday. Papa says I may, in the afternoon. Come on, Vicky."

"I'm not going with Andrew," said Vicky hotly.

"Why not?"

"He's a *servant*."

Roger looked at her for a moment in silence, then he said, "I didn't know you were like that," and, turning slowly, went back to the others.

She heard them setting off through the wood.

"Aren't you coming, Vicky?" called Mark.

"No," answered Vicky, in a voice choked by angry tears.

Their voices died away in the distance.

She sat there, pulling up the grass, her heart seething with anger and disappointment. It was her party and they'd deserted her—deserted her for Andrew, who was only a gardener's boy. . . .

Her anger burnt more fiercely against Andrew than against the other three. It was all his fault. It wouldn't have happened if he hadn't been here. Besides, he was *hers*. What right had they to take him away? He should have been standing in the background, watching her queening it over her party. . . . Her anger changed to a desolation of misery, and her eyes swam suddenly with tears. No one loved her. . . . She'd run away and never come back. Perhaps they'd be sorry then. . . .

Violet was still deeply engrossed in her novelette, quite unaware of what was happening around her. Vicky sprang up and began to run through the wood in the opposite direction to the one the others had taken, but she was crying so much that she didn't see where she was going. She caught her foot in a bramble and fell down, knocking her head against the stub of a tree. She got up and ran on, sobbing, and at last sank down behind a bush and lay there, giving herself up to an abandonment of misery.

Andrew and the Vicarage children came back to the clearing. Andrew had shown them a long-tailed tit's nest and a goldfinch's nest, whose occupants he had watched in the spring, and a squirrel's drey, as well as the fox's hole.

"Where's Vicky?" said Roger, looking round.

Violet raised her bemused eyes from her book. The hero had now been kidnapped, too, but he had managed to bring in a rope ladder concealed on his person, and there was every prospect of a happy ending.

"Wasn't she with you?" she said.

"No," said Roger.

He called "Vicky," but there was no answer.

"Let's go and look for her," he said.

"I'll look for her, Master Roger," said Andrew. "You go along to the dog-cart."

The Vicarage children set off down the path towards the gate.

Andrew made his way uncertainly along the woodland track. He knew that Miss Vicky was hiding somewhere. He knew that she was angry and unhappy. He'd been conscious of her all the time he was with the other children. He had an odd feeling of responsibility for Miss Vicky that he couldn't understand. It might be that he was all that was left of the old regime. It might be that, though he now knew all her faults, he couldn't quite dissociate her from the radiant vision of perfection who had set his heart racing when she came to the cottage with Miss Thompson. Her conceit and affectation irritated him, but he felt sorry for her, because he knew that life had borne rather hardly upon her lately and—it came back to that—he felt responsible for her. No one else—not even her parents—seemed to care what happened to her.

He called but no answer came. Perhaps she really was lost, and in that case Violet and he would get into trouble.

Suddenly he caught the sound of stifled sobs and made his way towards it.

Vicky looked up as he approached. Her face was swollen with crying. She'd meant to be cold and haughty when next she saw him, but she had a headache and felt sick and his coming filled her with a great relief. She was beginning to think that perhaps she really was lost, and then, of course, she would starve to death or be killed by robbers. She forgot that she'd considered him the cause of all her unhappiness. She gave him a faint tremulous smile.

"Oh, there you are!" she said in a voice that she strove to make airy and casual. "I felt tired, so I thought I'd come here and rest. . . ." She paused, then went on, "I fell down and hurt myself. That's why I've been crying."

Again something about her reminded him of the fat baby at home, and his heart melted towards her. He helped her to her feet, then straightened her dress, pushed her hair out of her eyes and, taking her handkerchief, gently wiped her wet cheeks.

"There!" he said at last. "Now we'll go to the others, shall we? Master Roger's picked some flowers for you. Them pretty blue ones you like. . . ."

"Scabious," she said, all her sense of superiority restored as she said the word.

"Yes, them," said Andrew. "He's got quite a big bunch of them."

She took his hand and walked slowly towards the gate. Roger was arranging the baskets in the back of the dogcart, Mark was sitting astride the horse's back, shouting, and Mabs stood by with her finger in her mouth. Violet was walking down the path towards the gate, her head still buried in her novelette.

"Did you show them the fox's hole, Andrew?" said Vicky.

"Yes, Miss Vicky."

"Will you show me some day?"

"Sure I will, Miss Vicky."

Chapter Four

TARNAWAY TOWERS, the school to which Vicky was sent, was a fair-sized country-house in Somerset, belonging to the three Misses Parfitt. Their social standing was irreproachable; for they were the daughters of the late Colonel Parfitt, the nieces of a bishop, and distantly related to a baronet. Together with Tarnaway Towers, Colonel Parfitt had inherited ample means from his father, but he had had extravagant tastes and little scruple in gratifying them, and when he died it was clear that their patrimony would not keep his daughters in comfort or even in decency. Their relatives advised them to sell Tarnaway Towers and apply for posts as governesses in the approved fashion of necessitous gentlewomen, and, as far as the two younger ones, Jessica and Irene, were concerned, they would have acquiesced meekly enough. It was the eldest, Amelia, who took matters into her own hands. She said that she would not sell Tarnaway Towers. She would stay there and turn it into a School for the Daughters of Gentlemen. When asked where she was going to find her capital, she replied quite calmly that they were going to lend it to her, and in the end they did. She bought beds and desks for her pupils, engaged a staff, and sent out her prospectuses, waving aside all consideration of risk, all prophecies of failure.

Her confidence was justified. The pupils arrived, and Tarnaway Towers had prospered ever since. Miss Amelia was very particular whom she admitted into her school. Credentials were carefully scrutinised, and the stigma of trade was avoided as carefully as if it had been a contagious disease. More than one pupil had been summarily despatched home on the discovery that a member of her family was engaged in the nefarious occupation.

She accepted forty pupils. She never had more, never less.

She was a woman of dominating personality, iron will, and a highly intermittent sense of humour. She made no attempt to understand the individualities of her pupils. She did not consider that they had any individualities to understand. She saw them, not as so many immature human beings carrying in themselves the germs of development, but as so much raw material to be moulded ruthlessly into the likeness of the Perfect Gentlewoman. Manners and deportment were ceaselessly inculcated, the slightest peccadilloes were magnified into crimes, and the more refractory of her charges spent a large portion of their time in solitary confinement. Her ideas of discipline were old-fashioned even in those days, and she was scrupulously conscientious, doing what she held to be her duty with a thoroughness that spared herself as little as it spared those around her.

She was, moreover, an inspiring teacher, herself a keen scholar, with the gift of making the subjects she taught interesting to her pupils. She exacted the same standard from them all, never differentiating between laziness and stupidity, accepting no excuses of any sort for neglected work, priding herself on a justice so gloriously impartial that it frequently took the form of the most flagrant injustice.

In appearance she was short and plump, but with a portentous dignity of figure and carriage. Her complexion was sallow, her mouth small, her nose beak-like. She could reduce a guilty child to tears by one glance of her piercing brown eyes.

Miss Jessica, the second of the three sisters, looked after the domestic side of the household, supervised the maids, and ordered the meals. She was a placid edition of Miss Amelia—the same small mouth, beak-like nose, and brown eyes—but in her case the mouth was mild, the eyes vague and short-sighted. She was fond of good living and inclined to be indolent, though too much in awe of her elder sister to indulge her weakness. She would have liked to prepare little treats for the girls in the way of special puddings or a change of fare, but Miss Amelia was adamant on the point. "Plain fare" was an essential of schoolroom life, and the girls must not be allowed to be "dainty."

So Miss Jessica contented herself by planning appetising little menus for the sisters' own meals, and the tantalising odour of roasts and grills would be wafted into the dining-room where the pupils sat eating their supper of dry buns and milk. Miss Jessica, however, would often manage to smuggle up some titbit for any of her favourites who were in disgrace.

She would have been popular had it not been for her habit of eavesdropping, in bedroom slippers, at the doors of classroom and dormitory and reporting what she heard to Miss Amelia.

Miss Irene, the third sister, was unlike either of the others—fair and slender, pretty in a haggard style, with timid blue eyes and hair that would not stay tidy. The story of her one love affair was still told in whispers, handed down through the generations from the girls who had been at Tarnaway Towers at the time. For Miss Irene had fallen in love with the father of one of the pupils and he with her. They had eloped together, but Miss Amelia had followed them that very night, torn her sister from the arms of her lover, and brought her back to Tarnaway Towers. The pupils had sat up in bed, holding their breath, listening to the sound of Miss Irene's convulsive heart-broken sobs. She had appeared in the schoolroom the next morning, white and desperate-looking, and had taught History and English with her usual inefficiency. She had no idea of discipline, but none of the pupils took advantage of this. Her love story made her sacrosanct, and they even conspired to hide her shortcomings from Miss Amelia, whom, they knew, she feared as much as they did themselves.

Miss Amelia showed herself as autocratic in her dealings with her staff as in her dealings with her pupils, and it was therefore continually changing. The only permanent member of it was a Miss Gilbert, who did all the secretarial work and taught any subject demanded by the time-table. She was hard-working and capable, but Miss Amelia secretly despised her, because she allowed herself to be bullied and overworked and accepted all Miss Amelia's snubs with apparent meekness. Miss Gilbert was not really meek, but she knew that she was too old to get another post, and she did not want to be dependent on her married brother, whose wife made no secret of her dislike of her. She was pallid and flabby and had a marked cast in one eye, which, she knew, detracted still further from her market value in the scholastic world. The married brother was in trade (actually he was a tailor), but she had carefully concealed this fact from everyone at Tarnaway Towers. When Miss Amelia was more than usually disagreeable to her, she was always afraid that her secret had been discovered.

It was into this little world that Vicky entered. She entered gaily and light-heartedly, confident as ever in the power of her charm and good looks to secure her the foremost place in it, seeing herself already in her dreams its indulged and established favourite. Her disillusionment was swift and sure. She was considered conceited and "stuck up" by her school-fellows, who promptly combined in the necessary and pleasant task of pricking the bubble of her self-esteem. They left her severely to herself, noticing her, when they noticed her at all, only to mimic her voice and manner. She was, moreover, the new girl, the youngest in the school, and they were determined that she should realise to the full the ignominy of that position.

The mistresses did little to help her. She was under Miss Gilbert's care, and Miss Gilbert, who made a practice of toadying the popular girls and bullying the unpopular ones, joined in the crusade against her.

Vicky cried herself to sleep every night, feeling homesick even for Nurse Tanner's grim rule, planning sensational escapes from the scene of her torments. If she ran away to her home, of course, Papa and Mama would send her back again, so she decided to run away to Andrew and ask him to hide her in the cottage with the solemn little boy and the fat baby.

But though these plans seemed quite possible at night, the day-time always brought the realisation that she had neither the courage nor the necessary money for them. She had imagined that she would shine at lessons, but somehow she didn't. She liked to do a thing slowly and thoroughly, to take her time over it, and she was chivied and harried from lesson to lesson, from classroom to classroom, by the hateful ever-clanging bell. She was bewildered and homesick and miserable, always losing her things (which her school-fellows "borrowed" without compunction), and being late, and getting into trouble.

She heaved a sigh of relief each day when the morning came to an end. The afternoon, however, allowed little respite. Except on Tuesdays and Thursdays there was a "crocodile" under the charge of Miss Gilbert, and, as no one ever asked either Vicky or Miss Gilbert to walk with them, they had to walk together at the back, an arrangement equally disliked by both.

On Tuesday afternoons the pupils had "musical drill" with Miss Irene, at which they bent up and down and to and fro, holding ribbon-trimmed "expanders" or poles. On Thursday afternoons a master came in from Taunton to teach dancing, a neat dapper little man, who played his own accompaniment on the fiddle, and footed it featly among his pupils, playing his fiddle as he danced.

Occasionally the Vicar came to give a Scripture lesson. He was a thin, middle-aged man, with timid eyes and an aggressive manner. It was said that he used to propose to Miss Irene every Sunday before she eloped.

Life was lived to an unchanging routine, but it was enlivened by an unceasing succession of "rows." Someone was always in spectacular disgrace, and Miss Amelia was generally followed in her progress through the day by a small procession of offenders, collected from the various classes she took.

As the term wore on to the accompaniment of punishments, rows, and very occasional treats, Vicky's memories of home took on a glamour that had little to do with reality.

The pupils wrote home once a term, the letters being dictated by Miss Jessica, then copied out in their best handwriting. Vicky's letter was passed at the third attempt. The next week she received a short impersonal reply from Mama, ending with the words, "Papa sends his love." That was enough to raise her spirits to the skies.

Papa sent his love. He loved her, he missed her. . . . Perhaps he wouldn't make her go back to this horrible school next term.

Her birthday fell on the day she went home. Rules were relaxed slightly at Tarnaway Towers on the last night of the term, but even with the prospect of home and freedom a few hours ahead the pupils were too much in awe of Miss Amelia to do anything really daring. There was a legend that a pupil had once been kept at school throughout the holidays for getting out onto the roof on the morning of the last day.

Vicky was so excited at the thought of going home to-morrow—her birthday—that she talked about it incessantly.

"My papa"—"My papa"—"My papa," was the oft-repeated burden of her song.

"Oh, shut up about your papa," said the others impatiently. "We're sick of the sound of him."

Vicky had talked so much about "my papa" that she was looked upon as the spoilt and petted darling of adoring parents, which in their eyes accounted for the conceit and affectation that had made her so unpopular.

"Wish her precious papa knew what *we* thought of her," said someone, speaking in a voice loud enough for Vicky to hear.

Vicky didn't mind. Their acceptance of her fiction seemed to make it a fiction no longer.

"Hello, papa's darling!" they sneered, and her heart leapt with happiness.

Miss Gilbert took them down to the station and arranged them in separate groups, according to the trains they were to go by, but now that they were actually on their way home, beyond range of Miss Amelia's eye and voice, they lost their fear of Authority and ran about excitedly, defying her orders.

Miss Gilbert contented herself by scolding and pushing about the smallest and most inoffensive little girls, who would not be likely to resist.

The more daring of them would lean out of the carriage windows at the last minute and call "Good-bye, Gilly," for, as the train began to move, Miss Amelia's majesty began to crumble away till she was nothing but a ludicrous old woman. They mimicked her and laughed at her and discussed the more sensational rows of the term. Every inch of the return journey in four weeks' time would give her back something of her majesty, till they would get out at the station they had just left quaking with fear at the thought of meeting her again, but that they ignored.

At the train's first stop they swarmed out upon the platform to buy the sweets and chocolates that were forbidden at Tarnaway Towers. Vicky sat in a corner of the carriage, munching happily at a bar of chocolate cream. Every minute, every inch took her nearer Home—the Home that had acquired such a rosy glamour in her eyes since she had left it. She saw the house, with the big hall, elegant drawing-room (she remembered those most clearly, though she had seldom been in them; the nursery, where she had spent most of her time, she hardly remembered at all, for Vicky's memories were well under control), the long gravelled drive, where the carriages rolled up and down, the spacious gardens, the greenhouses and—Andrew. Andrew would be raking the drive, perhaps, when she reached home. She would say "Good afternoon, Andrew" very graciously as she went into the house, and he would touch his forehead to her.

Papa and Mama would be with her, of course. They would have come down to the station in the carriage to meet her. Their birthday presents would be waiting for her indoors. Tea would be laid in the big drawing-room. She would sit down on the bearskin rug and chatter away, telling them all about Tarnaway Towers, and perhaps Papa would say, "You won't be going back there again, my darling, because we want you at home."

Her heart began to beat quickly as she neared the station. She took off her hat and leant out of the window, her curls streaming in the wind.

There wasn't anyone on the platform. Perhaps they were waiting for her in the carriage. She got out and looked round.

The station-master came forward. "Well, Miss Vicky," he said, "I didn't know you were coming back to-day. I'm afraid the carriage isn't here."

Vicky tossed back her curls.

"Oh no, I asked them not to send it," she said. "I thought it would be more fun to go in the cab."

He helped her into the cab and put her box by the cabman. Her spirits, which had sunk like lead at the sight of the empty platform, soared up again. After all, why should they have sent the carriage? They probably knew that she would rather come up in the cab. And it would be much nicer to meet them at home than on the station. Besides, they couldn't bring their presents down in the carriage, and, of course, they'd want to give her their presents as soon as they saw her. . . .

The cab swung into the big gates and up the gravelled drive. No, they weren't standing at the front door. The front door was shut. Perhaps they didn't expect her quite so early. . . . Perhaps they'd mistaken the day. But she'd addressed the "train-paper" envelope herself, and she had had to copy out the address four times before Miss Jessica was satisfied. It had been stamped and posted with the others. They *must* have got it.

A housemaid, whom Vicky had not seen before, opened the door.

The cabman put Vicky's trunk down in the hall. Vicky paid him with the change from the train money.

"Where are Papa and Mama?" she said to the housemaid.

"They're out, miss," said the girl uncertainly. "I don't think they were expecting you. . . . I'll ask Cook."

She went through the green baize door to the kitchen, and soon Cook came out with her, large and motherly and worried-looking.

"No, miss," she said, looking down at the small figure in the navy blue cashmere pelisse and round straw hat, "we've had no orders. But the master and mistress will be in to dinner. Shall I send your tea up to the nursery?"

"I don't want any tea," said Vicky.

"I'll get your trunk sent up."

"Thank you."

Cook and the housemaid withdrew through the baize door. Vicky went after them, intending to ask where her parents had gone. They didn't see that she was following them.

"The mistress did get some sort of a letter about her coming home," the housemaid was saying, "because I remember the master saying, 'What a nuisance!' "

Vicky closed the green baize door very quickly and went to the drawing-room. She felt a dispassionate interest in the fact that she wasn't going to cry, that she didn't even want to cry. She was angry, angrier than she'd ever been in her life before. She stood in the middle of the room and looked about her. Her eyes were very bright, her cheeks flushed, and even her breath seemed to be trembling. Her eyes rested on the cabinet by the window. It was full of Venetian glass that Papa had bought for Mama on their wedding journey, Vicky had heard Mama say how beautiful it was and how much she treasured it. The key was in the lock. Vicky opened it, took out the pieces of glass one by one and flung them into the fireplace as hard as she could. They shivered to atoms against the tiles.

She looked round again. There were two armchairs by the fire, and on a small table by one of them was a work-box and a piece of Berlin wool-work half done. Vicky took the needle-work and thrust it in the fire, then emptied the contents of the work-box after it, kneeling down on the hearthrug and pushing them into the flames with the poker.

A wild exaltation of lawlessness possessed her. She went upstairs to Mama's and Papa's bedroom. She had never been into it before—only sometimes peeped wistfully through the door when it happened to be left ajar. Now she entered boldly and looked about her.

Mama's crystal toilet set stood on the dressing-table. Vicky took up a small shining bowl and flung it on the floor. It rolled along without breaking. She picked it up and, opening the window, dropped it on the jutting-out roof of the porch that was just beneath. It smashed into tiny pieces, then rolled onto the drive. She did the same with each one till the dressing-table was empty. A strange, bitter-sweet delight filled her heart.

She'd go to the nursery now. She'd break all the cups in the nursery cupboard. Or should she break a window? Yes, she thought she'd break a window.

She opened the nursery door and stopped, catching her breath with surprise. A small cot stood in a corner by the fire, with curtains of frilled muslin, tied back with bows of blue ribbon. She went to it and peeped between the curtains. Blue eyes in a tiny face stared up at her. A hand no bigger than a rose petal lay on the coverlet Vicky slipped her finger into it and the tiny fingers tightened about it. Vicky smiled and said "Hello" rather shyly.

No, she wouldn't break a window here, after all.

The door opened and Nurse Tanner entered.

"We didn't expect you home to-day, Miss Vicky," she said.

Vicky gave her a hard unchildlike stare.

"When did you expect me home?" she said defiantly.

Nurse Tanner did not answer the question.

"Take your things off, and wash your hands. It's nearly tea-time."

Vicky looked at her. She was still upheld by that intoxication of lawlessness, that wild white flame of anger. And her whole being thrilled to the sudden knowledge that she wasn't afraid of Nurse Tanner any longer. She was nothing, nothing at all, compared with Miss Amelia.

"No, I won't," she said, "and I don't want any tea either."

Nurse Tanner shrugged her shoulders and went to the cot without speaking. Little Celia was her job, not Miss Vicky. She'd said from the beginning that she wouldn't be responsible for Miss Vicky when the baby came. Especially after she'd gone to boarding-school. Boarding-school ruined children. She'd noticed it again and again. They came back little heathens with no respect for anyone or anything. She always refused to be responsible for a child once it had gone to boarding-school. She'd never been fond of Miss Vicky, with her airs and graces and ready tears. And she looked as if she'd turned into a proper little termagant on top of it all. They'd have to get a holiday governess for her or send her away for the holidays. She wasn't going to have her in the nursery upsetting everything, and she'd tell Mrs. Carothers so straight.

She lifted the baby from the cot and held it in the crook of her arm, looking down at it, her grim face softened to tenderness. For babies in their first few months of helplessness Nurse Tanner felt an affection of which she was half ashamed.

Vicky walked slowly downstairs and out into the garden. Andrew was in one of the greenhouses.

"Hello, Andrew," she said.

She grinned at him as she spoke, the defiant exultant grin of the outlaw.

"Hello, Miss Vicky," said Andrew.

"I've broken all Mama's glass in the drawing-room and in her bedroom," said Vicky.

Andrew's freckled face was grave.

"You shouldn't have broke your mama's things," he said. "You'll get into trouble for that."

"I don't care," said Vicky. "I'm never going to do what anyone tells me ever again."

Chapter Five

Vicky stayed for four years at Tarnaway Towers. She was not unhappy there. Children do not resent discipline, as long as it is administered without malice, and certainly the pupils of Tarnaway Towers were never dull.

During Vicky's second term one of the new girls took her place by general tacit consent as the most unpopular girl in the school, and Vicky, rather to her surprise, found herself accepted and even liked by her school-fellows.

School life had taught her a good deal, apart from the official curriculum—to adapt herself to her surroundings, to give and take, to receive punishment and rewards lightly, without undue distress or exaltation. At Tarnaway Towers they succeeded each other so quickly that it afforded an excellent object lesson on the instability of human affairs. Miss Amelia considered it her duty to see that the proverbial fall trod closely on the heels of pride and vice versa, and would follow punishment by reward and reward by punishment with bewildering rapidity. Though prim and majestic outwardly, she was driven by a demon of inexhaustible vitality that must find outlet every moment of the day, and her passion of anger or approbation hovered over her pupils incessantly.

Though Vicky was now comparatively well-behaved at school, she continued her outlaw career during the holidays, becoming a reckless little firebrand the minute she set foot in the Hall. By this means, and this means alone, could she force her father to notice her. He could ignore her when she made timid attempts to win his love, but he could not ignore her when she turned the place upside down, caused the servants to give notice, and disobeyed his every order.

He was cold and distant when he reproved her, speaking in a tone of icy displeasure, looking at her with a revulsion of dislike that sent a wave of physical sickness through her, though she stared at him defiantly, and never cried till she was alone in her bedroom, and, even as she cried, was planning further ways of annoying him.

Once or twice she went to him to say that she was sorry, hoping against hope for the miracle of some dramatic reconciliation, some, sudden irrefutable evidence of his love. But he told her coldly, without even looking at her, that he hoped she would prove her sorrow by her conduct and brought the interview to an abrupt end.

Mrs. Carothers shrugged her handsome shoulders and went her way. The child was impossible, but she was determined not to fill the role of cruel stepmother (as, she shrewdly guessed, Vicky would have liked her to) and left her to the charge of a succession of holiday governesses, none of whom would ever take the position a second time, and some of whom left before the holidays were over.

Little Celia now complicated the situation. She was a plump, good-tempered little girl of four, adored by both father and mother. It wasn't easy, of course, for Vicky to see the child filling the position that she herself had longed for so passionately, to watch her father smile at her tenderly and take her on his knee, the servants and villagers pay court to her.

At first she did not know how to retaliate, for despite her naughtiness she was too kind-hearted to wish to hurt the child. Then Celia herself showed the way. For Celia, as she grew from baby to little girl, conceived a passionate affection for her elder sister. She was never so happy as when she could toddle by Vicky's side, holding her hand. She would struggle out of her father's and mother's arms to go to Vicky. She sobbed inconsolably on the days when Vicky went back to school.

It was indescribably galling to Mr. and Mrs. Carothers, and

Vicky made full use of her advantage, deliberately leading the child into mischief, inciting her to rudeness and disobedience.

"It isn't poor little Celia's fault," they said, and punished Vicky, but Vicky was hardened to punishment and delighted at having found the chink in her parents' armour.

Nurse Tanner, driven to despair, would give notice regularly each holiday, and Mrs. Carothers would implore her to stay. "It's only for a short time now, Nurse, you know. She'll be as good as gold once Miss Vicky's gone back."

They complained to Miss Amelia, but Miss Amelia never took much notice of complaints from parents. She had a profound contempt for them as a class, and considered them wholly unfitted to be entrusted with the care of children.

One afternoon, as Vicky was going through the hall from her music lesson to her dancing class, she saw Mama's parasol in the umbrella-stand. Mama, then, had come to see Miss Amelia, to tell her, probably, how naughty Vicky had been in the holidays. . . . A grin played about Vicky's mouth as she slipped back to her classroom for a penknife, then, taking the parasol from the stand, slit the rich flounced silk in half a dozen places.

Miss Amelia fixed a stern eye upon her that evening, but asked her no questions, for Mrs. Carothers had been to tell Miss Amelia that they had decided to take Vicky away from Tarnaway Towers and send her to a school in Switzerland, where she would spend the holidays. Miss Amelia had assented grimly. She despised Mrs. Carothers for not being able to manage the child.

"Vicky is very little trouble here," she said.

Mrs. Carothers had sighed.

"She's completely unmanageable at home, and she has a very bad influence on her little sister."

"How old is the other child?" asked Miss Amelia.

"Four," said Mrs. Carothers.

She spoke shortly. It was useless for Miss Amelia to take an interest in Celia. Celia was far too precious to be sent away from home. Why, her papa was restless if the child was out of his sight even for a few hours. He had moved his study so that he could watch her at play in the garden. He would go into the nursery to look at her in her cot. "Papa's sweetheart," he called her. Her affection for Vicky hurt him inexpressibly, though he tried to ignore it.

Vicky left Tarnaway Towers in good company. Both Miss Gilbert and Miss Irene left it at the same time. Miss Gilbert's secret had at last come to light. One of the pupils' brothers patronised the Gilbert tailoring establishment, and the man had told his customer that his sister was a mistress at a select Academy for young ladies called Tarnaway Towers, adding naively that, of course, it wouldn't do for the young ladies to know about his shop, so his sister had always kept it dark. The brother told his sister; the sister, a good-natured girl, told a few special friends as a great secret; and one fatal night Miss Jessica overheard them discussing it in the dormitory and reported the matter to Miss Amelia. Miss Amelia sent for Miss Gilbert the next morning and summarily dismissed her.

"A school of this standing," said Miss Amelia, "cannot afford to have any association with Trade. I have made the most searching enquiries in the case of all my pupils, and I cannot, in justice to the parents to whom I am responsible, be less particular in the case of my governesses."

Miss Gilbert accepted her dismissal meekly enough (she considered it quite just and reasonable) and spent the rest of the term trying to ingratiate herself with the more important pupils in the hope that it might "lead to something," and bullying the less important ones as an outlet to her feelings. Her toadying led to nothing, however, and she set off at the end of the term to the tailor's shop, her eyes red and her mouth grimly set.

Miss Irene was married to the Vicar in the last week of the term. The Vicar had begun to propose again, and Miss Amelia, who had dominated her all her life (her only gesture of independence had been her desperate flight with her lover), had now decided that she must accept him. Amelia had tried conscientiously to turn her into a successful schoolmistress, but at last even she recognised failure.

Irene was only fit to be a wife, and if she married the Vicar Amelia would still be able to keep an eye on her.

She was married from the school, wearing a black silk hat and jacket over a grey silk dress and carrying a bouquet of roses. Her eyes held that far-away look that they had held ever since her elopement, with an added something of fear.

Miss Jessica bustled about, making jellies and trifles for the wedding-breakfast, crying at intervals and feeling pleasantly sentimental and maternal, and Miss Amelia gave vent to whatever feelings she had by putting more girls into disgrace than had ever been known to happen before in the history of the school.

As the term drew to its close, Vicky found that she was sorry to leave Tarnaway Towers. She would miss the rambling old garden and the pleasant comradeship of schoolroom and dormitory.

Miss Amelia shook her head over her sadly as she said good-bye. Something might have been made of the child if she had stayed, but Miss Amelia regarded all other educational establishments than Tarnaway Towers as places where children were ruined by excessive pampering.

Vicky was unusually quiet and subdued at the beginning of the holidays. She felt depressed at the prospect of leaving the world she knew and going to a new world where she must stay till she was grown-up. Moreover, it didn't seem worth while defying authority any longer. She had given it a good trial, and it had been only partially successful. It had certainly forced Papa to notice her, but it had ended in her banishment from him and the home she loved.

She did not entirely abandon the fight, however, and she still used Celia as her chief weapon, now in a more subtle way. She did not lead Celia into mischief, but she paraded her power over the child, wielding it deliberately so as to hurt her father as much as possible. She was kinder to Celia than she had ever been before, and Celia's devotion increased.

"No, no," she would say, when her father offered to take her out with him or invited her down to his study. "I want to be with Vicky."

Celia was delighted that her birthday fell in the holidays.

"Vicky will be home for it!" she cried gleefully. "Vicky will be home for it! Isn't that lovely?"

Mr. Carothers said nothing. If the event had taken place in the term-time he would have instituted himself its presiding genius, for he loved to watch his darling's pleasure, but, as it was, he decided to ignore it. He would not share the place of honour with Vicky. Though he was ashamed of his dislike of the child, he found it impossible to overcome. And Vicky's behaviour certainly justified it to his conscience.

The birthday party was to consist of Celia, Vicky, the Vicarage children, and the doctor's little girl—a fat pale child called Dorothea, with a mass of tightly crimped hair, bandy legs, and a habit of falling asleep anywhere and at any time.

She arrived with her nurse at about half-past three and was committed to Nurse Tanner's charge with instructions not to take off the white shoulder shawl she was wearing till she was "warmed up."

The Vicarage children arrived in charge of Violet a few moments later. Roger seemed taller and thinner than ever. He was still quiet and grave and responsible, conscientiously snubbing Mark and keeping a protective eye on Mabs. Mark still shouted "Look at me," occasionally, but he was learning less direct methods of self-advertisement, acquiring a pretence of modesty that he was finding much more effective.

"Oh yes, I came in first," he would say, describing some race at school, "but it was just a fluke."

Mabs had lost a good deal of her shyness and was inclined to exploit her position as the only girl of the family by ordering the two boys about. Mark resisted strenuously, but Roger had got into the habit of waiting on her when she was a baby and did it as a matter of course.

Violet handed over her charges to Nurse Tanner.

"What a walk!" she panted. "I'm just about done up."

"It oughtn't to be anything to a great healthy girl like you," snapped Nurse Tanner.

"Maybe I'm not as healthy as I look," said Violet darkly. "I've often wondered if I am."

"Come back for them at six," said Nurse Tanner.

Violet lingered.

"You got Miss Vicky back," she said. "I hear she's a proper little devil."

"At six," repeated Nurse Tanner firmly.

Violet shrugged sulkily and took her departure. She'd never met anyone like that Nurse Tanner for jumping down your throat before you'd opened your mouth.

Roger and Mark and Mabs took their things off and went to the nursery, where Celia stood surrounded by her presents. She had had a doll's house from Papa and Mama, a picture book from Vicky, a doll from Nurse Tanner, some building bricks from the other servants, and a wooden horse from Andrew, carved and painted by himself.

Vicky had examined the wooden horse silently. Andrew had never given her anything for her birthday, but her birthdays had always fallen in term-time since that unlucky one four years ago. Her thoughts went back to that and she compared it with this birthday of Celia's—Celia, the petted feted darling. She couldn't dislike Celia, but she felt surging up within her the old resentment and with it the old reckless defiance.

The Vicarage children had brought a dolls' tea-set, which Roger presented to Celia with a ceremonial air.

"From all of us," he said, "with our love."

"Thank you very much indeed," said Celia, holding up her face to each of them for a kiss.

The tea was laid on the nursery table. There were jellies, sugared biscuits, and a large iced cake with "Celia, aged four" on it.

Nurse Tanner put on Celia's feeder, and settled them at the table, hovering over them with the usual stream of admonitions and reproofs.

"No, you finish that bread and butter, Miss Celia, or you'll have no jelly."—"I didn't hear you say Thank you, Miss Vicky." She did not exclude the visitors from her attentions. "Don't drink with your mouth full, Miss Mabs."—"That'll do, Master Mark."—"Get on with your tea, Miss Dorothea."

They ate and drank busily, chattering over the bread and butter on which Nurse Tanner insisted, becoming silent as they reached the more engrossing stage of jelly and sugared biscuits.

Nurse Tanner, seeing them so quietly occupied, thought that she might seize the opportunity to go down to the kitchen and get her own tea in peace.

"You can each have one slice of birthday cake," she said, "and mind you don't talk with your mouths full or make a noise while I'm away, or there'll be no Blind-man's-buff for you afterwards."

They finished their platefuls of jelly in silence, then Celia stood up and took hold of the glass cake-stand. Her round rosy face was shining with pleasure above her frilled white pinafore and embroidered feeder. Her neat golden-brown fringe hung just above her eyes. Her curls fell over her shoulders.

"There's a piece for each of us and one over," she said. "I'm going to give the one over to Andrew. My darling Andrew," she added affectionately.

A sudden gust of anger swept over Vicky.

"He's not your Andrew," she said.

"He is," said Celia. "He gives me rides in his wheel-barrow, and he lets me help him plant the flowers."

"He's mine," Vicky persisted. "I knew him before you were born. Why, I—I—I *engaged* him."

"All right, he's your Andrew, Vicky," said Celia pacifically. "He's not mine. He's yours."

Celia didn't want Andrew. She didn't want anyone but Vicky. . . .

Vicky's anger had passed, but in passing it had released the devil of mischief in her.

She took up a piece of icing from the cake.

"It's just like snow," she said. "Look out, Roger. I'm throwing a snowball at you."

The icing hit him on the nose, and they all laughed loudly.

"Look out, Mark," cried Celia, imitating her idol. "I'm throwing a snowball at you."

Mark retaliated promptly, and in a minute all five were throwing pieces of cake and icing at each other. Vicky snatched up a handful of jelly and flung it at Mark. They all began to throw jelly at each other, laughing and shouting excitedly.

Vicky made a ball of what was left of the bread and butter and rammed it down Celia's neck, while Celia giggled with delight.

It was at this point that Nurse Tanner entered. She stood in the doorway and took in the scene, her face darkening with anger.

"You *naughty* children!" she stormed. "How *dare* you! I'll tell your mama and papa of you, Miss Vicky, as soon as they come in; and, as for you, Miss Celia, you'll go to bed this minute and stay there the rest of the day."

She pushed the now weeping Celia before her into the night nursery, turning to make an angry gesture to the others, as if sweeping them off the universe.

"Off you go!" she said sternly. "And don't let me ever see any of you here again."

The children went slowly downstairs to the garden—all except Dorothea, who, feeling bewildered and frightened, made her way into one of the maids' bedrooms that was near the nursery, curled up on the bed, and went to sleep.

"We'd better go home," said Roger, abashed, and added, "We've been very naughty."

But Vicky was dancing about on one foot, still aflame with devilry.

"Let's rescue her," she said. "Come on. Let's rescue her. Let's rescue Celia from the enemy."

There was something infectious in her abandonment of lawlessness. Consequences seemed to lose their terror when Vicky laughed like that.

"Yes, let's," they shouted.

"Follow me," said Vicky, "and don't make a sound."

They crept on tiptoe after her up the back stairs, holding their breath.

The door of the day nursery was ajar, and through it they could see Nurse Tanner on her knees on the floor, clearing the jelly and icing from the carpet. Her professional pride would not allow such evidence of unruliness to be seen by any eyes but hers.

Vicky crept noiselessly up to the door, slammed it, and turned the key in the lock, then with a whoop of triumph ran to the night nursery and unlocked the door.

Celia sat up in bed.

"Vicky!" she said, her tear-stained face alight with sudden joy.

"Come on!" laughed Vicky. "We're rescuing you from the enemy. We've got the enemy locked in a dungeon. Never mind putting your clothes on. Here's your dressing-gown. ... Here are your slippers. Quick, quick, before she gets out again!"

Infected, like the others, by Vicky's exaltation, Celia leapt out of bed, slipping her feet into her bedroom slippers and her arms into the dressing-gown that Vicky held out. Then they all ran downstairs again and out into the garden.

Vicky began to dance about the lawn, and they all followed her, leaping over flower-beds, running in and out among the trees. Celia flung off her dressing-gown and bedroom slippers and danced about in her nightdress and bare feet on the grass.

Suddenly Vicky stooped and, taking up a handful of soil from one of the rose beds, flung it at Celia.

"A black snowball!" she shouted.

"Black snowballs!" they all shouted delightedly, and began to pelt each other with handfuls of soil.

An angry voice rose above the racket, and they looked up to see Nurse Tanner leaning out of the open window of the nursery. Her cap was askew, her face distorted, her whole body quivering with rage.

Vicky laughed and, snatching up another handful of soil, flung it up at the window. It missed its mark and fell with a plop on the window of Mrs. Carothers' boudoir just below.

Vicky laughed again, and was just taking up another handful of soil when Mrs. and Mr. Carothers appeared, coming round the corner of the house. They had returned from paying a call in the carriage and were about to take a turn in the garden before going indoors.

Mrs. Carothers was, as usual, an elegant figure, in her dress of garnet grenadine and a polonaise made from a fine Indian shawl. Her small hat of garnet velvet trimmed with ostrich tips was perched high on her fashionable coiffure. She stopped and stood for a moment motionless, as her eye fell upon the scene . . . Celia in her nightgown and bare feet, her face covered with mud where a "snowball" had hit her; Nurse Tanner, her dignity gone for the first time in her career, her usually deep commanding voice a hysterical scream.

There was no doubt as to who was the cause of the trouble—Vicky, dancing about exultantly, shouting defiance.

"Come here at once, Vicky," called Mrs. Carothers.

Still laughing, Vicky ran off in the opposite direction. Rather to her disappointment no one ran after her. She hid for an hour in the loft over the stable, and at last came slowly back to the garden.

There was no sign of the Vicarage children or her parents or Nurse Tanner. She went into the greenhouse, where Andrew was watering cinerarias with soot-water, and stood by him a few moments, watching. His freckled face was bent gravely over his task.

"What are you thinking about, Andrew?" she said at last.

"You shouldn't carry on like that, you know, Miss Vicky," he said. "It only makes trouble for yourself and everyone else."

"I know," said Vicky meekly.

The flame of rebellion had died down, and she felt weary and apprehensive.

"Where are they all now?" she said.

"I don't know, Miss Vicky."

There was a silence, in which Vicky suddenly remembered what Celia had said at tea.

"You don't like Celia better than me, do you, Andrew?"

He seemed to consider the question dispassionately.

"No," he said at last, as though faintly surprised by the result of his cogitations. "No, I don't, Miss Vicky," and added, "though she behaves a good sight better."

"I know she does," said Vicky. "Andrew . . ."

"Yes, Miss Vicky."

"I shan't be coming home again for years, when I've gone to this school in Switzerland."

"I know, Miss Vicky."

"Will you write to me sometimes? Papa and Mama won't write and Celia can't. Anyway, she's only a baby. Will you write and—and just tell me about the garden and things like that?"

"I'm but a poor writer, Miss Vicky. I've never had much schooling."

"That doesn't matter if you'll only write. Just tell me what flowers are out and things like that, so that I can keep a sort of picture of it in my mind. Will you? Will you promise to?"

"Yes, Miss Vicky."

Mrs. Carothers had reappeared on the terrace. She looked flushed and agitated. Nurse Tanner had given notice again, and this time it was clear that nothing would shake her resolution.

"No, ma'am," she had said. "A thing like that has never happened in my nursery before, and I must ask you to look upon my notice as final."

Vicky came out of the greenhouse.

"Come here at once, Vicky."

Vicky went slowly towards her stepmother.

Mrs. Carothers looked at her and spoke in a slow dispassionate voice, controlling her anger.

"You will go to bed at once, and your papa is making arrangements for you to go away to your new school first thing to-morrow."

Chapter Six

THE girls at the school in Switzerland were well looked after and allowed a good deal of freedom, but that curious zest of life that had been imparted to Tarnaway Towers by Miss Amelia's superabundant vitality was lacking. They were not bullied or overworked, but often Vicky found herself thinking wistfully of those days of stress and strain, when one row followed another so quickly that the whole school lived in a ferment of excitement and vaguely thrilling apprehension.

Her old school-fellows wrote to tell her the latest news, how Miss Irene, as the Vicar's wife, was growing pleasantly plump and matronly and beginning to patronise her sisters, even Miss Amelia, who was obviously disconcerted by the situation.

Andrew's letters came regularly, too, at first, badly spelt and badly written:

"The snodrops and krokuses is out now and the daffydils neerly the mistriss is having all the rosydendrons took up and a lorn laid there there's a good deel of blossom on the frute trees but there may be more frost on the way yet you never no Miss Celia shes riding better now but, doesn't keep her elbos in proper the spannial had pupies last week a nice lot all excep one that shud of been drown but Miss Celia beg for it the elm by the gat was blowed down by yesday storm laying right acrorst the rode."

At first Vicky awaited the letters eagerly, hungry for news of her beloved home, then she began to show them to her friends as a joke, with an odd nagging sense of disloyalty at her heart, and finally became ashamed of the illiterate handwriting and stopped answering, whereupon they gradually ceased to arrive.

As Celia grew older she also began to write—laborious, inky, affectionate letters. Celia's adoration did not cease with Vicky's absence, as her parents had hoped it would.

"Darling Vicky, do send me a photograph of you. The one I have is more than a year old. Do write often. You don't write half often enough. I do so love getting your letters."

She would send the news of the neighbourhood, especially of the Vicarage children.

"Roger and Mark went back to school yesterday. Mabs is going away to school next term. I shall miss them terribly. I wish Papa and Mama would let me go to school with you, but I've begged and begged and they won't. Don't forget me, darling Vicky, will you, and write to me again soon."

Mama wrote to her at rare intervals—short, impersonal letters, ending always, "Papa sends his love. He is too busy to write."

The picture of herself as beloved daughter had almost grown again in Vicky's mind with the years of absence. She had been rather a troublesome child, she remembered, but parents did not love their children the less on that account. They had sent her to Switzerland because there were good schools in Switzerland and they wanted her to be well educated. They did not have her home for the holidays because it was not worth while making a long journey for such a short time.

There were several English girls among the pupils who did not return home for the holidays, and they were all, according to themselves, adored by their parents.

Determinedly Vicky read pride and affection into Mama's short impersonal letters. It needed no effort to read them into Celia's long ones.

The days passed uneventfully enough. There was nothing to challenge the devil of mischief in her, and she became once more almost the docile little girl of Miss Thompson's regime, working painstakingly at her needlework, music, and languages during the term-time, and in the holidays going to concerts, museums, and picture galleries with the other pupils who did not return home.

When she was eighteen she began to expect to hear from Mama

or Papa that she was to leave school, but no word came. Once or twice she asked the headmistress if any arrangements had been made for her leaving, to be told always, "No, my dear. I have heard nothing from your parents."

Celia's affection for her half-sister continued to be a source of much secret exasperation to Mr. and Mrs. Carothers. Her devotion was due in part to memories of Vicky herself, idealised by lapse of time, but chiefly to the inevitable loneliness of the only child that is apt to fashion an imaginary companion for itself, and frequently to identify the companion with some real but inaccessible person.

Celia identified her imaginary companion with Vicky. She loved Mama and Papa, of course, but Mama was so brusque and matter-of-fact, and Papa belonged to another world, a man's world. It was Vicky who sat in the branches of the old apple tree with her, who raced across the lawn with her, who shared all her secrets. When Mama or Papa said something funny without knowing it was funny (as they frequently did, for neither had much sense of humour), Celia's eyes would twinkle at the invisible Vicky, and they would laugh over it together afterwards.

Andrew was part of this glamorous Vicky-world, for not only had Vicky claimed him passionately at that never-to-be-forgotten birthday party that was Celia's last memory of her ("He's mine," Vicky had said, "He's *mine*"), but also Celia was aware that Andrew had been at the Hall before Papa's marriage to Mama and had known Vicky as a little girl. Andrew, moreover, had some letters that Vicky had written to him when first she went to the school in Switzerland. They were grubby and worn and almost illegible, but there they were in Vicky's big childish handwriting. "I'm terribly, terribly homesick, Andrew. Do write again and tell me everything about everything." Celia was never tired of reading them, and Andrew would often bring them down with him carefully wrapped up in newspaper to show her. Vicky wrote to her now, of course, but they were grown-up letters in grown-up writing. It thrilled her to see the letters that Vicky had written when she was a little girl.

One day Mr. Carothers received with his morning's post a

communication that brought a frown to his brow and tightened the corners of his handsome mouth. He handed it to his wife without comment.

It was from Vicky, demanding to be taken away from school at the end of the term. "I shall be nineteen," she wrote, "and I can't stay here after I'm nineteen. No one does."

"I hadn't realised," said Mrs. Carothers. "Yes ... she will be nineteen. She'll have to come home, I suppose."

Mr. Carothers shrugged an unwilling acquiescence.

"The request is somewhat ungraciously put," he said, "but that, of course, is typical."

They could not know that only after a bitter struggle had Vicky subdued her pride sufficiently to make a suggestion that should, she felt, have come from them, and that the curt ungracious phrases hid a wistful longing for home.

Vicky came back to Six Elms in June, and Celia stood alone on the platform to receive her.

As the day drew near, Celia's excitement had been clouded by a doubt that had grown to an agony when the train drew in. Suppose that the real Vicky were not the Vicky of her dreams. Suppose someone dull and plain and ordinary stepped out of the train. ...

But it was Vicky—lovelier and more glamorous even than she had imagined her—and the relief and joy of the discovery brought a sudden catch to Celia's throat.

"Vicky, darling ... darling ..."

The tall and beautiful stranger, who was no stranger at all, bent down and kissed her.

"How nice of you to come, Celia!" she said. She glanced about her as she spoke.

"Mama had to go out and pay a tiresome call," explained Celia. "She sent her love. So did Papa. They'll be in for tea."

Well, at any rate, it was better than last time, thought Vicky. At least there was Celia. ...

The coachman touched his hat as they approached the carriage. He was new since Vicky had been home before. He stole a knowledgeable glance at her. She'll wake the place up, he said to himself.

In the carriage Celia leant forward eagerly, scanning the oval face—the flawless complexion, regular features, deep blue eyes, and the golden hair that escaped from the small flower-trimmed hat.

"Oh, Vicky, how beautiful you are!" she sighed. "You're even more beautiful than I thought you'd be."

Vicky was looking out of the window, watching the familiar landmarks with a quickly beating heart, noticing the slightest change—a tree cut down, a new barn, a gate where there had been a stile. Hardly a day had passed these eight years that she had not gone over every inch of it in her memory.

They passed the tiny cottage, buried in jasmine, at which she had called with Miss Thompson to interview Andrew (Celia had told her in a letter that Andrew's father had died); the general shop where she used to go with Nurse Tanner to spend her Saturday penny; the butcher's shop, so small and neat that it looked like a toy; the cluster of cottages, damp, unhealthy, but flauntingly picturesque with their thatched roofs and tangle of old-fashioned flowers; the squat Norman tower of the church and the chimneys of the Vicarage, peeping over the trees. . . .

"I told you Roger was at Cambridge, didn't I?" said Celia. "Mark's going next year. Mabs is still at school. She's got to be a governess when she leaves, but she doesn't want to be. I wish she needn't be."

"Perhaps she won't be," said Vicky absently, looking out over the field at the thick line of Darrock Wood on the horizon.

She and Roger and Mark and Mabs had picnicked there, and she had run away and cried because they'd gone off with Andrew and left her alone. . . .

"Of course, she might marry," went on Celia, with an air of deep wisdom, "but there's no one here for her to marry, and she goes to a Clergy Daughters' School, where they nearly all marry their fathers' curates, and hers hasn't a curate, so it's all very difficult. I expect she'll have to be a governess in the end."

"She can marry her employer's eldest son," said Vicky, amused.

"Yes, of course she can," said Celia. "That's a very good idea. And it would be much better than being a governess, though she'd make a much nicer one than Miss Standish."

"She's the latest one, isn't she? Don't you like her?"

Celia pulled a face.

"No. Just wait till you see her."

The carriage turned in at the big iron gates and rolled up the broad gravelled drive. In the distance Vicky could see the figure of a boy bending over a flower-bed.

"Is that Andrew?" she said.

Celia laughed.

"Of course not. That's the gardener's boy. Andrew's the under-gardener now. He helps with the horses, too, and drives the dog-cart. He's awfully good with horses. He is with all animals."

The carriage drew up at the big porticoed entrance, and a housemaid opened the front door. Vicky entered and stood looking about the hall, comparing it with the picture she had carried in her mind through the years. Those rugs were new. That huge mahogany hatstand was new. The oak chest and Landseer pictures had been there before. She had a mingled feeling of homecoming and strangeness—an exultant joy at being home again, and with it that heartbreak of loneliness that is the worst part of homesickness.

Celia was drawing her eagerly towards the staircase.

"Come and see your bedroom, Vicky. I do hope you'll like it. I chose it for you."

It was the bedroom that Vicky had once so longed to have for her own—spacious, bow-windowed, next to Papa's and Mama's. It had been papered with an opulent design of red roses and green ribbons and contained a handsome mahogany suite with marble-topped washstand and a large wardrobe with double doors. There were flowers everywhere, on table, dressing-table, and window-sill.

"I picked the flowers for you, darling," said Celia. "Andrew let me have all the nicest ones."

It spoilt it just a little that it was Celia who had insisted on this room for her, who had filled it with flowers, and yet it touched her, too. Her gaze went to a piece of paper that hung slightly askew over the bed, with "Welcome Home" painted on it in uneven childish capitals, the border decorated by an elaborate device in flowers that were evidently intended to represent forget-me-nots, and her eyes filled suddenly with tears.

"How nice of you, Celia!" she said.

"Oh, Vicky, I've been *living* for to-day," said Celia. "You will let me stay and help you unpack, won't you? Mama said you'd want all new things now you've left school. She said you could come out at the Hunt ball at Fenton. It's next month and everyone goes. . . . Vicky, how beautiful you'll look in a ball dress! Do take off your hat and let me see your lovely hair."

Vicky found that her hands were trembling so that she could hardly draw out her hat pins. She laid her hat on the dressing-table and stood for a moment trying to still the beating of her heart. She was actually here. She'd come home. . . .

Celia had run to the door and opened it.

"I believe Papa and Mama are back. Come on, Vicky. Let's go down to them."

She drew Vicky down the staircase, threw open the drawing-room door, and cried exultantly, "Here she is!"

Mrs. Carothers came forward, her hands outstretched in welcome. She had grown much stouter and wore a settled middle-aged look, though she was as handsome as ever. Silk petticoats rustled softly beneath the elaborately draped dress of prune-coloured Indian cashmere, as she moved across the room to Vicky.

"So glad to have you back, dear," she said, putting her arm about her and kissing her. "Now we must bestir ourselves and find some gaieties for you. There aren't many young people hereabouts, but we'll do our best."

Vicky wasn't listening. Her eyes were fixed on her father, who stood on the hearthrug looking at her. He seemed taller even than her memory of him, his moustache blacker and more flowing, his air of dignity more portentous. The colour had faded from his face at Vicky's entrance, and his heart was beating even more quickly than hers. It might have been Rosamund herself. She hadn't been

68

much older than Vicky when he married her. It might have been Rosamund entering the room as she had entered it so often in the past. It brought back vividly to his memory a phase of his life that had been one of acute humiliation and disillusionment, a phase his mind shrank from dwelling upon even now.

"How are you, Victoria?" he said, forcing himself to bend towards her and kiss the air near her head. Then he returned to the fireplace and stood frowning into space, his lips tightly set.

A cold shiver ran through Vicky's body. She couldn't pretend or deceive herself any longer. She shut her eyes for a second, wondering how she was going to endure his dislike, wondering desperately, resentfully, what she had done to deserve it.

Mrs. Carothers was fussing about her, drawing up a chair, asking questions about her journey. She felt annoyed with her husband. Really, he needn't have shown his feelings quite as plainly as that. The child had noticed. You could see that she had. . . .

The maid had brought in the tea, and Mrs. Carothers poured it out, handing a cup to Vicky and plying her with toasted scones and cakes, being just a little too affable, trying just a little too obviously to make up to her for her husband's coldness.

"So nice to have you back, dear!" she said again. "We've all been looking forward to it so much, haven't we, Celia?"

Celia watched them, her eyes shining with happiness. Papa had behaved rather oddly, but Celia understood it. He was overwhelmed at finding himself possessed of such a beautiful grown-up daughter. He remembered Vicky as a little girl, of course, and it gave him quite a shock to find her so grown-up and beautiful. He must be feeling terribly proud of her, but he didn't want to show it, because Papa never showed his feelings.

She moved a footstool and sat at Vicky's feet, looking up at her adoringly. It was the moment she had dreamed of for years. Vicky had come home. . . .

Mr. Carothers took a cup of tea, drained it hastily, muttered something about having some letters to write, and went abruptly out of the room. They heard him enter the library and close the door.

"You'd better go, too, Celia," said Mrs. Carothers. "Miss Standish will be waiting for you."

Celia rose reluctantly.

"I'll see you after tea, won't I, darling?" she said to Vicky.

"Yes," said Vicky absently.

Mrs. Carothers went on talking in her brisk rallying fashion after Celia had left them.

"You'd better keep up your painting and music, hadn't you, dear? There's a very good music master in Fenton. And I know that the Prescott girls have a sketching class every week. You must join that. And singing . . . that's very important. We must plan the days out carefully together. And we must see about some clothes——"

Vicky interrupted her.

"Mama," she said, "why does Papa dislike me?"

"He doesn't, dear," said Mrs. Carothers unconvincingly.

"He does. Why does he?"

There was a silence, in which Mrs. Carothers suddenly decided to tell her the truth.

"It's because you're so like your mother."

Vicky stared at her uncomprehendingly.

"But my mother died years ago."

Mrs. Carothers shook her head.

"She's not dead, my dear. Your father divorced her."

Vicky's stunned senses groped desperately towards enlightenment.

"Divorced? You mean— She loved someone else though she was married to Papa?"

Mrs. Carothers shrugged.

"It was worse than that, my dear. You may as well know the truth now as later. Someone's sure to tell you. Your father forgave her many many times before he divorced her. She was what people call a light woman."

Vicky's stunned mind groped towards the incredible truth. Her mother—her *mother*—had been a "light woman." She was as ignorant as were most girls of her age in 1884, but she knew what that meant. A light woman. She hadn't given much conscious thought to her mother, certainly, but she had always been there in the background—a grave sainted figure, mourned sincerely by her devoted husband. When she read the words in Proverbs, "Who can find a virtuous woman? For her price is far above rubies. The heart of her husband doth safely trust in her," her mind always went to her dead mother. And she wasn't dead, nor was she a virtuous woman. "Your father forgave her many many times before he divorced her."

A hot rush of shame swept over her, dying her cheeks scarlet.

Mrs. Carothers came across to her and patted her shoulders.

"There, there, child!" she said. "There's nothing for you to worry about. It all happened a long time ago. . . . As for your papa, he'll soon get over it. It was the shock of seeing you standing there so like her that upset him."

"He's always hated me," said Vicky unsteadily.

Mrs. Carothers laid her hand lightly on the coils of burnished gold.

"You must just do your best, my dear," she said. "Soon, I'm sure, he'll be very very proud of you."

To herself she was saying, "It's lovely hair—just like Rosamund's. She's every bit as beautiful as Rosamund was."

"He won't," said Vicky. "He never will. But it's no use talking about it, is it?" She rose and went over to the window. "I like those beds you've had cut in the lawn. What is it that's in them?"

"Heliotrope, dear, and begonias. I've always been so fond of begonias."

Mrs. Carothers sat down in the armchair and took up her needle-work with a sigh of relief. For a moment she'd been afraid the child was going to make a scene. Perhaps it had been a mistake to tell her, but she would have found out sooner or later. And she was taking it quite sensibly, after all.

"And you've got more greenhouses, haven't you?" went on Vicky in a voice that was almost steady, but that seemed to her to be someone else's voice speaking from a long way off.

"Yes, dear. Andrew's very good at indoor plants. We had the house full of them all last winter."

Celia burst tempestuously into the room.

"Miss Standish says I can have half an hour with Vicky before I do my practising. Isn't it lovely?"

"Take your sister round the garden then, dear," said Mrs. Carothers. "I think she'd like to see it."

"Darling," said Celia solicitously, "you look terribly tired."

"She's had a long journey," said Mrs. Carothers. "Don't let her walk too much."

Vicky went slowly from the room with Celia. She felt as if both she and everything round her were part of a dream. It had begun as a lovely rapturous dream, in which she had returned home, secure and happy, in the calm of a midsummer day. It had changed to a nightmare with Papa's first glance, and the nightmare had grown blacker and more terrifying each moment since. It couldn't be real. She would wake up soon to find herself in the clean bare dormitory in Switzerland, with its gaily papered walls and the blue curtains that billowed slightly in the breeze, as she had often awakened before from bad dreams.

Celia chattered away at her side.

"This croquet lawn's new since last year. We only had the big one till then, and Mama and her friends always wanted it, so she had this one made for me and Miss Standish. And sometimes Roger and Mark and Mabs come over for a game, too. . . . Miss Standish is awful, Vicky."

"Is she cross?" said Vicky absently.

"No; I wish she were. She's so terribly *friendly*. She's always trying to be an elder sister to me and it's dreadful. I've got the loveliest elder sister anyone ever had"—Vicky smiled wanly—"and I wouldn't want *her* even if I hadn't. Mama sent away Miss Mallory because she was so cross, but I didn't mind her half as much as I mind Miss Standish."

They entered one of the big greenhouses. A man was filling empty pots, with potting soil. He turned his pale freckled face to them as they entered.

"It's Andrew, isn't it?" said Vicky, unsmiling.

"Yes, miss," said Andrew, wiping his hands down his apron. He was part of the nightmare, of course, but one has to play one's part, even in a nightmare.

"How are you, Andrew?" she said in the correct tone of patronage that the young lady of the house should use to the under-gardener.

"Quite well, thank you, miss," said Andrew respectfully.

She hesitated for a moment.

"How are your brother and sister getting on? I suppose they're grown-up now?"

"Yes, miss. My brother's gone into a bicycle works, and my sister's kitchen-maid at Morton Manor."

"How nice!" she said vaguely.

Her *grande dame* manner was falling from her. She was frightened and hurt and unhappy, just as she had been when she had fallen from her pony and Andrew had picked her up.

Celia had gone outside and was removing some weeds from her own garden ready for Vicky's inspection.

"Andrew," said Vicky suddenly, "do you know about my mother?"

She hadn't meant to say it, but it slipped out.

"Yes, Miss Vicky," said Andrew quietly.

"Does everybody—the servants and the people in the village?"

"Yes, Miss Vicky."

She was silent. He went on filling the pots, then said, "There's nothing for you to worry about, Miss Vicky. That all belongs to the past. No one'll judge you except for what you are."

"Papa does," said Vicky.

It was absurd to be talking to him like this, but somehow she couldn't help it.

"Never mind your papa," said Andrew. "He's not everyone. . . . Move out of my way a minute, Miss Vicky. I want to get at them other pots."

She stood by in silence, watching him fill the pots and press down the soil, feeling strangely comforted.

Chapter Seven

"Vicky's home now," said Mabs. "She'll be coming this afternoon."

"I suppose so," said Roger, pausing for a moment in his task of carrying chairs across the lawn.

"Don't you remember her?" asked Mabs.

"No, hardly at all, and I'm sure you don't."

"I know I don't," admitted Mabs, "but I've seen her since she came home, you know. She's beautiful. Celia's terribly thrilled at having her back. Lucky beggar! I wish I'd left school."

"What d'you mean by 'beautiful'?" said Mark, who was lying full length on the grass, his head resting on his hands. "I expect you call anyone who doesn't squint beautiful. You've seen no one but those freaks at your school."

"Wait till you see her," said Mabs. "Then tell me if you don't think her beautiful."

"I bet you sixpence I shan't," said Mark. "I've seen a bit more of the world than you have."

"Well, I wish you'd do some work instead of lazing about like that," put in Roger. "There are all these chairs to bring out of the summer-house."

Mark rose slowly to his feet, and, going across to the summer-house, came out carrying three folding chairs on each arm. He stopped suddenly, having thought of a way of carrying four, but, finding it impracticable, put them all down and resumed his occupation of lying on the grass.

Mabs was arranging the chairs absently in little groups under the cedar tree, seeing them occupied, not by the expected guests, but by the opulent, eligible, romantic figures of her imagination.

Roger was tall and thin—good-looking, but slow in movement and abstracted in manner. He had won a scholarship to Cambridge and hoped to be ordained the year after he took his degree. Mabs felt for him a half-contemptuous affection. Though unfailingly kind and courteous, he was dreamy and absent-minded, and so short-sighted as to be useless at games. "Poor old Roger!" she would sigh. "He's Papa all over again."

Mark, on the contrary, had been the star athlete of his school, where, indeed, he had taken little interest in anything but games and sport. The Vicar, a scholar to whom his son's prowess at games meant less than nothing, was deeply distressed by his school reports, and coached him indefatigably in the holidays. He was coaching him now, but found him, as ever, a somewhat elusive pupil. Mark had innumerable friends, who were always asking him to visit them—wealthy people, for the most part, with country estates, where Mark shot and fished and hunted and picked up a good many expensive and, the Vicar considered, unnecessary tastes. There was, perhaps as the result of his association with these people, a faint suggestion of the gilded youth about Mark himself. He had an assured manner, a sound knowledge of dogs and horses, and was prepared to pronounce an opinion on any subject whatsoever, whether he knew anything about it or not. This aspect of him secretly thrilled Mabs, for the ordinary life of the Vicarage was as unreal to her as it was to Roger and the Vicar, but she did not, like them, live in the world of Ancient Greece. She lived in a world where dukes and earls and lords fell in love every day with penniless vicars' daughters and married them in spite of every obstacle. There were not many obstacles, however, because, even if the fathers of the young heroes (gouty irascible old gentlemen with bandaged legs supported on footstools) objected at first to the match, they invariably succumbed at the first sight of Mabs, saying either, "Gad, I wish I were a young man myself," or "Thank you, my boy, for giving me the daughter I have always longed for."

She was now sixteen, nearly seventeen—quite old enough, she considered, to marry. Mabs had boundless trust in the compliancy of fate. She had no doubt at all that a lover—young, handsome, wealthy—was waiting for her somewhere and might appear at any moment. He might be staying with Lady Sybil Beverley at Morton Manor and ride over to the Vicarage with a message, or get lost and call at the Vicarage to ask his way, and he would see her doing something picturesque, such as feeding the birds or cutting flowers in the garden, and—well, that would be the beginning. From that the affair would run smoothly on to the interview with the gouty earl and the marriage in the village church.

Every day when Mabs woke up in the morning, she expected something thrilling and romantic to happen to her before night, and even when it didn't she was not really disappointed, because there was still to-morrow. Life couldn't go on being dull and uneventful for ever.

A stocky clumsily-built youth came out by the side door onto the lawn. He had flabby cheeks, protruding eyes, and a loose mouth that hung slightly open.

"Hello, Walter," called Mark cheerfully.

"I say, can I help?" said the boy, speaking with a slight stammer.

"I should say you could," said Roger. "Bring some of those chairs out of the summer-house. Mark's no earthly use."

When his sons went to school the Vicar took a resident pupil into the Vicarage to help pay their school fees. He had had a succession of them, mostly of the "backward" type, very disappointing to Mabs and acute mental torture to the Vicar himself. He was not particularly successful as a coach, for he was a born scholar who would spend a whole morning searching for the right word and exploring every avenue it suggested when found, lacking entirely the crammer's technique.

Walter Pearson, the present pupil, was to take his exam in a few months' time, and Mabs, for one, was very anxious that he should pass, because the next pupil might always turn out to be the hero of her dreams.

He came across the lawn to her, blushing deeply. He had a peculiarly unbecoming blush that mounted from his neck and seemed to push his prominent eyes yet further out of their sockets.

"Let me do that, Miss Mabs," he said, taking from her the chair she was carrying.

"I'm going indoors to help Mama make the sandwiches," said Mabs coldly and turned away from him abruptly.

Walter Pearson was the only son of a wealthy Devonshire squire and the apple of his mother's eye. She had been very reluctant to entrust him to the Vicar's charge, because she was afraid of his getting "entangled" with the daughter. She had warned him solemnly of the danger of this, and told him to be sure to keep the girl at arm's length. She was slightly piqued when she found that it was the girl who was keeping Walter at arm's length, and that when Walter, whom she regarded as the most eligible *parti* in the west of England, had committed the supreme indiscretion of proposing, the girl had met him with a curt and uncompromising refusal.

Mabs went into the stone-flagged kitchen, where Mrs. Abbot and Violet were cutting bread and butter at the big wooden table.

"Can I help?" said Mabs.

"Yes, dear," said Mrs. Abbot, "though we've nearly finished, haven't we, Violet?"

"I should hope so, 'm," said Violet gloomily. "My hand's fair dropping off with all this cutting and spreading."

"Nonsense!" said Mrs. Abbot. "I've been at it far longer than you, and I'm not a bit tired."

Mrs. Abbot and Violet between them did all the work of the Vicarage, but by far the larger share fell to Mrs. Abbot, for Violet never did anything without first making quite sure that Mrs. Abbot was not going to do it, and Mrs. Abbot had an insatiable appetite for work of any kind.

Mrs. Abbot was a bright bustling eager little person, rather like a robin redbreast, who enjoyed to the full every minute of an extremely dull existence. She found as much excitement in altering the position of a sofa in the drawing-room as most people find in the redecorating of an entire house. She enjoyed housework and cooking and teaching in Sunday School and training the choir-boys and playing the harmonium and making clothes for the heathen (as well as herself) and planning and scheming and economising on the Vicar's very inadequate stipend. She was hard at work all day and every day from the moment she got up till the moment she went to bed, and she was utterly and supremely happy. She looked forward for weeks beforehand with a confident expectation of unclouded enjoyment that was never disappointed to the choir treat, the Sunday School outing, the Sale of Work, and, most of all, the annual Vicarage garden-party.

"Perhaps you'd get another cucumber, dear," she said to Mabs. "I don't think we shall need it, but I do so like to be on the safe side."

Mabs went out by the back door and made her way down to the kitchen garden, keeping in the shelter of the bushes, so that Walter should not see and follow her. She cut the cucumber slowly and dreamily. In reality she was dancing with a tall handsome man in a crowded ballroom (she didn't know how she'd got there) and he was whispering in her ear, "How beautiful you are! You are the most beautiful woman I have ever met."

She sighed as she closed the cucumber frame. When she was not actually looking at herself in a mirror she always imagined herself to be beautiful, but she knew really that she was dumpy and ungraceful and that her nose was just too short and her mouth too long. She wished that she were as beautiful as Vicky Carothers. . . . Vicky would be there this afternoon, of course. Everyone would be there. It was a pity that Lady Sybil's house-party had ended last week. She might have brought some of her guests over. Lady Sybil's house-parties were always a source of great interest in the neighbourhood. A crowd of smart people would periodically descend upon Morton Manor, ride and drive over the countryside, and fill the big Manor pew in Morton church on Sundays. These parties were the scene of a good many of Mabs' dream romances, though actually she had little share in them.

She took the cucumber into the kitchen.

"Anything else I can do, Mama?"

"Yes, dear," said Mrs. Abbot briskly. "You might put the cloths on the tables if Roger's got them set out. Violet and I will bring out the crockery as soon as we've finished this."

Mabs took the pile of tea-cloths from the drawer and went out onto the lawn.

Roger and Mark and Walter had arranged the chairs and tables and were now engaged in fetching the croquet mallets from under the seat of the summer-house.

Walter came up to her as soon as she appeared, and a spasm convulsed his face as he wrestled with his stammer.

"Let me do that for you, Miss Mabs," he managed to get out at last.

"No, thank you," said Mabs distantly, "I prefer to do it myself."

Crestfallen, he rejoined the others. Mabs looked after him, something of wistfulness invading her hauteur. What a pity he wasn't handsome and charming and titled!

It had been arranged that Celia and Miss Standish should accompany Vicky to the Vicarage, and that Andrew should fetch her home in the dog-cart. Mrs. Carothers had a slight headache and had decided to stay at home. She had chaperoned Vicky conscientiously to all the recent local festivities, but she felt that a chaperon was not necessary at the Vicarage garden-party. The same people would be there as had been there for the last ten years, and from none of them could Vicky possibly receive any harm. Lady Sybil's house-party had broken up last Friday, so there could not even be any unknown quantity threatening danger from that quarter.

Mrs. Carothers felt justified, therefore, in retiring to her bedroom, letting down her hair, taking off her corsets, and giving orders that she was not to be disturbed till tea-time. She was growing stouter and felt the heat a good deal.

Celia and Vicky walked on either side of Miss Standish down the shady country road. Vicky wore one of the dresses that her stepmother had sent for from London—white embroidered muslin with an overdress of pale blue faille—with long black gloves and a shady hat of crinoline straw.

Vicky had suffered acutely on learning the truth about her mother. She felt unwanted, unloved, an alien in the happy family atmosphere that enclosed the other three, and with the facile despair of youth saw no gleam of hope or consolation anywhere. She was not, of course, quite so unhappy as she imagined herself to be, for unconsciously she extracted a certain amount of satisfaction from the position of lonely and neglected heroine. It was rather annoying that Mrs. Carothers mistook her tragic mien for shyness and would rally her with a brisk, "Don't be afraid to talk to people, Vicky. You're out of the schoolroom now."

Mrs. Carothers had tried to stifle the faint compunction that the thought of Vicky always brought with it by buying her a large and elaborate outfit, and even Vicky could not help being delighted by the white evening dress of taffeta and tulle, the Sunday dress of green velvet trimmed with guipure, and the neat day dresses of cashmere and mohair, each gathered up behind by bows or knots onto the inevitable bustle.

Miss Standish kept up a ceaseless flow of animated conversation as they walked along the road. She was a thin worn-looking woman, with pale eyes always slightly inflamed and a mouth that was set in a permanent smile. The fixed brightness of her expression made her look older than she really was. She had obtained her first post as governess at the age of eighteen and, owing to her youth and good spirits, had been an unqualified success. She had constituted herself as sister to her pupils (she was only two years older than the eldest), allowed them to call her by her Christian name, and entered into all their pursuits with an eagerness that rivalled their own. She had repeated the same tactics, also with success, in her next post, and she saw no reason to change them now that she was forty-six, slightly deaf, and very rheumatic. They had certainly seemed less successful of late, so she had intensified the youthfulness of her manner in order to rectify matters. She made a point of cultivating all Celia's enthusiasms, and, as Vicky was one of them, she cultivated Vicky, trying to put their relationship on the footing of two elder sisters of Celia's, united by devotion to her and constantly planning little treats and surprises for her. She attributed to reserve Vicky's obvious reluctance to fulfil the role thus assigned her, and made ceaseless efforts to overcome it.

The bright staccato of her chatter cut sharply and in-harmoniously through the summer air.

"I remember once when I was about Vicky's age going to a garden-party at my uncle's—he was a dean of Winchester—and they were expecting a new housemaid that day and you'll never guess what happened. When——"

It appeared that Celia and Vicky were not listening to her.

"I wonder who'll be there," Celia was saying.

"Oh, *everyone*'ll be there," said Miss Standish. (She was always ready to abandon her own conversation in order to take the leading part in whatever conversation had ousted it.) "Simply *everyone*. Half the village has been to Miss Salter to have new dresses made, I hear. But I'm sure our darling Vicky will be the belle. I'll tell you something that happened at my first party, shall I? It's such an amusing little story. I'd got there too early, and I didn't want to be the first to arrive so——"

No, they weren't even pretending to be interested. Vicky was lost in her own thoughts, and Celia—Miss Standish tried hard not to see her—was flashing a little grimace of mockery at her sister.

They had reached the Vicarage now.

"Good-bye, Vicky," said Celia. "I wish I could come with you."

"You needn't," said Vicky. "It's sure to be deadly dull."

"You'll come to the schoolroom when you get back, won't you, darling?"

"Yes . . . if you like."

Vicky went in at the Vicarage gate, and Celia and Miss Standish turned to retrace their steps to the Hall. Miss Standish's whole body quivered with brightness as she rallied her forces for another effort.

Vicky walked up the Vicarage drive and round to the side lawn where the party was being held. Most of the guests had already arrived and were sitting in the chairs that had been arranged in groups about the lawn.

Mabs, in a dress of pink surah trimmed with bows of white ribbon, was being languorous and haughty like the heroines of her favourite novels, and, as there wasn't anyone else to be haughty to, she was being haughty to Walter, ordering him about and making him fetch and carry for her. Walter, his face shining with perspiration and pleasure, plunged to and fro at her bidding, dropping cups and spoons and plates, but supremely happy in the knowledge that Mabs was at least recognising his existence.

"How *stupid* you are, Walter!" said Mabs, raising her voice and showing off before Vicky. She was jealous of Vicky's looks and the dress that had so obviously come from London, and she wanted to stress the fact that Walter, at any rate, had no eyes for her.

Mrs. Abbot had come across the lawn to greet Vicky. Mrs. Abbot greeted each guest with a delight that would have seemed exaggerated in anyone else, but that was in her case only a feeble expression of the joy she really felt. She wore the same dress that she had worn at this garden-party for the past five years, but she had renovated it this year by new lace frills at the throat and wrists. Her hat was only two years old, and she had retrimmed it with black lace and several red roses, and thought with characteristic optimism that it looked as good as new. Mabs kept a stern eye on her and occasionally came across to straighten the hat or rearrange the frills, for Mrs. Abbot's eagerness always seemed to have a disintegrating effect upon her costumes.

"Vicky, darling! How nice to see you and how lovely you look!" she said, kissing Vicky affectionately. "So nice to have you home again. Here's Dr. Milner——"

The doctor and his wife and Dorothea were sitting under the cedar tree. Dorothea wore an enormous silver cross conspicuously displayed on the front of her plain white nun's-veiling dress. She greeted Vicky in an abstracted fashion, then sat in silence, her eyes fixed on the ground. Dorothea, after passing through a fairly normal childhood (her bandy legs had gradually straightened and she had lost her habit of going to sleep at inconvenient moments) had suddenly developed a form of religious mania that her parents found very disconcerting. She would sit in the drawing-room ostentatiously reading books of devotion while her mother did embroidery or read novels. She refused all food except the plainest.

She was reluctant to take part in any form of social entertainment. It had needed the united coaxing of her mother and threats of her father to bring her here this afternoon. She had told her parents last night that she had decided to go into a nunnery as soon as it could be arranged. She had a plump round face, with a snub nose and a large cheerful mouth, upon which her expression of sanctimonious martyrdom sat oddly. Her parents' only comfort was that the very devout mistress for whom Dorothea had conceived a schoolgirl adoration was leaving the school next term, and that Dorothea was extremely impressionable. After all, had she not gone through a phase of "culture" last year, when she could talk of nothing but Dante and Giotto and Leonardo da Vinci (that was the English mistress), and the year before that had she not developed alarming hypochondriac tendencies, demanding boiled milk and brown bread and insisting on her father's sounding her heart and weighing her every few days (that had been the geography mistress)?

Her parents were depressed but not despairing. They told her that they would look about for a good nunnery when she left school and hoped the best from the new mistress.

The Vicar came across the lawn to join them—a thin stooping figure, with kind blue eyes and a gentle dreamy mouth.

"What do you think of Gladstone's speech?" said the doctor. "Don't like all this soft soap he's handing out to Bismarck. 'Friend and ally in interests of human race and spread of civilisation' indeed! Don't trust 'em. Never have done."

The Vicar agreed vaguely. Pericles was to him a figure of blinding reality, but Gladstone and Bismarck were unreal shadowy creatures. He could have told you every detail of the Peloponnesian War, but he knew little or nothing of nineteenth-century Europe.

He had thrown a slightly apprehensive glance at Dorothea on joining the group. Lately Dorothea had been coming to consult him about her religious difficulties, and, though the Vicar was a deeply religious man, he was not good at religious difficulties.

There was a slight stir as Lady Sybil and her husband arrived. Lady Sybil had been a reigning beauty in her day, and though now over seventy still carried traces of her beauty buried deep behind a mask of cosmetics. She was dressed in the height of fashion and wore a luxuriant blonde wig.

Her first husband had been a handsome young spark who had run through her fortune and died, a prematurely old man, at the age of forty. Her second husband was a wealthy manufacturer, who had begun life as an errand boy and still bore the marks of his class. He was common in speech and manners, wholly uneducated, but generous and good-tempered, and the marriage was a very happy one. He admired her smartness and poise and capacity for spending his money, while she on her side found his un-couthness quaint and attractive, and delighted in teaching him social tricks as if he were a performing bear.

Her penetrating high-pitched voice rang through the Vicarage garden as she greeted Mrs. Abbot and introduced the guest she had brought with her. Everyone watched her with covert interest, for Lady Sybil's arrival always created a sensation. She arrived a little late in order to ensure this. As she never appeared more than once in the same costume, she liked it to be duly noticed.

Her husband followed her, stout, perspiring, smiling, immaculately dressed and irredeemably common.

The guest, who was introduced as Mr. Frensham, was a tall handsome man of about forty, with a military carriage and a somewhat arrogant manner. Mabs threw him a quick careless glance. He was a frequent visitor at Morton Manor and she knew him well by sight, but, though he lived apart from his wife, he was married, and therefore for Mabs, did not exist. Only eligible young men existed for Mabs.

Chapter Eight

VICKY too had looked quickly away on seeing Harold Frensham, but not, like Mabs, because he did not interest her. She had been to a tea-party at Morton Manor last week and had met him there. Taking a tea-cup from a tray held by a footman, she had looked up to find his bold handsome eyes fixed on her across the room, and something in them had set her heart beating rapidly.

After tea Lady Sybil had introduced him to her, and Vicky's heart-beats had quickened still further as he held her hand a little more tightly and a little longer than the formal introduction warranted.

Later he had managed to separate her from the rest of the visitors while they were being shown over the greenhouses, and, strolling with her behind the screen of a yew hedge, had slipped his arm about her waist.

She had been horrified, not so much at his doing it as at the thrill of delight that had shot through her in response. She had freed herself quickly and joined the others, ignoring him for the rest of the afternoon, but he did not seem abashed. There was triumph and speculation in his eyes as they followed her.

She had lain awake nearly all that night feeling ashamed and yet excited, for that strange sweet unrest pervaded her again at the memory of him.

She had thought about the incident a good deal, magnifying her instinctive response to his advances into a natural propensity to evil, dramatising herself as the inheritor of her mother's "lightness." She stiffened her resolution to fight it. . . . This particular episode was safely over, for Lady Sybil's house-party had broken up last week. She must be on her guard for the future.

But this particular episode was not over. Harold Frensham's easy passions had been inflamed, and he had made an excuse for staying on at the Manor after the rest of the party had gone home in order to meet Vicky again.

He was a connoisseur of women, a past master in the art of seduction, and Vicky's youth and innocence, which had made such a strong appeal to his senses, seemed also to ensure his speedy success. Her mother's history, too, he considered to be in his favour.

Vicky threw a quick hunted glance around her. Mark was arranging a croquet game on the lawn in his best school prefect manner, issuing orders in an unnecessarily loud voice, and looking aloof and important.

Dorothea Milner had refused to play. She had had a secret struggle with herself before refusing, because she liked croquet, but there was no getting away from the fact that it was worldly, so she sat, her eyes fixed on the ground, trying hard not to take an interest in it.

Vicky had been among the first to volunteer for the game. There, at least, she would be safe from her pursuer. (She thought of him as her pursuer, though she had not seen him since that first short meeting.) But she could not escape his eyes. As she moved to and fro with her mallet they followed her—dark eloquent eyes that seemed to melt her resolution like snow.

After the game she made her way to a chair as far away from Harold Frensham as she could. Roger brought her a cup of tea, and she began to talk to him with eager friendliness, as if begging him to stay with her and protect her, but it only increased his natural shyness, and he moved on with his gentle smile.

Mark came up to her with a cake-stand, but he could not stay long, either, for he was bringing all his powers of organisation to bear upon the croquet games. He had another game in progress and was keeping a stern eye upon the players to see that they did not cheat, and handing round cakes at the same time, so he had little attention for anything else, and he, too, passed on, swinging the cake-stand precariously to and fro as he went, shouting out instructions and admonitions.

Vicky watched him disappear among the other guests, then turned to meet the eyes of Harold Frensham, who had taken the empty chair at her side.

She was not really surprised. Something in her had known all the time that she could not escape. Her pulses pounding in her ears, she took the initiative, trying to speak lightly and casually.

"I didn't expect to meet you here. I thought you'd gone away last week."

"Can you guess why I stayed?" he said.

She tore her eyes from his and looked round again for protection. Roger was now talking to Dorothea Milner, and Mark was directing the players. Everyone was engrossed either in conversation or in the game. There was no one to help her. There never had been. . . . A sudden bitterness invaded the turmoil of her spirit. No one cared what happened to her. What did it matter what she did?

"Say you've thought of me . . . just a little . . . Vicky. . . ."

She made no response. Her eyes were fixed on the ground, and her cheeks were very pale. She dug the point of her parasol into the grass. He saw that she was trembling.

"Will you come for a stroll round the garden with me, Miss Carothers?" he said, speaking formally and in a voice that was loud enough for their neighbours to hear.

He stood up and gave Vicky his hand to assist her to her feet. Against her will, she obeyed.

They passed through the crowds of guests on the lawn, round the corner of the house, to the other lawn, now deserted, where a small summer-house stood.

"You're looking very pale," he said. "Come into the summer-house and sit down."

Of course she mustn't do that, she told herself, but, with his eyes upon her, she couldn't resist. She went with him up the sloping side of the lawn and, after hesitating a moment, entered the little wooden house. There was a rustic table in the middle, and a wooden seat running round the side. He followed her in and closed the door behind him.

She made a faint resistance when he took her in his arms—a resistance that convinced neither of them, for his kisses sent that wave of sweetness through her again, and she lay still in his arms, her eyes shut, surrendering herself to it.

"Vicky . . . tell me you love me . . ."

Terror stirred beneath the ecstasy. She felt trapped—not by him but by something in herself. A "light woman" like her mother. . . .

"Be kind to me."

"No, no," said Vicky, in a quick sobbing breath.

He held her closer.

"Where's Vicky?" said Mrs Abbot's voice faintly in the distance.

That broke the spell. She struggled to free herself.

"Let me go," she whispered.

He released her reluctantly, keeping his hands on her shoulders, looking down at her intently.

"Vicky . . . come for a walk with me to-night. In the moonlight. Just the two of us . . . with no one else to bother us. I'll be at the Hall gate at twelve. You can slip out, can't you? Just for a lark. . . ."

She shook her head. She felt stunned, shaken, caught up by an intolerable joy, beneath which loomed a black abyss of fear.

"Are you afraid?"

"No, no. It's not that."

"You'll come," he said quietly.

She turned from him blindly and went out onto the sunny lawn. He followed, smiling to himself. He had felt her surrender and had no doubt of ultimate victory.

"There you are, Vicky dear," said Mrs. Abbot. "Mark's getting up another game. Will you play?"

Vicky took the mallet that Mark handed her and began to play. It all seemed like a dream. She wouldn't go, of course. She had been mad to let him kiss her. She wouldn't go. She would never speak to him again. . . . But beneath it all something stronger than reason was saying, "You will go. Of course you'll go. You can't help it. . . ."

She was relieved when she heard that Andrew had come to fetch her. Mrs. Abbot, radiantly happy at the success of her party, kissed her affectionately and came round to the front door, where Andrew waited with the dog-cart. But it was Harold Frensham who helped her in, tucked the rug round her, and whispered, "Twelve o'clock. . . . Don't forget. I'll be there."

She didn't answer or look at him, but the blood crept into her cheeks, and again that strange sweet excitement surged through her.

As they drove home she was hardly aware of Andrew, sitting beside her, his pale freckled face grave and intent.

Celia came running into the hall to greet her.

"Darling, how lovely to see you again! Did you have a nice time?"

Miss Standish appeared in the background, laughing girlishly.

"Celia and I are longing to hear all about it," she said. "We can neither of us settle down to lessons till we've heard."

Vicky answered their questions absently.

Mrs. Carothers, stout, handsome, matronly, came out of the drawing-room.

"Here you are, my dear. You look rather tired. Hadn't you better go and rest before dinner?"

Vicky went upstairs and changed mechanically into her evening dress. The soft sensual haze that had drugged mind and body was departing, and her resolution was hardening. Of course she wouldn't go. It would be wicked. She was horrified to think that she had considered it even for a moment.

She came downstairs to the drawing-room. Mrs. Carothers sat on one side of the fireplace, her head bent over her embroidery, and on the other sat Mr. Carothers. Celia, in a cream cashmere dress embroidered with red, a red sash round her hips, her curls hanging over her shoulders, was perched on the arm of his chair, and, as Vicky entered, he was looking at her with an expression of tenderness that softened and transformed his stern features. Then his eyes turned to Vicky, and his face hardened into a mask of cold severity. He rose abruptly, said "Good evening, Victoria," and went from the room.

He generally found some excuse to leave a room as soon as Vicky entered it, but never before had he shown his aversion quite so openly, never before contrasted it quite so plainly with his love for his other daughter.

A hot rush of anger surged over Vicky. Why should she try to be good when nobody cared about her but Celia, Celia who was only a child, and for whom she felt this sudden bitter jealousy? A "light woman" like her mother? Very well, she would be like her mother. Perhaps that would hurt him. She hoped it would. She wanted to punish him even if she could only do it by bringing disgrace on him. Beneath her anger was the old wistful longing to be loved and made much of, the longing to which her lover's tenderness made such an irresistible appeal.

She went upstairs early and sat at her bedroom window, watching the light fade over the garden, till the trees stood like dark giants against a silvered sky. She sat there, taut and upright, her eyes unnaturally bright, little quivers of excitement creeping through her frame. Though it was a hot night, she had to clench her teeth to stop them chattering.

At last the clock struck twelve.

She put on her hat and coat and went noiselessly down the staircase.

She did not attempt the front door, which was locked and bolted and chained, but went round to the French window in the drawing-room, opened the catch, and stepped out upon the moonlit terrace.

A figure detached itself from the shadows, and came towards her. At first she thought it was Harold Frensham, then she saw that it was Andrew.

The servants' hall gossip about Harold Frensham had filtered down to Andrew's sister, who was kitchen-maid at Morton Manor. Wide-eyed with horror, she had repeated it in the kitchen of the jasmine-covered cottage. Andrew had paid little enough attention, but when he saw the hero of the unsavoury stories bending over

Miss Vicky, fixing his eyes on her, and whispering "Twelve o'clock. I'll be there," he remembered them with a feeling of uneasiness.

It was not his business, of course, and in any case "twelve o'clock" might have meant to-morrow morning, but the old unreasoning sense of responsibility nagged at his heart. Miss Vicky was young and thoughtless, and had no one but him to look after her. He must not let her do anything foolish if he could help it.

He went to bed with his brother as usual, then, as soon as his brother was asleep, got out of bed, dressed, and made his way across the fields to the Hall. Standing on the terrace in the shelter of the house, he waited till the clock struck twelve. Nothing happened, and he was on the point of turning away when a slender figure appeared behind the glass door of the drawing-room, deft fingers pushed back the catch, and Vicky appeared on the terrace.

She gave a start as he stepped in front of her.

"*Andrew!*" she gasped.

"Miss Vicky," he began, and words tumbled out, though he hardly knew what he was saying. "You mustn't, Miss Vicky. You can't. You don't know what you're doing. You don't know what he's like."

She turned on him with flashing eyes.

"How *dare* you!" she said.

"Miss Vicky, listen. I've known you since you were a little girl. I can't let you do this. I——"

She pushed him aside, white with anger, and began to walk down the drive.

He followed her, still pleading incoherently.

Half-way down the drive Harold Frensham came into sight, walking towards them with his leisurely arrogant stride, completely at his ease. His face darkened as his eyes fell on Andrew's stocky ungainly figure.

"Who's this?" he said shortly.

Andrew stepped forward. His pale freckled face was tense, his lips set.

"Miss Vicky's not coming with you, Mr. Frensham," he said.

Harold Frensham's lip curled.

"Oh, indeed," he said, "and who says so?"

"I am coming," put in Vicky hysterically, but Andrew motioned her back, and she obeyed almost without knowing she was doing so.

"I say she's not," said Andrew. "I'm here to stop her and I will stop her even if——"

"We'll soon see about that," said the other.

The two men made a striking contrast as they stood there face to face—the one tall, handsome, finely proportioned; the other plain, clumsy, common-looking.

Frensham's fist shot out, catching Andrew on the cheekbone and nearly throwing him off his balance. Andrew hit back gamely but at random, no match for his opponent. He returned to the attack again and again and was punished more savagely each time, till at last he fell onto the gravel and lay there motionless. Frensham looked down at him, breathing heavily, his teeth gleaming in the moonlight.

"Perhaps that'll be a lesson to you," he said, and vented the remnant of his rage in a contemptuous kick. It was the kick that woke Vicky from the stupor that held her. She flung herself on her knees beside Andrew, sobbing beneath her breath.

"Andrew ... Andrew. ... Oh, you've killed him."

"Nonsense!" said the man, straightening his coat and collar. Now that his anger had spent itself, he was feeling rather pleased by the situation. It was an auspicious beginning to the affair that Vicky should have seen him displaying his manly qualities to such advantage. Women admired physical strength. He almost wished he had had better material to try it on than that weed of a fellow.

"He's only knocked out and probably shamming at that. Come along, my dear."

His tone was complacent, possessive.

But she was still kneeling by Andrew.

"Andrew ... Andrew, look at me. ..."

Harold Frensham took her by the shoulders as if to raise her to her feet, but she shook him off angrily.

"Go away," she said. "I'm not coming with you. I hate you. I never want to see you again."

He stared at her, open-mouthed. She met his gaze with hostile blue eyes.

"But . . . Vicky . . ." he said.

"Go away," she repeated. "I hate you, I tell you. If you won't go I'll fetch Papa."

It was unlikely that she would fulfil the threat, but he had no wish to be confronted by an irate parent, and his presence there at that hour would be difficult to explain.

He turned on his heel and left her, thinking that he was probably well out of it after all. Women were the devil. She had obviously been on the point of coming with him, and then she'd suddenly changed to a raging spitfire, and all because of some wretched little cad of a manservant whose insolence he had justly punished. He made his way back to Morton Manor, feeling both chagrined and relieved. Perhaps the whole thing had been crazy and it was as well that he had seen the girl in her true colours before it was too late. . . .

Andrew was struggling to his feet. He was a pitiful object, with a bleeding nose, swiftly closing eye, and a cut lip.

He looked at Vicky's white tear-stained face.

"Don't take on, Miss Vicky," he said in a thick husky voice. "He wouldn't have been no good to you."

"Andrew, are you terribly hurt?"

"No, Miss Vicky," he said, still speaking with difficulty. "He isn't no good, you know, Miss Vicky. He hadn't no right to try to make you do a thing like that. You'd better go in now, Miss Vicky, quick, or there may be trouble."

"Yes," said Vicky meekly. "Good night, Andrew."

"Good night, Miss Vicky."

She went in by the French window, and Andrew walked stumblingly, unsteadily, down the drive.

Chapter Nine

VICKY sat tense and upright on the seat of the railway carriage, her hands folded in her lap, her blue eyes fixed absently on the fleeting scenery. It was just a week since Andrew's encounter with Harold Frensham. She had gone about since then pale and nerve-wracked, avoiding both Andrew (who had accounted for his disfigurement by the unconvincing story of a fall) and Celia, whose childish devotion and high spirits now irked her intolerably, spending most of her time alone in her bedroom.

Her thoughts had been turning more and more towards her own mother. It was there she belonged, not to these aliens—Celia, her stepmother, the father who hated her. The decision to go to her came quite suddenly while she lay awake one night, staring into the darkness. Apart from every other consideration, it would hurt her father almost as much as her going to Harold Frensham would have done. (She was still the little girl who had to punish her father for ignoring her by defiance and daring.) Moreover, there would be in it the thrill of the unknown, of breaking free from this life in which she had no part, of starting afresh.

"Mama," she said the next afternoon, as the two were having tea together in the drawing-room, "what does my mother call herself?"

"Your mother's name now is Mrs. Orell," said Mrs. Carothers rather shortly.

"Where does she live?"

It happened that Mrs. Carothers had received a letter from a friend only a few days previously, telling her, as a piece of idle gossip, where Rosamund was living. She hesitated for a moment, then took the letter from her desk and read out the address.

"Thank you," said Vicky.

Mrs. Carothers replaced the letter in her desk without comment or question. The child evidently meant to write to Rosamund. Well, it could do no harm. . . .

Vicky spent the next day in a kind of trance. I'm leaving them all for ever, she kept saying to herself. Perhaps I'll never see any of them again—not Papa or Mama or Celia or Andrew.

She wrote to her mother by the afternoon's post, packed her bag with a few necessities overnight, and, rising in the morning before anyone was about, slipped quietly down to the station.

Her plan worked with unexpected smoothness. She met no one. No one was on the platform. The train was practically empty. Her heart gave a leap as it started. The new life had begun. . . .

She tried to imagine what her mother would be like. All she knew of her was that she was a "light woman." Vicky's mental vision of a "light woman" was of someone standing on a table in the middle of a circle of men who were holding up wine-glasses or drinking out of a slipper. . . . Whatever sort of a life she lived, Vicky would now be part of it. It was her place—her home, her mother. The craving for love and understanding that had been with her ever since she could remember reached out hungrily, confident at last of satisfaction. Whatever her mother was like, she was her mother. She would love and care for her. Perhaps she had longed for her child all these years, just as Vicky had unconsciously longed for her mother.

It was a stopping train, and several other passengers got in and out. Some of them glanced curiously at the girl's pale lovely face, with its look of rapt exaltation, but Vicky did not see any of them, did not even know that the train had stopped or that other passengers had entered it. She was being clasped in her mother's arms, sobbing out her love and devotion on her shoulder.

At the London station she engaged a cab, gave the cabman the address, and set off through the crowded streets.

It was a small sedate house in Chelsea, with steps leading up to the front door flanked by curved railings of wrought iron, wrought iron balconies outside the upstairs windows, and an exquisitely traced fanlight over the door. Nottingham lace curtains were tied back with pale-green ribbon bows. Half-drawn Venetian blinds, like modestly lowered lids, accentuated the general air of demureness.

Vicky took her bag, paid the driver, and knocked at the front door. It was opened by an elderly housemaid in the regulation black dress, voluminous white starched apron, and white cap with long streamers.

"Is Mrs. Orell in?" said Vicky.

Her voice sounded shy and frightened, like a little girl's.

The maid ushered her into a small drawing-room just inside the door, and left her there, closing the door.

The room fulfilled the promise of the outside of the house. It was prim and elegant and demure. On the mantelpiece a pair of lustres flanked an ormolu clock. A table in the middle of the room supported a group of stuffed birds under a glass case. A small rosewood bureau stood in the window. The chairs and sofa were upholstered in green. Ornamental grasses filled the empty grate. There were no photographs—no personal belongings at all, except a mahogany inlaid work-box on a small tripod coffee-table near the fireplace.

Feeling faint with excitement, Vicky sat down on one of the green upholstered chairs and looked about her. This was her mother's house. She had come home. This room, now so strange, would soon become as familiar to her as her own features.

Then the door opened and Rosamund Orell entered. She was dressed in black, with touches of white at throat and wrists, and her hair was parted austerely in the centre and drawn back into a bun. It was fair, like Vicky's, but its golden tint had faded, and she obviously made no effort to conceal the few grey hairs that showed here and there. Her beautiful face was neither rouged nor powdered.

"Vicky!" she said.

Vicky threw herself, into the outstretched arms and was pressed for a second to the shapely black satin bosom against a large rather spiky mourning brooch. She was preparing to sob out her heart on the black satin, when she found herself released, held smilingly at arm's length, then pushed gently onto the green upholstered sofa.

Mrs. Orell took her seat beside her.

Vicky choked back her tears.

"You got my letter, didn't you, Mother?" she said.

She had decided to say Mother, because Mama could never mean anyone but Mrs. Carothers.

"Yes, darling," said Mrs. Orell. "It came about an hour ago. How stupidly slow the posts are, aren't they?"

"Mother, I want to live with you for always," said Vicky. "I've been so unhappy. I can't tell you how unhappy I've been." Tears quivered in her voice again. "Papa hates me, and Mama—she's not been unkind, but she's never liked me—and Celia's just a silly child, and there's really only been Andrew ever, and he's a servant and doesn't count."

Mrs. Orell patted her daughter's hand absently. There was a far-away look in her eyes, as if she were not listening.

"Darling," she said, "I can't tell you what it means to me to have you. My own little girl. . . . I hated leaving you. . . . I don't know what they've told you, but"—she looked faintly embarrassed—"I was terribly misunderstood, and I was too proud to justify myself. Whatever story they've told you isn't the true one, of course. You could never conceive how much I've suffered, my love. Misunderstood. Deserted by my friends. But that's all in the past. We won't think about that."

Vicky bent down impulsively and kissed the hand that was patting hers.

"My darling mother," she said. "We'll always be together now. . . ."

Again the thoughtful look came into Mrs. Orell's eyes.

"I can't let you do anything rash, dearest," she murmured. "I want you to consider this matter very carefully. I don't think that the life in this house is suitable for a young girl like you." Vicky opened her lips to protest, but Mrs. Orell waved the unspoken objection aside. "I lead such a very very quiet life. I am connected with various charitable organisations and my work for them takes all my time. I seldom go out except in connection with those. I never entertain and am in touch with no young people."

Vicky stared at her in amazement. This did not sound at all like the gay life in which she had been prepared to take her part, the vortex of pleasure in which she had been prepared to drown her youthful unhappiness.

Mrs. Orell fixed her eyes rather anxiously upon her daughter.

"Don't you think, dearest, that perhaps you would be happier with your papa? I don't mean that I wouldn't love to have you, but—well, as I say, it's a dull life for a young girl."

A wave of love and pity swept over Vicky. Her beautiful misunderstood mother, alone and friendless. Oh, why had she waited all these years before coming to her?

"Oh, but, Mother darling, it won't be dull. I shall have you. That's all I want. We shall be together at last."

Her eyes were starry with devotion. She made a shy movement as if to take her mother in her arms, but Mrs. Orell did not notice it. Her eyes were still fixed speculatively on the distance.

"Well . . . perhaps for the present, my love," she said, and added, "Do they know you've come to me?"

"Yes, I left a note."

"Of course, your papa may insist on your returning."

"He won't," said Vicky rather sadly. "He—he dislikes me, you know."

"Does he?" said Mrs. Orell, with an almost imperceptible shrug, and added, "How do he and Eleanor get on together?"

She asked the question in a casual, matter-of-fact tone, but Vicky felt embarrassed.

"Quite well," she said uncomfortably.

Mrs. Orell smiled faintly and said:

"She used to bore me dreadfully when we were girls. Is Edmund as pompous as ever?"

"I suppose so," said Vicky.

"What's the child like?"

"Celia? She's all right."

She spoke constrainedly. She didn't want to waste time talking about them. She wanted to begin the wonderful new life that lay before her—the life in which she was to be the help and comfort of her lovely misunderstood mother. Perhaps one day she would tell her the whole story of how she had been misunderstood. Probably she had been shielding a friend. She was innocent, of course ... Vicky had been sure of that as soon as she saw her. The dramatic story shaped itself in Vicky's mind. Deliberately she had let suspicion rest on her so that her friend might go free. Her friend was probably now a respectable highly honoured matron, while her mother lived here, alone and friendless.

Mrs. Orell glanced at the ormolu clock.

"Miss Tarrant should be in soon, dear," she said. "She's my secretary and companion. She's gone out to do some shopping, but she's coming in for tea. I'm expecting another friend, too—a clergyman who's on several committees with me. We have various pieces of business to talk over. I'm afraid you'll be terribly bored, my dear."

"Oh, I shan't. I shan't," protested Vicky earnestly. "I'm so happy just to be with you."

Again that speculative far-away look had come into Mrs. Orell's eyes.

"Dearest," she said. "I wonder—you see, it would really simplify things for both of us ... I mean, how would it be if we pretended that you were just a friend—or shall we say a distant relation?" She met the trusting ingenuous blue eyes and looked quickly away. "We'll let it be a lovely secret between you and me that you're really my little girl, shall we?"

The sudden hurt look vanished from the childish face and the colour flooded the soft cheeks. "A lovely secret between you and me." Vicky's heart was full. Here was someone at last who loved and needed her. ...

"You'd better go up, darling, and take your hat off, hadn't you?" Mrs. Orell was saying briskly. "What about your luggage?"

"I didn't bring any," said Vicky. "I wanted to get away without anyone seeing me. I'll write and tell them to send it on at once."

"You won't need much, darling. As I said, I lead a very quiet life."

"But they might as well send it all," said Vicky, "because I shan't be going back there ever again."

Mrs. Orell said nothing. Apparently she had not heard.

The elderly housemaid took Vicky up to a bedroom, with white muslin curtains, a dressing-table flounced in white muslin, and a very high single bed covered with a white crocheted counterpane. The walls were papered with a cheerful pattern of climbing roses and hung with framed texts. Over the mantelpiece was an engraving of Windsor Castle.

Vicky washed at the marble-topped washstand, then tidied her hair at the muslin-draped dressing-table. She felt bewildered—so much seemed to have happened in so short a time—but wildly, ecstatically happy. She was home, home, home. . . . This little room was already dearer to her than the large bedroom next to Papa's and Mama's had ever been.

She went to the window and looked out. A carriage and pair were passing down the quiet street, a powdered footman perched up majestically beside the coachman. The sun shone on the glossy coats of the high-stepping horses and on the gleaming polish of the carriage. It disappeared round the corner. Then came a hansom with a couple of ragamuffins hanging on behind. As it passed the window the cabby reached back with his whip and whipped them off, and they ran away, their rags fluttering in the breeze. A tradesman's cart came next, then a man and woman, the woman's face pretty and demure beneath her crinoline straw bonnet, one white gloved hand tucked into the man's arm, the other holding up her trailing skirts.

Vicky watched it all dreamily. If she'd been at the window of her bedroom at home, she would have been looking down at the garden—and perhaps Andrew working on the beds at the foot of the terrace steps. A sudden regret dimmed the ecstasy of happiness. The knowledge that Andrew was there in the background had always given her a feeling of safety and protection. Now, of course, Andrew would never be there again.

She pulled herself up sharply. The regret, however faint, seemed a disloyalty to her mother. It proved how lonely and unhappy she had been that she should ever have thought of a servant in that way.

She went from the room and stood hesitating for some moments at the top of the stairs before she plucked up courage to descend.

When she entered the drawing-room a woman who was evidently Miss Tarrant was sitting at the little rosewood writing-desk in the window. She had a vague unfinished sort of face—pale eyes that blinked behind thick steel-rimmed glasses, sallow cheeks, and a blunt putty-like nose. Her mouth was loose and tremulous, continually making vague little movements of its own accord even when she was not speaking.

Mrs. Orell, lying back on the sofa, held out her hand in welcome to Vicky.

"This is Miss Tarrant, dear, of whom I was speaking. She very kindly helps me and looks after me. This is the young cousin of mine, Miss Tarrant, who has paid us an unexpected visit. I've persuaded her to stay for a few days; haven't I, darling?"

She patted Vicky's hand affectionately as she spoke, as if to make up for relegating her to the position of a "young cousin."

Vicky returned her conspiratorial smile. It was rather fun to pretend to be a "young cousin"—"A lovely secret between you and me"—but part of her mind was unconsciously puzzling over it. Why had she to pretend? Why couldn't she just be Vicky, the beloved long-lost daughter?

During the half-hour that followed she was touched by her mother's kindness to her companion. Miss Tarrant, though well-meaning enough, was obviously incompetent and careless. She had mislaid the key to her employer's writing-case and forgotten to post two important letters.

"I'm so *sorry*, Mrs. Orell," she kept saying. "I can't *think* how it happened."

"Don't worry, my dear," said Mrs. Orell kindly. "The keys are sure to turn up. Things always do, and one day more or less doesn't make much difference to the letters. Don't bother about it any more. . . . Sit down and rest."

There was even a touch of deference in her manner that puzzled Vicky.

But Miss Tarrant refused to sit down and rest. She was in a state of great agitation over her carelessness (Vicky discovered in the next few days that Miss Tarrant passed her life in a state of agitation over her carelessness) and insisted on going out to the post at once with the letters.

As soon as she had gone from the room Mrs. Orell's brows came sharply together and her lips tightened.

"What a *fool* that woman is!" she said sharply.

Vicky laughed.

"You're so patient with her," she said.

"I try to be," said Mrs. Orell, with a shrug.

"I think you're wonderful," said Vicky.

An expression that on a less lovely face would have been called sanctimonious dispelled the ill-humour of eyes and mouth.

"I try to be kind," said Mrs. Orell. "Kindness to others is, after all, a Christian duty. But, my dear—" She leapt suddenly to her feet, and both sanctimoniousness and ill-humour were lost in a sudden gamin mischievousness as she began to burrow among the papers on her desk with large clumsy movements, her lips moving loosely as she muttered, "I'm so sorry, Mrs. Orell. . . . I can't *think* . . ."

It was a brilliant caricature of her companion, but there was a suspicion of vindictiveness behind it that made Vicky, despite her laughter, fear for its object on her return.

As soon as Miss Tarrant re-entered the room, however, Mrs. Orell's expression resumed its usual sweetness.

"Come and sit down, dear," she said kindly. "I'm sure you're tired with all that running about."

Miss Tarrant, panting and dishevelled (it was only two minutes' walk to the pillar-box, but that was sufficient to make Miss Tarrant panting and dishevelled), sat down and began to apologise once more for her forgetfulness.

Mrs. Orell waved aside her apologies.

"You aren't to think of it again, dear," she said; "is she, Vicky? I've just been telling Vicky how invaluable you are to me and that I simply shouldn't know what to do without you; haven't I, darling?"

She turned limpid blue eyes on Vicky, and Vicky, taken slightly aback, blushed and stammered, then quickly agreed, feeling herself taking part once more in a delightful conspiracy, this time to soothe Miss Tarrant's ruffled feelings.

Then the elderly housemaid threw open the door and announced "Mr. Thorburn."

A tall, thickset clergyman with neat wavy side whiskers, wearing a well-tailored clerical frock-coat, entered, and stood for a moment on the threshold with the air of one expecting and receiving an ovation. He had a large face whose small but decided features were crowded together in the centre, leaving, as it were, a disproportionate amount of it unoccupied. His manner was portentously dignified and impressive.

Vicky disliked him on sight, but her mother fluttered round him solicitously, settling him in his chair, fetching him a cushion, asking after his health. She introducing Vicky again as a "young cousin of mine."

Mr. Thorburn, however, ignored Vicky, concentrating his whole attention on Mrs. Orell. He had a deep well-modulated voice, and Vicky, despite her instinctive dislike, realised that there was something impressive and forceful about him.

The elderly housemaid brought in tea, and Mrs. Orell poured it out. Vicky thought how charming she looked, sitting there in the soft light that filtered through the lace curtains, her white hands moving gracefully among the tea-cups. . . . Their talk was serious and businesslike. They discussed the various charities with which they were both connected. Mrs. Orell was evidently a keen church worker and philanthropist. She must be rich, Vicky gathered, for she offered help freely to any case of distress mentioned by Mr. Thorburn, but she obviously lived very simply, spending far less on herself than she gave to others.

Miss Tarrant sat, large, nervous, clumsy, trying to help, but always just too late with the plates she passed or the remarks she made. Mrs. Orell treated her, as ever, with charming consideration, drawing her into the conversation, hiding her clumsiness, supplementing her inadequate service. Sometimes she flashed her bright smile at Vicky, so that Vicky shouldn't feel out of it either.

Vicky, listening and watching, thought how different it all was from the mental picture she had formed of it before she came. The gay life . . . champagne . . . standing on tables . . . drinking out of slippers. . . . A "light woman" indeed! She wished that Mama could see this quiet little room and hear Mother discussing charities and church work with Mr. Thorburn. Why, Mama, with her jewels and horses and elaborate clothes, was infinitely more worldly.

She listened carefully to the conversation. This was the new life. She must learn to take her part in it. She saw herself accompanying her mother on her errands of mercy. . . . They would sit in this cosy little room discussing their work together. She would even try to like Mr. Thorburn. . . . She was glad that Miss Tarrant was so inefficient. Perhaps soon they would be able to dispense with her altogether, if her mother's kindness of heart would allow her to. . . . How far away the other world seemed—Papa, Mama, Celia, Andrew! She wondered what they had said when they discovered her flight. She would never see any of them again, of course. Perhaps she would just write to Andrew to say good-bye, but she would never go back to the Hall. She wouldn't want to. She would be too happy here.

Mr. Thorburn took his leave, the elderly housemaid cleared away the table, while Miss Tarrant chattered in-consequently about everything that Mr. Thorburn had said. Miss Tarrant was usually silent, but she had periodic attacks of volubility, generally after some social occasion, when she would repeat everything that had been said as though no one but herself had heard it. She repeated it so confusedly, however, that it was almost unrecognisable.

Mrs. Orell sat with eyes downcast and a little smile on her lips. Quite obviously she was not listening to anything that Miss Tarrant said. Vicky wondered what she was thinking of. . . .

Miss Tarrant's conversation, as usual, came to a sudden stop as she remembered something that she had forgotten to do.

"Oh dear!" she said. "Here I am wasting time chattering when I ought to be hard at work. I did want to finish cutting out that calico to-day. I'll go and do them now, Mrs. Orell, shall I?"

Mrs. Orell woke with a start from her day-dreams and smiled pleasantly at her companion.

"Yes, my dear, do. I'll join you in a moment."

Miss Tarrant gathered up her reticule and went from the room.

"We make a certain number of calico garments each month for the heathen," explained Mrs. Orell to Vicky. "I often have to undo the ones Miss Tarrant makes, but, of course, I don't let her know."

"Mother, I think you're *sweet* to her," said Vicky impulsively. "She's so tiresome, and you're so patient. You're—wonderful."

Again that little smile played round the corners of Mrs. Orell's lips.

"She's very useful, dear," she said.

"Mother, let me help you, too," pleaded Vicky. "I do want to. You're so—so good and work so hard."

"Darling," murmured her mother absently, the faraway look returning to the blue eyes.

"I want to help you," went on Vicky in a voice that quivered with emotion, "and stay with you always now. I simply can't bear to think of you having been alone all these years. Alone and so terribly misunderstood. You will let me help, won't you?"

Mrs. Orell looked at her speculatively.

"Yes, darling," she said. "There are a few things you might do for me now. . . . Perhaps you'd copy out a list for me. Just a list of subscribers for one of the charities I'm interested in. . . ."

Vicky sprang up eagerly.

"I'd love to," she said.

She sat down at the little writing-desk and began to copy the list that her mother gave her into a thick black ledger. Her heart was full of love and hope and enthusiasm. . . .

Mrs. Orell sat staring into space. The smile had left her lips and her brows were drawn into a frown. Vicky's coming here like this was the worst thing that could possibly have happened just now. She felt so angry that it was all she could do to be polite to the child. She must get rid of her as soon as possible. Just as things were turning out so well, just as she was beginning to make headway at last. . . . The girl's presence would revive all the old scandals. Probably even Miss Tarrant, fool as she was, hadn't quite swallowed that lie about her being a "young cousin." Certainly Clement Thorburn hadn't. People had such damnably long memories.

Chapter Ten

Two days after Vicky's arrival in London she received a letter from her stepmother. It made no comment on her flight, but merely enquired if she had enough money and assured her that she would be welcomed at home whenever she chose to return. "I have told Celia that you were paying a visit to friends. I thought that best in the circumstances."

Vicky felt slightly piqued by the casual tone of the letter. She had imagined that her father and stepmother would be aghast and enraged at her daring, and they took it as calmly as if she had gone away on an ordinary visit. She handed the letter to her mother across the breakfast table, and Mrs. Orell read it with something of the same feeling. Eleanor might at least have mentioned her, if only to warn the child against her. It was humiliating to be ignored altogether.

"They don't seem very much upset, do they?" she said.

"I never want to see them or hear from them again," said Vicky angrily. "There!" She tore the letter into shreds and threw it into the fire. "That's the end of that. I can't think how I've endured it. . . ." The anger died out of her eyes. "If only I'd known about you before, I'd have come to you years ago."

Rosamund stirred her coffee in silence.

Rosamund Orell had spent her youth deliberately closing all the doors to whose entry her birth entitled her. She had delighted in shocking the dowagers and defying their rules of conduct. Their drawing-rooms were so dull that she would much rather be excluded, from them than admitted. The demi-monde was infinitely more

amusing. Gaily, irresponsibly, she closed door after door. ...
Immorality, carried on in a conventional fashion, might have been
condoned, but open immorality that brazenly mocked its censors
was quite another matter. Rosamund was light-hearted and
passionate and alluring, with thought for nothing but pleasure and
the lover of the moment. The years passed by and gradually she
realised that her youth had left her. Little by little her eyes turned
to the place that had been hers by birth, and she began to knock
tentatively at the doors that had been closed on her for so long.
Their refusal to open was a challenge to her, and now her sole aim
in life was to win back what she had so carelessly thrown away.
She shrank from no effort, no expense, no humiliation, that might
further this aim. She was a fairly wealthy woman, for she had
married her last lover, a rich city merchant, who had died
conveniently a few months after the marriage, leaving her his sole
heiress. The money was useful, of course, but did not solve the
problem. It could buy the entry to certain grades of society, but
not to that in which she had been born. Her own relations did
nothing to help, were indeed the most uncompromising in their
refusal to reinstate her. But her last campaign seemed to be on the
verge of success. It had been a stroke of genius to attack the enemy
from the side of philanthropy. Her money and quiet persistence
were gradually gaining her admittance to committees where those
who had closed their doors upon her socially had now to meet
her on friendly terms.

And it had been a glorious chance to find Miss Tarrant. For
Miss Tarrant, though penniless, was Lord Merrilow's cousin and
connected with various other strongholds of the aristocracy. And
Miss Tarrant's aristocratic relations patronised her, asking her to
tea on her free afternoon, letting her spend with them what holidays
she had. News of Mrs. Orell was sure to filter through to them—Mrs.
Orell, so good and kind and patient, so wholly given to good
works. No possible breath of scandal could touch Mrs. Orell, living
as she did with Miss Tarrant as her sole companion, going out
hardly at all, entertaining only as much as was necessary for her
philanthropic schemes, giving all her time and money to plans for

the regeneration of the heathen and the alleviation of the lot of the Poor. The impression would in time, she hoped, eradicate that other impression of Rosamund Carothers, taking lover after lover and brazenly flaunting her sin.

Mr. Thorburn, too, was a stroke of luck. His parish was peopled chiefly by the aristocracy, he was destined for a bishopric, and he was obviously willing to help Rosamund in her campaign. He was a shrewd, worldly man, and Rosamund felt that she could safely leave the pace of the return journey to him. He had his finger in a good many pies and he would never propose her for any committee unless he were sure that she would be acceptable to the other members. It was all going along smoothly, and she was beginning to feel confident of success when Vicky arrived, a bolt from the blue—Vicky, whose presence would set tongues wagging again, and dig up the past from its decent burial-place.

She had at first hoped that Edmund would send post-haste after the child, but he hadn't done so, and, judging from Vicky's account of his attitude, was not likely to, while Eleanor, who had always hated her even when they were girls together, was clever enough to realise how much the child's presence would embarrass her and enjoy the situation.

But she hid all signs of her irritation and continued to play her part. After all, even Vicky might prove useful one day. With her looks she ought to make a good match. She threw her a critical glance as she sat at the writing-desk in the window. Yes, she was lovely enough, as lovely as she herself had been at that age. She made a little grimace. No wonder Edmund disliked her. . . .

In the days that followed Vicky applied herself with youthful enthusiasm to the new life. She sat with Miss Tarrant sewing red braid onto unbleached calico for the heathen. She accompanied her mother on various little expeditions connected with her work—to the printer's, to collect subscriptions, to dispense charities. She copied out lists and added up figures. She did not somehow feel as much part of it all as she had hoped to, but she went on eagerly, blunderingly, doing far more than was asked of her and, at times, trying Rosamund's patience sorely.

She made tentative efforts to relieve her mother of the housekeeping, only to be snubbed by the elderly housemaid and by a still more elderly cook, who disliked the young on principle and was shrewdly aware that her mistress had a Past.

("Cousin!" she snorted derisively. "Cousin, me eye!")

One morning a coroneted envelope arrived for Vicky, addressed in a large firm handwriting. She opened it wonderingly.

DEAR VICTORIA [she read],

I have heard that you are staying in London and should be glad if you would kindly make it convenient to come and see me to-morrow at 4 o'clock.

Yours sincerely,

CHARLOTTE SKENE

She handed it to Rosamund, her blue eyes wide and puzzled. "Who is it?" she said.

Rosamund read it, her lips tight.

"It's Lady Skene, my mother," she said shortly.

"Your mother? Why, she must be my grandmother, then."

"Yes," said Rosamund.

Vicky was silent, digesting this new and startling piece of news. A grandmother. She had never even considered the possibility of having a grandmother.

"My grandmother," she said at last. "But—why did no one tell me?"

Rosamund shrugged.

"I suppose it never occurred to them," she said.

Vicky read the letter again.

"Why—it's to-day," she said.

"Yes," agreed Rosamund.

"Oh . . . she must mean you to come, too. You will come, won't you?"

Rosamund poured out another cup of coffee before she answered.

"No," she said at last, "I won't come. I'm very busy to-day."

"Oh, but *do* come," pleaded Vicky. "I shall be terrified alone, and I'd love it if you were there."

"I won't come, thank you," said Rosamund.

Her manner was so short and final that Vicky didn't dare press the matter.

Miss Tarrant fussed about her as she dressed for the visit, trying ineffectually to help with the preparations. Like Vicky, she believed firmly in Rosamund's innocence, and she had a muddled idea that Vicky was going to make a triumphant entry into Society and vindicate her much injured mother.

Vicky felt rather nervous when she set off alone in the cab that the elderly housemaid had summoned, but as it made its way through the bustling streets her nervousness vanished, and a feeling of excitement took its place. The visit was an adventure, only spoilt by the fact that her mother was too busy to accompany her. It had been raining when she started out, but the rain had stopped now and the sun had appeared, flooding the sky with blue and turning the wet streets into streams of gold. An old woman sat at the edge of the pavement selling flowers, and, as her eyes met Vicky's over her basket of roses, they smiled at each other suddenly. Vicky's smile was eager, joyous. The world was wonderful, and so was everyone in it, even the old flower woman. . . .

The cab stopped at a large house in Belgrave Square, and a footman opened the door to her. Her courage wavered as she entered the dim spacious hall, from which a wide staircase with elaborate banisters swept majestically up to a half landing where a draped marble woman stood holding a torch.

She followed another footman up the stairs, past the marble woman, then up another half flight to a massive inlaid mahogany door, from which came a confused sound of laughter and conversation.

The footman threw open the door and announced, "Miss Victoria Carothers."

Vicky entered and stood for a moment gazing round the crowded room. . . . Tall narrow windows overlooking the green square . . . an enormous candelabra hanging from a painted ceiling. . . .

Gainsborough portraits on grey panelled walls. . . . Chinese vases on a massive marble mantelpiece . . . a purple carpet. . . . The dull gleam of lacquer. . . .

The room was full of people standing about in groups or sitting on the damask-covered chairs drinking tea. Footmen moved about with trays. A young man, who stood by one of the windows, turned and looked at Vicky as she entered. He had flaming red hair and was a head taller than anyone else in the room. Their eyes met and held each other for a few seconds. . . .

Then there was a sudden movement near the mantel-piece, and Vicky's eyes left the young man and went to the Jacobean chair where sat an old lady with a yellow face, hooked nose, and sharp black eyes. She wore a lace cap with lappets and a heavily embroidered Chinese shawl. She bent forward as Vicky approached and fixed the piercing black eyes on her. One gnarled hand clutched the handle of an ebony stick.

"How do you do, Victoria?" she said, speaking as casually as if it were not the first time she and Vicky had met. Then she introduced her to a group of people near her chair and, turning away, began to talk to an old man with dyed hair and a face that might have been carved in ivory.

Vicky was tongue-tied by shyness, but she found that that did not matter. The group around her rapped out questions at her. (How long was she staying in London? Had she seen this? Had she seen that?) but hardly waited for her answers. They chattered gaily and inconsequently like so many birds each singing its own song. Half of what they said might have been in a foreign tongue for all it conveyed to Vicky. The jargon of the day was a secret code to which she had no key. Names that were household words were tossed lightly to and fro. This was Society . . . not particularly cultured or even intelligent, but the last exclusive stronghold, the ultimate if inaccessible goal of the social climber. . . .

Though Vicky never looked again in his direction, she was conscious all the time of the young man with red hair. He wandered restlessly about the room, hovering once near the group in which she was as if he contemplated joining it. His tall slender body was so vibrant and alive that even when still it seemed merely poised between one movement and another. The room was emptying now, and he took his leave of his hostess, throwing a challenging unsmiling glance at Vicky as he turned towards the door. Something of radiance and vitality seemed to go with him. The room was darker, less alive, when he had left it.

Though her grandmother had not spoken to her again since greeting her, Vicky knew that she was meant to stay after the others had gone in order to be interviewed. All her nervousness returned as the groups gradually melted away, leaving the two of them at last alone together.

The black piercing eyes were turned on her.

"Come here," said Lady Skene, pointing with her stick to a small gilt chair next hers.

Vicky obeyed.

"Mother didn't come with me," she explained eagerly, "because she was so very busy to-day."

"Your mother did not come with you," said Lady Skene slowly, "because she knew that I would not receive her."

Vicky stared, blue eyes wide with horror, as the meaning of this gradually dawned on her.

"But you can't," she protested, hardly knowing what she was saying. "You *can't* . . ."

The old lady shrugged.

"I owe a duty to my friends," she said in her tired old voice. "I could not allow them to run the risk of meeting in my house a woman whom it is impossible—and rightly impossible—for them to know socially."

The horror in Vicky's eyes deepened.

"But, surely," she gasped, "your own daughter,—all these years . . . surely you've visited her. You're——"

The old lady raised her hand as if to stop the flow of Vicky's protests.

"I do not visit where I do not receive," she said. "I have not seen my daughter since she left her husband's protection."

There was finality in the very weariness of her voice and Vicky was silent, sitting with hot cheeks and downcast eyes.

The old woman looked at her, noting the beauty that was Rosamund's, the air of innocence and vulnerability that was not. She felt no antagonism against her, no pride in her. She was too tired for either.

It was her duty to warn the child. That was why she had sent for her. The black eyes—curiously bright and alive in the dead old face—glanced at the portraits on the walls, then returned to Vicky.

"Victoria," she said slowly, "you must go home to your father at once. You cannot stay any longer where you are. It is social suicide. You are too young to understand, but——"

"I'm not too young to understand," flashed Vicky. "It's you who don't understand. You've never even tried to understand. She's not—what you think she is. It was all a mistake. It . . ."

She met the gaze of those piercing black eyes and her voice trailed away uncertainly.

"That is immaterial," said the old lady with a faint gesture of the thin gnarled hand. "The fact I am trying to impress on you is that she is not received in any reputable house in Society. For a young girl at the outset of her social career to stay with her even for a short time is madness. It will ruin your chances of marriage—of marriage, that is, into your own class."

"I don't care," said Vicky, who was now sobbing with anger. "I don't want to marry. I think you're cruel. She's wonderful. She's ever so much better than all those horrible people who're so beastly to her. I won't leave her. I'll stay with her always, always."

"You must leave her at once," said the old woman in her quiet imperious voice. "Your father and his wife must be insane to have allowed you to come. Put your handkerchief away, Victoria, and control yourself." Vicky obeyed automatically. "I am writing to your father to-night. I may have been wrong to drop all connection with him after my daughter disgraced us. I was—deeply pained and humiliated. He made no overtures on his side . . . but there is no reason why we should be estranged. How old are you?"

"Nineteen," sniffed Vicky.

"It's time you came out. Eleanor must bring you to London next season. Your father must be made to face his responsibilities towards you. I will give a dance for you. I trust that you realise what it means to you socially to have been received by me here this afternoon. But if you stay any longer with Mrs. Orell the effect will be undone. A young girl's reputation is easily tarnished and——"

"Oh, won't you understand?" burst out Vicky. "I don't care about all that. It means nothing to me, less than nothing. I love my mother. I only want to be with her, to help her, to——"

The footman opened the door and announced, "Mr. Lynnaker."

The young man with red hair entered. His hazel eyes danced mischievously, and there was a suggestion of impudent swagger about his tall slender figure.

"I must apologise for the intrusion, Lady Skene," he said, with a ceremoniousness that was belied by the twinkle in his eye, "but I believe I left my card-case here. I couldn't let your servant get it for me, because I couldn't really explain where it was." He glanced round the room. "I was standing over here, I believe." He went to the window, and took a thin silver case from a corner of the window-sill that was hidden by the heavy damask curtain. "Ah, here it is."

He came towards Lady Skene looking questioningly at Vicky.

"Mr. Lynnaker . . . my granddaughter, Miss Victoria Carothers," said the old lady, and added drily, "That was somewhat obvious, Philip."

"I know," agreed the young man with a disarming smile. "I quite realise that, but I hadn't time to think of anything more subtle." He turned to Vicky. "Are you staying long in town?"

"My granddaughter is returning to the country immediately," said the old lady.

Once more Vicky's eyes met the young man's, and, as they did so, all the tumult of her spirit seemed to die away and a new strange sense of peace possessed her.

The old lady broke the spell.

"I'm tired now, my dear. You'd better go."

"May I see her home?" asked the young man.

The old lady's lips twisted sardonically.

"From various things I've heard," she said, "I doubt whether you are a fit escort for any well-brought-up young lady."

The black eyes twinkled as she spoke, and a cold anger dimmed the new radiance at Vicky's heart. It wasn't fair. A man's lapses were only smiled at, while her mother's, even though she had not committed them, damned her for ever.

"How did you come, my dear?" the old lady was saying.

"In a cab."

"Alone?"

"Yes."

The old lady's lips tightened.

"You must go back with my maid."

The young man shot a conspiratorial smile at Vicky, a smile that snatched her up with him into another world, where old age and conventionality did not exist. Radiance flooded her heart again.

"I am trying to turn my granddaughter into a sensible young woman," went on Lady Skene.

"I hope you won't succeed," said the visitor.

"Why not?"

"I like her just as she is."

Lady Skene smiled grimly, but it was clear that she was not displeased by his impudence or by his admiration of Vicky.

"Be off with you!" she said, making a pass at him with her stick, and he took his leave, stealing a last look at Vicky as he went.

"That young man," said Lady Skene as the door closed on him, "is the son of a very old friend of mine. His parents died when he was a child, and he has been very much spoilt. He poses as an artist. Some people, I believe, take him seriously. Fortunately he has enough money to be able to afford not to take himself seriously. He obviously admired you, my dear, but he is notoriously impressionable. And now please ring the bell, and I will order the carriage and send for my maid."

When she had given her orders, she turned again to Vicky.

"I will say nothing more to you, Victoria," she said, "but please think over my words very seriously. Your whole future is at stake."

An elderly woman, dressed in a black cloak and bonnet, appeared in the doorway.

"I'm ready, m'lady," she said.

"Kindly accompany Miss Victoria in the carriage to the address that she will give you and return at once."

Leaning back in the chair, she seemed to have shrunk somehow, to have exhausted the vitality that had radiated from her when first Vicky came into the room. She looked old and tired and frail.

A sudden compunction of pity stirred at Vicky's heart. She was young and strong and alive, a-thrill with strange new emotions. She could afford to pity this old woman who knew nothing of the exaltation that was surging within her. She could hardly believe that she had ever felt afraid of her.

On an impulse she bent down and kissed the yellow withered cheek.

The old woman sat there motionless, neither responding nor withdrawing.

"That's all very well," she said, "all very well, all very well. . . . Do as you're told. Be a sensible girl."

Vicky shook her head, but some new understanding had come to her in the last few minutes and there was no defiance in the movement, only a sort of tenderness, as though she were the elder of the two and her grandmother a child begging a favour.

The maid accompanied her downstairs, stealing furtive glances of interest at her. As a girl she had waited on Miss Rosamund. The years seemed to have slipped back. . . .

Vicky was silent in the carriage, hardly conscious of the woman beside her. At first the strange new exaltation still upheld her, then gradually it died away, leaving a heavy depression. She would never see him again. His world was not hers. Hers lay with her mother.

Her determination hardened as she remembered the old woman's advice. Nothing, nothing would make her leave her mother. All her life she had longed to be loved and needed, as her mother loved and needed her. Would she be likely to throw away something so precious now that she had found it?

She got out of the carriage and almost ran up to the little front door, pushing past the elderly housemaid who came to open it.

Her mother sat alone in the drawing-room sewing. She looked up at Vicky curiously.

"Well?" she said.

"She wanted me to leave you," burst out Vicky.

There was triumph and contempt in her young voice. It exalted her love and despised the worldliness of the old woman who had tried to crush it.

But instead of the loving gratitude that she had expected a look of relief came into her mother's face.

"Perhaps that would be best, dearest," she said.

"But——" Vicky stopped, protestations and reassurances dying on her lips.

At first she couldn't believe it, but there it was, written plain enough on the smiling lips and in the blue eyes.

Her mother didn't want her. . . .

Chapter Eleven

MRS. ORELL continued to be sweetly affectionate up to the moment of Vicky's departure, but contrived to have Miss Tarrant always in attendance, so that Vicky could not discuss the situation with her or ask to be allowed to stay.

"It's been so lovely to have you, darling," she said, "and I shall miss you so terribly."

But Vicky couldn't forget the sudden unguarded relief in the blue eyes, when she thought that her grandmother had persuaded her to go home.

Miss Tarrant, too, was not sorry that Vicky was going. She liked her and was ashamed of her jealousy, but her love for her employer quickened her perception, and there was no doubt that dear Mrs. Orell had been a bit on edge and unlike herself while the young cousin was there. (Miss Tarrant had swallowed the "young cousin" unquestioningly, after all.) The young cousin hadn't been difficult to entertain, had, indeed, fitted into the household remarkably well, but the fact remained that it wasn't a household that catered for young visitors, and Miss Tarrant was glad that dear Mrs. Orell had not asked her to extend her visit.

Vicky shrank from the idea of returning home, defeated and humiliated, but it seemed the only possible course. At first she played with the idea of staying on in London by herself and getting work, but the saner part of her realised that this was impracticable, and something deep within her had been so hurt by her mother's rejection of her that all she wanted to do was to creep back and hide herself in the familiar surroundings of her home.

Her old capacity for dramatising herself helped a little, for she saw herself as the heroine of a tragedy—ill-used and unhappy—and that afforded her a certain bitter satisfaction.

She did not think any more of the young man with red hair. He was a radiant unreal figure belonging to a world of glamour and excitement and success, not to a world where things went wrong, where people were ill-used and unhappy. She couldn't even imagine him doing ordinary things—having breakfast or writing letters or missing trains. She could hardly believe now that she had ever met him.

She tried not to think of her mother, because the thought engulfed her in a sea of pain against which even her heroine feeling could make little headway.

Her mother said good-bye to her cheerfully and casually in the little drawing-room, and Vicky's pride kept her from showing the emotion she felt.

During the journey she sat tight-lipped, steeling herself for the scene that must meet her at the other end—reproaches, scolding, demands for an explanation.

She felt faintly disappointed when no scene took place. The carriage met her at the station, her father was out, and her stepmother received her as unconcernedly as if she merely had been into the village to do some shopping.

Celia, of course, flung herself upon her in wild welcome and followed her up to her bedroom, chattering eagerly.

"Darling, is London terribly exciting? Did you go to lots of dances? Did you buy lots of things?"

"Don't bother me, Celia," said Vicky. "Go away. I've got a headache. I'm going to lie down."

Celia tiptoed softly away, and Vicky unpacked her things, then sat by her bedroom window, looking down at the garden. Andrew wasn't in sight. She wondered what he was doing. . . .

Though she still tried not to think consciously of her mother, the thought was there all the time like a heavy weight of lead at her heart. Her depression changed to a kind of panic, to the desperate terror of something trapped. What was she going to do with herself? How was she going to fill her life? Always before there had been the conviction that something wonderful was going to happen to her, but now that had gone. She was only nineteen but with the ready despair of youth she looked on her life as over and finished. Nothing could ever happen to her now. . . .

The tea-bell rang and, after a brief inward struggle, she rose, tidied her half, and went downstairs. She didn't want to feel hungry and was slightly annoyed with herself for doing so, but she had had no lunch on the train, and despite her unhappiness the thought of tea was a welcome one. Besides, she would have to face Mama and Papa some time.

Mr. Carothers was still out. He had decided to be out till after Vicky had gone to bed. He had been infuriated by her flight to her mother. The girl seemed to have no decency or sense of shame. He had quarrelled with his wife when she made excuses for her. There seemed to be no end to the mischief Rosamund wrought in his life. Hadn't he suffered enough in those years of marriage with her, but that her evil influence must still reach out to poison his life?

In the first heat of anger he had said that he wouldn't take Vicky back if she came, but, even as he said it, he knew that it would be impossible to fulfil the threat. She was his daughter in the eyes of the world, if not in fact. His anger had been increased by the old woman's letter. Illogically enough, he blamed her for her daughter's failings. Annoyed because Rosamund wasn't a son, she had left her to her own devices. The girl had had lovers even before she married him. And now the old devil had the impudence to write to him, laying down the law about Victoria, ordering him to give her a season in London, as if he hadn't shown her plainly enough in the old days that he wanted none of her interference. The very thought of it brought to him a feeling of suffocation, so that he had to fight for breath. Any strong emotion or exertion did that nowadays. That was one of the reasons why he shrank from meeting Victoria again after her shameful escapade. He felt that he wouldn't be able to control himself, that this terrifying feeling of suffocation would catch him by the throat.

Mrs. Carothers looked up from the tea-table as Vicky entered.

"There you are, my dear," she said. "Come and have some tea."

She had always had a slight feeling of guilt towards Vicky. It wasn't the child's fault that Edmund had never liked her or, indeed, that she herself had never liked her. It was chiefly that fatal resemblance to Rosamund. They might both have forgotten if she hadn't been so like Rosamund. She and Rosamund Skene had disliked each other ever since they were children, and in the feud between them it was always Rosamund who scored. Even her marriage had been spoilt by the thought that she was, as her enemies put it, "taking Rosamund's leavings." She had honestly tried to like Vicky, and she might perhaps have succeeded, if every movement, every tone of her voice, hadn't been Rosamund's. . . .

Lady Skene's letter had not annoyed her. On the contrary, she had thought it very reasonable, despite its peremptory tone. But a season was out of the question as far as she was concerned. She was too lazy to uproot herself from the indolent country life she loved, and in any case she could not leave Edmund just now. He wasn't well and needed her at hand to save him exertion and see that he didn't get upset over anything.

She felt curious about Vicky's visit to her mother. One heard strange rumours about Rosamund—Rosamund leaving her world of laughter and gaiety and lovers . . . Rosamund wrapped in a garment of holiness, giving large sums to charity. . . . Rosamund's name beginning to appear on committees side by side with that of people who would have cut her dead a few years ago. She was clever, but it would take more than Rosamund's cleverness to win back what she had thrown away.

She glanced at Vicky again. The child looked pale and unhappy.

"We've had a letter from your grandmother, Vicky," she said. "She suggests a season in town for you. I agree that we ought to manage something, but I can't go to town myself just now. Your father, of course, wouldn't want to go in any case, and just at present he isn't very well, and I can't leave him."

For a moment, with a return of her childhood's power of make-believe, Vicky saw Papa frail and sweet and gentle, leaning on her arm, learning at last to love the daughter who nursed him so tenderly . . . but it wasn't a very convincing picture and it vanished almost as soon as it came.

"I've been thinking about it," went on Mrs. Carothers, "and there are several people we might ask to take you."

"I don't want to go," protested Vicky.

"But, Vicky——"

"Please, don't," said Vicky. "I've told you I don't want to. Leave me alone."

That look of pity in her stepmother's eye, the feeling of being a disagreeable responsibility, an alien (it was clear that her father had washed his hands of her), galled her pride intolerably.

Mrs. Carothers shrugged her shoulders. The girl was an ungrateful little creature. No, one couldn't question her about Rosamund, however curious one felt. . . .

Both were relieved when Celia burst into the room.

"Vicky, darling, Miss Standish says I can be with you till bedtime. . . . Oh, darling, it's lovely to have you. Have you finished tea? What are you going to do now?"

"I'm going upstairs."

"May I come too?"

"Yes, if you like."

After all, Celia's adoration helped a little to salve her hurt pride. And even Celia's company was better than being alone.

They went slowly upstairs, Celia hanging onto Vicky's arm.

Inside the bedroom she pulled Vicky down into an armchair and sat on the floor at her feet.

"Who did you go to stay with, Vicky?" she said. "They just said 'friends' and told me not to ask questions when I wanted to know the name. What was their name, Vicky?"

"I've been staying with my mother," said Vicky.

"Oh, Vicky!" Celia's eyes were wide. "Vicky, *why?*"

"Naturally she wanted to see me," said Vicky. "She hadn't seen me since I was a child. She—she'd been longing for me all these years. I felt I ought to go and see her—just for a few days, anyway."

"Oh, Vicky . . . what was it like?"

"My mother's been terribly misunderstood," said Vicky. "She—she was never bad at all. She took the blame to shield someone else—a friend—and let everyone think she was wicked, but she's terribly good really. She's a saint. I can't tell you how good she is. She gives her whole life to the Poor and Heathen and that sort of thing."

Celia clasped her arms round her knees and gazed up at Vicky with shining eyes.

"Vicky, it was splendid of you to go to her. . . . Then you didn't go out much, I suppose?"

"Oh yes, I went to parties at my grandmother's," said Vicky. Her hurt pride was gradually healing itself. "She's Lady Skene and she knows everyone in London. It was terribly gay and I met ever so many exciting people there. Duchesses and—and young men and that sort of thing. She wanted me to go to her for the season next year, but I said I'd rather not. I'm not really fond of gaiety. . . ."

Celia drew a deep sigh and leant her head against Vicky's knees.

"Oh, Vicky, you're . . . wonderful," she said.

Vicky felt almost happy when she went to bed that night, but the next morning Papa appeared at breakfast, silent and forbidding, ignoring her, hardly able to bring himself even to speak to his beloved Celia in her presence.

There followed long dull days that had to be filled somehow. Vicky was an indifferent pianist and had no artistic talent, and her music and painting lessons had gradually been dropped. Celia, of course, lived in the schoolroom, and, in any case, her attentions only emphasised the fact of Vicky's isolation. Miss Standish seemed more intolerable then ever, making excuses for visiting Vicky's bedroom and trying to have long confidential talks. Vicky avoided her, then felt ashamed and unhappy. Celia wanted to join in an offensive alliance with her against Miss Standish, but, though she had no place in the rest of the house, Vicky's pride would not allow her to be drawn into the life of the schoolroom, with its exaggerated emotions and magnifying of every detail, and she began to vent her unhappiness on Celia, snubbing and ignoring her. Celia would cry and there would be an emotional reconciliation, for

Vicky hated to be really unkind. It was all extremely unsatisfactory, and Vicky began to form vague plans for another flight. She would go to her grandmother this time. Perhaps she would meet the young man with red hair again. She often thought of him, not as one thinks of a real person, but as one might remember an exciting dream. Indeed, the whole visit to London now had a certain dreamlike quality in her memory. Certainly she never even considered the possibility of Philip Lynnaker's coming into her life again. She was so inexperienced that it never occurred to her to wonder whether she was in love with him or not. She had nothing to compare it with but that brief infatuation for Harold Frensham, and certainly it was different from that. That had been a hot heady excitement; this was something deep and calm.

Though she played with the idea of going to her grandmother, she knew that it was impossible, that the old woman would pack her straight back home even if she did. Restless, dissatisfied, unhappy, she threw herself into such diversions as the neighbourhood had to offer.

She took up riding again (she had learnt to ride in Switzerland but had dropped it on coming home) and rode daringly over the countryside. Her meeting with Philip had released unknown forces in her and, conscious suddenly of new powers, she began to take a pleasure in them.

She started on Roger, who hid at first beneath his armour of shyness, then yielded to the spell. She made him ride with her, walk with her, flirt with her. It provided the stimulus of excitement without which life now seemed dull and futile. The Vicar grew rather anxious, but Mrs. Abbot smiled and said that it was good for the boy. She was sure, she said, that Vicky was a nice girl at heart. . . .

Vicky, growing more skilful in the use of her weapons and tiring of Roger, began to look further afield. She found no lack of willing victims, and Roger, hurt and bewildered, returned to Plato's *Republic* and Butler's *Analogy*, from which one could at least expect consistency.

Vicky grew more daring. She was soon bored by her victims,

but the element of danger intoxicated her. There was a deep unhappiness somewhere at the heart of her, and in order to forget it she had to fill her life with noise and movement. If she could find nothing else to do, she would rout out her friends for impromptu parties. Matrons began to look at her askance, mothers to warn their sons against her, but Vicky only became the wilder. She took a delight in shocking people. Her mother's story was retold in whispers over the tea-cups. "What's bred in the bone . . ."

Mrs. Carothers knew nothing of all this. She was worried at having to let Vicky go about so much by herself, but glad that the child was making friends with the people in the neighbourhood and finding entertainment. Her husband had had a bad heart attack and was now confined to bed. Vicky had asked if she could help to nurse him, but he refused even to allow her to enter his room. Mrs. Carothers had dreaded having to tell the child that, but she hadn't seemed to care. She'd gone off at once on horseback and had brought a noisy party of young people back to tea. Mrs. Carothers, in fact, had had to ask them to be quieter as the noise was disturbing the invalid. After that she was glad that Vicky should be out as much as possible. . . .

When Vicky came back one day from a croquet party to find Philip Lynnaker in the drawing-room, she had a curious feeling of having known all the time that it would happen. She couldn't have gone on living through those weeks if she hadn't known. . . . As soon as she saw him it was as if she had been carrying a heavy weight and it had dropped from her. All that had happened since she saw him last ceased to exist. Happiness flooded her soul in wave upon golden wave—a deep serenity of happiness that went down to unknown depths of her being.

He explained that he was staying at Lady Sybil's and had ridden over to see her. He had already told Mrs. Carothers that he had been introduced to Vicky by Lady Skene. That had completely satisfied Mrs. Carothers, and in any case she was feeling too worried to give much attention to the affair. Her husband had had another attack in the night, and the doctor seemed less satisfied with him.

The visitor had brought an invitation to Vicky for to-morrow from Lady Sybil and asked if he could come in the morning to take her out riding. Mrs. Carothers gave her permission readily enough, glad of the prospect of peace for her invalid. Celia would be at home, of course, but Celia was very quiet nowadays. She was sulky because Vicky had, quite naturally, made friends of her own age and was out so much. In any case, Celia was needed at home now, for Edmund could hardly bear her to leave him.

Philip fixed his laughing hazel eyes on Vicky.

"You expected me, didn't you?" he said. "You knew I'd come?"

Vicky looked at him. She realised suddenly that she was tired—tired and radiantly happy.

"Yes, I think I did," she said.

Chapter Twelve

VICKY sat at the window of her hotel bedroom in Rome, waiting for Philip. It was three weeks since their marriage, and she still felt as if she were being swept along by a whirlwind—a delicious ecstatic whirlwind, but a whirlwind nevertheless.

Philip's love had changed the world. Even the colours around her were different—the trees more green, the blue of the sky more intense, the sunshine more golden, the moonlight more silver than they had been before. Her perceptions were quickened. A strong deep pulse of happiness beat in her all the time. Her life before she met him seemed now to have been so drab and empty that she wondered how she had endured it.

She could have no doubt of Philip's love for her, and yet sometimes his very love, though it was what she had longed for all her life, frightened her. Like everything else about him it knew no half measures. It was violent, tumultuous. He seemed literally to worship her beauty. He would make innumerable sketches of her, most of which he tore up in angry despair because they did not satisfy him. The same thing usually happened to the sketches he made of the places they visited. He had talent but no application. He could begin but he could not finish. Every plan they had made for their honeymoon had been changed at the last moment. They had meant to spend it in Switzerland, but just as he was buying the tickets he had decided that they would spend it in Paris instead. After two days in Paris, he had decided on an impulse to go to Venice, and after a week in Venice he had announced his decision to go back to Paris. He had spent two days in Paris planning a tour of the chateaux country, and then quite suddenly had taken tickets to Florence.

To Vicky it was all part of the glamorous dream, part of the rapture and bedazzlement of his love. What did it matter where they were or what they did, as long as he was with her—his magical presence casting a spell over everything, the very thought of him sufficient to thrill her nerves and send the blood coursing through her veins? His sudden changes of plan, his very incalculableness, only made the adventure more exciting, yet something in her seemed to hold itself aloof from the spell, to refuse to be bewitched, to stand apart, saying: "Yes, but what will happen when we get back to ordinary life? How will it fit in to that?"

Already she watched warily the swift variations of his mood, the bewildering alternations between serenity and depression or anger. His anger had never yet vented itself on her, but there had been a scene in a restaurant in Paris, when he had blazed out in fury at a waiter who had spilt some sauce on her dress, attracting the attention of everyone around them, and causing her acute humiliation. He had caused her humiliation on several other occasions, too. He loved big gestures and would be magnificently generous over large amounts of money, but amazingly mean over small ones. He would throw extravagant sums to beggars and spend money lavishly on jewels and dresses for her, but would argue and haggle and fly into a rage over a half-penny change or the most trivial overcharge on a bill.

She had been ill for a few days in Paris, and he had paced up and down the corridor, the sweat standing out on his brow, trying to summon courage to enter the room where she lay with closed eyes and colourless cheeks, all her zest for life and eager gaiety gone. His obvious shrinking distressed her, and she had got up and gone about with him long before the doctor wanted her to.

In Paris he had caught a chill, and had lain in bed in his turn, tossing and moaning, reproaching her for neglecting him, though she never left his side, telling her over and over again that he was dying. . . . His childishness woke a deep maternal tenderness in her, and, through it all, despite it all, her love for him strengthened, deepened. Each newly revealed weakness endeared him to her the more, and the elusive element of insecurity that underlay her happiness made it all the more precious.

She gazed absently over the Pincio gardens, where the trees stood motionless in the shimmering golden heat, thinking of Philip. . . . They had been to the Forum that morning and she had sat on a low wall in the courtyard of the Vestal Virgins in the sunshine, while Philip gathered a posy of the wild flowers that grew among the stones and fastened it in her dress.

The enclosed peace of the little place, with its still pools of water, its roses and irises, seemed to have laid a spell on both of them, and thrown a dreamlike quality over the whole morning.

Philip had been his most charming self—gay, tender, amusing—and Vicky had felt drowsy with content, like a bee heavy with its load of sweetness.

"Wouldn't it be lovely," she murmured, "if just this moment could go on for ever and ever and ever?"

He had laughed at her and said, "No, it would be terrible."

After lunch, Philip, despite the heat, had suddenly decided to go back to the Forum and sketch the little courtyard, and Vicky had taken the opportunity to lie down. She felt very tired. She usually felt tired when Philip was not there. His restless vitality upheld and stimulated her while he was with her, but when he had gone she felt drained and limp.

Her mind wandered back over the tempestuous weeks of their honeymoon, with its constant change of scene and plan, its movement and excitement and the rapt fulfilment of their love.

She was coming to understand him a little better, though she still felt bewildered by the innumerable conflicting aspects of himself that he could show in the space of a few moments. He was like a brilliant shifting kaleidoscope. His only constant quality was his love of beauty, and that was his passion, his religion. Anything ugly and sordid would throw him into an extravagant state of anger and despair. He had little sense of proportion. Everything to him was bigger than life-size, and his instinct was always to run away from whatever offended him. He had left Paris because of a wet day and Venice because he had seen a dog ill-treated. He was acutely sensitive to suffering, but it was its effect on himself rather than on the victim that concerned him. He had to leave the scene of it at once, so that he should not be offended by it any more. He bore a curiously equal resentment against the perpetrator of the cruelty and its victim.

Vicky always responded automatically to the stimulus of his mood, and, when he was in high spirits, would return to the daring irresponsible Vicky of her school-days, mocking him, playing tricks on him, inaugurating foolish little jokes. This side of her delighted him, and they would become like a couple of children, playing ridiculous pranks, shaken by gusts of reasonless laughter. But, even then, something in her of which she was only half conscious was watching him apprehensively, on the look-out for any change of mood.

Yes, there he was at last, crossing the street to the hotel, his sketching portfolio beneath his arm. She would see the brilliant darting eyes, the nervous mobile lips, beneath the broad-brimmed hat.

As he burst tempestuously into the room, his exuberance seemed to fill it with some potent magnetism, his vitality to flow into her veins, banishing her weariness and anxiety.

He took her in his arms and kissed her passionately, and she surrendered herself to the wave of happiness that surged over her, drowning for the moment the little nagging fear that lay always at the heart of her love.

He released her suddenly.

"I've done it, Vicky," he said exultantly. "I've been working like a demon all afternoon, and I've done it. I think it was the memory of you sitting there this morning. I've never done anything so good before. . . . Look!"

His eyes were shining with excitement as he tore open his case and took out the sketch. He held it at arm's length, then suddenly his whole expression changed. His face darkened and his cheeks flushed angrily. He tore the sketch across several times and flung it on the floor.

"Philip!" she cried in remonstrance, trying to stay his arm.

He shook her off.

"The whole thing's wrong," he said. "I'm a damned fool. I thought I'd done something worth while at last. I might have known. . . . I'm no good. I never shall be."

He sat down on a low chair and laid his head in his hands, sunk in deep dejection. She put her hand timidly on his shoulders and looked at the scraps of paper that lay scattered over the carpet. There was probably nothing much wrong with the sketch. A slight alteration, half an hour's more work on it, was probably all that was needed, but he never had the patience to alter or correct, and he would be satisfied with nothing short of perfection.

He started up.

"The one I did yesterday was better," he said. "I could make something of that one. Where is it? I gave it you."

"But, Philip," she faltered, "you told me to destroy it. You said you never wanted to see it again."

He stared at her, his hazel eyes suddenly cold and hard.

"Do you mean to say that you destroyed it?" he said slowly. "You destroyed what may be the best piece of work I've ever done in my life?"

"Philip, you told me to," she pleaded. "You said it was a failure and that I must never let you see it again."

His anger flowed over her like a black swirling flood. He stormed and shouted at her, striding to and fro, raising his hands above his head and shaking his fists. He said that she was ruining his life and his art, that he should never have married her, that he would never forgive her as long as he lived.

She bent before the storm of his rage, sinking onto her knees on the floor by the bed, sobbing in an utter abasement of misery. Then, suddenly, before she realised what was happening, he was lifting her up, crying out that he was a brute and a beast, not fit to touch her or breathe the same air, but that he loved her and couldn't live without her.

With their reconciliation, as sudden and passionate as their alienation had been, the ecstasy of happiness flooded her heart again. He loved her. Life was once more glamorous and golden. But behind the ecstasy was a faint, now familiar, weariness. The storms of emotion that seemed so necessary to him left her spent and exhausted. She longed for something stable to cling to amid the bewildering changes of his mood.

She stirred in his arms.

"When are we going home, Philip?"

"What does it matter?" he said restively. "When we feel like it."

Still fearful of annoying him, she went on:

"You said yesterday that we'd stay here for about another fortnight, and then go to Brindisi."

"Let's go to-morrow," he said suddenly.

His disappointment over the sketch had upset him. He wanted to get right away from the scene of it as quickly as possible.

"Very well," she agreed. "To Brindisi."

"Why Brindisi?" he said impatiently.

"I thought you said Brindisi."

"No, let's go to Ravenna, or Naples, or Genoa."

"All right. But which?"

"Ravenna," he laughed. "There are some wonderful mosaics at Ravenna."

"And when we get home," she said, "we'll buy a house somewhere, won't we?"

They were sitting on the bed, his arm round her.

"Anything you like," he said. "A dozen houses if you want them."

"No, I'd hate a dozen houses," she smiled. "I only want one. ... Where shall we live, Philip?"

She spoke timidly because she knew that he disliked her to ask him about his plans. It seemed to him as though she were trying to tie him down, to make him commit himself to something definite, which he always hated. He had refused even to consider the question of where they should live after the honeymoon.

Before he had time to answer, a waiter entered with a letter for Vicky.

"It's from Mama," she said, opening it.

He got up from the bed and walked about the room as she read it, his hands in his pockets, humming to himself, in high good humour.

"Papa's very ill," she said slowly, dropping the letter and staring in front of her.

He was at her side in a second, tenderly concerned.

"Darling, I'm so sorry. . . . Don't worry, sweetheart."

She was still staring in front of her.

"No, I'm not worrying. . . ." she said.

She was, in fact, dully surprised to realise how little the news meant to her. It seemed to come from a dim remote region of the past, a world of ghosts. Papa . . . Mama . . . Celia. . . . They were little mechanical figures moving against a painted background far away. Absurd to think that once they had been real . . . that once she had longed and prayed and hungered for Papa's love. And there swept over her a rush of gratitude to Philip, who had rescued her from that world of shadows and opened to her this new world, bathed in golden radiance.

And suddenly a cold breath of fear seemed to chill the warmth of her heart. She clung to him.

"Philip, you'll love me always, won't you? I couldn't bear it if you ever stopped."

He protested his love and she clung to him more passionately, her lips against his. Then gently she disengaged herself. The picture of her home had become clearer, less dreamlike—the red brick house, mellow with age, against its background of trees, the gravelled terrace with its grey stone balusters with the steps sweeping down to the lawn, Andrew bending over the herbaceous border, busy among the tall bushy plants.

"Where shall we live, Philip?" she said again.

"Wherever you like, darling."

"In the country, of course."

He was kissing the nape of her neck where little golden tendrils curled and twined.

"Of course," he agreed absently.

"We must have lots of greenhouses. Andrew loves greenhouses."

"Andrew?" said Philip. "Who on earth is Andrew?"

She looked at him in surprise. It seemed odd that Philip shouldn't know who Andrew was.

"Andrew? He's the gardener, of course."

"What gardener? Your father's?"

"Yes . . . I suppose so."

"Well, what's he got to do with it?"

"But . . . but, of course, he'll come to us when we get the house."

She felt slightly bewildered. She couldn't imagine an existence in which Andrew wasn't there in the background, bending over the flowers, moving to and fro with spade and fork. It was vitally important—she didn't know why—that he should be there. She had taken for granted always that he would be. . . .

"We can't walk off with your people's servants like that," protested Philip. "Besides, I don't know that I want to. I think I'd far rather start fresh with our own."

She stared at him, aghast.

"Oh, but we must have Andrew," she said breathlessly. "We *must*. He's always been there. You don't understand."

His mood hovered between irritation and amusement, but her loveliness—blue eyes fixed on him in childish appeal—turned the scale and he laughed delightedly.

"Have a hundred Andrews, have a thousand," he said, "as long as you'll go on looking like that. You mustn't ever change, Vicky, will you?"

"I shall grow old," she said dreamily.

He shivered.

"*Don't*," he said sharply. "You mustn't. I couldn't bear it. We won't grow old ever, either of us, will we?"

"No," she agreed, humouring his mood, "we won't. Ever. . . . But it's time to dress for dinner."

Mrs. Carothers had wanted Vicky to take a maid away with her, but Philip had objected. He would have no aliens in their Eden, and he loved to play the lady's maid to Vicky. He helped her to dress now—or rather hindered her—taking down the shining strands of her hair and burying his face in it, kissing the smooth whiteness of her arms.

"Philip," she said suddenly, "would you like me at all if I were ugly?"

"No," he laughed. "I hate ugly things."

She tried to hold him away from her.

"Do you only love me because I'm pretty?" she persisted.

"Don't ask silly questions," he said, and drew her into his arms again.

She surrendered once more with a little fluttering sigh. After all, what did it matter? She *was* pretty, so it was silly to worry about whether he'd love her if she weren't.

After dinner he sat in the armchair by the fireplace reading a book of travels that an acquaintance in the hotel had lent him. He seldom read and Vicky was always glad when he did, as it stilled temporarily the demon of unrest that drove him.

She stood at the window looking down at the darkening trees in the Pincio gardens. She was picturing the home they would have when they returned to England—trees, flowers, quiet lawns ... Andrew moving about amongst it all in his leggings and shirt-sleeves with his queer lolloping gait. It was odd how Andrew seemed to intrude himself into every picture of a home that her mind framed.

"We are going to Ravenna to-morrow, aren't we, Philip?" she said.

"Yes," he said absently. "Ravenna or somewhere else."

She sighed, thinking how nice it would be to know just where they were going and when. Beneath her eager careless young womanhood was still the methodical little girl who had lived by routine and put her things away so carefully under Miss Thompson's rule.

"I'll start packing, then," she said.

She went into the bedroom, took off her evening dress of white satin and gauze, put on her dressing-gown, and began to pack the big leather trunks.

"I'll help you if you'll wait a minute, darling," Philip murmured, but she knew that he wouldn't.

If a book interested him he went on reading it till he'd finished it, and everything else had to wait.

At the end of an hour she had packed almost everything, and came back to sit on the arm of his chair, leaning her cheek on his head. He put up his hand—a long thin nervous hand—to stroke her cheek.

"Let's go to bed now, Philip," she said. "I'm so tired."

He murmured, "Poor darling," but did not stir. She knew he wouldn't move till he'd finished the book.

At last he closed it, saying, "What did you say, dear?"

She kissed his hair.

"Let's go to bed," she said. "I've finished packing."

"You shouldn't have done it alone," he remonstrated. "You should have let me help."

"What's Ravenna like?"

"Ravenna?" he said vaguely. "Oh, I expect it's quite ordinary. Let's not go to Ravenna. Let's go to Egypt. Let's go there to-morrow. The desert, the temples, the Nile. . . . It's the most wonderful country in the world."

"But, Philip," she said, dismayed, "isn't it a long way?"

"What does that matter?" he said. "Let's never go home. Let's go to Japan, China, India. . . . What's the use of stagnating for the rest of our lives in some beastly little village? What a way to spend one's life! Let's go on and on and on and never stop anywhere." He got up and paced about the room. "That's what life ought to be. Movement, movement . . . always movement."

"Well, let's go to bed now, anyway," yawned Vicky.

About two o'clock he woke her. He was sitting up in bed looking at the window, where a silver moon rode high among the clouds.

"Isn't she lovely, Vicky?" he said. "Look at her." He sprang out of bed. "Come on. Put your clothes on and let's go out. It's too marvellous to waste. It's like being born again."

As usual his excitement communicated itself to her and she too sprang eagerly out of bed and dressed as quickly as she could, putting a long white cloak over her dress and leaving her head bare.

They crept softly down the stairs, rousing the sleepy night porter, who felt little astonishment, as he had decided long ago that Philip was mad. The empty streets echoed to their footsteps. The whole world about them was silvered with enchantment.

"Vicky," said Philip, "I know what was wrong with that sketch. I'll go there again directly after breakfast and I'll do it again."

Vicky stood still and looked at him.

"But—we're going to-morrow," she said.

"Going? Going where?"

"To Egypt . . . Ravenna."

"Nonsense! We can't leave a place like this after only five days. It's ridiculous."

"But you said we were going to-morrow," said Vicky. He frowned.

"My dear," he said impatiently, "I do wish you wouldn't try to tie me down to every casual suggestion I make. I may have vaguely mentioned it, but I wouldn't dream of leaving a place like this after only five days. The very idea's absurd."

His irritation, as always, frightened her, giving her a sudden terrifying glimpse of a dark world in which she wandered desolate, alone, bereft of his love.

"Very well," she said quickly. "I'd as soon stay as go on."

"Of course we'll stay," he laughed, his serenity restored by her acquiescence.

They reached the hotel about four o'clock. Philip was still in high spirits, but Vicky felt tired and depressed. She looked at the leather trunks standing packed at the foot of the bed and wondered whether she would be unpacking them in the morning, or whether Philip would have changed his mind during the night.

But in the morning she received a telegram, asking her to come home at once as Mr. Carothers had died the day before.

Chapter Thirteen

CELIA, wearing a dress of black serge hurriedly put together by Miss Salter and plentifully trimmed with crêpe, was standing at the front door as the carriage drew up. Her cheeks were pale, her eyes red-rimmed and swollen, for she had been crying all afternoon, less from sorrow than from remorse at feeling so little sorrow. There had been a certain element of excitement about Papa's death that had not been without its enjoyable side. It had raised her to unaccustomed heights of importance. The servants treated her with a new deference, furtive glances of interest were cast at her when she went into the village, her friends wrote her letters of sympathy in large copperplate handwriting and formal phraseology, dictated by their parents, and the mourning clothes, with their trimming of crêpe, gave her a thrilling sense of belonging to the grown-up world. Moreover, the sudden cessation of lessons and relaxing of schoolroom discipline lent an inevitable air of holiday-making to the occasion.

Celia was now promoted, as it were, into Mama's immediate circle, urged to be "Mama's comfort," reminded that she was "all Mama had left." Mama, it was true, did little to support this view. She went about, white and tight-lipped, ignoring Celia and everyone else, but Celia took advantage of her preoccupation to join the grown-up routine of the house—to bring her needle-work down to the drawing-room, and to take her meals in the dining-room. She felt little personal sense of loss. She was aware that Papa had loved her, but it had been a remote impersonal love, a love that made little difference to her ordinary life. He had been stiff and unapproachable, with no skill in winning her confidence, no art in sharing her childish interests. He had now gone to Heaven, but, to Celia, he had always been there—remote, aloof, God-like.

Then—most exciting of all—his death was bringing Vicky home—Vicky, the beloved, whom Celia had missed so terribly since her marriage. She had written long letters to her every day, telling her all the news of the schoolroom—how Miss Standish had gone and another governess, called Miss Boniface, had arrived, who was aesthetic and wore strange clothes and wrote poetry and filled the schoolroom with Japanese fans and painted milking-stools.

In reply she had only received hastily written postcards from Venice, Rome, Florence. . . . And now she was coming home, travelling post-haste across Europe—Vicky, with her golden hair and blue eyes and sudden lovely smile. No one in the whole world mattered as much as Vicky.

She had lain awake all last night, unable to sleep with excitement at the prospect of Vicky's homecoming, and to-day after lunch a sudden reaction had set in, and she had felt aghast at her own depravity. Why, she had *enjoyed* Papa's death. Actually *enjoyed* it. . . .

The thought overwhelmed her with horror, and she went to her room to lie on her bed and sob convulsively, working herself up into an agony of self-loathing and despair. Then, her emotion spent, she surveyed her swollen, tear-stained face in the mirror. The sight comforted her and she began to take a complacent pride in it. She looked so exactly as a little girl should look whose papa has just died. She wanted Vicky to see her like that, because it made her seem so much more interesting than she did ordinarily, so she rubbed her eyes surreptitiously every now and then to keep them red during the hour or so before Vicky's arrival.

As the carriage drew up at the door, Philip, tall and agile, sprang out and gave his hand to Vicky. The heavy black draperies (Vicky had spent a hurried few hours in Paris buying mourning on the way home) emphasised her grace and slenderness, and her face looked lovelier than ever beneath the filmy black veil.

Philip's handsome boyish face wore its blackest scowl. He had sulked all the way home, furious at having his honeymoon interrupted, and at being forced to surrender Vicky so soon to the claims of her own people.

"I've not had you to myself a month even," he kept grumbling. "It isn't fair. . . ."

He greeted Celia ungraciously. He had always been jealous of her affection for Vicky, and the sight of her standing there in the clumsy unbecoming black frock, her cheeks sallow, her eyes swollen with crying, infuriated him.

Vicky kissed Celia, then went into the drawing-room, where Mrs. Carothers sat upright by the fire, hung with crêpe and jet, looking majestic and unfamiliar. Mrs. Carothers had been greatly attached to her husband, and his death had left her life empty and meaningless, but her placidity concealed deep forces of pride and self-control, and she had given no outward signs of her sorrow, even to Celia.

She kissed Vicky, shook hands with Philip, who did not offer to kiss her, and rang for tea. Then she began to ask Vicky about her travels, speaking mechanically and obviously not listening to the answers.

Celia sat on a footstool at Vicky's feet, gazing up at her adoringly, and Philip sat glowering sulkily at everyone, especially Celia, for whom he was conceiving a quite irrational dislike.

Then Mrs. Carothers sent Celia to the schoolroom, where Miss Boniface, in a trailing sack-like gown, voluminously gathered at the neck and waist, read Tennyson to her, and Celia sniffled disconsolately, crying really because she had been banished from the drawing-room, but pretending to herself that she was crying because Papa was dead.

Downstairs, her departure removed something of the constraint.

"Your father died quite peacefully, Vicky," said Mrs. Carothers. "There was no hope from the beginning of the attack, but mercifully he had very little pain."

"Did he—did he mention me?" said Vicky.

"No," said Mrs. Carothers.

Vicky was silent, surprised once more to find how little it mattered, how remote it all seemed. . . .

"I shall move into a smaller house as soon as the business is settled," went on Mrs. Carothers. "I shall not go away from this neighbourhood as all my friends are here. I may build a small house if I can't find anything suitable, but, of course, I've made no definite plans yet."

Vicky felt a sudden pang of pity for her. She was majestic and controlled, as ever, but she was like some automaton going on being majestic and controlled after the mainspring had broken. She was an unconvincing copy of her old self. She must have loved him terribly, thought Vicky, with something of wonder.

Then pity was swallowed in a sudden blaze of terror as she put Philip into Papa's place. . . . Suppose Philip died and she was left alone. She caught her breath with a little gasp of anguish. She couldn't bear it. She couldn't go on living. . . . But at once reassurance came to her. It couldn't happen to her. Other women's husbands might die, but that was different, because they weren't Philip and Vicky. They were shadows, dim and unreal, their grief meaningless and vapid. . . .

"I expect you'd like to come upstairs to your room, dear," said Mrs. Carothers, rising. "I'll take you."

"Don't bother to come, Mama," said Vicky.

But Mrs. Carothers insisted. She took them up and stayed for a few minutes with them, straightening various things about the room and explaining the hours of meals, though, of course, Vicky knew them quite well, telling them several times to ring for anything they wanted.

Then she went downstairs to the drawing-room, took up her work-basket (the one whose contents Vicky had once flung into the fire) and, sitting by the fireplace, began to sew at a piece of embroidery with calm regular movement.

But she saw that despite her efforts her hands were trembling, so put it aside and went to her desk to check her household books again, though she had done it only that morning. Life was so long, and one must do something. . . .

Upstairs Vicky looked round the room. It was the best spare room, the same shape as Papa's and Mama's, with a big bay window in the corner overlooking the garden. She had sat on that broad window-seat when she was a little girl and watched the workmen papering the walls and putting in the marble mantelpiece, seeing herself as "Papa's darling," driving out in the carriage with him and the new mama. . . .

Philip was striding angrily up and down the room.

"It's damnable," he exploded. "Why need we have come back to this ghoulish place? I hate your sister. I hate your stepmother. We'd hardly begun our honeymoon. . . ."

"Darling," murmured Vicky absently.

She went to the window and looked down at the sunlit garden, where the trees stood motionless, each in the still pool of its own shadow. Andrew was mowing the lawn, moving backwards and forwards behind the large cumbersome machine. He was strong, despite his puny appearance.

She suddenly thought of him lying on the gravelled drive with Harold Frensham standing over him. That episode seemed faintly ridiculous now. How exactly like the handsome villain of melodrama Harold Frensham had been, with his fine dark eyes and curling moustache! She was glad that no one knew about it but Andrew.

She must remember to ask Mama about taking Andrew to their new house. They wouldn't go far away. They——

She wheeled round suddenly, her eyes shining.

"*Philip*," she said.

He stopped his angry pacing of the room.

"Well?"

"Philip . . . Mama said she was going . . . Philip, let's take this house. We could buy it from her. Philip, I'd *love* it, wouldn't you? It's just the sort of house we want. Philip, darling, do."

Her eagerness banished his depression, and her pleading roused his tenderness. He loved her to ask favours of him like that, her hands clasped, her blue eyes alight. Her mourning gave a dazzling ethereal quality to her fairness, and he thought he had never seen her look so beautiful.

"Vicky, I must paint you in that dress just like that . . . with the window behind you . . . and the sky and the trees . . ."

"Say *yes*, Philip. Let's live here!"

"We'll live wherever you like. Kiss me, Vicky. It's been so damnable having to come back to this cursed country when we might be still in Italy. These beastly grey skies and rain——"

She laughed.

"Do be sensible, darling. The sky's blue and it's not raining."

"Well, it's all damnable anyway. I hate your sister and I hate your stepmother, and I——"

She put her hand over his mouth.

"Don't, dearest. You've said it before, and anyway you don't mean it."

He caught her hand and kept it at his mouth, kissing it.

"Philip, we will live here, won't we?" she pleaded. "You have said 'Yes,' haven't you?"

"We'll live on the moon, if you like."

"Be serious, darling."

"I'm sick of being serious. I've been serious ever since we left Rome. I've been as serious as those numskulls downstairs."

"Philip, don't. Listen. . . . It *would* be lovely to live here, wouldn't it? Say 'Yes.' "

"Yes, yes, yes, yes, yes. Kiss me again, Vicky."

She tackled her stepmother on the subject that evening, terrified lest Philip, despite his complaisance upstairs, should raise objections, but he sat reading the current issue of the *Graphic*, and saying, "Just as you like, darling," whenever Vicky asked him anything.

Mrs. Carothers welcomed the suggestion, and the interest it awoke in her brought her, to a certain extent, out of her dreamlike state, so that she sent Celia to bed quite briskly at half-past seven. Celia went sulkily and reluctantly. No one had sent her to bed at half-past seven since Papa's death. Her brief and precarious reign as "Mama's comfort" was evidently over.

The next morning Vicky and Philip went into the garden after breakfast. Andrew was working on one of the borders, and Vicky greeted him with distant graciousness, then paraded about the path near, hanging onto Philip's arm, showing off his devotion and preening herself, disappointed that Andrew seemed to take so little notice of her.

She felt rather ashamed of the importance that the thought of Andrew had assumed in her memories of home. It was because she had had such a lonely childhood, she explained to herself once again. Even a gardener's boy had seemed important to her. But everything was different now. Her loneliness and unhappiness had come to an end, the fairy story had finished to the tune of wedding-bells, and there was nothing for her to do now but to live happy ever after.

"Queer-looking chap, that gardener," commented Philip.

"Yes, isn't he!" she agreed, looking down contemptuously on Andrew from the height of Philip's good looks. "You'll like living here, Philip, won't you?"

"I'd like living anywhere with you," he said, raising her hand to his lips, and Vicky laughed gaily and hoped that Andrew was watching.

Later in the day a sudden enthusiasm for the house and garden seized him, and he strode about suggesting alterations that left Vicky a little breathless beneath her delight at his acquiescence in her idea.

"That wing's wrong," he said. "We'll have it down altogether and build on at the back. And the door's wrong. It ought to have a portico, not that silly little porch. It's all out of proportion. I'd like to make a new front altogether."

"*Philip!*" she gasped.

"We could make a lovely place, Vicky. . . . And we ought to have a lake where the park is. Half of it could be made into a lake anyway. And an Italian garden. We must have an Italian garden. We'll go out to Italy again and get some statues."

It was probably the airs of ownership that he unconsciously assumed that sent Mrs. Carothers down to a house-agent a few days later. She found a small Georgian house called Ivy Lodge in the next village, with fruit trees growing against a high brick wall, and a little balcony of wrought iron over the front door. Celia was delighted that it was not too far away from the Hall ("I can drive over in the dog-cart every day, darling. It'll be lovely"), and Miss Boniface wrote a poem about it, called "The New Home," which she illustrated somewhat incongruously by the sketch of a Gothic ruin.

Then Philip suddenly became bored and went to visit a friend in Westmorland. To Vicky life seemed to stop short with his departure, to be merely marking time till he came back. She wasn't lonely or unhappy, but everything and everyone around her suddenly ceased to exist. Life would begin again where it had left off when he returned. She was dimly aware, too, as she always was when he was not there, of that faint something of relief. She could rest, relax. Philip never wanted to rest or relax. Even when he was tired his nerves drove him on relentlessly.

Mrs. Carothers went over to Ivy Lodge every day, choosing paint and wallpapers and carpets, harrying the builders in her old brisk fashion. She had definitely deposed Celia from her treasured position of privilege, and told Miss Boniface to begin schoolroom lessons again, to take her for the daily walk, and only allow her to come down to the drawing-room for the usual hour after tea.

Celia sulked, grumbled, and escaped to Vicky whenever she could, questioning her eagerly about Venice and Paris and Rome, and longing for the time when she, too, should be grown-up and have a tall handsome husband, and go abroad for her honeymoon. Her attitude of admiration, her acceptance of the "happy-ever-after" state, was an obscure comfort to Vicky, helping her to forget the vague sense of insecurity that lurked somewhere behind the radiance of her happiness, so slight that it had no power to dim it but never really absent.

She wandered about the garden or sat there with her embroidery, bathed in a soft roseate glow of contentment, thinking of Philip, dreaming of the time when their children would be playing on the lawn and racing up and down the grey stone terrace steps.

Celia, turning out her old toy cupboard, came upon a battered rag doll with indecipherable features that Miss Thompson had once made for Vicky, and that Vicky had handed on to Celia. Celia had treasured it throughout her childhood and now brought it to Vicky's bedroom in an important and secretive manner.

"You'd better have it for your children, Vicky," she said. "I shan't be having children for a long time yet, of course, and I'd like you to have it for yours first."

Vicky took it and looked at it dreamily. She saw Miss Thompson cutting it out at the schoolroom table, while she looked on excitedly ... saw them both stuffing the finished outline with scraps of material from the "rag bag" ... saw herself playing with it in a corner of the garden while Nurse Tanner sat grimly by, ready to punish any misdemeanour ... saw herself sitting at the nursery window hugging it as she watched Papa walking below in the garden with Mama, vainly hoping that he would look up and wave to her. ... She had dramatised her childhood and imagined herself to have been much more lonely and neglected than she actually was.

Her children wouldn't be lonely or neglected, she told herself exultantly. They would grow up in an atmosphere of love and understanding.

She looked down at the battered shapeless face, trying to pierce the future, wondering what her children's memories would be when they in their turn looked at their old toys. It thrilled her to think of them growing up, happy and cherished, in the same house where she had crept about, a little alien.

"Thank you, Celia," she said. "I'd love to have it."

Just then Philip burst into the room. He had written to her the day before saying that he would be staying in Westmorland four days longer, but it was characteristic of him to write that and then come back close on the heels of the letter. The definite formulation of any plan seemed to put prison bars around him that he had to break down at once in order to free himself.

"Darling!" cried Vicky, springing to her feet. "How lovely! But why didn't you let me know?"

The whole atmosphere of the room had changed the minute he entered it. It was as if a current of electricity had come in with him, exhilarating, revivifying.

Celia greeted him quietly and shyly and ran back to the schoolroom. She admired Philip but never felt at her ease with him.

"Had a good time, darling?" said Vicky.

The quick appraising glance she had thrown him as soon as he entered the room had told her that he was in a good humour.

"Splendid. Riding all day. Vicky, we must get horses at once. There is nothing like it. I'd forgotten how splendid it was. . . . And, Vicky, we must live there. It's the most glorious county I've ever seen. Wild and rugged and so far away from everywhere that you can forget that towns exist. . . . I saw a house that would just suit us. We could move into it almost at once——"

"But, *Philip!*" she protested, her eyes wide open in dismay. "We'd arranged to live here. We told Mama we'd take it off her hands."

He waved the reminder aside.

"Here!" he said. "What on earth do we want to live here for? Come to Westmorland and see it for yourself. It makes a place like this seem suburban. Your mother'll soon find someone else to buy the house. Besides, I'd rather take you right away where other people won't be constantly bothering you. That wretched brat Celia coming over every day!"

"But, Philip," she said. "You promised. You promised. . . ."

She stared at him in mute appeal, her blue eyes brimming with tears. Probably if she hadn't still been unconsciously hugging the rag doll to her he would have flown into a rage at her opposition to his plans, but the sight of her standing there, looking like an unhappy child, the battered doll at her breast, filled him suddenly with delight.

"Vicky, stay like that. I want to do a sketch of you. Just like that with the doll. I'll give it some silly sentimental title . . . but it's lovely."

He flung open a drawer and took out pencil and sketching block.

Obediently she retained the pose, her eyes still fixed on him pleadingly.

"Philip, we *must* live here," she said.

He was hard at work, frowning absorbedly.

"We'll live anywhere you like, sweetheart," he said, "if you'll just move your chin up a fraction of an inch. . . ."

Chapter Fourteen

VICKY stood before the full-length mirror in her bedroom, giving the final touches to her toilet. She was going to a tea-party at Lady Sybil's and she had put on a new dress of tartan silk, heavily flounced and trimmed with fringe. Her hair was done in a single loose curl on the top of her head, and she wore one of the tiny fashionable hats that were more like stringless bonnets.

She studied the effect anxiously, hoping that her pregnancy did not show too plainly. Philip had been extravagantly delighted when she told him that she was going to have a child, but already he was bored and irritated by the prospect, and any reminder of it was enough to dispel his precarious good humour. He hated specially to see her slender graceful figure growing large and ungainly, and she did her best to hide it, lacing her stays as tightly as she dared, and wearing dresses with flounces and furbelows.

They had been settled at the Hall for several months now. Mrs. Carothers had moved into Ivy Lodge, taking with her two maids and what furniture she wanted, Miss Boniface had been dismissed, and Celia packed off to a boarding-school. Mrs. Carothers filled her time with household tasks and parish work, but there was still something mechanical about her briskness, as though the essential part of her had died with her husband.

Vicky would have liked to draw nearer to her now that Papa was no longer there between them—she often felt the need of help and advice from an older woman in her new life—but Philip disliked her and would not allow Vicky to visit her or ask her to the Hall more often than convention demanded.

"I haven't got a mother-in-law, thank God," he said, "because your real mother doesn't count, and I'm damned if I'm going to let you give me one in that old harridan. I'm not having her or anyone coming over and telling us what to do and how to do it. I want you to myself, and I'm going to have you to myself."

He enjoyed being the master of a house and household and was still passionately in love with Vicky, bringing back some presents for her whenever he went to London—once a diamond brooch that had cost £200, and that he bought on an impulse when he had missed his train and had to wait an hour for the next. ("I couldn't just hang about the beastly station, so I thought: 'I'll go and buy Vicky something'.")

He had turned part of the park into an artificial lake, built a boat-house, and purchased two boats. His delight in it was like a child's delight in a new toy. He loved to paddle about by moonlight and would often make Vicky get up in the middle of the night to accompany him. Moonlight on water always held a strange fascination for him, and he would never tire of watching the reflections and the ripples made by the oars.

To Vicky's relief, he had abandoned his idea of altering the Hall itself. After Mrs. Carothers' departure, he had drawn up a plan that would have meant a complete rebuilding of the house, but when the builders he had sent for came to interview him about it he was in the garden, painting the front lawn and copper beech, and, furious at the interruption, sent them away and never gave the matter another thought.

The bill for the making of the artificial lake had staggered him (for he had made several additions to the original scheme while the work was in progress) and he had determined on a rigid policy of retrenchment.

"We can't go on like this, Vicky," he had said when his rage had cooled, speaking as sternly as if she alone were responsible. "We'll have to economise."

The next morning he came to her, smiling exultantly and rubbing his hands.

"I've started economising. I went to that gardener fellow—what's his name?——"

"Andrew?"

"Yes.—Andrew, or whatever it is. I told him that we found we'd have to reduce his wages by a shilling a week."

"*Philip!*"

"Yes, rather clever, wasn't it? I knew he'd think twice about giving up a good job. There aren't many of them round here. That saved us a shilling a week on wages, anyway."

"But, Philip, it was so mean."

"Not at all, my dear. It was business-like. I am business-like, though people don't think so. A shilling saved is a shilling gained. Of course, I'd have climbed down if he'd refused, but I was pretty sure he wouldn't."

He was so boyishly pleased with himself that she couldn't be angry with him, though she felt ashamed the next time she saw Andrew working in the greenhouse, and hurried past without speaking to him.

She had trembled for Andrew during the time that Philip had taken a—fortunately short-lived—interest in the garden. He would order extensive alterations and fly into a rage because they had not been carried out the next time he went into it. He had an unreasonable and quite disproportionate dislike for certain flowers and once smashed a dozen pots of geraniums, flinging them one by one against the wall by the greenhouse, his face dark with anger. Andrew went on his way unmoved, even continuing to address Vicky as "Miss Vicky" in spite of all Philip's orders to the contrary, but Vicky was still terrified of his anger, and when it was turned against her, as it not infrequently was nowadays, would be plunged into an abyss of misery and despair till he relented and consoled her.

The neighbours had duly left cards on them, but Philip had no wish for social intercourse and had not encouraged friendliness.

"They're all fools," he had said, "and we won't waste time on them. We only want each other."

"I'm a fool, too, you know," she said ruefully.

"You're a nice one, then," he replied, kissing her, "and you're all I want in the whole world."

He had bought horses, and they often cantered together over the countryside—on the commons, and along the bridle paths of the woods. He loved to see her on horseback in the long habit with the tall silk hat on her golden hair.

Sometimes when he was in an ill-humour and nothing at home could please him he would go out alone and ride hard till both he and his horse were spent, returning drugged with weariness, his good humour restored. He was a fearless rider (though not a particularly considerate one) and preferred a mount that other people found intractable.

Vicky's anxious eyes travelled slowly down her reflection in the mirror. It only mattered because of Philip, of course. She did not care what she looked like to other people as long as she could still be beautiful in Philip's eyes.

Her maid, Ellen, took down her coat from the wardrobe. She was a pale gentle girl, with a low voice and slim deft fingers that could build up the heavy coil of Vicky's hair in a few quick movements.

Vicky always felt apologetic towards her, because Philip disliked to see her in close attendance on his wife and treated her with scant courtesy, often dismissing her summarily as soon as he entered the room.

"It *does* show, doesn't it, Ellen?" said Vicky, her frowning gaze still fixed on her reflection in the glass.

"It does a little, madam," said Ellen.

They looked at each other—less maid and mistress than two women facing a common problem. Philip was in both their minds. Whatever happened, Philip must not be offended by the sight of his wife's pregnancy.

"I might pull your stays a little tighter, madam," the maid suggested.

"No, you'd better not," said Vicky. "It—it isn't really good for it, is it?"

The thought of the new life within her filled her suddenly with warm happiness, bringing a soft colour to her cheeks and a dreamy radiance to her eyes.

Philip entered, frowning (he had been sulking all day at the prospect of the tea-party), but, catching sight of the expression on Vicky's face, forgot his ill-humour.

He snatched the coat from Ellen's hands.

"You can go," he said curtly.

She took up the morning dress that Vicky had taken off and began to hang it in the wardrobe. He turned on her savagely.

"You heard what I said," he said. "Get out."

"Philip, you shouldn't speak like that to Ellen," said Vicky as the door closed.

He laughed.

"I'll kill her one of these days," he said, wrapping the coat about her and taking her in his arms.

They went down to the shining new carriage that they had used so little since they bought it. A wave of excitement surged through Vicky as she took her seat in it next to Philip. She was a real grown-up married woman, driving out with her handsome husband to a party. Across the years she smiled reassuringly at the Vicky who had longed so desperately to drive in the carriage with Papa and Mama. "It's all right, you see, after all," she said. "You *are* going out in the carriage, and a husband's much more exciting than Papa."

Vicky and Philip had appeared in public very little since their marriage, and as they shook hands with Lady Sybil, then made their way into the crowded drawing-room, a sudden fear clutched at Vicky's heart. Their joint life had so far been uncomplicated by outside influences. There had been just the two of them living in the small enclosed world of their own happiness. That couldn't go on for ever, of course, and—what were outside influences going to do to them? They wouldn't leave them just as they'd found them.

The Vicarage party was greeting her, Roger shyly, Mark with his irrepressible yet disarming self-assurance. Mark was in high favour at the Manor, for Lady Sybil had recently "discovered" him and now sent for him constantly to organise theatricals and croquet parties for her. She was fond of her husband but found him rather boring and liked to have a harmless flirtation in hand as an antidote.

Mark possessed all the qualities demanded by the situation. He was good-looking, entertaining, and athletic. She was ordering him about with an air of proprietorship, throwing him little intimate smiles and glances that her guests noted with interest. ("She's got hold of young Abbot now.") The Vicar was worried by the situation, not because of any possible scandal (he was too unworldly even to realise that there was any possible scandal), but because he was afraid that Mark would fail in his degree—the worst fate he could imagine for him. The boy was running off to the Manor every day and doing no work at all. ... His wife reassured him, saying, "Never mind, dear. It'll be all right," but he knew that even if Mark didn't get his degree she'd still go on saying, "Never mind, dear. It'll be all right," as if it didn't matter. He couldn't help being comforted by her gentle optimism, however, and perhaps it really would be all right, after all. ...

Roger hadn't wanted to come to the party. After his brief admiration for Vicky he had gone back to his work with renewed vigour, and it had taken all his mother's coaxings to bring him out this afternoon. "Darling," she had said, "I shall simply hate to think of you staying at home and working all by yourself. It will be a lovely party. *Everyone* will be there." They could never persuade Mrs. Abbot that anyone could actually prefer to stay away from a party, and had long ago given up trying.

So Roger stood in the background, shy and clumsy and ill-at-ease, longing for the time when he could get back to his beloved books. As he saw Mark hurrying about, greeting and being greeted on all sides, he felt an affectionate pity for him, a feeling that Mark, seeing Roger standing awkwardly by himself, reciprocated.

Mabs had spent a whole week making a new dress of yellow mousseline-de-laine for the occasion. It didn't fit very well on the bustle, and was too bulky all round, but fortunately Mabs saw it as she had meant it to be, and not as it had actually turned out, and was quite satisfied. The only blot on her pleasure was the fact that Walter had come with them. She had hoped that Walter would go home after his last examination failure, but he had written to his mother, begging her to give him another chance (he had been shrewd enough not to mention Mabs), and to his great joy she had consented.

He now followed Mabs about the drawing-room devotedly, as usual, and, as usual, she ignored him, thinking dispassionately that he looked more dreadful than ever, his nose longer, his chin more sloping. Her eager glance roved round the room. She had been sure that she was going to meet her future husband here to-day. She had had a feeling, almost a presentiment, ever since she received the invitation. He would be there—young, handsome, wealthy. He would fall in love with her at first sight, and would demand to be introduced to her. She was waiting happily, expectantly, for Lady Sybil to bring him to her through the crowd.

A short man with longish hair and a monocle was in attendance upon Vicky. He told her that he had just had a book of poems published, and Vicky congratulated him absently, her eyes fixed on Philip, who was standing with a group of men near her. Except for that brief glimpse in her grandmother's drawing-room, she had never seen him before taking his part in a social gathering among his equals, and she watched him curiously, trying to judge him as a stranger might. Everyone in his neighbourhood was throwing glances of interest at him, attracted by that curiously compelling quality of magnetism that emanated from him. His tall virile figure and flaming red hair seemed to dominate the room.

"Who's that handsome man over there?" the poet asked her. "The one like Apollo?"

"It's my husband," said Vicky in a soft exultant voice.

Suddenly she wished that all these people would vanish, so that she could be alone with Philip again.

The poet began to describe a dramatic poem that he had once written about Apollo, but Vicky didn't listen. All her attention was given to Philip. Though the youngest man in the group, he was speaking authoritatively, laying down the law in his usual fashion.

"If the Tories think they're going to gain anything by coquetting with the fellow Parnell and his gang," he was saying, "they'll find they're mistaken. I wouldn't trust one of them an inch."

"Oh, I don't know," said a small white-haired man mildly. "And they've got some pretty real grievances when you come to look into the question."

"Nonsense!" said Philip. "They've no legitimate grievances at all. A horde of savages. They ought to be exterminated."

He spoke angrily with raised voice, and there was a sudden constrained silence.

Footmen were bringing round tea, and Mr. Beverley was moving about among his guests, beaming happily. He was feeling intensely proud of his wife and glad that she had got young Abbot in tow. She was always a little nervy and irritable when she hadn't a young man in tow. He dreaded the interregnums in her succession of youthful admirers, and often tried to find one for her himself when there wasn't one on the horizon. She had been charming to him ever since young Abbot had appeared, and, for his part, her husband hoped that his reign would be a long one. He was a nip young man and probably wouldn't annoy poor Syb by wanting to go too far.

Mabs Abbot caught sight of herself in a mirror on the wall opposite, and for a few seconds did not realise that the reflection was her own. During these few seconds her dress looked badly fitting and dowdy. As soon as she knew that it was hers it became again just what she had meant it to be, but something of depression remained. The figure in the mirror had looked not only dowdy, but forlorn and neglected, standing there alone in the window recess. Not so must her future husband see her. ... She at once summoned Walter and began to talk to him with unusual animation, trying to look popular and sought after. Walter, delighted and bewildered by her sudden affability, stammered incoherently in reply.

A long-haired musician was sitting at the grand piano, playing one of Liszt's Hungarian Rhapsodies, with many tossings of the long hair and glances of scorn at the assembly that was talking and laughing and clattering its tea-cups so unconcernedly around him. As a matter of fact, he would have been disappointed had his audience listened to him in silence, for he enjoyed the feeling of contempt and artistic isolation that their Philistine behaviour gave him.

Vicky looked round again for Philip. The group of men he had been talking with had broken up, and at first she could not see him. Then suddenly she saw him standing at the far end of the room by a woman whom Vicky did not know, leaning over her chair as he talked.

The woman was strikingly beautiful, with raven black hair, a creamy skin, and deep-set violet eyes. She wore a dress of dove grey, perfectly cut, and a grey hat trimmed with soft curling feathers. She was smiling up at Philip as she talked to him.

A sharp stab of jealousy shot through Vicky's heart. She tore her eyes away from them reluctantly as Lady Sybil, pinched and padded and dressed in an exaggeration of the fashionable mode, her face heavily rouged beneath the towering blonde wig, came across the room to speak to her.

"I'm so glad we're going to keep you in the neighbourhood, my dear," she said. "I hope we shall be great friends."

"I'm sure we shall," murmured Vicky vaguely, and went on, "Who's that very pretty woman my husband's talking to?"

She was relieved to find how calm and unconcerned her voice sounded.

"Mrs. Coverdale," said Lady Sybil. "Isn't she beautiful? Now come along, dear. I want you to meet a very great friend of mine."

As she moved among the guests, being introduced to all Lady Sybil's house-party, Vicky's eyes kept wandering to Philip and Mrs. Coverdale. He had taken the empty seat by her now and was still leaning towards her as he talked, his hand on the back of her chair. She was smiling at him intimately, encouragingly.

The jealousy in Vicky's heart sharpened to a physical pain. The room grew hotter and she began to feel faint and dizzy. People surged to and fro around her.

Dorothea Milner came to speak to her, wearing a long shapeless green garment, tied at the waist with a girdle and embroidered with a design of sunflowers. Her large feet were encased in brown sandals and her hair cut short beneath a home-made rush hat.

Dorothea's religious phase had proved of short duration, for the new mistress had been athletic, and for the next few months Dorothea had stridden about in stout shoes and what were considered indecently short skirts, talking slang in a loud voice, and introducing a (not very successful) overhand service into her tennis game, to the dismay of both her partners and opponents. The present craze was due to the influenceof Celia's governess, Miss Boniface, with whom Dorothea had struck up one of her sudden friendships just before Celia went to boarding-school.

Her mother, in particular, found it trying, as it involved a home dyeing vat that had completely ruined the walls and carpet of Dorothea's room, and a weaving machine in which Dorothea became inextricably entangled whenever she tried to use it.

The pianist finished his recital and was standing up to bow with an ironical smile which he had practised in front of his mirror and brought to a fine perfection.

The Abbots (except Mark, who was staying to dinner) were taking their departure. Mabs was looking rather depressed but telling everyone with much vivacity that she'd had a lovely time and enjoyed it tremendously.

She was very disagreeable to Walter on the way home, but he was not particularly worried by it, as it was her usual manner, and he still felt uplifted by her recent affability, which was quite new.

Philip tucked the carriage rug carefully about Vicky.

"You look tired, darling," he said solicitously, noticing her pale cheeks and the shadows beneath her eyes.

"I am rather tired," she murmured, sinking back in her seat.

They drove in silence for some minutes, then Vicky said in a small voice,

"You seemed to admire Mrs. Coverdale very much, Philip."

"She's lovely, isn't she?" burst out Philip with enthusiasm. "That *marvellous* colouring! Her hair and her white skin and those deep violet eyes. . . . And she's charming."

Vicky said nothing and he gave a sudden exultant shout of laughter.

"I believe you're jealous, Vicky. Vicky, are you jealous? Tell me."

"It was—the way you looked at her," said Vicky.

He bent over and kissed her.

"Dearest, you needn't be jealous. Ever. You're my wife. You're different from every other woman in the world. But—didn't you think her beautiful?" and he enlarged on Mrs. Coverdale's charms for the rest of the way home.

The next day he was sulky and irritable. He went into the garden to finish a sketch that he had begun the morning before, but he complained that the light was different and was finally driven in by a sudden shower of rain. He stormed into the drawing-room where Vicky was sitting sewing her baby clothes.

"It's damnable," he raged. "The best thing I've ever done, and I shall never finish it now!" He turned on her savagely. "Don't sit there staring at me like that. It doesn't matter to *you*, of course, does it? I tell you I'm sick of this damned place. There is nothing to do in it."

He snatched up an ugly blue vase that Celia had given Vicky and that he had always disliked, and threw it violently into the hearth, where it shivered to atoms.

"I won't have trash like that in the place," he shouted, then flung out of the house, ordered his horse to be saddled, and galloped off through the rain, while Vicky, who never could believe that his anger did not mean the final closing of Paradise to her, spent the day in an agony of despair and misery.

He returned at nightfall, radiant with exercise and good spirits, and Vicky, in the reaction of discovery that the gates of Paradise were still open, was hilarious with joy and relief, and for that evening they were again the two light-hearted children of their honeymoon.

But as the weeks passed his bursts of irritability became more frequent, and Vicky's nerves began to suffer. Once, when he took something out of his pocket-book, a slip of paper fell from it, and Vicky saw Mrs. Coverdale's name, followed by a London address.

"What's that, Philip?" she said sharply.

He picked it up, unconcerned.

"Oh ... she told me her address, and I promised to look her

up. I want to paint her some time, if she'll let me. I've never seen such colouring. Her eyes . . ."

Then Vicky, to her own horror, grew hysterical, telling him between her sobs that he didn't love her and never had loved her and that he could go to Mrs. Coverdale if he wanted her.

He became angry and they railed at each other, then made it up in one of those passionate scenes of reconciliation that were even more wearing than the quarrels they followed, after which Philip dramatically tore up the piece of paper and burnt it and said that the woman could go to hell for all he cared.

Vicky felt so ill the next morning that the doctor was sent for and ordered her to stay in bed for several days.

Philip had made the acquaintance of an artist called Peter Lorrimer who lived in the next village, and now began to ride over to visit him regularly. Lorrimer was well known in artistic circles, and Philip was pleased and flattered by his friendship, while Vicky, lying in bed and revelling in the peace and quiet of the house, was glad that he should have this new interest.

On the first day she was allowed downstairs it had been arranged that Lorrimer should come to tea to see Philip's sketches. He was a tall man with a black pointed beard and keen grey eyes.

Vicky, wrapped in a shawl, sitting by the drawing-room fire, found him a charming companion, and Philip was in his best mood.

After tea Philip brought his portfolios down and Lorrimer took out the sketches one by one, praising or criticising each. Vicky was delighted by his tone, for it was clear that he accepted Philip as a serious artist and was willing to help him, but Philip's brow darkened at each criticism till in the end he snatched the sketches from Lorrimer's hand and shut up the portfolio.

Lorrimer looked at him in surprise.

"What's the matter?" he said.

"Nothing," said Philip, "but I think you've said quite enough. When I want your criticism I'll ask for it."

It was evident that he was controlling his anger with difficulty. Lorrimer shrugged.

"I'm sorry," he said. "I took for granted—However—" He took his leave immediately afterwards.

When he had gone Philip paced angrily about the room.

"He'll never set foot in this house again," he said. "The confounded insolence of it!"

"But, Philip——?" began Vicky. She wanted to point out how much Lorrimer's criticism might help him, how grateful many artists would be for it. He wheeled round on her.

"Well?" he said.

She relaxed against the pillows. What was the good of saying anything? It would only make him angrier. And she felt so tired. . . .

"Nothing," she said. "Be nice to me, Philip."

He knelt by her tenderly, and she lay back in his arms with a sigh. All she wanted was his love. What did anyone or anything else matter?

But it was becoming more and more difficult to hide the ungainliness of her figure, and his revulsion from it increased. He would speak to her without looking at her. He would set his teeth and turn away sharply when she entered a room.

Curiously, she did not resent this. So near to him was she that she could feel his irritation and revulsion as if it were her own.

"Vicky," he said suddenly one afternoon, "I'm going away. Just for a little time. Do you mind? I'll come back— before it happens."

Rather to her surprise she was conscious of relief.

"Why, yes, Philip," she said. "I think it would be a good idea. Where will you go?"

"Switzerland, India, China—anywhere," he said. "I'll start next week. Sure it will be all right, darling?"

"Of course it will."

"I—I just must get away," he said. He looked like a shamefaced schoolboy.

"I know. I understand," she said gently.

He went about for the next few days in high spirits, singing to himself as he collected his things, strewing the place with maps and atlases. Then quite suddenly his good spirits seemed to vanish.

He had longed for solitude, but now that it was within reach he was frightened of it and wanted Vicky's familiar beloved presence.

He burst in on her one evening when she sat sewing in the drawing-room.

"Vicky, come with me," he pleaded. "I'll take such care of you. We'll be back in time for it, and if we're not there are doctors everywhere. It'll be all right. I don't want to go without you."

She looked at him in surprise.

"But, Philip, you——"

She stopped.

"I know," he said, "but it's only because I'm so sick of everything here. I shan't mind a bit if you'll come away with me. We'll have a lovely time—another honeymoon."

She dropped her sewing onto her knee. His excitement seemed, as usual, to enter her and make her its own.

"Vicky, will you?" he pleaded.

"Yes, I'd love to," she said eagerly.

All that evening he talked of places and routes and arrangements. He was tender and charming, his revulsion forgotten. His eagerness still upheld her. It would be lovely to go away with him. How could she ever have thought that she could bear to be left behind? There seemed to be two parts of her—one that was exhausted by him and longed to rest, the other that loved him so desperately it could not bear to be away from him for a moment. The former part always vanished when he was actually present. And his excitement could always recall the eager high-spirited little girl who lived behind her newly acquired dignity.

All that evening they discussed their plans.

"Though it doesn't matter what we say we'll do," laughed Vicky. "You'll do just the opposite."

She stifled some slight doubts about the wisdom of the trip by repeating to herself Philip's careless "It'll be all right. There are doctors everywhere." Of course it would be all right. There were doctors everywhere. And the prospect had dispelled all Philip's moodiness. He was sunny-tempered and loverlike. . . .

The next morning they went into the garden arm-in-arm. "Let's go abroad every year," said Philip. "Let's live abroad. Let's buy a fortress in Arabia. . . ."

They were passing the border where Andrew was working, and he touched his forehead as they passed. Vicky wondered vaguely what Andrew thought of Philip. Philip had restored the shilling cut in wages after one week, being apparently under the impression that he had then fully compensated himself for his extravagance over the artificial lake. The other day, too, when Andrew had asked to go home early as his mother was ill, Philip had carelessly taken out a five-pound note and given it to him for the expenses of her illness. On the other hand, he would often irritably refuse to give him money for some quite necessary garden expense.

Vicky stopped in front of him.

"We're going abroad again, Andrew," she said. "I don't know how long we shall be away. Till next year, perhaps. Anyway, you'll keep an eye on things in the garden, won't you, and we'll send your wages."

Andrew looked slowly from her to Philip. He had felt relieved when he heard that Miss Vicky was going to be married, because now she would have someone to look after her, and he could shake off his sense of responsibility. But—as the weeks went on he had felt less and less sure, and in the end the old sense of responsibility had descended heavily upon him again. The master wasn't fit to look after her. He couldn't even look after himself.

He fixed his eyes, grave and intent in his pale freckled face, on Philip.

"You can't take Miss Vicky away now, sir," he said slowly. "She ought to stay here quietly till the child comes."

Philip went red, then white, and for a moment Vicky thought that he was going to strike him. Andrew didn't flinch or change countenance. He went on looking earnestly at Philip.

And suddenly Philip flung back his head with a roar of laughter.

"That's the most colossal piece of impudence I ever heard in my life," he said, "but, by God, Vicky, he's right."

And the next day he set off alone.

Chapter Fifteen

THE child (a son, whom Vicky called Lionel after Philip's father) was born while Philip was still abroad.

Mrs. Carothers came over from Ivy Lodge to take charge of the situation, and Celia was allowed to come home from school for the day of the christening. She arrived in a state of wild excitement, laden with highly unsuitable presents for her nephew—sweets, toys, and a muslin frock that would have fitted a child of three.

Vicky, who still felt weak and listless, shrank from her exuberance and from her persistent questioning, for Celia was trying to reconcile her mother's account of the depositing of a fully grown baby Lionel by an angel in Vicky's bed with certain quite different information given her by her school-fellows.

Mrs. Carothers returned to Ivy Lodge the day after the christening. Vicky had been glad of her help, but there had never been any confidence between them, and, just as her father had once seemed to separate them, so Philip did now, even in his absence. He had shown his dislike of his stepmother-in-law plainly from the first, and she never mentioned him to Vicky unless it were necessary, so that there was still the old feeling of constraint between the two women, and Vicky was not sorry when she left the Hall.

Life now settled down into a happy jog-trot existence. It was strange, thought Vicky sometimes, how little she missed Philip in practical matters. The household seemed quite complete without him. He wrote to her from Germany, Italy, Norway, Greece. . . . Following his erratic course across Europe, she felt grateful to Andrew for having prevented her from accompanying him.

Her world now consisted of the nurse, Andrew, and Ellen—a

warm, peaceful, sheltered little world, where the days followed each other happily and uneventfully, and she lay in the sunshine, wrapped in a dreamy languor, regaining health and strength.

The baby filled her whole life, and she was glad to leave everything else to the others. Ellen took her orders to the kitchen and quietly and tactfully performed the office of housekeeper in Vicky's place. Her devotion to Vicky seemed, strangely, to have been increased rather than diminished by Philip's discourtesy to her.

Andrew was there, too, as always, in the background. It was Andrew who carried chairs and cushions out into the garden on the warm spring days, who tucked the rug round her knees and set a footstool at her feet.

Andrew and Ellen would consult together in the morning as to whether she should stay indoors or sit out. Sometimes Andrew would order the carriage for her in the afternoon, and she would go for a short drive.

When the monthly nurse went, she engaged a young girl, who had been nursemaid in a large family, and who would not object to Vicky's supervising her nursery. She was a small, apple-cheeked, smiling little person called Flossie, and she worshipped Lionel from the moment she saw him. She worshipped Vicky, too, and was glad for her to spend a large part of the day in the nursery. It was before the régime of Truby King, and Vicky would sit rocking her baby to sleep in her arms, happily unconscious of the horror the sight would have caused her daughters.

Then, quite suddenly, and, as usual, with no warning, Philip returned. And at once the time during which he had been away ceased to exist, and life returned to the quick exhilarating tempo that Philip's presence always meant. He came back in high spirits, delighted to be with her again, thrilled at the possession of a son.

"You ought to have come, Vicky," he said. "It was a marvellous trip. I can't think why I took any notice of that crazy gardener of yours. You'd have been all right—but it's heaven to get back to you."

He was bronzed and handsome, and he had grown a Vandyke beard, that made him look very distinguished. He had brought home a portfolio full of sketches and showed them proudly to Vicky the first evening. She knew little about the technical side of art, but she was struck by their beauty and spirit.

"Philip," she said, "couldn't you have an exhibition of them in London? They're so lovely. I'm sure it would be a success. Why not consult Mr. Lorrimer about them?"

But his face darkened at the mention of the name. He had never forgiven Lorrimer for his criticism of the sketches he had shown him the year before.

"Nonsense!" he said impatiently. "Why should I expose my work to a set of ignorant fools?"

She learnt later that he had once given an exhibition of his work in London, which had been very successful on the whole, but the few adverse criticisms he had received had so enraged him that he had resolved never to give another.

Now that he had returned, she forgot the timeless peace of his absence and imagined that she had missed him poignantly.

"Don't go away again," she pleaded. "I don't know how I lived through it."

"I don't know how I have, either, now I've got back to you," he replied. "I kept trying to draw your face from memory and it maddened me that I couldn't get it right."

He had brought her a silk shawl embroidered in rich shades of blue and green, and he draped it over her shoulders and made her sit on the sofa, gazing out of the window, her profile turned to him, while he sketched her.

Not for the first time something in his worship of her beauty frightened her. It was so impersonal, so remote from any understanding, any real love of her.

The few days immediately after his return were passed in a state of dreamy happiness. He was delighted with everything. He loved to watch Vicky with the child in her arms and made innumerable sketches of them.

Then gradually he began to resent the child's claims on her. She couldn't ride with him because she had to stay indoors to feed the child.

"Good God!" he exploded angrily. "What on earth does it matter? Surely the nurse can give him a bottle just this once?"

But she knew that "just this once" would mean "always" and remained obstinate.

He resented, too, her going into the nursery so frequently.

"What do we pay a nurse for?" he would storm.

And, though he loved the child and was proud of it, he was revolted and infuriated by the more intimate details of its toilet, and, once it had been sick over his coat, refused to hold it again. His restlessness gradually increased till it came to a head one evening.

It had been Flossie's afternoon out, and Vicky had insisted on taking her place in the nursery.

"I believe you only do it to annoy me," he had said sulkily. "Here's a house full of maids who could easily look after the child, but you must needs make a drudge of yourself."

"The maids have their work to do," said Vicky firmly. "Besides, I couldn't trust anyone else to look after him. He's got a cold and——"

He interrupted her angrily. Her solicitude for the child seemed a personal slight to him. He was always pointing out to her how the village children throve under a regime of neglect.

"Our child isn't a village child," Vicky would reply calmly.

Insensibly since the birth of the child she had grown a little firmer, a little less yielding and pliable. His anger still had power to distress her, but it no longer meant the end of the world to her. Even while she reasoned and pleaded with him—even while she wept—she was aware of the child, and if it were time for his walk or his food, would break off the scene to go to the nursery.

Philip felt bewildered and aggrieved. This exquisite being (he never thought of Vicky apart from her hair and eyes, the flawlessness of her skin, the lovely line of chin and throat) had seemed to belong to him entirely, had seemed created to respond to his moods, to minister to his needs; and now his empire was threatened by the son who should have perfected his happiness, cemented his empire. What he resented most was the subtle change in Vicky herself, the hint of maturity and individuality in her. She no longer existed solely as his reflection. He resented this vaguely, almost unconsciously, not knowing quite what it was he resented. Vicky was "different." She didn't love him as she used to. Striding angrily over the countryside, he decided suddenly to go to London for a week or so and leave her here alone. She would miss him then. She would perhaps be her old self when he returned.

He originated the idea as a piece of childish revenge, in the spirit of a boy who runs away from home because he thinks he is not sufficiently appreciated, but, as he walked back to the Hall, the idea took more definite shape in his mind, and the mood in which he had conceived it altered. He was deeply, if erratically, attached to his art, and he was secretly pleased with the work he had done on his recent holiday abroad. Moreover, though personal contact with his equals generally ended by irking his pride and intolerance, something in him craved the society of his fellow-artists. He would try a fresh line, a line he'd always been interested in. Portrait painting. . . . He had taken it up once before, and abandoned it because his sitters had got on his nerves, but, after all, one needn't paint people who got on one's nerves. There were quite a lot of people who didn't. Mrs. Coverdale had said "You must paint me," when she heard that he was an artist, and, though he had laughed and said, "One doesn't try to paint goddesses," he knew that she had really wanted him to paint her portrait. He would take a studio in London and divide his time between that and the country. When the child was older, Vicky would be able to come to London with him. He could never stay away from Vicky for long. . . .

By the time he reached home, he had quite forgotten the grievance that had driven him out. Vicky, waiting apprehensively for his return, was relieved to see him coming whistling into the house, obviously in high good-humour. He poured out his plans to her eagerly.

"You see, Vicky, I can take up portrait painting in earnest and get sitters in London. You must come and stay there as soon as you can, and we'll go about a bit. You've hardly seen London, have you?"

"No, I haven't," said Vicky dreamily. London. . . . It meant that strange remote interlude of her visit to Rosamund . . . the little sitting-room with Miss Tarrant hunting in the rosewood bureau for papers that were just beneath her nose. . . . Mr. Thorburn, large and pale and curiously impressive. . . . Rosamund sitting by the fire with that secret smile on her lips. . . . Lady Skene, her black eyes bright and vigilant in her wizened yellow face . . . and Philip . . . Philip . . . Philip. . . .

The others had all stayed in the dream, but Philip had come out of it to rescue her from her loneliness and bewilderment, to give her happiness, security, and love. . . . She put her arms about his neck.

"Don't stay away long, darling," she said. "I couldn't live without you."

"And you'll come too?"

"Of course. When you're settled. I'll be one of your first sitters."

In the days that followed their love seemed deepened, revivified. Philip included Lionel in his expansive affection, making no further objections to the child's claims on Vicky and even helping her nurse him one night when he was feverish with teething.

Vicky felt depressed and apprehensive as the day of his departure drew near.

"As soon as I get settled I'll come up and fetch you to see it," he said. "I'm going to work like hell."

She accompanied him to the station, and he set off, still eager and excited, with the innumerable trunks that he always seemed to take with him, wherever he was going and for however short a time. The last she saw was his head out of the window with the flaming red hair and beard.

She returned home, feeling sad and lonely, her heart heavy with vague fears.

After tea she went into the garden and found Andrew waiting for her at the bottom of the terrace steps with Ellen.

"Miss Vicky," said Andrew, "me and Ellen here would like to get married."

He looked, as always, earnest and intent, not embarrassed in any way. Ellen's pale face had flushed. She fixed her grey eyes on Vicky's face.

"It'll be all right, won't it, 'm?" she said. "We're going to live at the cottage with Andrew's mother and I'll look after her. She needs someone now the others have gone, and she's almost bedridden. I'll always come back here to help if I'm needed."

"Oh, but I'm so glad," said Vicky. "It's lovely. I'm so *glad*. . . ."

Andrew would never go away now. He would always live in the village near her. . . . He would always be there . . . always. The sense of security returned to her, and with it a sudden rush of happiness.

Chapter Sixteen

PHILIP'S studio was furnished in sombre magnificent fashion, with pieces of rich velvet and brocade flung carelessly over carved oak chairs, a massive inlaid Italian chest, glints of armour against the dark walls, and a tall cloisonné vase on the floor by the door. There was a model's throne in a corner of the room, and in the middle a table littered with palettes and paint tubes. On an easel, just under the skylight, stood a half-finished portrait of Mrs. Coverdale. It was radiantly alive and beautiful. The white neck, rising from the dark furs, gleamed like satin, the deep blue eyes were serene and arrogant, the dark hair held the gloss of a raven's wing.

Vicky felt a moment of sheer triumph at her husband's talent before the little stab of jealousy shot through her heart again.

"She is beautiful, isn't she?" she said wistfully.

"She's marvellous," said Philip. "Every movement's perfect. I couldn't decide which pose to do at first, but in the end I chose this. Just turning to look over her shoulder. ... I can't do her justice, of course."

The unqualified impersonal praise somehow stilled Vicky's jealousy. She remembered that beauty was his religion, that he would rhapsodise with equal enthusiasm over the texture of her skin and a silver birch sapling in a wood.

She shrugged faintly and let the problem go. Anyway, she had seldom seen him as well and happy as he was now—pleased with his work, stimulated by the new interest and the friendships that it had brought into his life. He mentioned carelessly the names of men, well known in the artistic world, whom he had come to know since he began work in London, and Vicky listened with ever increasing pride. He was handsome, brilliant, successful, and he was hers, hers, hers. . . .

She was staying in London for a week, and Philip had left the small austerely furnished room off the studio where he generally slept to join her at an hotel. It had been a bewildering week, for Philip dashed about here, there, and everywhere, and she seldom knew where she was going till she got there. She had to see sunrise at Covent Garden and sunset on the river. She had to see Richmond, Kew, Hampstead, Hampton Court, and the Zoo. She had to see the pre-Raphaelite exhibition at the Grosvenor Gallery and the Doré Gallery in Bond Street. London was *en fête* for the Queen's Jubilee, and there was an air of festivity over everything. Vicky loved to watch the crowds in the streets, to drive through them with Philip in a hansom or on one of the brightly coloured horse-drawn buses. She enjoyed walking, too, but when they walked Philip would stride along so fast that it was all she could do to keep up with him. She was rather nervous of the traffic, and was often left hesitating on one side of the street after Philip had crossed to the other. Once, taken up by his own thoughts and intent on reaching his objective, he had forged ahead so quickly over roads and crossings that she was hopelessly lost and had to find her way back alone to the hotel. She was afraid that he would be angry, but he was only concerned and remorseful.

He proved a delightful companion on these expeditions—amusing, interesting, and good-tempered. London seemed to have wrought some magic in him, and his high spirits seldom flagged. There were, it is true, one or two of the old scenes when he haggled with cabmen over a few coppers, losing his temper and attracting a crowd, but Vicky was growing hardened to them now.

She wrote to Rosamund, offering tentatively to visit her, and Rosamund wrote back very affectionately but so vaguely that Vicky did not follow it up. Rosamund was too busy working her way through the outskirts of Society to have time for a Mrs. Lynnaker who lived in the country and had no social footing in London. Had Vicky married someone with an established position, it would, of course, have been very different. She had dropped Miss Tarrant, who had now served her purpose, and was looking forward to the time when she could afford to drop Mr. Thorburn, whom she found intolerably boring, but whom in the meantime she continued to humour and flatter. Her name had lately been seen among the guests at several important Society functions. Only at the most exclusive houses, such as Lady Skene's, was she still not received.

Vicky had visited Lady Skene the day after her arrival in London. She had found her suffering from an attack of bronchitis, propped up in bed, and looking very frail.

"Yes, my dear," she said, fixing her piercing eyes on Vicky, "I think you did right. If you had waited I daresay you could have made a better match, but your background was so ambiguous that I think you were quite right not to wait. You are beautiful, but your likeness to your mother has been, of course, unfortunate." She looked Vicky up and down with a little nod of approval. "Yes, you've improved, my dear. You've improved a great deal. Are you in love with your husband?"

"Yes," said Vicky shyly, "of course."

"No 'of course' about it," said the old woman tartly. "It's rather a drawback, in fact. One can manage them so much better if one isn't in love with them. Philip Lynnaker will be a handful. Better that than dull. My husband was excessively moral and indescribably dull. . . ."

Philip had arranged a tea-party in the studio the day before Vicky's return to Six Elms. Mrs. Coverdale was to be there and several other friends of Philip's whom Vicky had not yet met.

He had sent out for flowers and food in enormous quantities and given elaborate orders to the Rembrandt-esque old woman who looked after the studio. He was in his most genial mood, delighted at the prospect of showing off Vicky to his friends, and proud of the paintings that were ranged round the room.

Vicky had bought a sheaf of lilies of the valley to wear on her dress, but Philip, who hated to see flowers worn as a decoration, took them off and fastened round her throat a string of moonstones that he had bought for her the day before.

"They're like you," he said, drawing her to him and kissing her. "You are enjoying it, aren't you, darling?"

"I'm loving it," she said happily.

She looked round at his preparations—banks of sandwiches and cakes of every description, caviare, jellies, trifles, urns of tea and coffee, bottles of champagne.

"How many people are coming?" she asked.

"About twenty or so."

"You've provided for fifty at the least."

He made a sweeping gesture with his hand.

"Oh, well . . . I hate anything mean."

She smiled, thinking of the scene he had made that morning over sixpence. One couldn't expect Philip to be consistent. . . . One hardly even wanted him to be.

The guests had nearly all arrived, but still there was an air of expectancy, of waiting for something. Then Mrs. Coverdale entered. She looked poised and disdainful and very, very beautiful as she swept in, wearing a dress of white China crape, trimmed with turquoise embroidery and crystal beads. Her small hat was fashionably high and massed with flowers and ribbons.

Vicky, who had been feeling pleasantly grown-up and matronly, suddenly felt young and shy and immature. Everyone was praising the portrait, and Mrs. Coverdale stood by it, displaying her beauty with languid arrogance. She seemed to make no effort to entertain or interest, but everyone in the room was aware of her.

A little group of Philip's friends (they mostly had beards and flowing neckties) was standing round Vicky, and she was talking to them with shy childish enthusiasm, telling them all she and Philip had done during her visit. Her confidence gradually increased. A glance into one of the brocade-draped mirrors told her that she was looking her prettiest, and the knowledge sent a little thrill of exultation through her, an exultation that had nothing in it of vanity, for she only looked on her beauty as something that enhanced her value in Philip's eyes.

She heard two men near her agreeing that Philip had real talent, and her heart glowed with pride.

One by one the guests were taking their departure. . . .

Philip brought Mrs. Coverdale over to Vicky, and she began to talk to her in the deep musical drawl that seemed to hold in it the secret of her glamour. She asked Vicky if she had been to various places, and if she knew various people, and they were all places she hadn't been to and people she hadn't met.

"You see, I've never been in London properly till this week," explained Vicky. "I don't really know anyone."

"That must be remedied," drawled Mrs. Coverdale. "We must introduce you to people."

Vicky smiled.

"Oh no," she said. "I'm going home to-morrow. I've got my baby to look after, you know. I should hate to live in London."

"Should you?" Mrs. Coverdale's violet-dark eyes dwelt on her speculatively.

"Yes, I've always lived in the country."

"But now that your husband's living in London?"

"Philip isn't actually living in London; are you, Philip? He's just got his studio here. It's his *pied-à-terre*, that's all." She glanced shyly from the portrait to its original. "I think it's lovely."

"Do you?" said the original carelessly. She turned her head in Philip's direction. "Have you the other sketches you made of me? Perhaps your wife would like to see them."

"I'd love to," said Vicky.

The other woman's proprietary manner towards Philip did not annoy her, for Philip seemed hardly to glance in her direction. He was sitting on the arm of Vicky's chair, arranging the lace at her neck with little lover-like touches. She had that sweet sense of triumph that a woman feels when another woman makes obvious efforts to attract a man whom she knows to be wholly hers.

"Do show me them, Philip," pleaded Vicky.

The others had gone now, and the three of them were alone.

Philip rather reluctantly fetched a big portfolio from a corner of the room.

Mrs. Coverdale's eyes wandered up and down Vicky.

"If you're staying in town," she said, "do let me give you the name of my dressmaker—that is, of course, if you haven't one already. And my hairdresser. One can waste such a lot of time and money looking for the right people."

"Leave her alone," said Philip shortly, untying the strings of the portfolio. "I don't want her any different."

"Of course, she's perfect," drawled Mrs. Coverdale. "I didn't mean that. But she's just said that she's always lived in the country." There was something faintly mocking in her smile. "If you'd let me take her in hand and advise her where to go for her things she'd be what they used to call in the old days the toast of London."

"I don't want her the toast of London," said Philip.

"No, you'll have to leave me as I am," smiled Vicky. "I belong to the country."

"You belong to me," said Philip.

He had opened the portfolio and taken out several sketches, handing them to Vicky one by one.

"I tried every possible attitude, didn't I?" he said, "before I fixed on that," nodding towards the almost finished portrait.

Again Vicky felt ashamed of the faint jealousy that had invaded her as she turned over the sketches. His interest was purely that of the artist in his sitter. And how lovely the woman was! Suddenly Vicky wished that she had dark eyes, creamy skin, and black hair. . . .

Among the sketches was a small water-colour of the terrace steps of the Hall, showing the lawn and part of the house. Vicky looked at it in silence, surrendering herself to a rush of homesickness. That was where she belonged. Perhaps Lionel was there now, sitting up in his pram at the bottom of the steps, throwing his toys out. Flossie would be upstairs, getting his bath ready, and Andrew, working on the long herbaceous border, would be keeping an eye on him, leaving his work to pick up the toys as he threw them out.

"It looks a most delightful spot," Mrs. Coverdale was saying.

"I've been telling Mrs. Coverdale that she must come over for a day and see it," said Philip.

"Oh, longer than a day," said Vicky. "Come and spend a week with us. The country round is lovely. And there's the baby. . . ."

"Ah, of course, the baby," said Mrs. Coverdale, with her faint smile. "I should love to come."

They arranged the day on which she was to come before she went home.

Vicky regretted the invitation as soon as she had given it. The thought of it spoilt her home-coming, hanging over her spirit like some heavy foreboding of disaster. She didn't like the woman and neither did Philip (he had shown his dislike quite plainly in the studio). She couldn't think why they had asked her. The memory of that beautiful arrogant face, that faint disdainful smile, seemed to spoil everything, even the pleasant sunny nursery where Lionel lay in his cot, rosy with sleep and surfeited with milk.

Flossie had little less than an epic to recount to Vicky about Lionel. Everything he had done, every expression of his face, every movement of his sturdy limbs, had to be described in detail. And Vicky listened eagerly, holding the warm sleeping bundle in her arms ... but she kept remembering that disdainful smile, that mocking arrogant glance.

"It's going to be hateful," she said to herself. "She'll sneer at everything. I'll have nothing to talk to her about. A *week*. It'll never go. And just when I want to be alone with them—Lionel and Philip and Andrew and the others. Oh, why did I ask her? Why did Philip *let* me ask her?"

Philip came down alone to Six Elms the day before Mrs. Coverdale was expected. He laughed at Vicky's apprehensions, but seemed nervous and on edge himself, roaming from room to room, flying into a passion because there was a pot of begonias on a window-sill in one of the upstairs passages, and flinging it violently down through the open window onto the terrace below.

Andrew came slowly from his work in the garden to clear away the mess, without looking up at the window, and Vicky, who was standing by, said "*Philip!*", her face so grave and reproachful that it suddenly made him laugh and his good temper returned.

It was very precarious, however, and both of them were aware of a sense of strain connected unmistakably with the prospect of the expected visitor.

Vicky went down to the station in the carriage to meet her the next afternoon. The weather had turned rather cold and Mrs. Coverdale wore a long velvet cloak edged with sable that gave a regal quality to her beauty. She was very pleasant to Vicky as they drove back to the Hall, but there was still that hint of mockery in her smile, and Vicky felt self-conscious and ill at ease.

It was all right when they reached home, for Philip was his most charming self, welcoming the guest with unusual geniality and slipping an arm round Vicky's shoulder affectionately as he did so.

They took Mrs. Coverdale into the garden before tea. She seemed interested and appreciative, but Vicky still seemed to detect a hidden amusement that she couldn't understand.

Andrew was working in one of the greenhouses, and Vicky saw him throw a glance at the visitor that took her in from the elaborately trimmed hat to the tips of her elegant boots. Vicky wondered what he thought of her. His face was, as usual, quite expressionless. The sight of him working there gave Vicky an odd homesick feeling. He represented the security that she had always longed for and that even Philip, whom she loved so dearly, could not give her.

She wished again that she had not invited this beautiful disturbing stranger to her home. Security? It couldn't exist within miles of her.

After tea they went into the nursery to watch Lionel have his bath and he showed off obligingly, crowing and smiling and kicking in Flossie's arms.

After dinner Vicky and Mrs. Coverdale worked at their embroidery, and Philip read the newspaper and occasionally threw them scraps of news. A pleasant sense of domestic intimacy crept over the group, and Vicky began to think that the visit might prove quite pleasant after all.

Then they discussed the next day's programme, and decided to drive over to Bartleham Abbey, a local beauty spot, and have a picnic lunch among the ruins.

The visitor stole many glances at Philip from her violet-blue eyes, but Philip ignored them all, showing himself affectionately attentive to Vicky, and Vicky enjoyed parading her husband's devotion before a woman who probably had found it easy enough to detach other men from their wives. Still—she grew rather thoughtful—perhaps it was as well she had only been invited for a week. . . .

Philip went out for a walk about half-past nine, and the two women sat sewing by the fire. Mrs. Coverdale exerted herself to ask questions about the neighbourhood and countryside, and displayed interest in Lendale Rocks—a supposedly Druid circle—when Vicky described it.

Finally they decided to go there the next day instead of to the Abbey, and both went to bed soon after ten.

Vicky was half asleep when Philip entered the bedroom. She murmured "Darling . . ." sleepily, then drifted off again into a sleep in which she dreamed that Lionel was lost and that she was searching desperately for him everywhere, only to discover that Mrs. Coverdale had stolen him. . . .

When she awoke in the morning, Philip was still sleeping. She roused him, but he only grunted and went to sleep again.

"Philip, darling," she said at last, "won't you have your bath now? The breakfast gong will be going soon."

He did not answer or move. In this, as in everything else, he seemed to know no mean. He would sometimes get up at about five o'clock and try to make her get up, too, and at other times would lie in bed till the middle of the morning.

The breakfast bell rang and Vicky went downstairs. Mrs. Coverdale had put on a dress of red ottoman silk that showed off her dark hair and clear skin to perfection. She was pleasant, almost animated, and Vicky began to look forward to the expedition to Lendale Rocks. She remembered that she hadn't told Philip about their change of plan, and went upstairs to her bedroom as soon as breakfast was over.

She found him dressed, standing in front of the looking-glass in his shirt-sleeves, brushing his hair and whistling.

"Hello, darling," he said cheerfully. "Everything all right?"

She had opened her mouth to tell him of the change of plan when suddenly he said:

"If we're going to Lendale Rocks we ought to start soon, I suppose. It's further than the Abbey."

She sat down on the bed and looked at him with a puzzled expression.

"But—Philip——" She stopped.

"Well?"

"How did you know? We arranged it after you'd gone out."

"You told me last night, I suppose."

"I didn't, Philip."

Her expression of bewilderment was changing to one of incredulity and dawning horror.

"This morning, then."

His voice was studiously careless, and he didn't turn round from the looking-glass.

"I didn't. You know I didn't. *Philip!*"

He turned round at last to meet her horrified gaze.

"What?" he said defensively.

Her face had gone very white.

"Philip—you——"

He shrugged.

"All right. I just looked into her bedroom when I came in last night. She told me."

She closed her eyes for a second as if at a stab of physical pain, then said:

"Philip—you didn't—say you didn't——"

He was suddenly angry.

"Good God, Vicky, of course not. What do you think I am? Do you think that *here* under my own roof I'd——"

"But before," she persisted, "in London—while you were painting her——" She looked at his face, then turned her head away sharply. "Oh, you needn't tell me. I know."

Something of his blustering died away.

"But, Vicky, it didn't mean anything. ... My God, can't you

understand? It didn't mean a *thing*. I don't care two pins about her. It's you I love."

She was silent, remembering that party in his studio, when she had felt so exultantly confident of his loyalty, when she had watched Mrs. Coverdale's proprietary manner to him with triumphant amusement. And all the time they had been lovers, even then. . . .

She dropped her face into her hands.

"Oh, send her away," she cried. "I won't ever see her again. How dared she come here? How *dared* she?"

"Of course, I'll send her away," said Philip. "I'll send her away at once. Vicky, darling. . . ."

He laid his hand on her shoulders. She shook him off.

"Don't touch me," she sobbed. "I can't bear it."

Philip went downstairs and had a short interview with the guest. He was furious with himself and her and made no attempt to gloss things over.

"She says you'll have to go," he said when he had finished the story. "She says she won't have you in the house."

Mrs. Coverdale laughed.

"Naturally," she said suavely. "My dear Philip, what a mess you've made of things! I never thought you were such a fool."

"You were a fool to come here," he said. "It's all finished, anyway, and you can get out."

"How charmingly you put it!" said Mrs. Coverdale. "What a tender lovers' parting!"

"Get out," he said savagely.

The servants were informed that Mrs. Coverdale had received a letter by that morning's post summoning her back to London and that the mistress was incapacitated by a sudden headache.

The carriage was brought to the door and the guest drove off, magnificent in the sable-trimmed cloak, the faint disdainful smile still on her lips.

Philip returned to Vicky, who lay sobbing on the bed, her spirit groping blindly in a black underworld. Philip and that woman . . . Philip . . . Philip . . . Philip. . . .

He knelt by the bed pouring out protestations of penitence. He loved no one but her. He never had loved anyone but her. He'd spend the rest of his life proving it to her.

She believed him, because she had to believe him, because life couldn't go on unless she believed him. Yet her mind was still groping in that black underworld. Philip and that woman . . . Philip . . . Philip . . . Philip. . . .

She let him take her in his arms and kiss away her tears. . . . Her sobs grew slower, less convulsive.

Then Lionel's shrill wail cut sharply through the air. The sound seemed to drag Vicky up from the darkness into the wholesome light of day. She disengaged herself gently.

"I must go to him," she said unsteadily. "Flossie's in the kitchen. She won't have heard."

"Vicky, do you believe me? You *do* forgive me?" he pleaded passionately.

"Yes, yes," she said, and went to Lionel.

He stayed for another week, tender, adoring, assiduous in his attention. Before he returned to London she knew that she was to have another child.

Chapter Seventeen

PAULA, Vicky's second child, was born on her twenty-third birthday, and she had two more children, Noel and Margery, within the next three years. Her whole life now centred in the nursery. It was a happy enclosed life—feeding babies, dressing them, washing them, nursing them, adoring them—a life whose high lights of excitement were Lionel's first tooth, Paula's first tottering steps, Noel's whooping-cough, Margery's fall from the copper beech. . . .

Philip came and went in meteor-like flashes, leaving generally a train of disturbance in his rear.

Vicky had become philosophical with regard to his infidelities, though the knowledge of them tinged her love for him with bitterness. They passed as quickly as his other interests. She learnt to ask no questions, but she always knew by his restlessness when another affair was beginning, and by his sudden devotion to her when it was at an end.

He loved his children and was proud of them, but his fastidiousness shrank from their exuberance, and he was jealous of the part they played in Vicky's life. His selfishness was the instinctive unconscious selfishness of a child. He had to come first and was angry and resentful at any sign that he didn't. He never grudged money spent on the nursery; he insisted, in fact, that the children must have the best of everything, and, in a shy wistful fashion, he hungered for their love, but their childish high spirits irritated him.

Vicky herself was now unmoved by his frequent anger. No longer did she sob in desolation and abasement when he stormed at her. She shrugged her shoulders and returned to her babies. And that, of course, made him angrier still. He complained that the children were all over the place. There always seemed to be a baby sleeping in the cot by Vicky's bed, crawling over the drawing-room carpet, toddling about the hall.

"My God!" he would rage. "Can't you keep the children in the nursery? What on earth do we pay a nurse for?"

When Vicky kept them in the nursery he sulked because she was always there with them herself.

The paraphernalia of childhood—nurses, baths, prams, chamber-pots—disgusted him, and he would be driven to fury by the table manners of a child who had hardly yet learned to use its fingers. He did not understand how terrifying he was to the children in his rages, and was continually being hurt by their shrinking from him.

He came home unexpectedly on Paula's second birthday, genial, happy, laden with toys, but her last memories of him were of a red angry face, blazing eyes, and a voice that roared like an enraged lion, and she clung to Vicky for protection, refusing to go to him, despite all Vicky's efforts.

Then his anger returned, and he flung the toys upon the floor and went back to London by the next train.

Occasionally he would bring a friend down with him, but Vicky had long ago stopped trying to keep pace with his friendships. He made friends easily but was too touchy and intolerant to keep them. No one's opinion but his own could exist on any subject. He would take offence at the slightest shadow of criticism. His interests changed as quickly as his friendships. He gave up portrait painting and began to design wall-paper in the fashion of Morris; that was followed by a craze for beaten metal and wood-carving; then quite suddenly he threw everything else up for sculpture.

His restlessness would drive him abroad for months at a time, and invariably, when he had been away for several weeks, Vicky's relief would be succeeded by a longing for his return, a hunger for the stimulus of his eager mercurial presence. Always she was aware of his deep love for her unaltered beneath his infatuations and changes of mood.

Lady Skene died the year that Margery was born. She had been an invalid for some time, but had entertained her own exclusive circle right up to the end, sitting in her chair in the drawing-room, her maid hovering unobtrusively near with the tablets that alleviated her pain.

Mrs. Orell had continued her slow demure reconquest of Society. She had sent Mr. Thorburn about his business as soon as she could afford to (and with scant ceremony, to that gentleman's indignant amazement), dropping the mask of piety whose object was now achieved and taking a house in Curzon Street. Her triumph was made complete by her marriage to Lord Attley—a notorious rip, but a nobleman whose social position was unquestioned. Rosamund's one regret was that her mother had died before being forced to recognise her.

She flaunted herself in the drawing-rooms of Mayfair, patronising various people for whose patronage she had worked so hard a short time ago, and paying off a few old scores that she had zealously treasured through the years.

Then, having vindicated her position, she took a villa in the South of France, and went there with her enamoured old husband, to become the centre of a demi-monde that she found much more amusing than the circles of Mayfair.

Vicky had written to congratulate her on the announcement of her marriage but had received no reply.

The days flowed by happily and uneventfully at the Hall, their peace broken only by Philip's sudden appearances. Celia spent as much time as she could spare from her mother with Vicky and the children. She still adored Vicky and included the children in her adoration, playing with them indefatigably, spending her pocket-money on toys for them, and working industriously at little garments for them.

She was eighteen now, but had changed very little since childhood. She was still short and plump, with curly dark hair and a boisterous vivacious manner. Her boisterousness sometimes frightened Noel, who was a timid nervous child, but on the whole Auntie Celia was a great favourite in the nursery.

Mrs. Carothers seemed to have grown old quickly since her husband's death, and seldom left Ivy Lodge, where she occupied herself pottering in the garden and making flannel petticoats for the poor. Her majestic person seemed to have shrunk somewhat, and she dressed always in black, with caps of lace, trimmed with imitation violets, and a small black silk apron.

Andrew and Ellen lived in the jasmine-covered cottage. Andrew's mother was quite bedridden now, and Ellen looked after her, coming to help at the Hall whenever Vicky was short-handed. They had one child—a stocky quiet little boy called Bill, very like Andrew.

Flossie, after presiding over the nursery for six years, left to get married. Vicky found her difficult to replace, for she had been capable, energetic, and supremely good-tempered. After interviewing several applicants, she chose a middle-aged woman, with an expressionless face but excellent references, whose last charge had just gone to boarding-school, and who professed a deep love and understanding of children.

The nursery seemed to settle down quietly under her rule, and Vicky was glad that she had chosen an experienced woman, for Philip made one of his sudden descents on her, and she had no time for her children or their concerns. He had taken up photography—then an affair of large box cameras and heavy plates—and Vicky had to go with him all over the countryside, pose for her photograph against every possible background, and watch all his proceedings in the "dark room."

He was passionately in love with her again and she let herself relax in his love, responding to his high spirits with that childish merriment that always lay hidden beneath her young dignity, agreeing to his wildest suggestions, forgetting all the ordered routine that she had built up so carefully for herself and her household.

Then one morning she heard sounds of raised voices in the garden—Andrew's voice shouting and the nurse's screaming shrilly. She ran out to find them both by the baby's pram, Andrew holding up a bottle and the nurse struggling to get it from him. She had never seen Andrew angry before. His face was a dull red, his voice harsh, his eyes blazing.

"Give it me back! How dare you!" the nurse was saying.

"No, you don't!" he answered. "This goes to Miss Vicky. I've had my eye on you for long enough——"

"What is it?" said Vicky breathlessly.

"It's this, Miss Vicky," said Andrew. "This stuff she gives the children to make them sleep. I'd like to know what's in it. And that's not all." He raised his voice above the woman's shrill protests. "She doesn't treat them right. Frightening them out of their lives with tales of ghosts and such-like. Locking little Master Noel in the boot cupboard."

"What do you know about it, you prying beast?" screamed the woman.

It appeared that Andrew knew everything there was to know about it. Andrew had made it his business to find out. He had watched her in the garden with her charges, he had taken the opportunity of sawing off the dead branches of the copper beech on the lawn to watch her in the nursery. He had seen the frequent use of the dark mixture in the bottle and its immediate effect.

The woman screamed abuse at him and at Vicky.

"Taking a gardener's word against mine. . . . Prying and poking. . . . Queer sort of house where the gardener says what's to be done and what isn't."

The bottle was sent to the doctor and found to contain a dangerous percentage of narcotic. The children were questioned, and it became clear that the woman had terrified them by stories of goblins and ghosts and had punished them by imprisonment in a small dark cupboard in the passage just outside the nursery.

She was packed off that afternoon, still abusing Vicky.

Vicky told Philip about it when he came in. He was much concerned, for he was tender-hearted and could not endure the thought of suffering.

"Poor little things!" he said. "What a good thing you found out!"

"I didn't, I'm afraid," she said ruefully. "Andrew did."

"Andrew? The gardener?"

"Yes."

"What the devil business is it of his?" he said, half amused.

Vicky stared at him, amazed that he should not realise how vitally important to Andrew was the well-being of her children. But it was something she could not explain or even understand. It just existed, like the sun or the moon or the rocks or the trees, without any reason.

The incident brought her back sharply to ordinary life. She felt deeply ashamed of having left her children for so long to the unsupervised care of a hireling.

She engaged a young girl, and set to work to train her, taking her share in the work of the nursery, ordering her household again—businesslike, abstracted, remote.

Philip sulked and raged. His playmate had suddenly left him. He hated the method and routine that she now tried to impose on him. He would come in an hour late for lunch, and fly into a rage because the meal was tepid or burnt.

"I'm sorry. They tried to keep it hot. We have lunch at one, Philip. . . . I don't care, we *must* keep to regular hours. The work of the house would never get done if we didn't."

"Damn the work of the house!" he exploded.

"Well, there are the children to be considered. They must have their midday meal regularly, and you can't expect the cook to prepare two hot midday meals at two different times."

It enraged him when she seemed to put the children before him.

"My God, Vicky!" he would shout. "I won't be treated like a nonentity in my own house."

She would reason with him patiently, as though he were a fractious child.

"I'm not treating you like a nonentity, Philip," she would say, "but a house *must* be run to regular hours. One can't just do things when one feels like it."

She had a quiet persistence that infuriated him. He called her obstinate and pigheaded. She learnt to avoid the sentence "I must put the children first," as it was to him as the proverbial red rag to a bull. His anger wearied her, but didn't frighten her any more.

Despite all her persuasions, he refused to go out on his

photographic expeditions without her. He attempted some camera studies of the children, but they wouldn't keep still and he lost his temper with them and they fled from him in tears.

He was so restless and irritable that Vicky wished he would go back to London, or on one of his aimless journeys abroad. Instead, he began to spend his time at Morton Manor, where one of Lady Sybil's famous house-parties was in progress. Vicky supposed that he found some attraction there, but felt such relief in his absence that she did not worry much about it. Beauty drew Philip like a magnet. He had no power of resistance against it. The affairs generally ended in the same way. The woman would begin to presume on his admiration, to adopt a possessive attitude towards him, and, as the faintest shadow of possessiveness enraged and terrified him, he would bring matters to an abrupt conclusion.

Andrew was looking tired, his face white and drawn. The little boy in the jasmine-covered cottage had whooping-cough, and there was little sleep for either Andrew or Ellen.

Vicky sent down everything the doctor ordered and asked Andrew about him anxiously every morning.

Philip was suddenly in good spirits again. Lady Sybil's house-party was getting up some private theatricals, and he was to take the chief part. Vicky had been asked to join the cast, too, but had refused on the score of her household duties. There was evidently no special feminine attraction at the Manor, after all, but Philip had thrown himself heart and soul into the new interest, letting all his others go. He was in a state of childish excitement, refusing to tell Vicky anything about the performance. "You'll see it on the night," he said. "I want it to be a surprise."

Lady Sybil was giving a dinner-party before the play, and Philip was anxious that Vicky should outshine all the other guests. He insisted on taking her to London to buy a new dress—white satin veiled in cobwebby white lace with a long train. Philip always liked her best in white. He even wanted to have a hairdresser from London to do her hair, but Vicky laughingly refused, and indeed her hair, with its soft natural waves and golden sheen, needed no artificial aid. Philip himself supervised the twisting of the loose coils at the back of her head, then, the process completed, held her at arm's length.

"You'll knock them all into the middle of next week, sweetheart," he said exultantly. "I'm so proud of you."

"Oh, Philip! Just because I look nice?"

"No, of course not. But you look wonderful. I've got you the best seat in the hall. Specially reserved it for you."

He was as eager as a child for her to see and acclaim his performance and excited at the prospect of showing himself in public by the side of her golden beauty. His love and pride in her touched her deeply, as it always did.

There was a knock at the door, and a housemaid entered.

"Please'm, Andrew would like to speak to you. He's at the side door."

"Damn the fellow!" exploded Philip. "What the devil does he want? Tell him to go to hell with his cabbages or potatoes or whatever it is."

"I won't be a minute, darling," said Vicky reassuringly, and, slipping a shawl over her shoulders, went out, radiant in the shimmering white satin.

Andrew stood at the side door. He looked small and shabby, his face white beneath the day's accumulation of grime.

"Do you mind if I go now, Miss Vicky," he said in a low toneless voice, "without finishing my time? I want to get back to the boy. Ellen's wore out."

"Is he worse, Andrew?" said Vicky anxiously.

He nodded, and his mouth twisted slightly.

"Yes, Miss Vicky. I've just had word. They say he's goin'."

She caught her breath sharply.

"Andrew! He's not. I'll come. I'll come at once. They said Noel was going, but I pulled him round. Go to Ellen and tell her I'm coming."

He looked at her in dull surprise.

"You can't, Miss Vicky. Not to-night. You're going out."

"Of course I can. Go to Ellen, Andrew. I'll be over there in a few minutes."

She ran up to her bedroom and began pulling off her dress. Philip stared at her.

"What on earth——?" he began.

"I'm sorry, Philip," she said breathlessly. "I can't come. I've got to go to Andrew. His little boy's worse and Ellen's done up. I must go. I shan't be back to-night. . . . Philip, I'm *sorry*. I can't help it. What else can I do? I know I can pull him through. I pulled Noel through. I won't let him die. . . . Philip, do stop *shouting* like that. I've said I'm sorry. I can't help it, I tell you. I can't let Andrew's child——" She had dragged her everyday dress over her head now. "I can't stop to do it up. Where's my cape?"

She flung it on, snatched up a hat, and ran out. Philip's anger pursued her loudly down the stairs. She ran all the way to the cottage.

Chapter Eighteen

SHE swept into the cottage like a breath of new life, flung off her cape and hat without a word, and took the child from Ellen's aching arms. She sat all night holding him on her knee, her eyes fixed on him, willing life and health back into him, and toward dawn the paroxysms grew less violent, and in the end he fell into a quiet sleep. The doctor was surprised to find him alive the next morning. In a few days he was convalescent.

When she returned home Philip was silent and sulky. Then his sulkiness left him and he became puzzled. Vicky's relations with Andrew had puzzled him from the beginning.

"I'd understand it if you were in love with the fellow," he said. "I've known lots of women who've fallen in love with good-looking men-servants, but God knows he's not good-looking, and even I know you aren't in love with him. What is it, then?"

"I don't know," said Vicky. "It's just that—he's Andrew."

She asked Philip how the play had gone, but he would tell her nothing about it. He went to London the next day, and Vicky returned to the beloved jog-trot routine of her household.

As the children grew out of babyhood their different characters began to develop.

Lionel was the benevolent autocrat of the nursery. He was a grave silent child, thoughtful beyond his years, oppressed by an ever-present sense of responsibility towards his younger brother and sisters. He was worried by Paula's wildness, by Noel's timidity, and Margery's lapses from truth. He made rules and insisted on their being kept, inflicting penalties on the transgressors. He was as strict with himself as with the others, as worried by his own failings as by theirs. They accepted his rule as a matter of course, seldom rebelling, pleased by his praise, abashed by his displeasure.

Part of the code was a passionate loyalty to Vicky.

"She's the queen," said Lionel, "and I'm the prime minister. You've got to do as I tell you and not let her be worried."

He was good-tempered and kind, exquisitely tender to the little ones, especially to Margery, the baby.

Philip teased him as "the bookworm," for he would spend hours reading, and loved to learn long pieces of poetry by heart even though he did not understand it. During the half-hour or so he stayed up after the others he would sit motionless at the nursery or schoolroom table, his head on his hands, his eyes fixed intently on the book. Vicky felt for him a deeper love than for any of the others. There seemed to be a strange understanding between them, and an elusive quality of protectiveness in his devotion to her set their relations apart from the ordinary relations of child and parent.

Paula was the only one who was like Vicky in appearance. She had her colouring and her spun gold hair. In temperament, however, she was more like Philip—wild and turbulent, flying into rages on the least provocation, tiring of every pursuit as soon as she had taken it up, difficult to manage, but adorable when in a good mood. She worshipped Lionel, who could quell her rages by a look, when all Vicky's reasoning and punishment had failed.

Noel was a nervous sensitive child, obsessed by imaginary terrors, afraid of the dark, painfully shy. One of his secret fears (implanted in him, perhaps, by the nurse whom Vicky had dismissed) was that the pleasant life of nursery and schoolroom was only a dream, and that he might wake up at any minute to find himself the child of cruel parents in the slums who would ill-treat him. When the others were punished it was Noel who was distressed far more than the culprits themselves. He was deeply attached to Paula, and dreaded for her the punishments she took so lightly, putting away her things for her when she left them about, trying in every way he could to cover the traces of her frequent misdemeanours. Paula on her side despised him, feeling personally humiliated by his tendency to tears.

Margery lived in a world of her own, a world of strange

excitements and odd taboos. As she ate her meals at the nursery table or took her walks with Nurse, she was a princess, a fairy, a goblin, or a king. . . . There were certain things she must or must not do—she didn't know why—or dread results would follow—she didn't know what. She must always go downstairs on the right-hand side of the staircase and up on the left; she must never step on one of the small red squares in the dining-room carpet; she must hop, not walk, along the paved path that enclosed the rose-garden; she must always dip the first finger of her right hand into the garden tank as she passed it. There were some things—the little statue of a faun that Philip had brought from Italy and that stood at the end of the lawn, the stump of a tree at the end of the shrubbery, the old pump just outside the kitchen door—that were hostile and had to be propitiated by a murmured spell as she passed them.

Her wildly untrue statements worried Lionel ("A witch comes in to see me every morning before the rest of you are awake." . . . "I was out all last night in the woods. I saw the fairies dancing there." . . . "I know the Lord Mayor of London quite well") and he evolved a secret sign for her to give him, unknown to the others, to tell him that she was "only 'magining." It fitted in with the spells and incantations that formed part of her secret life, and both were satisfied.

In appearance she was not unlike an elf herself, with her mop of thick red curls and her pale freckled pointed face.

The nursery was now under the nominal charge of a large kind-hearted, good-natured Irishwoman called Biddy, who looked after the children's physical well-being meticulously, but otherwise left them pretty much to their own devices.

It was Lionel who made himself responsible for the discipline of the nursery, Lionel from whose word there was no appeal.

Andrew, of course, played an important part in their lives. They followed him about the garden, riding in the wheelbarrow, "helping" him push the mower, crowding into the greenhouse to watch him at his work, each tending a small garden under his direction.

They would run out from nursery lessons, calling "Andrew! Andrew!" till they found him.

They loved to be given little tasks and would dig with small spades in the borders, ply their small wooden carts full of grass cuttings from lawn to rubbish heap, water the plants (and themselves) with their miniature watering-cans.

"We've been helping Andrew," they would say proudly at lunch.

Philip had given them a pony, and Andrew taught them all to ride. He was as silent as ever, and they were immensely proud of his rare words of commendation.

Vicky began to play her part again in the small activities of the neighbourhood. Mabs Abbot had obtained a post on the staff of a girls' boarding-school in the North, but after one term her engagement to Walter Pearson was announced. Having decided to marry him, she decided at the same time to endow him with all the qualities of her dream lover and bored her friends and acquaintances with descriptions of his virtues and good looks, for she now apparently actually saw him with a chin and an average-sized nose. She referred to him as "distinguished-looking."

They were married in Six Elms Church, then went to live in Devonshire, but they frequently came over to stay at the Vicarage with their little girl Elaine—a tiny creature, so delicate and fairy-like as hardly to seem real.

The Vicar had died suddenly two years ago, and the distant cousin, in whose gift the living was, had given it to Roger, then a curate in an East End parish. Roger slipped easily and naturally into his father's rut, pottering about the garden, preparing his sermons in the shabby comfortable book-lined study. He was retiring and absent-minded—more, indeed, like a middle-aged man than a youth—but he was popular in the neighbourhood, and Vicky's children were devoted to him, glad of any excuse to run over to the Vicarage and invade him in his study.

Mrs. Abbot had grieved sincerely for her husband's death, but it had made little actual difference in her life, for she fussed round Roger as she had fussed round her husband, and still looked forward eagerly to all the parish functions.

Mark had, for the last few years, been "bear leading" a slightly subnormal aristocrat on the Continent, and Roger was rather worried about it. He was staying at the best hotels, learning expensive tastes, and as an employment it seemed something of a blind alley.

Mark, however, was, as usual, completely satisfied with himself, his occupation, and his way of life.

The first incident to upset the even tenor of Vicky's life was Celia's engagement. She had gone to stay with a school friend and had written home after a fortnight to announce her engagement to her friend's eldest brother. He was coming home with her at the end of her visit, and she wrote to Vicky to ask if she could bring him to the Hall the next day, which would be Paula's birthday. He was a doctor, she said, with a good practice, and they hoped to be married quite soon. . . .

Paula woke up early, ran to Vicky's bedroom, and took a flying leap onto the bed. She would not have dared to do that, of course, if Philip had been at home, but Philip was in Egypt and not expected back for several months.

"It's my birthday, Mummy," she shouted. "I'm seven."

Vicky looked up, her golden hair rumpled, her blue eyes blinking sleepily.

"Oh, darling! So it is. I'm so sleepy I can't remember anything. Don't sit on my tummy. I can't breathe."

Paula bounced up and down, and Vicky began to tickle her. The two of them tumbled about in the bed, laughing, wrestling. They looked ridiculously alike. . . .

"You haven't said Many Happy Returns," said Paula reproachfully.

"I'm so sorry," said Vicky. "Many Happy Returns, darling."

"Can I start looking now?"

"Get dressed first, then you can."

On the children's birthdays Vicky would hide their presents all over the house, and they had to hunt for them. It was part of the nursery tradition. Because Vicky's own childhood had contained so little of the usual pageantry of childhood, she treasured it in the case of her children—the Easter eggs, the Christmas tree, the

November fireworks and bonfire, the New Year gifts, the culminating ceremony of the Birthday. With her children Vicky seemed to relive her own childhood, remoulding it to serenity, surrounding it with love. ... For her children she now reserved that gaiety that had once so delighted Philip. She would enter into their games as zestfully as if she had been one of them. She had little intimate jokes with each, played foolish little tricks on them and they on her. Often she would put small presents, elaborately wrapped up, under their pillows so that they should find them when they went to bed. She was the—always appreciative—audience of their nursery plays, the reading public of the nursery magazines that Lionel edited, and to which they all contributed. When they had anything serious to communicate to her they would write a note and leave it on her dressing-table. These notes were generally in the nature of ultimatums and Vicky always acceded to the demand. "Please, Mummy, we think it's time Noel went into proper boys' suits."—"Please, Mummy, may we not have sago so often? We don't like it."—"Please, Mummy, will you send Cook away? She makes Katie [the kitchen-maid] cry."

The last had caused great trouble, as that particular cook was the best they had ever had, and Philip was furious when he learnt why Vicky had dismissed her.

Paula ran back to her room and struggled into her garments, pulling her petticoats over her head and not bothering to button them up. The blue drill sailor suit was difficult to get into. The white front, embroidered with its dark blue anchor, had to be slipped over her head, and its tapes tied round her chest. The same had to be done with the collar, then came the cord with the whistle that went into her pocket.

The others were awake now, crowding round her and thrusting their presents upon her. Then they trooped, breathless and laughing, into the dining-room.

They had breakfast with Vicky when Philip wasn't at home. Philip did not object to their presence at breakfast, but his uncertain temper made things difficult. He would laugh at them one morning as they wrote their names in treacle on their porridge, even inspiring the addition of dots and dashes, and the next morning be angry with them for doing it.

Paula was his favourite, and even she was afraid of him.

Most of the children of the neighbourhood had been invited to the party. Mabs happened to be staying at the Vicarage and arrived with Elaine, well wrapped in shawls and chest protector, for Mabs was a firm believer in the harmful effect of fresh air. She unwrapped her carefully before the fire like a small porcelain doll, combed out the ash-blonde hair, and arranged the large pink hair-ribbon and the elaborate pink tulle frock.

Celia swept in tumultuously, flinging off her cloak, scattering her parcels around her, snatching up Paula to kiss her, rushing at Vicky, then at all the others, picking up her parcels and thrusting them into their hands. . . . So boisterous was her entrance that for a few minutes no one noticed the man who stood in the doorway behind her, looking about him.

Then Vicky turned and their eyes met across the crowded room under the strings of paper-chains that Lionel and Andrew had put up the night before.

"Celia . . ." Vicky reminded her gently.

"Oh, darling, I'm sorry," said Celia breathlessly, "but it's so lovely to see them all again. This is Hubert." She smiled at her lover. "The children might as well start calling him Uncle straight away, mightn't they?"

The children accepted him joyfully and pulled him across the room to look at Paula's presents, but his eyes still followed Vicky as she moved to and fro among her little guests.

Vicky, on her side, watched him with covert interest. He had a thin keen face with a good-humoured expression, and he looked much older than Celia. Vicky decided that he would be an asset to the family. He would make a pleasant brother-in-law and a delightful uncle. Already Margery was on his knee and Paula hanging over his shoulder.

"Isn't it *lovely*!" said Noel earnestly. "I've always wanted an uncle."

They surged into the dining-room for tea, and took their places round the table, decorated with fairy lamps and piles of crackers.

Noel threw a slightly apprehensive glance at the latter, afraid of betraying his terror of them when the moment came for the bangs. Lionel, however, always allowed him to open his own without pulling it. . . .

Vicky glanced round the table with pride. What darlings they looked—Paula and Margery in their white muslin party frocks and blue sashes, Lionel and Noel in black velvet knickers and white silk blouses! How much nicer they looked than that overdressed little doll of Mabs'!

The party was being a success. The children were laughing and chattering, and the jellies and blancmanges and iced biscuits and cakes were disappearing fast. There was a burst of laughter as "Uncle Hubert" pretended to be taken in by the "poached eggs on toast," which were really stewed apricots and whipped cream on little squares of sponge-cake.

Celia's eyes grew soft and dreamy as they rested on him. She was radiantly happy and in love. But, when the table was cleared and the games began—Blind-man's-buff, Nuts in May, London Bridge is Falling Down—it was Vicky to whom the newcomer's eyes turned as if against their will—Vicky, her golden hair piled high on her head, her full skirt swaying from her slender waist, as she moved about, directing the games.

Celia followed his eyes, and her happiness deepened till it was almost intolerable. The two beings whom she loved best in all the world. . . . She had hoped so desperately that they would like each other, and now she knew they did.

"Let's play Turn the Trencher," Noel was shouting.

He hadn't even flinched when the crackers were pulled at tea, and Lionel had thrown him a glance of approval. He was feeling brave and big and a little above himself.

Margery, too, was happy, but so quiet that Hubert whispered to Vicky, "She's very shy, isn't she?" and Vicky said, "No, she isn't really shy . . ."; for Vicky knew that Margery had brought a lot of guests of her own to the party—goblins and fairies and princesses and witches—and was busy looking after them.

Paula was dancing, singing, darting about everywhere like a piece of quicksilver. She was wildly, exultantly happy. The table was covered with the presents the guests had brought her. Uncle Hubert had carried her round the room on his shoulder. Auntie Celia had chosen her in every one of the choosing games. . . . It was the loveliest birthday she had ever had in her life.

Mabs was rather sulky because there were evidently to be no performances of any kind by the guests. Elaine could say a little piece and do a little dance, holding out the pink tulle skirts, and Mabs had rehearsed her carefully this morning so that she should do her credit and outshine all the others, and she naturally felt a little annoyed with Vicky for so firmly vetoing the suggestion.

"Jealous," she said to herself. "Probably hers can't do anything," and the reflection brought a certain amount of comfort.

Nurses and mothers began to arrive and to wrap their charges in shawls and cloaks. Carriages drew up at the door. . . . Biddy came down for the children. ("They've all been as good as gold," said Vicky. "Bless their little hearts," said Biddy.)

Vicky and Celia and Hubert, left alone, set to work to clear up the disorder, moving the furniture back into its place, picking up the papers dropped from the crackers, laughing as they went over episodes of the afternoon, and remembered Mabs' affronted expression when she learnt that Elaine was not to dance or recite.

Celia was ordering her fiancé about with a charming air of proprietorship. She looked prettier than Vicky had ever seen her, and had obviously taken more pains with her appearance than she usually did.

Then they went upstairs to say good night to the children and tuck them up, and Hubert sat on Margery's bed, telling her stories about a gnome whom (he said) he had met in Ireland the year before. She listened entranced, her hands clasped round her ankles, her chin on her knees. . . .

They shouted for him from room to room, "Uncle Hubert, come to *me*."

Celia squeezed Vicky's hand, her brown eyes shining, and Vicky felt a sudden compunction that she didn't quite understand.

After that, Hubert and Celia came over every day. The children adored him. He went for walks with them, played games with them, and took them on the lake in the boat (the last a great treat as the children were not allowed to go near the lake alone).

It was late May, and the fields were gay with buttercups, the woods with bluebells, the hedges with the delicate lacy flowers of the corn parsley. In the orchards sheep drowsed beneath a roof of apple blossom. In the gardens the air was sweet with the scent of wallflowers and sweet-briar, clamorous everywhere with the song of the birds.

Andrew moved about among his borders, where flaming tulips rose from a sea of forget-me-nots. The hawthorns were not yet in bloom, but their greenness was as sharp and vivid as a sword.

Through the sunny and unclouded days the children ranged the countryside with the beloved new uncle.

Auntie Celia, their old favourite, was deposed from her supremacy, and even Biddy grew a little jealous.

"You and your Uncle Hubert!" she said.

"He'll make a lovely father, won't he?" said Celia.

But it was not to Celia that he turned his quick amused glance when Noel got his words muddled up as he sometimes did, when Margery narrated one of her imaginary adventures; it was not Celia whom his eyes followed when the three of them were together.

Vicky tried to absent herself from these expeditions, but Celia would not allow it.

"You must come, dearest," she said. "It's not the same without you. Hubert likes you awfully. I can tell he does. ... Vicky, darling"—her voice grew tremulous—"you don't know what it means to me—you and Hubert taking to each other like this. It would have spoilt everything if you hadn't done."

Celia lived in a dream of happiness. Hubert loved her. He had told her so. She loved Hubert. They were going to be married. ... These facts surrounded her like a golden wall of rapture. She saw nothing beyond them. There was nothing to see beyond them. How could there be?

She was much quieter than she had been before her engagement—quiet, with a new deep serenity.

To Vicky the sunny days took on a nightmare quality. Every word, every look, revealed Hubert's love for her. It was almost incredible that Celia didn't see it. . . . She lay awake through the long warm nights, tossing from side to side and wondering how it was going to end.

It ended quite abruptly one afternoon when Hubert had been there a fortnight. He had come over alone, bringing a message that Celia had had to stay with her mother, who had slipped that morning and sprained her ankle. He went out into the garden with the children, then, finding that Vicky remained indoors, came back into the drawing-room to her. She was sitting by the window, her head bent over a little blue smock she was making for Margery. He sat watching her in silence.

She began to talk, quickly, nervously, saying anything that came into her head, trying to stave off the moment that she knew couldn't be staved off much longer.

Suddenly he caught her hand in his.

"Vicky, I can't go on pretending. I love you. You know I do."

"But Celia . . ." began Vicky, her heart beating wildly.

"She means nothing. I was mad. I wanted a wife and home and children, and I thought she'd make a good wife. I thought I loved her. But the moment I saw you I knew I didn't, knew I never had done. Vicky, my love for you is—my whole self. I haven't any existence apart from it. . . . I can't go on living without you. Vicky, you can't——"

"Celia loves you," said Vicky.

He waved the reminder aside impatiently.

"That doesn't matter," he said. "I'm sorry, but—it doesn't. I suppose I'm every kind of villain there is, but—Celia doesn't matter. Only you matter. Vicky, do you love me? For God's sake, tell me."

Vicky looked at the dark narrow face, at the kindness and sincerity and humour of the grey eyes, the firmness of the finely moulded lips, and was conscious of a pang of regret. He was the husband of every woman's dreams—tender, patient, protective. One could always feel safe with him. . . . But it was too late. And—she didn't love him. It was Philip—unreliable, blustering, incalculable, faithless—whom she loved and would love for ever with all her soul and body.

She shook her head.

"I'm sorry . . ." she said.

He went out.

She heard him telling the children that he couldn't stay, that he had to go back at once to Auntie Celia.

The next day Celia came over. Her face was white and drawn.

"Hubert's gone home, Vicky," she said.

"Why?" asked Vicky, aware that her voice sounded forced and unnatural.

"He—we broke off the engagement last night."

Then the children called her and she went up to the nursery and played with them noisily all afternoon.

Neither she nor Vicky ever made any other reference to the affair.

Chapter Nineteen

THERE was an air of bustle and activity over the Hall, particularly the nursery and schoolroom. Lionel and Noel were coming back from school to-day, and Paula and Margery were busy hanging up the decorations—the flags, the festoons, the "Welcome Homes"—that were part of the day's ceremony.

Before going to school the two boys had had daily lessons from Roger at the Vicarage. Roger, despite his dreaminess, was an excellent teacher and had a knack of getting on with children. Then Lionel went to school, and Noel fretted for him so much that he was allowed to join him the next term. Noel, striving ever to mould himself on Lionel, was already less timid and sensitive, his life so completely filled by a schoolboy's normal interests that he had little time to brood over imaginary slights and unkindnesses as he had so often done at home.

They had all been deeply distressed when Lionel first went away, but it had made less difference than they had expected. While taking his full part in the school life, he managed still to organise the activities of the nursery at home, demanding regular reports of their doings, editing the magazine, and even carrying on their favourite "paper games" by correspondence.

Vicky had engaged a governess for Paula and Margery—an eager enthusiastic young person called Diana Everett, who was an ardent champion of the "New Woman" movement and aggressively masculine in dress and manner. Philip detested her, but she was conscientious and good-tempered and taught the children well, though she found them disappointing from the point of view of the Cause. Paula (now fourteen) was completely uninterested in her sex's wrongs, but deeply interested in the other sex, and ready instinctively to try to attract any member of it who entered her orbit, while Margery wept so bitterly over stories of sweated female labour that Vicky forbade Miss Everett to mention the subject to her again.

Margery, emerging from her childhood's world of dreams, was difficult and stormy tempered, given to fits of naughtiness, followed by fits of exaggerated despair and remorse. Paula was wild and intractable as ever, but with a sunny gaiety that forgot both offence and punishment as soon as they were over.

Miss Everett was only engaged for the term time and went home the day the boys came back from school. She never knew whether to be pleased or offended at this arrangement. It gave her three months' holiday in the year, for which her friends envied her, but, on the other hand, it prevented her having any influence over Lionel and Noel, and "the men of to-morrow" were, of course, vitally important to the Cause.

Paula and Margery were besieging Andrew in one of the greenhouses, begging for his potted fuchsias and heliotropes to put on the schoolroom window-sill.

"It's to make it look nice for Lionel and Noel," pleaded Paula. "Do let us have them, Andrew darling."

Philip was in London, and Vicky, who always found it difficult to reconcile his claims on her with the children's, was conscious of a half-guilty wish that he would not come home these holidays. He had spent a week at home last month and had been thrown by his horse on the first day of his visit and twisted his ankle. It had only been a slight sprain, but pain of any sort terrified him, and he had groaned aloud all night, so that neither of them could sleep. Vicky had tried to be sympathetic, but it had been impossible to keep up indefinitely the excessive sympathy he demanded—especially when she had to go about her usual household duties in the morning.

"My God, Vicky!" he had moaned. "Are you made of *stone*? Don't you care *how* much I suffer?"

He had been even more difficult when Noel had pneumonia last year. He had been distracted by anxiety for the child, unable to remain still for a moment, pacing the corridors, bursting noisily into the sick-room with armfuls of fruit and sweets and toys, pestering the child continually with questions as to how he felt. When told that his presence upset the invalid and asked to keep away from him, he had, of course, been desperately hurt. . . .

Andrew came across the lawn to where Vicky sat in a basket-chair busy with her mending, his impassive freckled face relaxed into a half smile.

"They'll leave me nothing in my greenhouses before they've finished, Miss Vicky," he said (even Philip had now given up trying to break him of the "Miss Vicky"), and added, "What time are you expecting them?"

"The 3.15. We're all going to the station. You'll fetch their luggage in the cart, won't you, Andrew? Any time will do. They'll have their handbags with their night things."

"I'll go after tea," he said. "I've got the gooseberries and currant bushes to prune, but Bill can come up and help me do that to-morrow."

"What are you going to do with Bill when he leaves school, Andrew?" said Vicky. "Would you like him to come here?"

"Well, Miss Vicky, George—my brother, you know—wants to take him into his bicycle shop, and the boy's keen to go. All for machinery, boys are, nowadays—bicycles and such-like."

The solemn little boy had done well for himself, and now had a bicycle shop of his own in Fenton. Vicky occasionally saw him in the village. He still looked very solemn, but there was a prosperous air about him. He belonged to a different class from Andrew. He was an employer of labour, a man with a stake in the country.

"I suppose Ellen wants him to go there?" said Vicky.

Ellen's and Andrew's marriage had turned out happily. Ellen was as quiet and gentle as ever, Andrew as uncommunicative, but there was a bond of understanding between them that went deeper than words.

"Yes," said Andrew. "She says she'd like the boy to come to you, but one must think of what's for his good."

"I know . . ." said Vicky.

"Andrew," called Paula. "Do come and help us. We can't get the tennis net right."

Andrew went off to them with his slow clumsy gait.

There was a sudden jangle of a bicycle bell and Celia swept up the drive.

Hubert had passed completely out of Celia's life, and no other suitor had appeared, and now at twenty-eight she seemed to have settled down into the traditional spinster's rut. She was very bright and energetic and helpful, and spent her time running the various parish organisations and acting as a sort of unofficial curate to Roger. The local gossips often put their heads together and wondered if anything would come of it, but even the sharpest-eyed of them had failed as yet to discover anything lover-like in the demeanour of either.

Celia laughed just a little too much and too often, and could talk of nothing but her parish work, and Vicky—still with the old familiar sense of compunction—found her rather boring.

As the children emerged from childhood, Celia became less popular with them. Her boisterousness embarrassed them, and she continued to treat them as if they were small children. They had begun to avoid her, making little grimaces at the mention of her name. A visit to Ivy Lodge to have tea with Auntie Celia was no longer a nursery treat. Paula even mimicked her vivacious, faintly spinsterish manner.

She propped her bicycle against the terrace balustrade, took a parcel from the basket carrier on the handle-bars, and came down the steps to Vicky.

"Hallo, darling," she said, kissing her exuberantly. "Isn't it terribly thrilling? I hardly slept a wink last night, I was so excited. When are they coming? The 3.15, isn't it?"

"Yes," said Vicky, thinking that Celia's absorption in the young nieces and nephews who treated her so cavalierly was rather pathetic.

Celia was tearing the brown paper from the parcel she was carrying.

"I brought a few sweets for them and these little dolls for the girls and the pencils for the boys. I'll just pop up and put them under their pillows."

Vicky couldn't, of course, tell her that to the children her appropriating Vicky's habit of putting little presents under their pillows was a sort of desecration and made them furious. In any case both Paula and Margery had long ago given up playing with dolls.

"You'll all be back for tea, of course?" went on Celia, with a studied carelessness that had a wistful note behind it.

Celia used to be asked to tea on the first day of the holidays as a matter of course, but lately the children had insisted that she shouldn't be.

"*Not* Auntie Celia," they groaned. "She spoils everything. She's such an old ass."

So Vicky, feeling self-conscious and guilty, had not asked her. But she couldn't refuse the pleading in her eyes, especially with her presents scattered on the grass at their feet.

"You'll come to tea, dear, won't you?" she said, as carelessly as Celia, steeling herself to endure the children's reproaches. ("Oh, Mummy, why *did* you? It's all spoilt now.")

Everything in Celia seemed to bubble up in delight.

"Of course, I'd *love* to, darling. How *sweet* of you! I'll settle Mama for her nap, then I'll come straight over, shall I?"

"How is Mama?"

"Much better. It's one of her good days, to-day."

Mrs. Carothers was growing slightly—very slightly—senile. On her good days she was quite normal. On her bad ones she would ask where she was several times an hour and mistake Celia for an afternoon caller, entertaining her with the conversational topics of twenty years ago.

"What are they doing to-morrow?" went on Celia. "Would they like to come over to Ivy Lodge to tea?"

"I'm sure they'd have loved to," said Vicky insincerely, "but Roger's asked them to the Vicarage."

"Perhaps they'll come to Ivy Lodge another day, then. Mabs is at the Vicarage, isn't she?"

"Yes. And Mark and his wife. Mrs. Abbot's rushed off her feet and simply adoring it."

"It's rather a pity they've come just now, because it's a very busy week for Roger with the scouts going into camp on Monday. However—I must go and find the poppets. Where are they?"

She always called Paula and Margery "the poppets," much to their disgust.

"Somewhere in the garden, I think," said Vicky. "Worrying the life out of Andrew."

"I'll go and find them."

Celia ran off towards the greenhouses calling "Poppets! Poppets!" as she ran.

Vicky slowly folded up her mending and put it away in her basket. She had a hundred household matters to see to, and it would be her last chance of seeing to them in peace for a month. The children couldn't bear her not to be with them even on the smallest expeditions. ("Oh, do come, Mummy. Never mind about the old house. It won't be any fun at all without you.")

As she went up the terrace steps, she heard Celia's voice raised in a peal of laughter, in which Paula and Margery joined somewhat half-heartedly.

The smile faded from her lips. If it hadn't been for her, Celia would perhaps have had children of her own to play with. ...

The Vicarage, usually so quiet, was full of life and activity. Mabs and Walter and Elaine were there, as well as Mark and Helen. Mark had married a cousin of the subnormal aristocrat and held now a lucrative post in the city. He was a good-looking man, his heaviness of build redeemed by his height and the perfection of his tailoring. His old absorption in sport had resolved itself into an occasional game of golf at the week-end, and the bombastic manner of his boyhood had grown into a pleasant geniality that had nothing of conceit in it.

His wife was a slender exquisite creature, radiantly fair but with a Chinese cast of countenance that gave a faintly exotic impression. The two of them seemed to bring the atmosphere of another world into the quiet Vicarage—a sophisticated world of wealth and fashion, of seasons in London and holidays on the Riviera.

Mrs. Abbot was flustered and delighted. She always found it difficult to believe that this handsome man of the world was her son, but the new daughter-in-law removed him yet further from the realms of credibility.

Roger was still slightly worried by Mark's "worldliness," and Mark by Roger's complete sinking into their father's rut, but, beneath the changes that had separated them, their old affection was as strong as ever.

Mabs was secretly chagrined by the elegance of her new sister-in-law. She was so exactly the sort of person that Mabs would have liked to be herself, and knew she wasn't. She was slightly aggressive in manner, making much of Walter and putting on what Philip called her "young mother airs" with Elaine.

Elaine was fulfilling her baby promise of prettiness, though her delicate complexion, ash-blonde hair, china blue eyes, and elaborate little frocks still suggested one of the more expensive kinds of doll. Despite her prettiness, there was an elusive likeness to Walter about her that confirmed Mabs in her determination to regard Walter as a handsome man.

Walter jumped up and down continually—moving Mabs' chair out of the sun, going indoors to fetch snapshots, sweets, cigarettes, toys for Elaine, cushions for everyone. With his pointed nose and amiable foolish expression, he reminded Vicky of a fox-terrier running joyously after sticks. He was as devoted to Mabs as ever and felt toward Elaine as a man might feel to an angel who has deigned to form part of his household. It gave him an indescribable feeling of elation to revisit the scenes of a courtship that had seemed so hopeless as the husband of Mabs and father of Elaine.

The children played on the lawn, and Vicky sat with the grown-ups on the verandah. Roger and Mark talked happily and affectionately of old times, and Helen sat with her slender white hands crossed on her lap, her golden head resting on the back of her chair, occasionally stifling a yawn and glancing surreptitiously at her watch.

Mrs. Abbot had invited Dorothea Milner to tea, but, to the relief of everyone except Mrs. Abbot, she had not been able to come. She was now fired by an enthusiasm for nursing and insisted on attending her father's patients, making up their medicines and dressing their wounds and fractures. She had already lost her father several important patients, and the village nurse had given notice three times in one week.

Mrs. Abbot was in the kitchen with Violet, cutting bread and butter at the big wooden table. Violet had grown into a large robust woman with a gift for looking busy when she was doing nothing at all. She was now making great play with a few cups and a tray and leaving Mrs. Abbot, as usual, to do the real work.

The tea-bell rang and the children came running in from the garden. Lionel held Elaine protectively by the hand. She had fallen and grazed her knee, and he had comforted her and dried her tears. She refused to be separated from him.

"I want to sit next to Lionel," she pleaded when places were assigned for tea.

Before they went home plans were made for a picnic in the wood the next day.

"We'll all go in the wagonette and take our tea," said Vicky.

"Can I sit next to Lionel in the wagonette, please?" Elaine asked anxiously.

"What a soppy kid!" said Paula scornfully as they went home.

"Oh, I don't know," said Lionel tolerantly.

"Did you think she was pretty?" said Margery, who, like Paula, had resented the newcomer's appropriation of Lionel.

"Yes," said Lionel. "Didn't you?"

"No, not a bit," said Paula and Margery simultaneously.

The next week Philip came home. He arrived late one night and went straight to bed. He was still asleep when Vicky got up the next morning and did not appear till about eleven, when he came onto the lawn where the children were playing, smiling genially, obviously in a good humour.

"Well," he said, "who's coming for a walk with me?"

There was a sudden silence, then Lionel said, "I will, Dad," but he said it just a second too late.

All Philip's good humour vanished. He was hurt and annoyed. They shouldn't have stood and looked at him guardedly like that. They should have run up to him in welcome, clustered round him with cries of "I'll come, Daddy." Instead, they had shrunk back as if afraid of him. He couldn't understand it. He was always thinking of them, always doing what he could for them. He had presents for all of them in his bag now, but he wouldn't bother to give them. He'd looked forward eagerly to his home-coming and now it was spoilt. . . .

Vicky followed him indoors and tried to coax him back into a good humour, but he was morose and sullen, and refused to go out to the children again.

After dinner, however, when the children had gone to bed, he forgot his grievances, and his good temper returned.

Vicky listened dreamily as he described the work he had done in London. She knew that it would be difficult to adjust his claims to the children's, but something of the old excitement had as usual swept over her at his return. Her love for him was ineradicable, interwoven in the very tissues of her being. Part of her still leapt in delight at sight and sound of him.

"I've brought some sketches I've done of the river to show you," he said. "They're in my portfolio. I'll get it."

He fetched the portfolio and handed her the sketches, one by one. They had the boldness, the originality, the sheer talent divorced from discipline that marked all his work. She realised as she looked at them what a fine artist he might have been.

"They're lovely, Philip," she said sincerely.

As he put them back a sketch fell out of the portfolio, and she picked it up to give it him. Then—she sat motionless looking at it. It was the painting of a woman with deep auburn hair, a white transparent skin, and grey-green eyes.

"Who's this, Philip?" she asked.

She spoke casually, for Philip could never see a beautiful woman without wanting to paint her, and his portfolios were full of sketches of them—finished, half-finished, just begun.

He took it from her quickly and put it back in the portfolio. His hands were trembling as he tied the strings and a faint dusky colour had crept into his cheeks.

"Just a friend," he muttered.

Vicky looked at him in surprise. Always before when she found a portrait of one of his "fair sitters" (as she called them in jest) he had expatiated at length on their charms, pointing out the beauty of colour, of feature, of contour. . . . She had never known him like this before. He had stood up and was putting the portfolio away, his back turned to her.

"Who is it, Philip?" she said again.

"Lilian Hindely," he answered shortly, and added, as if finally dismissing the subject, "You don't know her."

She realised suddenly that there had been a subtle difference in him ever since he came home. On the surface he had been as usual, but beneath the surface his spirit wandered in some dark region of torment where she could not reach it. . . . She sat in silence, gazing unseeingly in front of her. His other infidelities had, she knew, meant little. They had not touched his essential love of her. This was different.

"Philip . . ." she began, and stopped as he wheeled round, scowling, on the defensive, still darkly flushed. He could not bear, of course, to be questioned and examined. It would only drive him into one of his senseless tearing rages.

"Well?"

"Nothing," she said. She tried to speak lightly though her throat was dry. "I think I'll go to bed now."

Chapter Twenty

VICKY sat in the shade of the copper beech, a pile of mending on the table by her chair. The children were all out. They were generally out nowadays. Vicky spent a good deal of her time sitting alone in the house or garden, mending socks and household linen. She wore glasses for working and reading, and her hair had lost its golden sheen. She had been forty on her last birthday and, as she often said in half jest, was beginning to feel middle-aged.

Lionel's engagement to Elaine had been announced last month, though Lionel, who was a medical student at Guy's, would not be able to marry for some years. The childish attraction between the two that had begun at the Vicarage on the day when Lionel had consoled her for her grazed knee had grown with their growth. Elaine had continued to adore Lionel throughout her childhood, writing inky badly spelt letters to him from school, and always insisting on coming to stay with Uncle Roger during the holidays so that she could see her idol.

Lionel had taken her under his wing with the rest of his flock, including her in the old nursery activities that were still carried on by post when the children were separated.

As the childhood bonds between the brothers and sisters loosened, however, the bond uniting Lionel and Elaine had become firmer, and their first relationship of worship on Elaine's side and grave protectiveness on Lionel's ripened into a deep friendship.

Elaine, now eighteen, was lovely—ash-blonde hair, blue eyes, and a skin of transparent fairness, and Mabs had seen to it that she had met plenty of eligible young men. She had a great many admirers and had already received several proposals, but no one existed for her beside Lionel. He coloured her every thought and action. Lionel, on his side, was conservative, shy of forming new friendships and interests, clinging to old ties and associations. He did not know exactly when the tenderness for the child had turned into love for the woman, but the engagement had grown so naturally out of their friendship that it seemed to mark no particular stage of it. For years now neither of them had contemplated any future apart from the other. Mabs, of course, was not pleased, and would describe at length to Vicky Elaine's other "chances"—all much superior to the "chance" represented by Lionel—where-upon Vicky would indignantly enlarge on Lionel's virtues and prospects, implying that even Elaine was not good enough for him.

("What an old fool I am!" she would say to herself as she did so. "Why do I always rise? Why don't I just let her talk? What a ghastly pair of mothers-in-law we shall make—always harring and jarring!")

She had been to the Vicarage yesterday and had steeled herself to endure another attack from Mabs, but it happened that Mark had come over for the week-end, and so the atmosphere was friendly and genial. Mark, who was fond of both Lionel and Elaine, was delighted by the match, and Mabs contented herself by sighing deeply whenever Lionel's name was mentioned.

Mark often ran down to the Vicarage for the week-end nowadays. He came alone, for he and Helen had separated the year before. They were on friendly terms and met occasionally at other people's houses, but their passion had long ago burnt itself out and there had never been any real basis for comradeship. Mark did not seem happier or unhappier since the separation. He lived behind a wall of sophisticated geniality. He was good-tempered, amusing, well-informed, always perfectly turned out, and an authority on food and drink. He still deplored the Vicarage *ménage*, saying that Roger had no palate at all, and that Violet's ideas began and ended with mince and rice pudding. He was, however, genuinely fond of his mother and brother (he was less fond of Mabs, who, he said, should have married a wife-beater, not the devoted Walter), and, since his separation from his wife, visited them much more frequently.

Vicky took up a pair of Paula's stockings from the mending-basket and shook her head, less over the large hole at the toe than over Paula herself.

Paula was nineteen now—as gay and wild and irresponsible as when she had been a child. She demanded constant change and excitement and became bored and irritable when nothing was going on. Amos Beverly had died two years ago, and the Manor, after standing empty for some time (Lady Sybil had removed to London), had been bought by a Mr. Allwood, a stockbroker, who brought with him a plump comfortable wife and a large family of high-spirited young people, with whom Paula was very friendly. They came over to the Hall or fetched her to the Manor almost every day.

Vicky was glad for her to have the new friends and interests, but felt secretly worried about her, and wished that she could fall in love with someone nice and steady, like Lionel, and settle down. She had a large number of boy friends, but they all seemed as wild and irresponsible as Paula herself.

Noel was at Oxford, very precious and aesthetic and dilettante. He edited a high-brow journal, wrote ultramodern poetry, wore soft collars and flowing ties, and spoke with a newly acquired drawl. The timid nervous little boy was still there, but well concealed.

Margery was at the boarding-school in Harrogate to which she and Paula had been sent when Miss Everett left to devote herself entirely to the Cause. She had inherited something of Philip's artistic talent and took little interest in any other study.

As the children grew older, a subtle change had taken place in their relations with Vicky. It had been, like most changes, so gradual that it had actually taken place before Vicky herself realised it. She no longer held the foremost position in their lives. They no longer wanted her to accompany them on all their expeditions, to take part in all their activities. They were embarrassed and disconcerted when she offered her company. They no longer needed her as guide and helper and object for their childish hero-worship, and as companions they preferred their own contemporaries. They stood to Vicky now in the relationship of adult to adult, and between them yawned the impassable gulf of a generation. They still loved her, but she had to learn to recede into the background of their lives, to be there when they needed her, and not when they didn't.

Their love, too, was no longer uncritical. They no longer accepted her as perfect. They found her, she knew, slightly old-fashioned. Her absorption in the house and insistence on its routine irritated them. ("Mother says we can't have the rehearsal in the dining-room to-morrow morning because the maids want to turn it out. Did you ever hear anything so ridiculous?")

It was strange to remember that only a few years ago they had refused to go anywhere, do anything, without her, that she had formed their whole world. Only Lionel was still as loving, as considerate, as ever, but his devotion was now given to Elaine, and Vicky sensed something of tolerance even in his attitude, something very far removed from the old unquestioning worship.

She was gradually learning to resign herself to it. They weren't hers any longer, but Philip was left. It was time for her and Philip to draw closer to each other. . . . They were growing old; there was nothing but loneliness ahead for either of them unless they drew closer to each other.

Her thoughts went back to the day when she had discovered the painting of Lilian Hindely among his sketches. Her fears had been justified. It had proved more than a passing infatuation. She would have known that from the change in Philip himself, even if kind friends and acquaintances had not taken the trouble to write to her from London describing the utter lack of restraint with which he was pursuing the affair. She knew, too, that he was not happy, that he had more than once tried to break with the woman, but always some irresistible attraction drew him back to her. He couldn't live without her, yet she made life intolerable for him.

It was as if she had been chosen by Fate to avenge all those other women whom his intolerance and fickleness had hurt so deeply.

Sad at heart, Vicky had watched the gradual change in him. The old fierce pride and independence had gone. The very rages that had been like tempests clearing the air, over almost as soon as they began, became sultry and vicious. His restlessness was brooding, tormented.

When he was at home he would sit for hours in silence, his fingers drumming on the arms of his chair, his eyes, hot and desperate, staring in front of him. In his anger now he no longer raved blindly, making wild and unfounded accusations for which he was immediately penitent. His insults were calculated, cruelly and deliberately designed to hurt. . . . He took no pleasure in his work. It was more than a year now since he had even touched canvas or sketching block. Vicky had never seen him the worse for drink before his infatuation for Mrs. Hindely, but it had happened with increasing frequency lately.

She roused herself from her day-dreams. It wasn't any use just thinking that Philip had changed. She was to blame for doing nothing to help him, for just sitting there waiting for him to come back to her. She had been so sure at first that he would come back to her, but he hadn't done, and she must face the fact now that he wouldn't, unless—

She took from her pocket the post card she had received from him that morning. He was coming over to-day. It was probably one of those swift visits when he sometimes stayed only an hour or so, driven there and driven away by his compelling restlessness. But—he'd never let her know before that he was coming. There must be something unusual about this visit.

And suddenly an explanation occurred to her. He had realised what she was realising—that old age lay before them, an old age that could be sweetened and lightened by their mutual affection and comradeship. He was wearying at last of his restlessness and philandering. He had at last decided to break with the woman who had been his evil genius for so long. He was turning again to Vicky, his wife. . . .

She stiffened her resolution. She would help him by every means in her power, bear with his restlessness and sudden gusts of temper, strive to interest and amuse him, give up for him her absorption in the house and garden, go where he wanted to go and do what he wanted to do. She would never again behave as she had done in the past—letting her pride and sensitiveness stand as a barrier between them.

He loved her still. He wanted to return to her. He was asking her help. Looking down at the post card with its few curt words, she wondered why she hadn't read at first sight its message of love, its cry for aid.

A heavy weight seemed to fall from her, and she looked forward eagerly into the future, seeing herself and Philip, the tempest and tumult of their youth over, finding peace and companionship together at last.

The children came running down the terrace steps, and flung themselves breathlessly on the grass at her feet. Elaine was with them and several of the young people from Morton Manor. Most of the girls wore light blouses with dark, trimly belted skirts, their hair done into neat buns beneath their shady straw hats. Elaine looked very smart and pretty in one of the new "motor hats," tied under her chin by a veil.

They had been rehearsing a play that Lionel was getting up, and they all talked at the same time, laughing, chaffing each other, beginning to tell Vicky about the rehearsal but interrupting each other continually, so that they never got to the end.

"And we met Auntie Celia free-wheeling gaily down the hill with parish magazines dropping from her carrier at every yard. She'd left a trail of them all the way from the Vicarage."

"Lionel went back to pick them up for her. The poor old dear was a bit flustered. She said it was one of Granny's bad days."

"Mummy, darling, may we go and forage in the larder? We want to take our lunch over to Lendale Rocks. It's the last week of Lionel's vac. and we want to celebrate wildly every day."

Vicky forgot everything else—even Philip—in the indignation of the careful housewife.

"But, Paula, it's nearly one. Cook's got the lunch on."

"Surely she can take it off," said Paula impatiently.

"Of course she can't."

"Then she can keep it and heat it up some time."

"Don't be ridiculous, Paula."

"It's not ridiculous. Anyway, cold meat's always useful, and what on earth do a few potatoes and a cabbage matter?"

"It's so inconsiderate," said Vicky. "You might make your plans earlier in the day, instead of suddenly springing a picnic lunch on me at this hour, when everything's in train for lunch indoors."

They looked at her in silence for a moment, and she sensed their youthful impatience with her "fussiness" and that faint hostility that it always brought with it.

"Darling, we're not springing a picnic lunch on you," said Paula in the tone in which one would reason with a fractious child. "You talk as if we were asking you to provide something elaborate. We're only asking if we can forage for something. We don't mind bread and cheese and fruit."

"But the lunch will be completely wasted."

"No more than if we'd eaten it, my pet," said Noel with his clear-cut drawl. "All food's wasted, anyway, when you come to think of it."

"And, darling," said Margery coaxingly, "it will be a good thing for us all to be out of the way when Daddy comes home, then if he's in a bad temper you can get him into a good one before we appear on the scene."

"That's all very well, Margery," said Vicky, "but about this lunch. . . ."

"We might be able to find something at the Vicarage," suggested Elaine.

"No, don't bother the Vicarage," said Vicky. "You can go and see what you can find in the larder, but don't take anything without asking Cook. She'll be furious anyway."

"No, she won't. We'll send Lionel in to break the news to her. She adores Lionel. She's never cross with him."

"If you really mind terribly, Mummy . . ." said Lionel, looking at her with loving anxiety.

She smiled at him. "No, it's all right. . . . Only," she returned to her perennial grievance, "you call me fussy for running the house properly and having things on time, but you wouldn't really like it if I didn't, though you think you would. I don't know how you can expect the maids to put up with it."

"Oh, darling, don't start that again," groaned Paula.

"You've said we could, anyway, haven't you?" said Margery, springing up. "And don't worry, sweetheart. We promise we'll make it all right with Cook. Come on."

"She'll probably give notice," said Vicky resignedly.

They went indoors in a laughing excited group.

Vicky looked after them, frowning slightly, but she didn't feel as ruffled as she would have felt ordinarily. Her thoughts had turned to Philip again. She would be so kind, so patient. He would never regret having come back to her. Why shouldn't they go abroad together again? In a week Lionel would be back at Guy's, Noel at Oxford, Margery at school. Paula could go and stay with the Allwoods.

The children came out again and crowded round her chair, showing her their spoils and laughing as they described the interview with Cook.

"She was wild at first, then Noel kissed her and began to polka round the kitchen with her, and we got a band with saucepans and trays and Elaine's pocket-comb in tissue paper, and she was laughing so much in the end that she could hardly speak. She's given us a steak and kidney pie and some custard cakes and bread and cheese and apples. Isn't she a sport? Don't worry about it, darling. She's quite forgiven us."

(Yes, thought Vicky, she's forgiven *you*, but she'll sulk with me for weeks.)

They went off gaily, carrying the picnic baskets, turning to wave and blow kisses to Vicky before they vanished from sight.

Paula lingered to pick a rose for her waistbelt, but, seeing Andrew coming towards her with a "Now, you leave them roses alone, Miss Paula" look on his face, tossed her head haughtily and went after the others. They all resented Andrew's way of treating them as if they were still small children and the garden his private property. They, on their side (except when they wanted his help in anything), would be cold and distant to him, trying to put him in his place by an exaggeration of youthful dignity that had no effect on him whatever.

The sound of their voices died away and Vicky leaned back in her chair again. The peace of the garden enclosed her, shut her in with the warm comforting thought of Philip.

After lunch she went to her bedroom and put on a dress of lilac-coloured muslin with a black velvet belt that Philip had once carelessly admired, and coiled her hair low in the nape of her neck as he liked to see it.

He arrived as soon as she had reached the drawing-room. She heard the sound of wheels on the gravel, and almost as soon as they stopped he burst into the room. His arrival was always dynamic, but he seemed driven now less by his own restlessness than by some ruthless force outside. She noticed again that the old suggestion of glorious freedom had gone from him. With his flaming hair and restlessness he used to remind her of a comet. Now he was like a dull smouldering fire.

She went forward to him, her hands outstretched.

"Philip . . ." she began.

He interrupted her, speaking quickly as if he had rehearsed the words and were repeating a lesson.

"I can't stay, Vicky. I've only come for a moment. . . . Vicky, I want you to divorce me. . . . Will you?"

The room swam before her eyes. She put her hand on a chair-back to steady herself.

"It's—Mrs. Hindely?" she said.

"Yes. . . ."

He averted his eyes from her face, not in pity or compunction, but just as he had always turned away from anything he found unpleasant or distressing.

"Philip . . ."

She wanted to plead with him, to tell him how she loved him, to show him the vision she had just had of an old age sweetened by their comradeship, but the words would not come.

"Will you?" he persisted.

She found words at last, halting, incoherent.

"But, Philip . . . if only . . . the children . . ."

He made a gesture of impatience.

"Will you, Vicky? I can't stand here all day arguing with you. Will you divorce me? It won't make any difference as far as you're concerned whether you do or not. I mean——"

"You mean—you won't—come back to me in any case?" she supplied.

"Yes. Oh, what's the use of talking about it? I want your answer."

She was aware of his restless anger rising against her.

"Will you divorce me?"

Again she tried to plead with him, but her throat was too dry. She could hardly see his face—angry, unhappy— through the mist that enveloped her.

"Yes, if you want me to," she said at last.

He was off almost at once, running down the steps, plunging into the waiting cab, disappearing round the bend of the drive.

Philip Lynnaker stepped onto the pavement from Mrs. Hindely's house in Bruton Street and stood looking about him dazedly. Then he began to walk away from the house, swaying slightly as he walked, colliding with any passer-by who did not get out of his way in time. They glanced at him with idle interest, thinking that he was drunk, but he wasn't drunk, though he heard nothing, saw nothing around him. All he saw was Lilian's scornful face, all he heard was her voice, as cruel as the sting of a lash.

"I don't care whether she divorces you or not. I've finished with you. Can't you understand that? Have I to put it in so many words? Haven't I shown you plainly enough . . . ?"

"But I thought it was because—You said you'd marry me if I could get her to divorce me. You promised."

"How long was that ago? Well, if I ever said it, I've changed my mind. I'm sick of you. Sick of you, I tell you. I never want to see you again. . . . I've stood your moods and jealousy and meanness till I can stand them no more. It's the end. I don't even hate you, you crazy fool. And now get out."

He had pleaded and raged, wept and grovelled. He had knelt

on the ground at her feet, and she had looked down at him and laughed.

"You fool!" she said again. "Are you blind or deaf? Do you want me to ring and have you thrown out? I am going to be married, but not to you. Can you understand that? Go back to your bread-and-butter miss, you dolt! She's all you're good for. And the next time you set foot in this house you'll be thrown out by the servants."

He had gone at last, and she had hurled after him the name of the man she was going to marry.

"D'you think I'd *look* at you now, you miserable fool? D'you think we haven't laughed at you together often enough?"

He had crept away like a whipped cur, groping blindly with his hands, half sobbing beneath his breath.

He didn't know where he was going till he found himself in the train on the way to Six Elms. He dimly remembered hearing the sound of his own voice asking for the ticket as if it were the voice of someone else. He was an automaton doing he didn't know what, he didn't know why. . . . He wondered dully if that was the way madness came.

His stunned senses began to awake slowly to life, and, at the memory of her scorn and laughter, shame and despair rushed over him in wave upon hot wave.

At Six Elms station he got out of the train and began to walk quickly in the direction of the Hall. He didn't know why he was going there, or what he was going to do when he got there, but he half ran through the village in his haste, as if the whip of her scorn still goaded him on.

In at the gate, up the long drive. . . . At the front door he stopped. No, he couldn't go in. He drew back and began to walk dazedly, unsteadily, along the terrace, down the steps, across the lawn to the lake. There he stood in the moonlight, looking down at the still water. . . . He couldn't live without her. His lust for her was like the craving of a sick man for his drug. He'd tried to break himself of it time after time, but he hadn't been able to. It was no use even trying any more. Already he was in torment—every nerve in his body aching for her.

He glanced towards the house, dark and silent in the shadow of the trees, its unlighted windows shining faintly in the moonlight. Vicky was there alone, thinking of him, waiting for him. Vicky with her gentleness, her serenity, her shy fastidiousness. The thought stirred only revulsion in him. Lilian had spoilt him for Vicky, for any decent woman. . . . And he couldn't live without her, her sweet rottenness, her glamour of corruption.

All at once he knew what he was going to do, what some part of him, of which he had been unconscious, had decided to do the moment he realised that Lilian's dismissal was final. He went into the boat-house, took a piece of paper from his pocket, wrote some words with a suddenly steady hand, propped it up on the shelf among the tools and tins of paint, and walked to the end of the little mooring-stage.

There was only a small rippling sound as he slid into the water.

Andrew never knew what made him awake that night and sit up in bed, listening to the sound of footsteps in the village street, what made him get up and hold back the holland blind to look out.

It was the master, walking swiftly, purposefully, and yet in some queer way as if he were being driven. The moonlight fell full upon the white set face, the blank blazing eyes, the tortured twisted lines of the mouth.

Andrew stood still for some moments, his heart racing, then with swift noiseless movements began to put on his clothes. There was going to be trouble at the house and he must be there to protect Miss Vicky. . . .

Ellen lay asleep in the big double bed. She stirred and flung an arm over the empty pillow, then sank back into sleep again. Through the open door he could hear Bill's deep breathing from the little room beyond. He took his boots in his hand and crept silently down the wooden staircase. . . .

Up the village street, in at the big gates, up the moon-flooded drive. Then he stood looking at the house that lay silent and sleeping before him. There was no light in Miss Vicky's bedroom, nor in the master's dressing-room. He didn't quite know what he had expected—lights, shouts, violence, perhaps Miss Vicky's voice crying for help, for there had been murder in the face he had looked down on from behind the holland blind.

Then some instinct took him round to the lake and into the boat-house. There he saw the square of white paper that Philip had left on the shelf. He opened it and, taking it to the door, read it by the light of the moon:

"I'm sorry, Vicky, but life's so damnable I can't go on. Lilian's thrown me over and there's nothing left to live for."

He crumpled it up and slipped it into the pocket of his corduroy breeches. Then he stood and gazed down at the smooth surface of the water, his pale freckled face grave and frowning. No one used the lake now, and it was long enough since the weeds had been cleared out. And the master, he remembered, couldn't swim, would never be bothered to learn.

He stood as motionless as a statue, while the minutes passed by. ... Suddenly, as if coming to a decision, he went back into the boat-house, untied the boat, and began laboriously to turn it over till it floated upside down. Then, with the help of the oars, he pushed it out into the lake, thrusting the oars after it. That done, he stood again considering. ... Near the boat-house was a small summer-house where Philip used to keep some painting kit. He went to it, and, taking a sketching block from a pile of things on the rustic table, returned to the lake and threw it after the boat.

He looked again at the house. All was dark and silent. The upturned boat rocked softly on the moonlit surface of the lake.

Slowly, with his plodding clumsy gait, he made his way back to the cottage. In the kitchen he knelt by the smouldering fire, took the note from his pocket, and thrust it between the bars, waiting till it had burnt down to a fluff of grey ash. He did not know that he was breaking a law of the land, nor would he have cared if he had known.

Then he took off his boots, went upstairs, undressed, and slipped into bed beside the still sleeping Ellen.

Chapter Twenty-One

It was late March. In the woods the willows were splashes of gold and the birch saplings held a ruddy glow. Overhead, the delicate tracery of the bare branches stood out against a blue rain-washed sky. In the fields farm horses, brown and patient as the earth they tilled, moved slowly to and fro drawing the harrow. Vicky loved this time of early spring before the leaves came out, when the world lay silver and russet in the pale sunshine.

She had been for a walk through the woods, as she did almost every afternoon, and was now hurrying home to be ready to receive the children.

She had had her forty-fifth birthday last week, but none of the children had been able to come over, so they had arranged to come to-day instead, except Lionel, who could not leave his practice. Celia had asked her to Ivy Lodge for tea on her birthday and had provided a nursery birthday tea for the two of them, with crackers and fairy lights and a tiny "birthday tree" hung with small and quite useless gifts. Vicky had felt touched and slightly foolish. . . .

Celia still lived in a world of perpetual childhood, with its accompaniment of anniversaries and treats and surprises. She bustled about happily at little childish tasks from morning to night—her gardening, her needle-work, her parish duties. Somehow, even when she undertook any really difficult piece of organisation her attitude made it seem childish and unimportant.

It had been one of Mrs. Carothers' bad days. She had not recognised Vicky and had addressed Celia as Miss Standish, asking her several times how Celia was getting on with her lessons. People said that Mrs. Carothers ought to be "put away," but the very suggestion made Celia indignant. She loved to fuss over the old lady, humouring her delusions with tact and patience, and yet even in this she suggested a little girl playing with a large unwieldy doll. It was as if something in Celia that had been emerging into a sweet grave maturity with her first and only love affair had been driven back in terror, and ever since had shrunk from reality, using every possible subterfuge of childishness to avoid it. Sometimes, under the boisterous carefree manner, Vicky caught a glimpse of a fear and bewilderment of which Celia herself was unaware, and would think sadly, "I couldn't have helped it. It wasn't my fault. . . ." She knew that even at the time Celia had not borne her the shadow of a grudge.

She took off her outdoor things, changed her dress, and went down to the drawing-room.

The house seemed very big and empty now that none of the children lived there. She was always saying that she must look out for a smaller one, but her whole being was so firmly rooted in the old house and garden that she kept putting off a definite decision.

Apart from every other consideration, however, she knew that she could not afford to stay at the Hall. Philip had lavished money and gifts on Mrs. Hindely so recklessly that his affairs were in hopeless confusion when he died.

She glanced at the portrait of Philip that hung over the mantelpiece. The red-gold hair and beard seemed to catch the light, the grey-green eyes were afire with restless purpose. . . . Her mind went back over the five years since his death, and she felt again the flood of glad thankfulness that had at first almost quenched her sorrow. He had come back to her. He had changed his mind at the last minute and come back to her. . . . There was no other possible explanation of his return on the same night on which he had said he was leaving her for ever. Like her he had realised that nothing could take the place of the love that had united them for so long; he had seen, as she had seen, the vision of the old age that lay before them, and realised that he needed her help and comfort. And then—well, after all, it was typical of the man. Hurrying home to her, he had caught sight of the lake, tranquil and beautiful in the moonlight, and had decided on an impulse to take the boat out onto it before going indoors. He had probably meant to do some sketching. His sketching block had been found not far from the body. There was nothing strange in it to anyone who knew Philip. He obeyed every passing impulse, and it was common knowledge that he could not swim, that, once before, his restless movements had upset the boat and he had been rescued with some difficulty by Lionel who was with him.

There was not the slightest doubt in Vicky's mind—or in the minds of any of the jury—that his death was an accident. The inquest had been a purely formal affair and the verdict "Death by misadventure" a foregone conclusion.

Vicky's sorrow at his death had been very real, but even now, after all these years, that feeling of thankfulness and joy still predominated. He had come back to her at the end. She hadn't lost him, after all. . . .

Her face hardened as she thought of Mrs. Hindely. She had consoled herself soon enough. Vicky had read the announcement of her marriage only a month afterwards.

She thought over the arrangements for the day. There really wasn't very much to arrange. The children were coming in time for tea and going back the next afternoon; all except Margery, who would be staying for a few days.

Paula had said she couldn't come at first, but had wired early this morning to say she was coming down with Noel and Margery.

Vicky was rather worried about Paula. She had been engaged three times and had broken off each engagement for no valid reason. As a result, she had got the reputation of a jilt, and the mothers of local eligibles looked at her askance.

This did not worry Paula, for she spent as little time in Six Elms as she could, and professed a great contempt for its inhabitants.

A year ago she had suddenly decided to train as a dancer, and had gone to live at a hostel in London while she attended a dancing school. Vicky had asked Mark to see that both dancing school and hostel were respectable and to keep an eye on her, and he had sent reassuring reports, but still Vicky couldn't help feeling worried.

After her training she had got a small part in a musical comedy, which, however, only ran for a short time. Now she seemed to spend her time going about with a crowd of noisy young people, whom she sometimes brought over to Six Elms at the week-end. They screamed and laughed and romped and chaffed each other and made up their faces and wore clothes that Vicky secretly thought outrageous.

"She's no right to bring them over, Miss Vicky," Andrew would say indignantly, seeing how depressed Vicky was after these invasions.

"Oh, but, Andrew, don't you see," Vicky would answer, "it's all right as long as she brings them. I'm *sure* it is. . . . But I do wish she'd make nicer friends."

She had seen little of Lionel since his wedding to Elaine last year, but Mabs, she knew, stayed with the young couple frequently. Elaine was pregnant, and the baby was expected in about four months' time.

Noel had taken a post in a boys' school after leaving Oxford, but he had soon tired of teaching and now lived in a small flat in Bloomsbury and contributed poems and articles to high-brow reviews. He was very proud of his flat, but Vicky secretly considered the rooms bleak and comfortless, with their bare stained boards, plain distempered walls and sparse bits of furniture. She found it harder to keep in touch with Noel than with any of the others. He would insist on talking to her about Bernard Shaw and Edward Carpenter when she wanted to gossip about the occupants of the other flats.

Margery had gone to the Slade School of Art immediately on leaving school. She was quiet and reserved, only occasionally now showing the moodiness and gusts of temper that had made her adolescence so trying. She shared rooms with another girl student—an earnest, rather plain, girl of whom Vicky heartily approved. As in the case of Paula, she had asked Mark to keep an eye on her, but Vicky felt no anxiety about Margery. She was working hard and deeply interested in her work.

She had said that she wanted to rent a studio in London and

take up portrait painting when she had finished her training. Vicky made no objection, but she thought that Margery would probably marry and did not take the idea of a career for her very seriously. Already Brian Halstone, a friend of the Allwoods, had begun to haunt the Hall whenever Margery was at home. A short time ago he had come to see Vicky and, stammering with embarrassment, had asked if she thought he had any chance. She had told him that Margery was so reserved it was difficult to know what she felt, but that, at any rate, she was sure there was no one else.

He was a good-looking pleasant youth, modest and unassuming in manner, and Vicky felt drawn to him. He also had the necessary "prospects"—a good post under his uncle, who owned a large leather factory in Fenton.

The next time Margery was at home he had come over almost every day, and Vicky, watching the child, had noticed a subtle change in her—a soft new radiance, a mellowing of her youthful austerity. Before she went back to London Vicky was sure that she was in love.

Brian was coming over to see her to-morrow. Perhaps he would propose then. Margery would be the next to marry, she thought dreamily. They were all gradually leaving her. She could do nothing more to help them ... only resign herself now to the insidious onset of old age.

The carriage, which had gone to the station to fetch them, drew up at the front door, and they tumbled out, talking and laughing.

"Mummy, you're too absurd not to have a car. *Everybody's* got one nowadays."

"Darling, old Tompkins would be so hurt and he'd never learn to drive one. ... Give me your coat, dear."

"Well, it's time he retired. You never take him out in the rain because of his rheumatism, so I don't see what good he is, anyway. You ought to pension him off and scrap the carriage and buy a car. If you don't do it soon you'll be the laughing-stock of England."

"Don't be so absurd, Paula. And I don't like motor-cars. They're noisy and smelly and never get anywhere. Now come in and have some tea and tell me all your news."

Paula linked her arm affectionately in Vicky's as they went into the drawing-room.

"Dearest, I've had an offer to go out to Paris. A sort of cabaret job. An awfully good one."

"*Paula!*"

"Oh, Mummy, don't be so ridiculous. Honestly, we might all be about six by the way you fuss. Queen Victoria's dead and it's nineteen hundred and ten. I'm perfectly capable of taking care of myself in Paris or anywhere else. Anyway, I'm not going."

"Oh!" gasped Vicky in relief.

"I think I'd miss London even in Paris. Do you remember Frances Merton?"

"No, dear," said Vicky, taking her seat at the tea-table. "Have I met her?"

"She's been over here ever so often, darling. She raves about you. You're the most beautiful woman she's ever seen. She says I'm like a copy of you by a very bad artist."

"How ridiculous!" said Vicky indignantly, and they all laughed.

"Anyway she says so. . . . But the point is that she's opened a place in Bond Street for lessons in ballroom dancing and she's asked me to help her. I went last week to see what it was like and it was quite fun."

"It sounds more sensible than the other," said Vicky. "I do hope you'll like it. I'd love to think that you'd really settled to something."

"*Settled!*" mocked Paula. "I hope I never settle to anything. It's the most ghastly thing that could ever happen to anyone. I know it was the ideal and ambition of the Victorian age, but Heaven preserve me from it!"

"I think you're very absurd," said Vicky, feeling, as usual, just a little bewildered by them all. They had such odd and dangerous ideas. She couldn't believe that they had ever been the shy trusting children who had clung to her and looked to her for everything.

"You've got too many ornaments in this room, Mummy," said Noel. "You're obsessed by the *horror vacui* which is one of the marks of a primitive civilisation. Why not leave a foot or two of wall uncovered?"

"They're very nice pictures," said Vicky, looking round. "We paid quite a lot for some of them."

She wished that Noel would have his hair cut shorter and not wear such curious neckties. It gave her an obscure comfort to see that he was making an enormous tea, picking out the iced cakes and obviously enjoying them.

"And just *look* at that," said Paula, pointing to the table that was covered with photographs of them all at various stages of childhood.

"And that and that," laughed Margery, pointing to the mantelpiece and grand piano whose surfaces also were covered by little Lynnakers in silver frames.

"I like them," said Vicky firmly. "Especially that of you all together."

"The one with the waterfall-and-rustic-bridge background or the tessellated castle?"

"I adore the one of Noel with nothing on sitting on the tiger skin."

"Really, Mother!" said Noel, outraged, noticing it for the first time. "I say, that really *is* the limit!"

"You were just like that," said Vicky dreamily. "You had the loveliest curls."

They laughed, then Paula said:

"When I was helping Frances last week, I had to deal with the funniest client you ever saw. He was enormous and as clumsy as an elephant and completely unselfconscious. He'd come to learn the tango and he was going to learn the tango. He was utterly absorbed in learning the tango. I've never seen anyone so earnest and solemn and so perfectly hopeless as a dancer."

"I expect you get some very funny people there," said Vicky, with a sigh.

"If by 'funny' you mean common, of course we do, but this particular man happened to be Sir somebody something, a baronet, and has quite a large estate in Hampshire."

"I daresay," said Vicky darkly, "but even so . . . I do hope you'll be careful, Paula."

"She's starting again," moaned Paula. "Gag her, someone."

"Will you teach me the tango cheap, Paula, if I come to you?" said Margery.

"I'll teach you here after tea for nothing at all," said Paula. "Honestly, Gerry, you ought to go about more. It's dreadful the way you stick round with a crowd of girl art students. I'd be ashamed."

"I'm quite happy, thanks," said Margery.

Her blue eyes were soft and dreamy, there was a faint wild-rose colour in her pale cheeks. She *is* in love, said Vicky to herself. Her thoughts hovered over her with brooding tenderness. Little Margery ... her baby ...

"You never go out with any man but Mark," went on Paula.

"How do you know she doesn't?" said Noel. "She's what our fathers would have termed a sly little puss. By the way and to change the subject, what a horrible mess they're making of the station end of the village!"

"Do you mean the new villas?" said Vicky.

" 'Villas' forsooth! Yes, aren't they ghastly? Who's responsible for them?"

"I think they look rather nice," said Vicky.

"Good God!" burst out Noel. "The foul proportions, the utter lack of taste!"

"They're fascinating inside," said Vicky. "They've got electric light and a new sort of boiler in the kitchen that uses much less coal than the open ranges and heats all the house. They make this big old house seem terribly behind the times. Noel, dear, if you'd like more of those little iced cakes, just ring. There are heaps in the kitchen."

"Me?" said Noel, as if bewildered and affronted by the suggestion. "No, thank you. I never eat much at tea."

"Dorothea Milner's gone to prison again," said Paula. "Did you read about it in the paper?"

"What was it this time? Putting a bomb in a pillar-box or serenading Asquith with 'Votes for Women'?"

"Trying to set fire to a church, I think. Funny to think of her and Miss Everett as leaders of the Movement, isn't it?"

"I think it jolly fine of them," said Margery. "I'd join them myself if I'd got the pluck."

"Well, thank Heaven you haven't then," said Noel. "But never mind the shrieking sisterhood just now." He gathered the glances of the other two significantly and went on, "We've really come down to talk to you seriously, Mother."

"I thought you'd come down to see me because it was my birthday last week," said Vicky.

"Well, so we have, but we've been thinking about you a good deal lately. This house is far too big for you, and we've come to the conclusion that you ought to find something smaller."

"I know I ought, dear, but——"

"It's a lot of trouble to run and it needs an enormous staff of servants and it simply eats money and it's a long way from us all and——"

"Yes?" said Vicky.

"Well, we've all been talking it over, and Lionel's found an ideal flat for you in Hampstead. You could run it easily with two maids or even one, and it's within easy reach of Lionel and the rest of us. We can keep an eye on you and you can keep an eye on us——"

"And you can scrap half this rubbish," said Noel, including the whole room in a sweeping gesture.

Vicky stared at them, bewildered.

"But—but what about Andrew?" she said at last.

"Andrew?" repeated Noel incredulously.

"Yes. What will he do?"

"Good God! What should he do? Get another place, of course. What on earth has Andrew to do with it?"

"He'd easily get another place, darling, if that's what you're worrying about," said Paula. "Now that Ellen's dead, he could go anywhere. For the matter of that, his brother would take him into his motor-cycle works. I believe he's offered him a job there more than once."

"Andrew! Good God!" exploded Noel again.

"You *will* take the flat, won't you, dearest?" coaxed Paula. "Lionel will see to all the business part of it. You can sell this house and just keep enough furniture for the flat. Lionel will see to everything. . . . It's a darling flat, isn't it, Gerry?"

Margery roused herself from her day-dreams.

"It's lovely," she said.

"And Noel's terribly good at decoration and that sort of thing. He's got wonderful ideas for it, all planned out ready."

"Plain walls," said Noel, "and just one picture in each room. And just a few good pieces of furniture. Half the stuff you've got here is sheer junk, but I can pick enough out to furnish the flat perfectly, and we'll get rid of the rest."

Paula was looking at her, head on one side.

"Frances was right, you know, Mummy. You *are* beautiful. But you simply take no trouble with yourself. I mean, you do your hair the same way you did it when we were children, and you *don't* dress well. . . . Yes, I know Miss Popkins or whatever she's called does her best, but she's only a village dressmaker, and she's made your dresses exactly like that for years and years and years. It would smarten you up all round to come and live in town."

Vicky gave a little laugh in which surprise, dismay, amusement, and a faint indignation, were mingled.

"Darlings, you must really give me time to think it over."

"We've thought over it for you, my sweet, from every possible angle," said Noel patiently. "If you'll only say 'Yes' we can get the thing in train at once."

"I want to think it over," repeated Vicky obstinately.

"She belongs to the generation that thought things over," sighed Paula. "Mummy, it would be terribly good for your soul to do something on impulse for once in your life."

"Perhaps," said Vicky dryly, "but it's not going to be this. . . . Now, if you've finished tea, do be good children and run over to Ivy Lodge to see Auntie Celia. She'll be so hurt if you don't."

They didn't mention the matter again, but, as Vicky thought over what they had said, her indignation increased. The calm way they were taking possession and disposing of her! She was to be uprooted from the place where she had spent her whole life, she was to be robbed of all her treasures, she was to be deprived even of Andrew, she was to be planted in a horrible flat, furnished by Noel, with plain walls and nothing pretty anywhere. Once they got her there, of course, they'd have her completely under their thumbs. Paula would make her wear uncomfortable clothes, and Noel would make her live in rooms like barns, and she'd have to do all sorts of things she didn't want to do and meet all sorts of people she didn't want to meet. She set her lips. Oh, will I? she thought grimly. We'll see about that. . . .

"Promise you'll let us know about the flat by the end of the week," said Noel, as he and Paula were setting off for the station the next day.

"Yes, I promise," said Vicky.

Paula looked at her critically.

"You'll be quite an asset, darling," she said, "when we've smartened you up."

When they had gone, Vicky and Margery turned back into the house.

"I think I'll go over to the Vicarage," said Margery, taking her hat from the hall chest.

"Yes, do, dear. They'll be glad to see you. I believe Mark's there."

"I know."

"I told you that Brian was coming to tea, didn't I?"

"Yes."

As soon as Margery had gone, Vicky went out to Andrew.

"Andrew," she said, "I want you to get out the dog-cart and drive me down to those new villas by the station. I want to look over them."

"Very good, Miss Vicky," said Andrew.

A few minutes later the dog-cart drove to the front door, and Andrew helped Vicky up to the front seat by him.

"The children want me to go and live in London," she said. "In a flat."

Andrew considered the idea in silence for some moments, and finally said:

"I shouldn't do that if I was you, Miss Vicky."

"No, I'm not going to," said Vicky with spirit. "But I know I ought to leave the Hall, and if I don't do something about it myself they'll be hatching some other wild scheme between them."

The horse clip-clopped along the country road, past the little cottage where Andrew had lived alone since Ellen died of pneumonia last year. Andrew had felt deeply the loss of the silent gentle woman who had been his wife for twenty-five years. Ellen had understood everything without being told. She had understood from the beginning about Miss Vicky, and how Miss Vicky must always come first. He couldn't have explained it to her, couldn't have explained it to himself—but she'd understood.

Bill was now a smart young man in George's motorcycle works. Andrew's brother had gradually turned the bicycle shop into a motor-cycle works and was doing very well. Bill could talk of nothing but dynamos and ignition and cylinders and cooling-fins. Andrew would listen to him contemptuously. He had a boundless distrust of motorcars and motor-cycles and everything to do with them.

"Dirty noisy things!" he would say. "Driving horses off the roads! Ought to forbid by law."

"Horses!" Bill would echo with a contempt as fierce as Andrew's.

"They want me to get rid of all my nice ornaments and pictures," went on Vicky ruefully. "They say they aren't artistic."

"Don't you take no notice of them, Miss Vicky," said Andrew. "Don't you let them boss you about."

He felt a deep resentment against Miss Vicky's children now they were grown-up. They were always coming over and laying down the law and bossing and criticising and upsetting things. . . .

"I hate plain walls," went on Vicky. "I like papers with a pretty pattern."

"Quite right, Miss Vicky," said Andrew approvingly.

They had reached the little block of new villas now, and Andrew drew up and helped Vicky down.

"Come in with me and look at it, Andrew," she said.

She beckoned a boy who was hanging about among the piles of builders' materials.

"Will you hold the horse for us while we look round? We shan't be long. . . . Come on, Andrew."

They went over the house together. It was almost finished, and Vicky exclaimed with delight at the toylike appointments and the light airy kitchen on the ground floor.

"It's lovely, Andrew, isn't it? Don't you think so? Quite big enough for what we want, and so easy to run."

They went out into the garden, picking their way among planks and buckets of cement, and surveyed the long rectangle of bare trodden earth that was the "garden."

"I suppose it would be awfully hard work at first," said Vicky, "but once you'd got it going it would be all right, wouldn't it? You could have a little greenhouse in that corner. And a tool-shed there. . . . We couldn't keep the carriage, of course, or even the dog-cart here, but—*Andrew!*" as a sudden idea occurred to her. "Would you simply *hate* to learn to drive a car?"

He stared at her, aghast.

"I know you don't like them. I don't either. But we must have something, and"—with a sigh—"I suppose one ought to try to move with the times. I wouldn't have one, of course, unless you'd drive it."

"Well . . ." Andrew considered, frowning. "I've never had nothing to do with them. . . ."

"But, Andrew, you could learn."

There was a minute's silence, in which he threw over the prejudices of a lifetime.

"Very well, Miss Vicky," he said. "I'll do my best."

She made a quick little movement that reminded him of how the child Vicky used to jump up and down and clap her hands when she was pleased.

"Come along," she said. "Let's get it fixed up before the children find out and stop me. After all, why should I live in London if I don't want to?"

Andrew drove her first to the house-agents, where she arranged the purchase of the house, then to the builders, where she insisted on choosing the wall-papers, though she was told that they could not be put on till the distemper had "dried out." She chose red roses growing up silver and black trellis ... big yellow chrysanthemums on a pale-blue ground ... blue wavy stripes like watered ribbons. ...

"I think wall-paper's so dull without a pattern," she said.

They drove home in silence. Andrew was secretly dismayed by the decision he had taken. Vicky felt pleased and excited and apprehensive, like a child who has enjoyed an afternoon of lawlessness, but for whom the hour of reckoning was now drawing near.

"They'll be furious," she kept saying to herself, "but, after all, why *shouldn't* I do what I like?"

Andrew helped her alight, then took the dog-cart round to the stable, while Vicky went indoors.

As she entered the drawing-room, Mark turned slowly from the window. She looked round the room.

"Where's Margery?" she said, drawing off her gloves.

"She was here till we heard you coming, then I made her go away, because I wanted to talk to you alone."

The smile faded from Vicky's face, and her heart began to beat unevenly. She'd never seen Mark like this before—pale, serious, stripped of his urbane geniality. For a moment she thought that something dreadful had happened to one of the children, and that Mark had been deputed to break the news to her.

"What is it?" she said. "Tell me quickly ... Lionel. ..."

"No, no." He shook his head. "It's nothing like that. . . . It's—Vicky, I suppose this will be rather a shock to you, but Margery and I love each other. We want to get married."

"*You!*" she stammered foolishly. She couldn't believe the words. "You and *Margery?*"

"Yes, you see—well, we've been seeing a good deal of each other in London and——"

"But—but I thought you were just keeping an eye on her and——"

"It began like that," he said gently. "I'm sorry, Vicky. I know you'll hate this, but I've never loved anyone in my life as I love Margery, and she feels the same."

"Oh, you'd no right," said Vicky hotly. "A child like Margery!"

"Yes, I know how it must seem to you, but—you've got to face it. We love each other."

"And you talk of marriage! You're married already. Helen's your wife."

"That can be arranged. We've meant nothing to each other for years. Helen always said that she'd divorce me if ever I wanted her to."

"Mark, how *can* you!" said Vicky angrily. "How can you even *think* of dragging Margery through the mud of a divorce court!"

"I think it can be managed so that Margery's name doesn't come into it at all."

"Don't be so absurd. Of course Margery's name would come into it. Mark, she's only a child. She can't realise what this means. Do you think I'd allow her in any circumstances at all to marry a divorced man?"

She was trembling with anger. Margery ... her baby ... her darling. It was strange to remember how only this afternoon she had felt that they didn't need her any more, that her part as mother was over. And now she felt that she would fight to her last breath to save Margery.

"Can't you see, Mark?" she went on. "She'd be ruined for the rest of her life. No decent people could know her. She'd lose all her friends."

He was looking at her gravely, gently.

"Things are changing, you know, Vicky. Women get a fairer deal than they did a few years ago."

Vicky compressed her lips.

"Standards generally may be looser than they were, but if you think that for that reason I'm going to let Margery—Divorce is wrong and the re-marriage of a divorced person isn't recognised by the Church. It would break my heart and ruin Margery's life." Her voice trembled. "Mark, how *can* you do this!"

He looked so troubled and grave and kind that it was difficult to feel as angry with him as she wanted to.

"I knew how it would hurt you, Vicky. I've been wretched about it—for your sake."

"How did it happen?"

"I don't know how it happened. I knew I was in love with her some time ago, but I thought that as long as she didn't know no great harm was done, then I found out almost by chance that she loved me, too, and—well, that's how it happened. ... Vicky, I promise you I won't let her regret it. I know that the circumstances aren't ideal, but I promise you I won't let it hurt her in any way."

"How can you help it? Oh, Mark, her whole life's happiness is at stake. Can't you see?"

"I know. That's how I look at it. I know she loves me or I wouldn't take up this attitude. I'm fighting for her as well as myself."

"Do Roger and your mother know about it?"

"No. No one knows but you. Vicky——"

She cut him short with a gesture.

"It's no use, Mark. It doesn't matter what you say, I'll never allow it. And she's under age. She can't marry without my permission."

His face hardened.

"Then we'll just have to wait till she's twenty-one. I warn you I'll never give her up unless she gives me up."

Vicky's mind was working quickly.

"Will you just do one thing, Mark?"

"What's that?"

"Let me take her right away, just for a month. Don't write or come to see her just for that time."

He hesitated, then said:

"Very well. I can see her once before she goes, I suppose?"

"Yes," she held out her hand. "Now, please go, Mark. It's been a dreadful shock to me. I want to speak to Margery."

"Mayn't I just say one word to her now?"

"No. Good-bye."

"Good-bye."

She went slowly upstairs to Margery's bedroom. Margery sat on her bed, her slender form tense and rigid, clutching the edge of the bedstead with both hands. Her delicate oval face looked very white under the mop of red-gold curls.

Vicky sat down by her and put an arm tenderly about her shoulder.

"Margery, darling," she said, "I can't let you do this."

"But, Mummy, you don't understand," protested Margery. "I love him. I can't live without him."

"Darling, he's married already."

"But Helen will divorce him. She always said she would."

"Margery, dear, you *can't* marry a man who's been divorced. You're too young to understand what it means, but it'll ruin your whole life."

"Mark says people aren't like that nowadays."

"Mark knows nothing about it. You're only a child. I can't bear to think of your being smirched by a thing like that almost before your life's begun. You've no knowledge of the world. You don't understand what you're doing."

"But, Mummy, if it's just people not wanting to know me, I don't mind. I don't want anyone in the whole world but Mark."

"What a *child* you are, Margery! Even if it weren't for Helen, I should still disapprove. Mark's far too old for you."

"Mummy, I know there are lots of things against it. That's why I tried to stop caring for him at first. So did he . . . but we couldn't, either of us. I love him so much that he's—part of me. I think I'd die if you didn't let me marry him."

"Margery, darling, listen to me. I want you to come away with me, just to get a perspective on things. Mark's agreed to it. Just a month without seeing him or hearing from him. Then if you still feel the same we'll—we'll consider the whole question again. You're infatuated by him. So often, darling, a girl falls in love with an older man at your age and forgets all about it in a few years. I suppose you've not met many young men—except Brian——"

"I don't like young men, Mummy. I'm not Paula. I never liked men at all till I got to know Mark. I don't like them now. It's only Mark I like."

"Darling, will you promise to come away with me?"

"Where?" reluctantly.

"Abroad. . . . Somewhere on the Italian Riviera, perhaps."

Right away, she told herself—away from anything that could remind the child of her infatuation.

"For how long?"

"A month." A lot could happen in a month. "Mark's agreed, dearest."

"Very well."

Vicky went downstairs. Brian was just being shown into the drawing-room. He turned to her with his eager boyish smile.

"She is here, isn't she?" he said.

Her heart warmed to his youth, to his vulnerability, to the something of immaturity and inexperience that contrasted so sharply with Mark's man-of-the-world manner. How blind the child was! Here surely was all she could want. This boy and she could set out together on life's path, sharing its adventures, could grow and develop side by side. Mark would be an old man when Margery was still young. . . . Youth . . . she was too young to value it, of course.

She closed the door before she answered him.

"Yes, she's here," she said, "but—you haven't any chance at present, I'm afraid, Brian. She's in love with someone else, and I'm terribly distressed by it. I'll do all I possibly can for you." She smiled faintly. "Don't look so tragic. It mayn't be anything serious. I hope it isn't. We're going abroad for a month—she and I—and I want you to join us. Will you?"

She felt mean and sly and hateful as she spoke, but—one must fight. One couldn't just stand by and do nothing.

The boy's handsome face was flushed and unhappy.

"I say—that's awfully decent of you," he stammered.

"I'm sorry," said Vicky. "I'm afraid it's been a shock to you. It has to me, too. I'll let you know where we go. Don't do it too obviously. Come and stay somewhere near, and then—we'll leave it to fate. . . . And now you'd better go. She won't want to see you to-day."

Chapter Twenty-Two

VICKY was packing her things ready for the journey to Paula's, where she was to spend Christmas. She was trying hard to look forward to it, telling herself how nice it would be to see the children again, but really she hated to leave the little house even for a few days. In the three years she had lived in it she had grown deeply attached to it, though Noel still sneered at its lack of every artistic merit, and they all still tried occasionally to persuade her to come nearer London.

Andrew drove the car and looked after the garden and occupied the little room over the garage, while Katie, who had come to the Hall as kitchen-maid eighteen years ago, did all the work of the house.

Andrew drove the car well if somewhat over cautiously, but he still felt a vague resentment towards it and was very stupid about finding his way. On a long drive he would get lost several times, and Vicky often thought that he did it on purpose in order to emphasise his contempt of the whole process. She bought him innumerable maps, but none of them seemed to convey anything to him.

They lived at very close quarters in the little house, and there were many sources of contention between them. The garden, of course, was a small one, and Vicky, who had left the garden at the Hall entirely to Andrew, began to take an interest in it, buying weekly gardening papers and doing bits of work in it herself. This irritated Andrew, and his mouth would set in an obstinate line when he saw Vicky coming out to him with one of the little papers in her hand. He felt all the professional's scorn of the amateur, and would say, "Oh, them papers! I s'pose they've got to put in something," then dismiss the matter from his mind. Even though he had been going to do some piece of work, it was a point of honour with him not to do it—till, at any rate, a decent interval had elapsed—if Vicky's paper told him to. He couldn't bear "new-fangled" notions, either. Everything must be done as it had been done in his boyhood. He was faithful even to his rows of geraniums, calceolarias, and lobelias, which he persisted in planting on either side of the walk from gate to front door.

Another source of friction between them was the chauffeur's uniform, which he seemed to include in the contempt he felt for the car. He would go straight into the garden when he had been out with the car, and, to Vicky's indignation, begin to work there in his beautiful navy blue trousers and shining leggings.

Vicky, on her side, irked him by her fussiness, her insistence on details, her over punctuality, and her interference with what he considered his province. When he felt particularly annoyed with her, he would drop the "Miss Vicky" and address her distantly and respectfully as "Madam."

But, though the little irritations of everyday life ebbed and flowed between them, the bond that united them was stronger than ever. Neither had ever understood it—or even tried to understand it—but neither could have contemplated a life that did not include the other. In the first hour of Andrew's meeting with her more than forty years ago he had seen her as a fairy princess, a conceited and irritating little girl, and a frightened baby, and something of the feelings each had roused in him still remained. He resented fiercely what he considered her children's undue claims on her, and was always rather sulky when any of them were visiting her.

He was going to his brother's for Christmas. He didn't expect to enjoy it, but Bill would be there, and he wanted to see the boy. Besides, he couldn't stay at home alone (Katie was going to her mother's), and he'd nowhere else to go. George had grown a bit too grand for him of late years, and had married a wife who was ashamed of having a "common gardener" as a brother-in-law.

George's new grandeur—the maid in cap and apron, the dress

clothes, the visiting cards—tickled Andrew immensely, though he was fond of George, for George was a good fellow and personally unspoilt by his success. He sent money regularly to their sister, who was married to a farmer in Canada and had a large family of children. He was anxious, too, to help Andrew to rise in the social scale and still at intervals, though now without much hope, offered him well-paid posts in his firm.

"Honestly, old chap," he would say seriously, "you ought to get out of your rut and into something better. It'll be too late in a few years."

"It's too late now," grinned Andrew. "I like my job and that's all that matters."

"There's no money in it," persisted George.

"I don't want money," said Andrew. "I've never thought that money was all it's cracked up to be. I'm quite happy without it, anyway."

And that worried George, because it didn't seem natural. He couldn't, of course, refer to what worried him most—the fact that the social gulf between them was widening slowly but surely with the years, and that Andrew seemed to make no attempt to help him bridge it. Andrew's eyes would twinkle disconcertingly when his brother made stumbling suggestions as to the improvement of his speech and manners.

George was afraid that this was the last time Bella would let him ask Andrew for Christmas. She'd sulked about it last year, and made quite a scene about it this. There was, of course, something to be said on her side. Her father had been a dentist, unqualified but with a good manner, and they had always had a parlour to sit in on Sunday afternoon and a maid to open the door. It was natural that she should resent Andrew. She'd only married George because she thought that he would get on, and she was anxious to prevent him from being dragged back by old associations.

Bill, of course, was quite a different matter—a good-looking, well-turned-out young man, as sharp as a needle, and a credit to anyone. Bill, however, was fond of his father, and it was more on his account than George's that Bella had given in over this Christmas visit.

Vicky was a little worried by the thought of Andrew's going to George's, for she had met George's wife, an overdressed woman with a tight mouth and aggressive manner, and disliked her intensely.

"I don't think either of us really wants to go away," she said. "Never mind. It'll soon be over, and we'll be back here again."

"Yes, Miss Vicky," said Andrew. "That's what I keep telling myself."

As Vicky put her things into her suitcase, her thoughts turned to the children.

Paula had been married for three years now. She had announced her engagement to Sir Peter Daventry, her large clumsy dancing pupil, very soon after that day when they had all met at the Hall and she had first mentioned him. He was a simple, kind-hearted, somewhat conventional young man, and he worshipped Paula with an old-fashioned devotion that Vicky found rather touching. Fortunately Paula on her side was deeply in love with him and had almost unconsciously adapted herself to his ideals, moulding herself into the likeness of the wife he had always dreamed of. From the beginning she had entered his world and made it her own, presiding with a dignity that amazed those who had known the old Paula over his house in Hampshire. The inexhaustible vitality that had been the cause of her youthful wildness was diverted now to running her home, organising local activities, opening bazaars and flower-shows, attending functions. She was growing more and more correct and conventional, careful to set a good example to the village, to wear the right clothes, and to know the right people. She and her old friends had dropped each other by tacit consent.

She had had two children in the three years of her marriage, and announced her intention of having ten altogether. Already there was a hint of matronly plumpness about her figure, already something quelling in her eye when she was annoyed; already you saw in her the handsome majestic dominating woman she would be in twenty years' time. She was revealing undreamed-of powers of organisation, showing herself unexpectedly capable in all her new duties. Her nurseries were models of what modern nurseries should be.

"It's ridiculous," grumbled Vicky, forbidden to take the babies out of their cots and nurse them when they cried. "I used to take you all out of your cots and nurse you whenever I wanted to and you've turned out all right."

Lionel and Elaine were as devoted to each other as ever, but Vicky didn't feel happy about the marriage. Elaine had had a bad miscarriage with her first child and had been so ill that it was thought she would not recover, and after that she had refused even to consider having another child. Lionel had supported her, growing angry when Vicky remonstrated with him.

"She was desperately ill, Mother. Surely you remember."

"But she's perfectly well again now, Lionel."

"She had a bad shock. It frightened her. A woman doesn't get over those things. She's delicate and highly strung."

Vicky felt that he was arguing to convince himself as well as her. Elaine, lovely and childish-looking as ever, poured out what maternal tenderness she had upon her Pekinese, cuddling it and crooning over it, talking baby language to it, and decking it out in ribbons. It made Vicky feel a little sick to see her holding it out to Lionel and saying, "Div oo's Daddy a tiss, den." And it was worse still to watch Lionel respond, to see him, too, giving to the grotesque little creature a tenderness that he secretly longed to give to his own children. He would have made, of all the men Vicky had ever known, the most perfect father. And something in him hungered for children, was incomplete and frustrated without them.

Vicky had been afraid that Mabs would wreck the marriage by her interference, but that fear had proved unfounded. During one of her visits Mabs had criticised Lionel too unguardedly, and Elaine had taken offence. Mabs had departed in high displeasure, and, though the quarrel between them had been patched up, their relations were still strained and Mabs now seldom visited her daughter.

Elaine's loveliness made it inevitable that men should admire her, but all her love was still given to her husband. It was too intense, too possessive a love, thought Vicky. She was jealous of everything that separated him from her, even his work. She had persuaded him to take a partner, though he didn't want to and could easily have managed the practice alone.

"Darling, don't go . . ." she would plead when he was summoned to a case. "Don't leave me. Let Jim see to it. What's the good of having a partner if you do all the work yourself? You were out all yesterday evening, and I was so lonely here by myself."

He tried to persuade her to make friends, but she wouldn't.

"I don't want anybody but you," she persisted. "I hate every minute I'm not with you."

She would persuade him to go away with her, leaving his cases to his partner.

"Just for a week. Do, darling. I just never get you to myself at home. Jim can see to everything. . . . Well, darling, he can always ring you up and tell you how they're going on. Do, Lionel. Popsy wants an 'ickle holiday, doesn't 'oo, darling? Tell Daddy 'oo doos. Tell Daddy Mummy wants to have him all to herself for a bit wivout his silly patients bowering him all the time."

She took no interest in his cases and would not even let him tell her about them.

"No, don't, darling. I hate them. I wish they didn't exist, then you'd have to stay with me all day."

The thought of her waiting for him at home, the prospect of her reproaches, however loving, when he got back to her, the feeling of compunction that oppressed him whenever he had to stay away from her longer than usual, poisoned all his pleasure in his work. There was a look of strain in his face nowadays that worried Vicky. It would have been better if he loved his wife less, or if she could have found some distraction.

And Margery? Somehow Vicky didn't like thinking of Margery's marriage, either, especially because in Margery's case there nagged a tiny sense of guilt. If it hadn't been for that holiday in San Remo, perhaps Margery wouldn't have married Brian. If Brian hadn't been there, courteous, considerate, charming, handsome, with an unobtrusive air of sympathy and understanding, if Vicky hadn't perpetually enlarged upon what marriage to a divorced man would mean to Margery, to her children, even to Mark himself—but it was no use thinking of that now.

They had come back from San Remo engaged, Margery pale and listless but somehow at peace, as if the very making of her decision had brought relief. She had written to Mark to tell him of her engagement and had not seen him again. And it wasn't really an unhappy marriage. Vicky kept assuring herself of that. Certainly at first Margery had been happy and in love with her husband. It was just that Brian was rather unfortunate. He had quarrelled with his uncle soon after the marriage, and after leaving his uncle's firm had got a job as a commission agent that hadn't turned out well.

Perhaps Brian wasn't quite as steady as they'd thought he was, but he was unfailingly pleasant and kind. Nothing could ruffle his good humour. And Margery was devoted to Sandy, her baby. That must compensate for a lot. . . .

Noel was the only one of them who didn't seem to have changed at all in the last few years. He was still living in his rooms in Bloomsbury and wearing his hair too long and dressing oddly and writing poetry that didn't rhyme and forgathering with an earnest crowd of long-haired men and short-haired women. Vicky was secretly amused by it all. As long as Noel was happy she didn't care how odd he was. . . .

Andrew drove her down to the station, bought her ticket, and put her into a carriage.

"Take care of yourself, Miss Vicky," he said as he wrapped the rug carefully over her knees.

"Yes," said Vicky, "and take care of yourself."

Andrew was thinking resentfully of Miss Vicky's children, who, he considered, were selfish and thoughtless and "put on" her shamefully.

Vicky was thinking resentfully of Andrew's sister-in-law, who would probably snub or ignore him throughout his visit.

"Oh, well," she said, "we'll both soon be back—won't we?—settled nicely down in our rut again."

Their eyes dwelt on each other rather wistfully as they said good-bye.

253

Vicky sat at the long dining-table and looked around her. The centre of the table was filled with crackers and holly and lit by tall candles. Peter, at the head of the table, was a typical country squire, red-faced and jovial. Paula, opposite him, glowed with health and happiness. She dressed in too matronly a style for her age, thought Vicky, but Peter liked it, and that was all that mattered.

Noel, in deference to Peter's well-known conventionality, wore a dinner-jacket instead of the purple velvet coat that was his usual evening attire. He wore, too, a monocle—a recent acquisition, which, he thought, gave him an air of distinction. He had assumed an expression of detached amusement as suitable to the affair, but he had nevertheless taken a good deal of trouble in his choice of presents and had been very much pleased with the presents he received in return.

"I adore Christmas," he said. "It's such an amusing blend of the Roman Saturnalia and the nineteenth-century Dickens."

Elaine's eyes kept seeking Lionel's across the table. She was very quiet and shy. She never seemed to have much to say to anyone but Lionel. And Lionel was too responsive, too sensitive, too conscious of her need of him, too ready against his will and instinct to confine himself to the narrow world she made for them. They both should have married other people, thought Vicky, with a sigh.

Brian was making himself pleasant to Peter, talking of dogs and horses and sport and hunting. Brian didn't take any interest in such things, but he had the knack of being able to talk to people about what interested them as if it interested him too. He had the jargon of anything at his fingers' ends. He *was* charming, thought Vicky, watching him—too charming, perhaps. Too pleasant, too adaptable, too conciliatory. He agreed with everyone on every subject. He was agreeing with Peter now that the country was the only possible place to live in, but he would just as easily have agreed with someone else that it was only possible to live in town. Perhaps he really hadn't any views of his own. Strange that it should have been the very pleasantness she distrusted now that had first attracted her to him. She had thought: He may not be clever or rich, but he's good-tempered and kind and straightforward. She was a little less certain of the last now. His eyes had a curious way of shifting from yours as he talked, as if he were afraid of their giving something away.

A pity he hadn't a better job. It meant that he was living on Margery's money and, of course, she hadn't very much. Margery was watching Brian as he talked, and Vicky tried to read her expression. Her mouth was rather tight, and there was a hard look in her eyes that had not been there before her marriage.

Then Peter made some reference to Sandy and her whole-face softened. . . .

Peter enjoyed having his wife's relations round the Christmas table like this, but he was looking forward to the time when their numbers should be swelled by his own children. He was by nature a patriarch. Home life satisfied the deepest needs of his nature. He wanted a large family, children at every stage of development growing up around him, opening like flowers in the sun of his love and protection. Already he seemed to see a crowd of laughing boys and girls round the old mahogany table.

"Shall we pull the crackers now, Mother?" he said to Vicky.

He always addressed her as mother and treated her with a deference and consideration that made her feel she ought to be wearing a shawl and a cap.

They pulled the crackers, then began to examine their contents, laughing and exclaiming. The noise had made Vicky's head ache and she became suddenly drowsy.

She wondered what Andrew was doing and hoped that his sister-in-law wasn't being unkind to him, then realised that it didn't matter if she was, because Andrew wouldn't care. They would be back again soon in their comfortable rut in the ugly little house that she had grown to love so dearly.

She thought of the tiny overcrowded drawing-room, with the children's photographs and Philip's portrait over the mantelpiece. Her eyes grew dreamy and the room with its chattering occupants seemed to fade away.

She was conscious only of Philip—Philip who had come back to her in the end. . . .

Chapter Twenty-Three

ANDREW really was tiresome, thought Vicky, as she sat down with a flop of exasperation in her deck-chair and took up her book. Every year she showed him the piece in the gardening paper that said the climbers should not be pruned with the ramblers, and every year he did them together. She'd found him doing it again this afternoon, and when she remonstrated he had said, "Very good, madam," and had gone off in a huff to hoe the herbaceous border, leaving both ramblers and climbers altogether. He'd sulk now, perhaps, for the rest of the day, but it did her good to "have it out" with him occasionally, though she always began to feel a little lonely and desolate if his respectful manner lasted for long.

Although she allowed herself to criticise Andrew, she never allowed anyone else to, and would defend him vehemently when the children attacked him. They attacked him frequently, resenting, in particular, what they called his "familiarity."

"The way he speaks to you, Mother! He might be your equal."

"Well, dear," Vicky would say mildly, "when you really come to think of it, he is."

They referred to him as "mother's mascot" and were angry when they found, as they often did, that she had discussed their affairs with him. Vicky had only to begin "Andrew says—" for them all to groan in unison.

Katie had had to go home for a year to nurse her mother, and Vicky's domestic arrangements had been somewhat uncertain, as maids were now difficult to get in the country. She herself suffered from rheumatism and could not do much housework, and more than once in a crisis Andrew had done the whole work of the house.

"What *is* that man supposed to be," said Paula to Margery when they were discussing Vicky's affairs together, "a chauffeur or a charwoman? The last time I went there he was scrubbing out the bathroom."

"Or a sick nurse?" said Margery. "The last time I was there Mother was in bed and he was cooking all her meals and taking them up to her."

It was a warm September afternoon, and Vicky began to doze over her book. She roused herself, sitting up straight and fixing her eyes resolutely on the print. She mustn't get into the habit of dozing like that. It marked her as an old woman, and she wasn't really old yet. . . . Only fifty-eight. Fifty-eight was nothing.

The book wasn't very interesting, though the librarian had told her that it had had excellent reviews and that everyone was reading it. Books nowadays were never as interesting as they used to be.

She laid it on her knee, and her gaze wandered round the garden again. The little lead figure in the middle of the rose garden had been given her by Lionel. He had bought it for her on his last leave before he was killed. Only a week after he went back the casualty station where he was working had been hit by a shell and there were no survivors.

Vicky had been in the drawing-room when the telegram was brought to her. She had sat there, staring dry-eyed at the photograph of Lionel in his uniform on the mantelpiece, unable to believe that it was true.

Andrew, who had seen the telegraph boy come to the door, entered the drawing-room and clumsily laid his dirt-ingrained hand on her shoulder. Then she had broken down and sobbed, and Andrew had knelt by her, murmuring, "There, there, Miss Vicky. Don't take on like that. . . . There, there. . . ."

Elaine had been so completely prostrated by the news that for a time the doctors had feared for her reason. She could neither eat nor sleep. She locked herself up for hours in Lionel's room and refused to allow anyone to touch his things. Finally she took some prussic acid that she found in the dispensary and raged weakly at them for trying to save her.

"Let me die," she pleaded. "I can't bear to go on living without him. . . . I can't bear it. . . ."

She looked a ghost of herself when she recovered, so weak that she could hardly raise her hand. Then Mabs and Walter took her abroad with them—to India, Ceylon, Java—and gradually life seemed to return to her. She had married again two years later and was now the blooming mother of two children. She was fond of Vicky and often came to see her, but Vicky couldn't quite forgive her for those children—the children of which she had cheated Lionel. She sent Vicky photographs of them, but Vicky, whose display of photographs was the joke and despair of her children, put the photographs of Elaine's little girls away in a drawer and never took them out again.

She returned to her book, but she was using a letter from Paula as a bookmark and that took her thoughts to Paula—Paula, the mother of seven children with an eighth on the way, undisputed aristocrat of home and village. Peter was passionately proud of her, of her beauty and energy and the forcefulness of character that made her so dominating a figure in his world. He loved everything about her, even the stoutness that marred her once lovely proportions. He himself was stout, too—stout and mahogany-faced and generous and imperturbable. He spoilt his young brood shamefully, delighting in their good looks and health and daring. They ran wild over the countryside with ponies and dogs, and were all accomplished riders almost as soon as they could walk.

"I think I'm the happiest man in the world," he had said solemnly to Vicky the last time she had seen him.

She glanced through the letter again. "Daphne won a first in the children's jumping competition at the Horse Show last week. . . . Jill's pony's gone a little lame, and the poor child is so upset about it. . . . Frankie went out with the guns last week, and Peter said he's really quite a good shot for his age. . . . Patsy had her first riding lesson yesterday. She was rather frightened, but Peter says she'll soon get over it. Do come over and spend a week or so with us, darling. The children say it's years since they saw you."

Vicky shook her head gently as she put back her letter in the pages of the book. No, she didn't want to go and stay with Paula. The children were darlings but terribly noisy, and no one in the house ever seemed to sit down from morning to night. They were always out riding or walking or playing games or seeing to their dogs and horses and other live-stock. And they had loud voices and all talked at once. Even Paula's voice had acquired a ringing tone suggestive of the barrack square. It had had to acquire it, of course, in order to make itself heard above the uproar. Paula's family made Vicky feel very much a grandmother. . . .

Of the others, Margery now had two boys and Noel one daughter. Four years ago Noel had married a tall sinuous woman called Salome (she had been christened Ethel), and they had a solid foursquare little girl called Undine, of whom they were inordinately proud.

Vicky had only met Noel's wife once before marriage, and still did not feel quite at ease with her. Noel said she was the "Rossetti type," and certainly she was very striking looking, with her great eyes, full lips, and masses of untidy auburn hair. She dressed in exotic styles and shades, was perpetually horrified by the ugliness of modern life, and considered Noel a great poet. They had moved to a small house in St. John's Wood, which was as bare and, in Vicky's eyes, as comfortless as Noel's Bloomsbury rooms had been.

Her reveries were interrupted by the sound of Celia's noisy little car drawing up at the gate. Then Celia bustled into the garden, stout, cheerful, untidy, her greying hair done in an erratic bun beneath a lop-sided hat, carrying the large shopping basket which always accompanied her and which she used as a sort of travelling desk, for it contained her correspondence, account-books, and all the papers relating to the many parish affairs she conducted.

Mrs. Carothers had died the year before, and Celia now lived alone in Ivy Lodge, still filling her life with a succession of little duties, to each of which she seemed to give every ounce of energy she possessed.

Mrs. Abbot, too, had died after a stroke that had left her helpless for several months, and since then Celia had looked after both Roger and his parish.

Roger was a dreamy scholar, with hardly half a foot in the world of reality, and even the most determined matchmakers had resigned themselves to the fact that nothing would come of his lifelong friendship with Celia.

Mark very seldom came to the Vicarage now, and when he did he and Vicky avoided each other by tacit consent.

After Mrs. Carothers' death the air of spick-and-spanness had vanished from Ivy Lodge (none of her delusions had prevented Mrs. Carothers from keeping a sharp lookout for dust and disorder) and Celia's natural untidiness found full vent. All the rooms were now cluttered up with her belongings—the materials for the Women's Institute classes (raffia, leather, basket-work), badges and uniforms belonging to the Girl Guides, the choir surplices she was mending, the hymn-books and prayer-books she was looking over for missing pages, account-books, minute-books, and food for her pets—for she kept two cats, a canary, a tortoise, and a hutch full of Angora rabbits.

"There you are, Vicky, darling," she said. "Do you think you ought to be sitting out with your rheumatism?"

"Well, I can't sit out without it," said Vicky. "No, I'm all right, Celia. It's sheltered here and the sun's quite warm. Get a deck-chair from the summer-house and sit down yourself."

"Well, only for a second, dear. I'm just on my way to clean the church brasses and do the flowers. That's what I came for really. May I steal some of your chrysanthemums? I don't seem to have any decent ones this year."

"Yes, take as many as you like," said Vicky.

"As many as Andrew will let me have, you mean," said Celia. "As soon as I start picking them he'll come up and say, 'You stop pulling them flowers about, Miss Celia.'"

"No, he won't," smiled Vicky. "He's sulking. He'll let you do what you like this afternoon."

Celia sat down in the deck-chair.

"Oh dear! It's nice to sit down. I've just been up to the Vicarage. Roger's got such a nasty cold and I've been trying to persuade him not to go out to his confirmation class, but he will, of course. I've been telling Mrs. Bird" [Mrs. Bird was Roger's housekeeper] "to give him hot lemon last thing at night, but she's so stupid. I'm sure she'll forget or not make it really hot. I'm very worried about it. A neglected cold leads to all sorts of things, and Roger never takes any care of himself."

Vicky laughed.

"You're a fussy old hen, Celia. Roger's all right. He always has a cold all through the winter. He has done ever since he was a little boy."

"He ought to be more careful," persisted Celia. "He's not really strong. And he *will* fast on Fridays. Naturally he can't keep up his strength. I simply dread Lent for him every year. I can't see any merit in starvation, but it's no use talking to him. He won't look after himself. I found out yesterday that he was still wearing his summer underclothing."

"Well, it's only September, after all."

"It's very cold in the mornings and at night. There were several degrees of frost the night before last. I put all his summer things away and told Mrs. Bird she was to be sure to put out his winter things on Sunday."

Vicky thought that it would be rather interesting to hear Mrs. Bird's opinion of Celia. Mrs. Bird was a pleasant easygoing old woman, but even her patience must be sorely strained at times.

"I haven't seen you since I came back from the Women's Congress, have I?" said Celia suddenly. "I managed to get over to see Margery. It was only six miles from where the Congress was."

"How was she?"

"Well, Vicky, is she——? You know what I mean, dear. Is there another little one——?"

Vicky stared at her.

"Oh, I'm *sure* not, Celia. She'd have told me."

"Well, dear, I thought so. I *really* thought so."

"Did she say anything?"

"No, she didn't say anything, and I didn't like to ask, but—well, dear, it was beginning to show. Vicky, wouldn't it be lovely to have another little one in the family?"

Celia's face radiated a tenderness that took from it its usual look of amiable foolishness.

Vicky's heart contracted anxiously. She could never think of Margery without that contraction of the heart. She knew so little of her affairs. The child was so passionately proudly reserved. But Vicky was aware whenever she saw her of her unhappiness and disillusionment.

The marriage was turning out badly. Brian was dishonest, drank too much, and had affairs with women. His work as a commission agent brought in very little money, and he could never settle to a steady job. Peter had found him several, but he had lost them all. Vicky knew that behind her mask of proud reserve Margery suffered acutely. She was not the type of woman who can compromise or lower her ideals. She lived for her two little boys—Sandy, who was now ten, and Tony, who was eight—struggling to bring them up well and protect them from Brian's influence, a struggle against heavy odds. Sometimes she looked worn out with work and worry. Another child. . . . Vicky's heart sank still lower at the thought.

"Such a dear, Brian, isn't he?" Celia was saying with a smile that was almost coy.

Brian, of course, still had a way with him. He was handsome, charming, and looked appealingly boyish, and Celia, who took everything at its face value, had never even suspected the unhappiness of Margery's married life.

"Is he?" said Vicky shortly.

"Of course he is," said Celia. "Not many young men would go out of their way to be nice to an old woman like me, but Brian does. You know, Vicky——" She stopped.

"Yes?" said Vicky.

"I know Margery's splendid and manages wonderfully and all that, but—well, I do think she might be a little nicer to Brian. I'm not criticising her, dear, but I *do* think she might. She seems so hard and so—sharp with him sometimes, and he's *so* sweet and patient always, and so responsive. I've never heard him say a hard word to her, however sharp she is with him. You know, Vicky, I wish you'd speak to her. A woman could do anything with Brian if she'd take him the right way."

Brian had always been able to make women feel like that, thought Vicky bitterly, but she said nothing. She, too, had heard that rasping note in Margery's voice when she spoke to Brian, and it had sent a pang through her heart. To hear her gentle dreamy little Margery nag like a shrew. . . . It was so unlike her, and it must come from such a deep well of bitterness. . . .

"I do wish you'd find out definitely, dear," Celia went on. "I mean, about the little one. Paula's is due in March, and if Margery's— Well, I'd like to know in good time because of the christening robe. I must get it laundered between the two christenings, if Margery is——"

Celia had a christening robe that had been in her mother's family for over a hundred years. It was trimmed with lace that was supposed to be priceless, but it was ugly and cumbersome and yellow with age. It was the apple of Celia's eye, however. It gave her a pleasant sense of importance and made her feel the pivot on which the family revolved. Every niece and nephew had to be christened in it, and it had to be laundered and fussed over by Celia in between.

"I wish to goodness the wretched thing would get lost in the post," Paula would say, but it always arrived safely the day before the christening, and it would have broken Celia's heart had Paula suggested not using it. Even Salome had not dared refuse it for Undine, though the rosettes of lace and ribbon had sent a shudder through her. "So baroque . . ." she said to Noel.

"Well, dear, I really must go," said Celia, rising from her chair. "I'll just get the chrysanthemums, shall I? Don't bother to come with me, dear."

She went to the other side of the garden, tore up an armful of yellow chrysanthemums, watched disapprovingly by Andrew, waved them in a gesture of farewell to Vicky, and returned to her car. It started up noisily, then roared furiously away into the distance.

Vicky sat still gazing in front of her, that heavy oppression over her spirit that the thought of Margery always brought with it. She did not see how another child could do anything but make the situation worse than it was.

The sun had gone in now, and a wind had sprung up from the east. She saw Andrew glancing in her direction and knew that he was thinking it was time she went indoors, but was reluctant to come to her because of their recent tiff. She shivered ostentatiously and drew her coat closer round her shoulders. The thought of Margery had made her feel unhappy and frightened, and she wanted the consolation of Andrew's devotion. She saw him lay down his spade and pretended to be deeply interested in her book, looking up with a start when he reached her chair.

"It's time you went in, Miss Vicky," he said. "You'll be getting your rheumatics bad again if you aren't careful."

She smiled at him and he smiled back, their difference forgotten.

She felt more cheerful when she got indoors. A fire was lighted in the grate and the tea-table drawn up to it. Even Vicky acknowledged to herself that the room deserved a little of the scorn Noel poured on it. It was completely cluttered up with furniture—occasional tables, pictures, ornaments, photographs—but they were all her personal friends. They had lived with her so long, known her happy and unhappy, anxious, afraid, triumphant, despairing. They consoled her by their familiar presence when things went wrong. They seemed to rejoice with her in her triumphs and happiness. To get rid of any of them—even the what-not that Noel hated most of all—would be like turning one of the family out of doors. The only stranger among them was a small lacquered desk that her mother's executors had sent last year, thinking that she would like to have some personal memento of her.

Two years ago Vicky, much to her surprise, had received an invitation from Lady Attley to visit her at Cannes. Vicky hadn't seen her mother since that visit to London before her marriage, and she found her a travesty of the woman she remembered. Her face was heavily made up, her hair dyed a bright golden. She was almost incredibly thin and sharp and dry and witty. She defied convention as outrageously as when she had been a girl, but with no other apparent result than that of increasing her circle of admirers. It was strange to remember how demure and pious she had been as inhabitant of the demi-monde and how glaringly demi-monde she was now that as Lady Attley she had an impregnable position in Society.

She seemed amused by the fact that Vicky was her daughter.

"Isn't it absurd, my dear! I simply don't believe it."

"You've got grandchildren," said Vicky.

"I believe I have. At least I've been told so. Tell me about them. How many? What are they like?"

Vicky began to tell her, but she soon lost interest and turned the conversation to the more congenial topics of Paris fashions and London gossip.

She had died in her sleep last year after a particularly riotous champagne supper.

Vicky's head nodded over her book and she began to doze.

At first she thought that Margery's entrance was part of her dream. She seemed to appear so suddenly in the room, her face white and set, her blue eyes hard. Sandy and Tony were with her—Tony merry and roguish-looking as usual, Sandy worried and anxious.

One glance at Margery's figure told Vicky that what Celia had said was true. But the wonder of that was swallowed up in the larger wonder of Margery's unheralded arrival.

"Margery!" she cried, dragging herself from the haze of sleep. "What's the matter? Has anything happened?"

Margery flashed a warning glance at the children.

"We just thought it would be nice to have a little holiday with you, Mother," she said. "I said to the children, 'Let's go down and see Granny for a bit,' and they were awfully pleased; weren't you, Sandy?"

Sandy looked at her, puzzled and afraid—afraid of the dull weary tone of her voice and the bitter unhappiness of her eyes.

"Sandy, dear," said Vicky gently, "take Tony into the garden and find Andrew."

The boys went out, and Vicky turned to Margery, noticing with sudden concern her pallor and the heavy shadows beneath her eyes.

"Margery, darling, you're ill. You——"

"I'm perfectly all right," said Margery, still in the hard toneless voice.

"But how did you come?" went on Vicky, bewildered.

"We came from the station in a cab. Didn't you hear us?"

"No. . . . I think I'd just dozed off." She put out her hands to the bell. "You must have some tea, dear, at once."

Margery stopped her with an impatient gesture.

"No, don't, Mother, I couldn't. It would make me sick. Mother——" She spoke as if with an effort.

"Yes, dear?" said Vicky anxiously.

"May we—may we come to you—the children and I? To live, I mean?"

"Darling, of course, but——"

"I just can't stand it any longer—living with Brian. I can't go on. I've tried. I'd have left him long ago, but—I've hardly any money now. I've had to—pay his debts. I couldn't let him go on owing money to—to people we knew and trades people. I'll get a job when——"

She stopped, pressing her white lips together. It was as if every word she had to say were torture.

Vicky longed to gather her into her arms and comfort her, but one couldn't—not with Margery. One daren't risk outraging the pride that had been so besmirched and yet was still inviolate.

"Margery," she said timidly, "are you——?"

"Oh yes," said Margery bitterly. "I'm as much a fool as that." She turned her head away, and a hot flush suddenly stained her pale cheeks. "He'd been—worse than usual, and I'd told him I was leaving him, and he didn't want me to go. He—cares for me in his own way, I suppose. He worked himself up into a hysterical state over it, and he swore he'd be different, and, like a fool, I believed him." She was sitting on the sofa, rigidly upright. "We—said we'd make a fresh start. I believed him, you see. I thought it was going to be all right, God knows why. Anyway—that's what happened. And then——"

She stopped again.

"And then?" Vicky prompted gently.

"And then—things did seem better at first. I only found out yesterday. He"—she fixed her eyes unseeingly on the distance and spoke as if each word cost a supreme effort—"he—forged—my name—to a cheque."

"Margery!"

"He did it last month, but I only found out yesterday. I had to go away. I couldn't stay there any longer. He's taken money from my purse before and—he's written to ask you for money to pay bills for the children, when he knew I'd paid them. I put up with it for the children's sake. But—this! It can't go on. . . . I told the children that we were coming here for a holiday. They know nothing about it, of course."

"Margery, darling." Vicky's tenderness flowed out to her, but still she dared not even touch her hand. "Brian knows you've come?"

Margery's white lips curled scornfully.

"Oh yes. He cried. He cries very easily, you know. It used to do the trick at once in the early days. It only makes me feel sick now." She turned her head slowly and fixed her haggard eyes on Vicky. "Mother, do you mind? Will you have us here? I thought once I'd have killed myself rather than come back on you like this, but—it isn't only me. I've Sandy and Tony and—the other child. I've got to get them away."

"Margery, darling, I shall love to have you."

One part of her held out arms of welcome to Margery in a passion of love and pity; another almost subconscious part contemplated with dismay the addition of three extra members to the household, tried to cope with the task of adjusting its machinery, altering its arrangements. . . .

"I mean to get a job, but I can't till—after the baby's come. You do understand, don't you, Mother?"

"Darling, of course."

Margery put her hand to her head and closed her eyes, as if a stab of pain had shot through it.

"Come upstairs and lie down, darling," said Vicky.

Margery stood up obediently, then swayed in sudden faintness.

Vicky helped her upstairs to her bedroom, where Margery sat on the bed, staring in front of her as if at the ruins of her life.

Through the open window came the sound of Andrew's and the children's voices and a burst of laughter from Tony.

"Margery," said Vicky slowly, "I'm so terribly sorry. I've always known that it's my fault, in a way. I mean, it was Mark you wanted to marry and I——"

"Oh, I don't suppose it would have been any better if I'd married Mark," said Margery.

The note of weary bitterness in the voice tore at Vicky's heart. Better if she'd kept her dream of Mark, blamed Vicky. . . .

"I've never told you this before," went on Margery, "but—Brian took for granted that I'd been Mark's mistress. He thought that that was what you meant when you spoke to him about it."

Vicky swung round from the window.

"*No!*" she said.

"Oh yes. He still believes it. And he doesn't mind. That's the worst part of it. He doesn't see why I shouldn't have been if I wanted to any more than why he shouldn't——"

She broke down suddenly and lay on the bed, convulsed by slow difficult sobs.

Vicky ran to her and gathered her into her arms at last, murmuring broken words of comfort, the tears running down her cheeks.

Chapter Twenty-Four

Vicky was sitting in the drawing-room, waiting for Margery and the children to come in from their afternoon walk.

They had been with her now for over a year. The baby, a girl, had been born in the spring, and Margery looked after the three of them without help. There was no room in the house for a nurse, and, in any case, she could not have afforded one.

She was acutely sensitive about her position, insisting on "paying her way," taking offence at any suggestion that she was living at Vicky's expense. Vicky had to walk very carefully, so as not to hurt her over-sensitive pride. Her new freedom seemed to have brought her little happiness. She went about her work dogged and unhappy.

She had taken a correspondence course in commercial art and hoped to be able to earn money at home by it. Every afternoon Vicky took the children out while Margery worked at her designs. She had no influence or knowledge of the market, but she sent samples of her work persistently and unavailingly to manufacturers of wallpapers and cretonnes and china, to publishers of books and Christmas cards, and even to theatre managers. They came back with monotonous regularity and each time Margery's lips would take on that tight narrow line that Vicky dreaded, though she never dared to sympathise or even to mention the disappointments.

Brian wrote several times, but Margery burnt his letters unread.

"Margery, darling," Vicky once ventured, "hadn't you better just read what he says?"

"No," said Margery. "It's no use, Mother. It's over. It's finished. I never want to see him again."

"But, darling——"

"Please don't talk about it."

Once he sent a registered letter with a ten-pound note inside, but Margery burnt that letter, too, without reading it, and returned the note.

"I'd rather starve than touch his money," she said passionately.

"But, Margery, there are the children to consider." Vicky was looking uneasily into the future. Three children to be educated and launched in the world. Her own funds would be insufficient, and Margery's money seemed to have been largely dissipated by Brian in the first few years of their marriage. "If Brian can help he ought to."

Margery's face flamed in sudden anger.

"I'd rather they went to board schools than let him help," she said. "It's useless to talk about it. It—frightens me sometimes, to think that they're his children, that there must be something of him in them. . . ."

The whole stream of her passionate brooding love was now turned onto the children. She was, Vicky thought, unnecessarily severe, looking always for Brian's faults in them, treating the most ordinary childish misdemeanours as an evil heritage to be ruthlessly stamped out.

Vicky would often intercede for the small culprit or furtively try to circumvent the punishment, and that, of course, would cause more trouble.

"Darling, he didn't really mean to be naughty."

"Please don't interfere, Mother."

Sandy, the eldest, was a quiet sensitive child, serious beyond his years, passionately devoted to Margery, but Tony, the younger boy, was strikingly like Brian both in ways and appearance. He was sunny-tempered and amiable, and had already an easy charm of manner that was Brian's own.

Margery watched him anxiously, seeing Brian's dishonesty in the slightest prevarication, Brian's shiftlessness in any shirking of duty. Once, finding that Vicky had given him a penny to comfort him when he was in disgrace, she flamed out in sudden anger.

"Don't you see that that's how Brian was ruined? Do you want

Tony to go the same way? People gave in to Brian just because he was attractive. All his life they have done. And look what he is now. For God's sake, let's save Tony from it."

Oddly enough, it was Tony whom she loved the best of the three, though she hid her preference under a mask of severity. Tony loved her, too, and took all his punishments in a philosophical fashion, forgetting them as easily as Brian himself forgot all the failures and rebuffs of life.

The little girl, Sheila, was a placid healthy child, though even over her Margery's love brooded with unremitting anxiety.

Vicky often wished that Margery could enjoy her children as she, Vicky, had enjoyed hers. But life had treated Margery badly and she could not trust it even in the slightest detail.

She had gone to a nursing home in Fenton for Sheila's birth, which had taken place a week or so before it was expected. Vicky had been awakened one morning at five o'clock by Margery's coming into her room, fully dressed and in her hat and coat. She looked white and ravaged.

"I'm sorry to disturb you, Mother," she said quietly, "but I think I shall have to go now. It's—begun. Andrew's getting the car out."

Vicky dressed quickly, and they both went down to the garage and stood there watching Andrew. It was a cold morning, and despite all his efforts the engine was sulky and refused to start. Vicky grew desperate with anxiety, but Margery remained quiet and composed, digging her teeth into her lip as a spasm of pain shook her but making no sound.

At last the car started, and Andrew drove to the nursing home in Fenton as fast as he could, without losing his way once, though he had never been there before. ("Which just *shows*," said Vicky.)

Vicky got on well with the two boys while Margery was away, but when Margery and the baby came home things became difficult again. It wasn't easy to accommodate a nursery in the little house. The children seemed to be all over the place, getting in everyone's way, and the cramped quarters gave endless sources of friction to frayed nerves.

Celia would have been willing to help, but her sympathies were so obviously with Brian, and she made such tactless attempts to defend him, that, after an open quarrel in which Celia called Margery hard and unforgiving and Margery called Celia a fool, they avoided each other, and Margery refused even to allow the children to go to Ivy Lodge.

Vicky did her best to avoid giving offence, but to Margery's tormented pride the most trivial incidents assumed colossal proportions. Vicky's tidying up of the drawing-room after the children had played there, her deploring quite innocently the high cost of something she had had to buy for them, were all accepted by Margery as reproaches and brooded over in silent unhappiness. Vicky, on her side, was secretly hurt by Margery's strictures on the smallness and inconvenience of the house and her impatience with Vicky's fussy over-methodical ways and arrangements. Often she longed guiltily for the peace and quiet of the little house before Margery came there. She had no time to herself now from morning to night. She looked after the children or went out with them every afternoon, so that Margery could go on with her work. People commiserated with her on looking tired, and that, also, Margery took as a reproach.

The two loved each other deeply, and their very love tended to estrange them. Margery could not bear the thought of the trouble and upset that she knew she must be bringing into Vicky's life, and Vicky, on her side, was worried by Margery's weariness and unhappiness. They both looked with apprehension into the future. . . .

Samples of Margery's work continued to return as regularly as they were sent out.

"I'm a failure all round," she burst out suddenly one evening. "I failed with Brian, and I'm a failure at my work."

"Darling, you're not," protested Vicky.

"I'm a burden to you here."

"You're not. . . . I love having you. . . ."

Such scenes were wearing to both of them.

Roger called occasionally—a tall dreamy-looking man with grey hair and a confirmed stoop, impractical and saintly in his life, shy in his dealings with other people.

He had been to tea yesterday and, pressed by Margery for his opinion, had said that he thought she had done wrong in leaving her husband.

"You married him for better, for worse," he said. "You are breaking your marriage vows."

"But it isn't only for myself," she had persisted hotly. "It's for the children. It would be wrong to expose them to an influence like Brian's."

"As long as you are doing your duty," said Roger, "God will protect both them and you."

"Oh, Roger," sighed Vicky, "it's so easy to talk. You've never been Brian's wife."

He smiled.

"No," he said, and added, "I admit it's a difficult question." His eyes dwelt anxiously on Vicky's face. "You're looking tired out, Vicky," he went on. "You ought to rest more than you do."

Margery put her cup down and went abruptly from the room.

This morning, too, there had been trouble. A friend of Vicky's in the next village had rung her up and asked her to tea, and Vicky had said—somewhat regretfully, thinking of the old days when such an invitation would have been welcome—"I'm so sorry, but I'm afraid I can't. Margery's with me, you know, and I generally go for a walk with the children in the afternoon."

Margery quickly dressed the children in their outdoor things and took them out, her lips set, not speaking to Vicky when Vicky questioned her. Vicky had passed a morning of tense anxiety, afraid suddenly and for the first time that Margery might do something desperate in her misery, but they returned at lunch-time, Margery white and tired, having spent the morning in an ineffectual attempt to find rooms for herself and the children in the neighbourhood.

Vicky comforted and reassured and petted her, and Margery relaxed at last into a weary resignation. But she had insisted on taking the children out herself in the afternoon, so that Vicky could rest. Vicky, however, couldn't rest. She felt uneasy and apprehensive.

She sat in the drawing-room for an hour working at the pile of mending that she had made her own particular job, darning small socks and sewing buttons onto small articles of underwear.

Then she went into the garden, where Andrew came slowly down the path as soon as she appeared and stood for a moment looking at her solemnly in silence.

"Miss Vicky," he began.

"Yes, Andrew?" she said, surprised by the expression on his face.

"I've got to tell you something."

"Yes?" she said again.

"I wired for Miss Margery's husband this morning."

Vicky stared at him.

"You—? Andrew, how *dared* you?"

"I had to," he said doggedly. "It's his job, not yours. It's killing you. I couldn't stand by and watch it any longer."

"But——" She was still staring at him aghast. "Margery will be furious. She'll never forgive you."

"I can't help that," he said. "I had to do something."

Vicky glanced around her desperately.

"I must stop him somehow, anyhow. . . . Andrew, what were you *thinking* of?"

"You," he said simply. "It's too late to stop him, Miss Vicky. I sent it first thing this morning. If he's coming he's on his way, and if he hasn't started now he won't be coming anyway."

"It's—it's unpardonable of you," gasped Vicky and turned back to the house.

She was trembling, her heart beating unevenly. How *dared* Andrew do it? And how could she break the news to Margery? She would have gone out to meet her, but she did not know from which direction she would be coming.

She turned to look at Andrew. He was placidly digging in the garden as if he hadn't just shaken their universe to its foundations. Brian on his way here, now. . . . Brian, whom Margery had sworn never to see again.

A wave of anger surged over her. How dared he? The children

275

were right. He was impossible. . . . Something would have to be done about it.

She stood at the drawing-room window, her eyes fixed on the gate, dreading to see either Brian or Margery entering it. Then her feeling of panic abated somewhat. Probably he wouldn't come. For weeks now he had not written. He had probably adjusted his life to bachelor existence and had no desire to take back the responsibility of wife and children (not that responsibility had ever worried Brian, she thought bitterly). Perhaps it would be better not even to tell Margery that Andrew had wired.

Someone was approaching the gate . . . but at once she realised that it was Margery with the pram, followed by the two boys. How white and strained her face was! Another batch of her designs had come back from a manufacturer this morning.

She went to the door to help her in with the pram and to lift out Sheila—a soft warm bundle, who smiled at her suddenly, crinkling up a button-like immature nose.

Vicky adored babies in the old-fashioned way that Margery and her contemporaries despised, and poured forth a flood of baby talk while Margery silently gathered the rugs and blankets from the pram.

No, Vicky decided, she wouldn't tell her about Andrew's wire. It was absurd to suppose that Brian would come after the long silence. Anyway, Andrew had wired first thing in the morning. He'd have been here now if he were coming at all. She wouldn't give another thought to the matter.

Katie came out of the kitchen to take Sheila, and carried her upstairs, crooning happily.

"Come and sit down, darling," said Vicky to Margery, "and let Katie see to Sheila."

The two boys went into the drawing-room with them. Sandy stood by the window.

"Here's Daddy," he said suddenly.

Vicky's heart raced tumultuously.

"Sandy, take Tony away," she said breathlessly. "In the garden or upstairs or anywhere."

Sandy, anxious and puzzled, took Tony's arm and pushed him out of the room, out of the side door, and into the garden.

Brian came straight in. The front door was open, and he had seen Margery and Vicky through the window. His face was as white as Margery's. She sat motionless, staring at him in silence.

He opened his lips as if to speak, then suddenly dropped on his knees by her chair and hid his face on her lap. She bent over him, her mouth twisted into lines of bitter tortured tenderness, and Vicky saw that, however much she despised herself for her love, she had not been able quite to kill it.

"Brian," she said softly. "Oh, Brian. . . ."

Vicky crept silently from the room.

Chapter Twenty-Five

IT was Christmas Day. There was a sharp tang of frost in the sunny air. The roads were pleasantly empty, and Andrew had not once lost his way.

Vicky felt exhilarated by the keenness of the atmosphere and by an enjoyable sense of truancy. She ought, of course, to be at Paula's, sitting with the noisy crowd of young people round the big mahogany table in the dining-room. She had been there each Christmas for more than twenty years, watching the family grow and develop, for Paula and Peter had had only one short of the ten children they'd promised themselves. Moreover, the number each Christmas seemed to increase even out of proportion to Paula's increasing family, for the children invited their friends, and Peter dug out for the occasion all the unattached relations, however distant, that he could find. There seemed to be no limit to Peter's patriarchal tendencies, and Christmas, of course, was the culminating family festival of the year. Nothing that tradition associated with the ceremony had to be omitted. They were merry, hilarious, noisy gatherings. Just a little too noisy for Vicky. After all, she was seventy now. . . .

For years she'd been thinking, somewhat guiltily, that she would like to spend a Christmas quietly at home, and this year she had suddenly decided that she would. She had made the most of a slight cold that ordinarily she would hardly have noticed, and had written to Paula to say that she was afraid she would not be able to come.

It hadn't been allowed to end there, of course. She was "Grannie," one of the pivots of the patriarchal machine, and as such her presence was necessary to the occasion.

Peter wrote to her and rang her up and sent wires. He offered quite seriously to fetch her by car, ambulance, or aeroplane. He consulted his doctor and sent pages of advice on how to treat a cold so as to get rid of it overnight.

His persistence hardened Vicky's obstinacy, and by a policy of masterly inaction (she left most of his wires and letters unanswered) and prevarication (she exaggerated her symptoms till they sounded quite ominous) she tided over the days preceding Christmas Day. She had felt rather nervous yesterday and had half expected Peter or one of the boys to arrive for her with a car and bear her off willy-nilly, but they hadn't done and now she was safe. She could have her Christmas by herself—with Andrew, of course. (Katie had gone home to spend Christmas with her father.)

Andrew had brought breakfast to her in bed and then packed the luncheon basket.

"No newspaper this morning, you know, Miss Vicky," Andrew had said when she appeared downstairs. He generally had the newspaper ready by the chair where she was going to sit.

"I don't mind," said Vicky. "Newspapers aren't what they used to be."

She said it half in joke, but it was true, of course. Newspapers used to be a pleasant accompaniment to breakfast, blending happily with the coffee and toast and bacon and kidneys, but nowadays they took one's appetite away instead.

Politics . . . they used to be just a sort of game that had to be played skilfully according to definite rules, but that wasn't really of much importance to anyone but the players. There were Conservatives and Liberals and a few bad but negligible people called Socialists. But now . . . it was like Alice Through the Looking-Glass, where the pieces of a game suddenly became real. The Red Queen in a rage. Italy and Germany and Russia. Whole nations going mad, for, as it seemed, no reason at all.

The Poor and the Unemployed. . . . No longer the grateful respectful Poor of Vicky's childhood who bobbed curtseys and were

279

kept well supplied with tea and soup by the local Ladies Bountiful. You couldn't say any longer, "Unemployed indeed! They could find work if they wanted it." Whole districts destitute and derelict as if an enemy had laid them waste. No, it didn't blend any more with the coffee and toast and bacon and kidneys. . . . But it didn't seem to matter very much. . . . Nothing mattered very much when you were old. And how quickly the years flew by! Ten years seemed more like one. . . .

Andrew had the car ready and they set off at once, past the rows of little newly built houses and the Vicarage. As they passed the Vicarage the sound of children's voices cut sharply through the air, and Vicky could see three little girls in red coats running about among the trees, shouting and laughing. It was nice to see children in the Vicarage garden again. It took her back to the days when she had played there with Roger and Mark and Mabs.

Celia had been heart-broken by Roger's death last year, but she had "carried on" doggedly, refusing to give up any of her work and making herself an intolerable nuisance to the new vicar and his wife. It had really been a relief to everyone concerned when she died this spring, just a year after Roger.

Dame Dorothea Milner—now a famous woman surgeon—had come down to operate on her, but it was too late. Poor Celia! She had been so well-meaning, so generous, so kind-hearted, and yet she had never really mattered to anyone, except to Papa in those far-off days of childhood.

They were passing the Hall now. A group of young people were just setting off from the gates with brogues and stout sticks. The Hall had been turned into a guesthouse two years ago, and the lake was now an up-to-date swimming-pool, with white tiles, a sun-bathing lounge, and a row of changing huts. Through the bare trees Vicky could see the front door, where the child Vicky had stood, her cheeks hot with tears, watching Papa drive off in the station cab . . . where later an older Vicky had stood, an anguish too deep for tears at her heart, and watched Philip go away from her for ever. . . . Now a fat man stood there in brown plus-fours, smoking a cigar and looking up at the sky. Vicky didn't at all resent the fact that her old home was a guest-house. She felt rather pleased than otherwise. She liked to watch the people in the village, and wonder what they did, and guess which was married to which.

As they cruised along the lanes in the bright crisp sunshine, Vicky thought of the children sitting round the table at Paula's, but somehow it was her own children she saw, with Philip at the head of the table and herself at the foot, the table filled with crackers, a Christmas tree in the middle, Philip genial and kindly, the children happy and excited. There had in reality been few Christmases like that and many more when they had waited in vain for Philip to come home, or when he had arrived sullen or irritable, but memory had purged Philip of his faults. He lived in her mind as the tender loving husband, the kindly genial father, he had so seldom shown himself to be. Her eyes grew dreamy. How sweet the children had been, how dear! Isolated memories came to her. She saw Margery, small and serious, laying bits of bramble round the lawn, so that the birds could hop about in safety there ("It's a cat trap, Mummy. You see, it'll prick their toes so they won't want to tread on it") ... saw Paula's wild mischievous face laughing down from her "wigwam" in the old apple tree ... saw again the letter Lionel wrote to her when he was in the sanatorium at school, "I felt wrotten at first. But I am all wright now," in large uneven writing ... sat next to Noel again during his first term watching a cricket match, leaning slightly back, as if accidentally, in order to inspect his neck and ears, met his stern eye that read her manoeuvre and dared her to make any comment or ask any question.

Paula's children, though dears, weren't as interesting as hers had been. What a noise there would be now round the big table! Peter, stout and red-faced, at the head, teasing them, roaring with laughter at all their jokes. Paula, placid and matronly, at the foot, murmuring "Darlings ... darlings," when the noise became unbearable.

Vicky was glad she wasn't there. It was lovely in the quiet country lanes. She would go to Paula's next year and always in the future for as many Christmases as were left to her, but she'd wanted to have just one quiet Christmas all by herself.

Andrew had been invited to Bill's, but he had refused the invitation.

Bill was quite a big man now, a director in the motor-cycle firm, with a car and a chauffeur of his own. Like George he had grown tired of offering Andrew good posts in the firm only to have them refused, and of sending him money only to have it returned, for Andrew said that his wages were more than enough for his needs. Both Bill and George found Andrew's contempt for money disconcerting. Bill, however, was fond of "the old man," though too busy to see much of him, and Andrew was quite content that their lives should lie in different worlds. ("It won't do him any harm," he would say, referring indulgently to the wealth and comfort in which his son now lived. "He's a good boy, is Bill. Ellen'd have been proud of him, if she'd lived.")

Vicky's children still vaguely resented Andrew, but her grandchildren delighted in him. To them he was a character, a family institution. "Isn't Andrew a *pet*!" they would say when they had been to see her.

Paula's two eldest girls had spent a day with Vicky last month. Daphne had been staying with friends near, and Jill had been passing through in a small green sports car, and they had met at Six Elms to see Vicky.

"I can't really stay a minute," Jill had said. (She was radiantly pretty, with red hair of a darker shade than Philip's and blue eyes.) "I'm dining with Hugh to-night and we're going to a show."

"Good for you!" Daphne had laughed. "Does Mother know?"

"I should think not!" said Jill. "She thinks I'm safely anchored with the Carlows. Swear you won't tell her."

"Course I won't tell her," said Daphne. "What d'you take me for?"

"What's all this?" Vicky had put in, smiling. "Who's Hugh and why is your mother not to know about him?"

"Oh, Gran, be a sport," pleaded Jill. "Hugh's a darling, isn't he, Daphne?"

"Course he is," said Daphne.

"But his people aren't the anybodies of anywhere," continued Jill, "and you know what Mother is."

"Are you in love with him?" said Vicky.

"Yes, I think I am."

So it was all beginning again, thought Vicky—love troubles, love complications—but it wasn't her business now. It was Paula's. And it wasn't real as her own children's love affairs had been real. . . .

"Gran, be a sport. Promise you won't tell Mother."

Vicky chuckled.

"I won't say anything unless she asks me," she said.

She remembered how desperately she had worried over Paula's love affairs in the past, and it amused her that Paula's children should be turning the tables on her like this. It was what always happened, she supposed. Life was really rather entertaining as you got on and could look back at it.

"How are things at home?" said Jill to Daphne.

"Same as usual," said Daphne. "Mother just as fussy as ever. I wasn't in time for breakfast once while I was there and—well, you know the song and dance she makes about it. Going on about the maids and household routine and habits of method and punctuality. It's too ridiculous, all this fuss about running a house. I'm sure your generation didn't make it, Gran, did they?"

"Of course we didn't," said Vicky, and really believed it.

"Mum seems to think that the world will come to an end if the whole family isn't waiting on the mat for its bone the second the bell rings. I tell her that this worship of household routine is the mark of the bourgeoisie. It's gradually turning me into a Communist, anyway. Animals just eat when they're hungry. Why shouldn't we?"

"Is Undine still at home?" said Jill.

"Oh yes. Seems to be fixed there for months to come. Doesn't want to go home at all, I believe." She turned to Vicky: "Isn't it odd, Gran, that Undine adores dogs and horses and hunting and all the things that make poor old Uncle Noel and Aunt Salome turn green? It would break Uncle Noel's heart if Patsy weren't just the opposite. Patsy thinks that Uncle Noel's marvellous and spouts his poems and tries to wear awful garments like Aunt Salome. It worries poor old Daddy terribly. So, when Undine comes to us, Patsy generally trots over to Uncle Noel. I think they ought to swop permanently."

"Poor old Uncle Noel!" laughed Jill. "He *is* a scream. He went over to see Tony and Frankie at Oxford last term, and he wanted to meet the men who were running some high-brow magazine there. He thought they'd be kindred souls, I suppose. Anyway, Tony and Frankie trotted him along to the leading spirit of it—a man called Bessimer—for a high-brow chat. Bessimer happens to be crazy on Victorian stuff, and he's got some perfectly marvellous wax flowers under glass cases and antimacassars and a what-not and a *tête-à-tête* seat—you know, the sort that turns round on itself—not to speak of a genuine horsehair sofa. Anyway, old Uncle Noel just sat and stared at them as if they were ghosts. Frankie said afterwards that he supposed the poor old chap had led the revolt against them in his wild youth and couldn't tumble to the fact that they were coming back into their own. Frankie said he seemed quite dazed. . . ."

They had both gone off together very noisily and at a dangerous speed in the little green sports car.

They would be sitting at the big table with the others now, and perhaps Jill would be thinking of Hugh who was a darling, but whose people weren't the anybodies of anywhere. . . .

Margery and Brian would be there, too, with Sandy and Tony and Sheila. People said that Margery "wore the trousers," and had "got Brian where she wanted him." Certainly she was hard and a little shrewish, and Brian was afraid of her. With Peter's help she had got him a post in a house-agent's firm, and she kept him to it, driving him there every morning and watching all his doings with a sharp eye. She made him hand over his salary to her and she ran the household, doling out pocket-money to him sparingly. He still carried on an occasional furtive "affair," but lived in terror of Margery's discovering them. He had lost a good deal of his charm, and his ingratiating manner was becoming less attractive as he grew older. It reminded one of the fawning of a dog that expects a beating. Beneath Margery's resentment against Brian for his instability was another deeper resentment. He had forced her, against her nature and instinct, to be hard and domineering. She had wanted to be soft and gentle and kind, and he had made it impossible. The saving factor in the situation was Sheila. Both Margery and Brian were devoted to her and shrank from doing anything that might endanger her security. Whatever happened, Sheila must have a happy normal home life. She adored Daddy, and Brian was at his best with her, while Margery was careful to do or say nothing that would show her contempt for him when the child was there.

"Let's sit at the back and put the little tables up," said Vicky.

There were small hinged flaps attached to the back of the front seats, which formed tables. Vicky took a childish delight in them and had chosen the car solely on their account.

They went into the back seat, and Vicky spread out the contents of the picnic basket. There was cold chicken and ham, rolls and butter, some fruit and cheese, a thermos flask of coffee for Vicky, and a bottle of beer for Andrew.

"Isn't it fun?" she said. "Much better than if I'd gone to Paula's and you'd gone to Bill's. ... Perhaps Paula or Peter will ring up to ask how I am this afternoon and find no one in the house. ... Won't they be angry?"

She laughed, feeling like a naughty child playing truant from school.

"It'll be me that'll get into trouble over it, not you," said Andrew grimly, "and they'll be quite right. You've got a cold, and you've no business to be gallivanting about in the car like this."

"Nonsense!" said Vicky. "Don't be so ridiculous, Andrew. Gallivanting indeed! And I've hardly got a cold at all. ... Did you remember the salt?"

Another car passed, and its occupants looked with interest and faint amusement at the old lady and her elderly chauffeur, sitting at the back of the car, having their lunch together. Vicky glanced at Andrew as if suddenly seeing him through their eyes. Yes, he was an old man. It seemed absurd, but it was true. His hair was grey, and he looked smaller than he used to look, shrunken, wizened. Funny how he still suggested horses, though he'd never had very much to do with them. He'd always looked more like a groom than a gardener, with his thin spindly legs and awkward rolling gait.

"We've known each other a long time now, haven't we, Andrew?" she said suddenly.

"Yes," said Andrew. "I was thirteen and you were seven."

"I came to the cottage with Miss Thompson. Do you remember?"

"I do."

"I was hoping you thought me pretty."

"I know you were."

"You needn't say it like that," said Vicky with spirit. "I *was* pretty."

He grinned.

"You thought you were."

"Well, I don't care. I was. I'm not bad looking now considering I'm over seventy."

"You've not changed much," he said dryly.

She laughed.

"Neither have you. . . . Life's not been bad on the whole, has it, Andrew? We've both had happy marriages, at any rate, and that's a lot. You and Ellen were happy, and so were Philip and I. . . . You knew that he'd left me, didn't you, Andrew? But he came back to me in the end."

"Yes," said Andrew, "I know."

He'd almost forgotten that night when he'd pushed the boat out into the lake and burnt the letter at the kitchen fire. He remembered it now dimly as if it were a dream.

They were silent. Vicky was thinking of Philip, her king of men, her lover, her husband, so kind and tender and gay and faithful. She thought of him with longing and something of the old ecstasy.

"I don't think I shall mind dying, Andrew," she said suddenly; "will you? Not with Philip and Ellen there already."

"Now, don't you start talking about dying, Miss Vicky," Andrew rallied her, "and we aren't old yet, not by a long chalk."

"We're both over seventy."

"That's not old," he said stoutly, and went on after a pause: "They say there are more horses on the road now than there were ten years ago. I knew they couldn't get along without them. All this machinery's not natural."

"No," agreed Vicky absently; then, "Andrew, did you notice the little heath garden in front of that house we passed about a mile back? It looked so pretty. Some heaths flower all through the winter. Couldn't we have one?"

"We'll see about it," he said shortly. (There she was again, with her new-fangled notions. Heath garden indeed!)

"There's nothing to see about," snapped Vicky. (There he was again, being obstinate even on Christmas Day.) "Of course we could have one."

"Just as you like, of course," said Andrew distantly.

"Very well," she said. "We won't if you don't want to."

"Why shouldn't I want to?" he said a little aggressively. "I can grow a few heaths as well as anyone else, I hope."

"All right," smiled Vicky, and added, "Shall we pack up and go on now?"

They packed the picnic basket, got into the front seats again, and set off.

The sun was a red ball on the horizon. There was a touch of ice in the air. Andrew put up the window and stopped to tuck the rug more securely round Vicky.

"Mustn't get that cold worse, Miss Vicky," he said.

"Oh, don't fuss, Andrew," said Vicky drowsily.

They drove on at the leisurely pace that Andrew liked. His thoughts hovered round Vicky anxiously, protectively. He must look after that cold of hers. She ought to go to bed early and have some hot lemon and whisky. Couldn't have Miss Vicky ill. . . . Andrew had never analysed his feelings for Vicky. It wasn't a question of admiration or even liking. There was indeed something strangely impersonal in his devotion. She annoyed him frequently, but—she was Miss Vicky. He was her liege man. He would willingly and without question have given his life for her. All feudal England lay at the heart of their relationship.

Vicky's thoughts went back again over her life. It hadn't been very eventful, but then few people's lives were eventful. It had consisted chiefly in a gradual shifting of relationships. Andrew was the most stable relationship that life had given her. . . . He was maddeningly obstinate, deliberately stupid and careless sometimes, but he was Andrew. It began and ended there. Life without his help and loyalty was unthinkable. She was growing old, so was Andrew. She wouldn't say anything more about the heath garden. Andrew hated anything new. How lovely the sky looked—a pale primrose faintly flushed towards the west, where the great red ball still hung. The world was very beautiful. It was a pity that people were generally too busy or worried to notice it. She remembered Philip—or was it Noel?—reading her a poem that began:

> Look thy last on all things lovely
> Every hour . . .

You had time, of course, to notice how beautiful the world was when you were old . . . She was growing drowsy. . . . Philip . . . Lionel . . . Paula . . . Noel . . . Margery. . . . Poor little Margery! She'd been such a dear little girl. Lionel had been so fond of her. He'd have been so sorry if he'd known about Brian. But perhaps he did know even now . . . perhaps he helped.

Philip . . . Philip who'd fastened a string of moonstones round her neck and held her laughing and breathless in his arms while he rained kisses on her . . . Philip who'd come back to her in the end. . . .

Her head dropped forward.

She was asleep.

THE END